The Mersey Girls

It would have been nice to take Lucy, though Maeve thought rather wistfully, heaving the sheet up over her shoulders. Nice for Linnet to meet her sister at last, nice for Maeve herself to have the company. But no point in even considering it. Lucy was doing well at school, she was useful on the farm, sensible and helpful. Padraig would do very well with Lucy and with one of his other daughters to keep an eye on things, and the twins would meet up again soon enough, for Maeve was determined to bring Linnet back with her. She hugged herself at the thought of that other fourteen-year-old, waiting in New York, about to get the surprise of her life when her Auntie Maeve turned up to rescue her.

And still smiling at the thought, Maeve fell asleep at last.

Katie Flynn has lived for many years in the Northwest. A compulsive writer, she started with short stories and articles and many of her early stories were broadcast on Radio Mersey. She decided to write her Liverpool series after hearing the reminiscences of family members about life in the city in the early years of the century. She also writes as Judith Saxton.

Also by Katie Flynn

The Mersey Girls

Katie Flynn

arrow books

Reprinted by Arrow Books in 2002

3 5 7 9 10 8 6 4 2

First published in the United Kingdom in 1994
by William Heinemann Ltd

This edition first published in 1995
by Mandarin Paperbacks and reprinted ten times,
then published by Arrow and reprinted twelve times

Arrow Books
The Random House Group Limited
20 Vauxhall Bridge Road, London SW1V 2SA

Random House Australia (Pty) Limited
20 Alfred Street, Milsons Point, Sydney
New South Wales 2061, Australia

Random House New Zealand Limited
18 Poland Road, Glenfield
Auckland 10, New Zealand

Random House (Pty) Limited
Endulini, 5a Jubilee Road, Parktown 2193, South Africa

The Random House Group Limited Reg. No. 954009

www.randomhouse.co.uk

A CIP catalogue record for this book
is available from the British Library

ISBN 978 0 09 956224 5

The Random House Group Limited supports The Forest Stewardship
Council (FSC®), the leading international forest certification organisation.
Our books carrying the FSC label are printed on FSC® certified paper.
FSC is the only forest certification scheme endorsed by the leading
environmental organisations, including Greenpeace. Our
paper procurement policy can be found at
www.randomhouse.co.uk/environment

Printed and bound in Great Britain by Clays Ltd, St Ives PLC

**For Olive Edwards, because she has
promised to enjoy it!**

As always, the staff of the Liverpool Local History Library on William Brown Street were both patient and helpful in finding me the material I needed, and Rosemarie Hague told me what Exchange Flags had looked like many years ago – and how to find it now!

And in Ireland, Elaine Walsh of Waterford was enormously helpful, telling us how to get where, and advising us not simply to head for one particular place but to wander, which is the best way to enjoy the country and to meet the people. We accordingly wandered down to Kerry and on to Cahersiveen, with its half-a-dozen different spellings, its fascinating sea-lough-cum-river, its gently rolling countryside and its weird, Eastern-looking barracks, to say nothing of the stump of a castle which I 'borrowed' for Lucy, Caitlin, Finn and Granny Mogg. Even the views are all there as described – and so is the delightful Evelyn Brennan, who, with her daughter, runs Brennan's Restaurant in the town and not only introduced us to brack, which is absolutely delicious, but told me a great deal about her town and the surrounding countryside – and put me straight on the state of the railways in the thirties.

And thanks to Maggie O'Driscoll and Nick Evans, who shared their knowledge of Irish tinkers in the thirties with me and helped me with the language of the travellers and their ways.

Chapter One

May 1913

As the faint chimes from the church clock stole across the dark waters of the lough, Maeve Murphy sat up on one elbow, struggling out of the depths of sleep. She did not know what had woken her, only that something had. A sound? A voice, perhaps? She turned her head cautiously and checked that Nora, with whom she shared her bed, was still fast asleep, then glanced across the small attic room towards the bed shared by two of her three younger sisters. Had one of them stirred, called out? But the girls slept, Clodagh curled up into a tight little ball, Éanna sprawled on her back, her beautiful lips just parted, a tiny snore curling rhythmically from her mouth. Maeve listened again. Yes, there had been a sound – a creak, and not just the usual creak of an old house settling either. This was the sort of creak, lively yet furtive, which meant that someone was awake and trying to move about the house without disturbing others.

Was it time to get up, then? Maeve glanced towards the uncurtained window; the sky was still dark, she could see stars twinkling, and there was not a sound from outside, not even a bird cheeped, forestalling the dawn chorus. Later the farmyard cock would start to clear his throat ready for his first cock-a-doodle, but right now the household should be wrapped in slumber, not prowling around. The last creak, Maeve was fairly sure, had come as a foot landed gently on the last stair but one.

Still, it was probably only a cat having a snoop round whilst the rest of the house slept. Maeve was about to lie

1

down again when it occurred to her that her sister, Evie, who had slept in the small bedroom next door to their father's room ever since her twin daughters had been born, might be up and doing. Immediately Maeve swung her feet out of bed, listening more intently than ever. Evie was barely seventeen and Maeve, the oldest of the five Murphy girls, had taken upon herself the care of the smallest, frailest twin. If Evie had gone down to feed them or change them she would appreciate Maeve's presence.

Maeve shuffled a bit further down the bed and reached for her shawl, draped across the bedpost. She wrapped it firmly around her shoulders, glad of its soft, woolly warmth. Although the month was May it was still chilly in the early hours and her flannel petticoat wasn't much protection against the cold. Then she stood up, carefully tucked her side of the bed in – Nora did not even stir – and tiptoed over to the door. It opened silently, because when five lively young girls share a house with an elderly father it behoves them to keep their door-hinges well-oiled, and Maeve slid out on to the steps which, ladderlike, descended to the upper landing.

Outside Evie's room she hesitated; should she peep inside, just make sure? No one would burgle the Murphys because there was nothing to steal, but there was usually food in the pantry and there were always gipsies and tramps eager to fill their bellies. She put a hand on the door knob, then drew it back as a sound from downstairs reached her ears; there was definitely someone in the kitchen, she could hear quiet footsteps padding across the hard earth floor!

That settled it: they either had an intruder, in which case two people were better than one, or Evie had got up. Quickly, before she could change her mind, she opened Evie's door. One glance at the bed showed her that it was

2

empty, the covers pushed back, the pillow still dented from the impression of Evie's head.

Relief washed over Maeve in waves. She turned away from her sister's room and ran down the stairs, not bothering to go particularly quietly. At the bottom, in the small, square hall, she turned at once to the kitchen, though she opened the door softly enough.

At first she thought the room was empty: moonlight streamed through the two low windows overlooking the farmyard, turning the room into a symphony of black and silver. Puzzled, Maeve took a step into the room . . . then stopped short, a hand flying to her heart.

By the fireplace, something moved. A figure stood there, on tiptoe, reaching up for the battered teapot which stood directly under the grandmother clock. A hand, white in the moonlight, was already curled round the blackened pewter pot.

'Evie! What on earth . . . ?'

Evie spun round, leaving the teapot still rocking from her touch. Her face looked white as a ghost, her eyes black pits. She gasped, then relaxed. 'Maeve! Dear God, girl, I nearly died. What are you doing down here at this time of night? I thought everyone was asleep, so I did.'

Maeve walked over to the fire and took a taper from the box by the hearth. She lit it, then held the flame to the candle on the end of the dresser. Her mind was working furiously; Evie was fully dressed, this was no trip downstairs to fetch something for one of her babies, this was . . .

'What are *you* doing, Evie?' she said evenly. 'I came down because I heard you creepin' down the stairs. Where's the babies?'

'In bed, Maeve, me love, it's the middle of the night; where else would me darlin's be but in their bed?'

In the candlelight, Maeve looked hard and long at her

3

younger sister. Evie was so beautiful, that was the trouble, it became difficult not to believe every word uttered by those pink, perfect lips!

'Evie, you're fully dressed,' Maeve said, changing tack. 'Where were you going?'

'Were going, Maeve?' Evie sighed and turned back to the mantelpiece. She reached up and took the teapot down, then stood there cradling it. And when she spoke again it was with more than a touch of defiance. 'I *am* going. In ten minutes or so a cart'll pull in off the main road. I arranged it a day or so ago, it'll take me down to the station. Oh, Maeve, you know I can't stay here for the rest of me life – you wouldn't want it for me, would you? The disapproval's enough to break my heart, and besides, I'm wasted here. I'll never get anywhere, do anything . . . *be* anyone, come to that, whilst I stay in Cahersiveen. So I'm leaving, going to – to seek me fortune, you could say.'

'And you're taking the housekeeping money,' Maeve stated calmly, jerking her head at the pewter teapot. 'That's stealing, Evie, no matter how you justify it. And what about your little girls, then?'

'I'm taking Linnet with me, but I can't burden meself with two of them,' Evie said defensively. 'Besides, what'ud you do, Maeve me darlin', if I took Lucy as well? You'd miss them both sore, you know you would. And leaving Lucy shows I mean to come back – but I can't take 'em both or I'll never get rich and famous!'

The last words were almost a wail. Despite herself, Maeve smiled.

'Oh, Evie, what does rich and famous matter, after all? Isn't it better to be happy here, with your two little girls? To live a good life?'

Evie shrugged her shoulders and set the teapot down on the table. She took the lid off it and tipped the contents

4

very gently out onto a cloth she had already placed there to receive it. Then she wrapped the money in the cloth and pushed the small bundle down into the shabby bag which Maeve now saw at her sister's feet.

'I can't settle to it and never could,' she said honestly. 'Country living's always drove me mad . . . I should've gone a year back, only it seemed a big thing to do. And then Jan didn't want me to leave, said to wait a while, so I stayed . . . and look what happened!'

'Jan Wilde's a good feller and would have taken you and the babies on, if only you'd let him,' Maeve reminded her sister. 'But if you don't want Jan why in God's name didn't you marry the Ronald feller from England? You let him give you the babies, so you must have liked him. Or at least you could've got his address, so our Dad could have sent someone looking for him, told him what he'd done.'

'I don't want to marry anyone,' Evie said pettishly. 'You don't understand about babies, Maeve, that Englishman was dull as ditchwater; if I hadn't been so bored I'd never have let him do more than kiss me, so there!'

'Indeed, madam? Then why not marry Jan Wilde if you weren't in love with that blackhearted English? He'd be good to you, treat you right.'

'Because I can't bear the thought of scratching a living from a poor little place all me life, because I know there's more to me than Jan could possibly appreciate. I'm a good actress; I sing like an angel and dance like a . . . a dervish, and I can imitate voices so folk don't know it's me,' Evie said definitely. 'And it isn't just me that thinks so, Maeve me love; that Ronald feller knew a thing or two and he said I was talented, in the right hands he said I'd go far.'

'He was a big-mouth,' Maeve said bitterly. 'He comes

5

for a holiday after an illness, turns your head, gets you pregnant and then leaves, never realising the harm he's done. I hope the good God has shown him the error of his ways, even if 'tis too late for you to come to your senses.'

'Well, I am talented, and I shall go far despite all of you,' Evie said hotly. 'Did you think I'd stay here for ever, rotting away, while other girls went to Dublin, to England, and had all the fun and excitement?'

'Once you'd had the babies . . .' Maeve began patiently, only to be briskly interrupted.

'Oh, the babies, the babies! One little slip from grace and you'd condemn me for the rest of me life! You're as bad as the others, Maeve Murphy, and I always thought you understood!'

'I do understand, alanna, and I know you're a good actress and beautiful, too. But how can you go back to Dublin with a child under each arm? Who'll take you seriously as an actress when you're hung about with babies? Leave it a few years, until they're older . . .'

'Until I'm older you mean,' Evie snapped. 'I've got to strike whilst the iron's hot, Maeve – I've got to! And it'll work, I promise you, because I've learned me lesson. This time I'll steer clear of the fellers and be single-minded and really work at my career, I won't listen to any man, no matter how sweetly he talks. I'll make a name for myself and then . . . then you and little Lucy can come and visit me in London, or Paris, or – or New York, and I'll buy a mansion and we'll all live happily ever after!'

'They're just daydreams, alanna,' Maeve said gently. 'Put the money back like a good girl and go and get into your bed. I'll make us a cup of tea and by the time you've drunk it you'll be sleepy again and tomorrow you'll realise that there's a good life for you here – a good man, too. Why, half the young men in the town would give their eye-teeth for a smile from Miss Evie Murphy!'

'I don't care about local fellers and that's no more'n the truth. I'm going, Maeve, and if you try to stop me then I promise you'll never set eyes on me again, as long as I live,' Evie said hysterically. 'I can't stay here and rot – I won't! You can stop me tonight, but you can't stand guard over me for the rest of my life. I'll get away, and if I do it that way I'll never come back, I swear it.'

The two girls stood on opposite sides of the table, the teapot between them, the candle casting its flickering shadows over the smooth oval of Evie's face and the rich glory of her thickly curling wheat-coloured locks. Maeve knew that the same shadows danced over her own plain and bony visage, over tear-filled eyes and lank, dust-coloured hair; but right now it was not Evie's beauty nor her own ugliness which was in question, it was whose will would prove stronger.

For what seemed like an eternity they stood there, eyes locked, then Maeve sighed and let her glance drop before the icy determination in her little sister's gaze. If she held out, she knew, she would lose Evie and she could not bear that.

'All right. If you must go, you must. Take Linnet and come back for Lucy when you're able,' Maeve said in a small, colourless voice. 'Remember, Evie, that we love you. Don't forget us, whatever happens. We'll always be here for you.'

The ice in Evie's glance melted and tears brimmed over and trickled down her cheeks. She ran round to her sister and put her arms round her, giving her a hard hug.

'Maeve, me darling, as if I could ever forget you. You're the best thing that happened to me, you've been like a mother to me – better than most mothers from what I've seen. And I'll come back to you, I swear it, when I'm

7

rich and famous. And – and I'll take great care of Linnet
... I'll write to you every week. Oh, darling Maeve, you'll
never regret what you've done tonight.'

'Don't wait till you're rich and famous,' Maeve said
with a slight smile. 'I'll fetch Linnet for you, shall I?'

'She's already in the sling you made for me, sleepin'
like a little angel,' Evie said with a sparkling look towards
the big fireside chair. 'Did you not see her, in the shadows? Oh, Maeve, look at the time – give me a kiss, dear,
then I must run. I dare not lose me lift into town.'

The sisters kissed, Evie clinging for a moment, then
Maeve went over to the big fireside chair and lifted the
sling and its rosy, sleeping occupant, helping Evie to
arrange the sling so that the baby lay comfortably against
her breast, leaving the young mother's hands free.

'Now isn't that grand?' Evie murmured. 'I've got a bag
with a few things in ...'

'The bag's awful light,' Maeve said uneasily, picking
the shabby little holdall up from the floor. 'Are you not
taking food and drink for your journey?'

'No need,' Evie assured her. She took the bag and put
a hand on the back door latch. 'I've got me best dress and
some stuff for Linnet ... hark, can you hear that rumbling? It's me lift coming across the river-bridge. Oh,
Maeve, I do love you; hold onto that! And take care of
Lucy for me.'

'I will alanna, but I wish ...' Maeve began, but her
sister had slipped out of the doorway and was crossing
the dark farmyard on quick, light feet. Maeve went and
stood on the big, cold flags, watching the younger girl
while tears ran down her cheeks, but Evie did not look
back. She turned out of the yard and into the lane and
Maeve strained her eyes but could see only Evie's hair,
pale as the moon's glow, and her slim ankles beneath the
dark coat. She watched, a hand pressed to her mouth,

until a bend in the lane hid Evie from her view. Only then did she turn back into the candlelit kitchen.

Gone! Maeve doused the candle and crossed the dark room, suddenly aware of ice-cold feet and a heavy heart. She had let Evie go – but how could she have stopped her? She could have insisted that Evie take both babies but it would have been wickedly unfair on little Lucy. The smaller of the twins was not a bouncing, rosy-cheeked child like her sister, she was pale and frail. At four months old Linnet had not seemed at all bothered when her mother had weaned her from the breast onto bottled cow's milk, whereas little Lucy had not taken to the bottle at all. She cried a lot, drank a small quantity from her bottle very slowly and reluctantly and then sicked half of it up again, usually all over whoever was bringing up her wind. Placid, fat Linnet seldom cried, played with her pink toes and chuckled and cooed. But Lucy suffered from colic, bringing her pointed knees hard up into her small stomach whilst she screamed with pain. Maeve had noticed that even the slightest change in her routine brought about an attack, and weaning the smaller twin was a painful process which Evie had left almost entirely to Maeve.

I should thank the good Lord that Evie didn't suggest taking Lucy, Maeve told herself, wearily climbing the stairs on her ice-cold feet. Evie could never manage the smaller twin – at least with a healthy, happy child like Linnet she has a head start, and I can manage Lucy meself, no problem.

Outside Evie's bedroom door, she paused. If she left Lucy to slumber on undisturbed the child would not waken until six or so, but then, with Maeve having had such a disturbed night, would she herself wake before Lucy's howls had aroused the entire household? Their

9

father was not a particularly patient man and had been heartbroken when his favourite daughter had produced twin girls and no husband to go with them. Indeed, Padraig Murphy had been deeply disappointed when the wife of his bosom had presented him with no fewer than five daughters and not one single son, though he had grieved over her death for they had been a fond couple. Nevertheless, he felt that fate had dealt unfairly with him.

'Fine it is for herself, a-choirin' wi' the angels on high,' he had observed sourly in the hearing of the eleven-year-old Maeve. 'And here am I, left lit'rally holdin' the babby.'

But it had been Maeve who had brought Evie up, with very little help from her other sisters, and even less from Padraig, though he had adored his youngest daughter and revelled in her pretty, loving ways. Plain old Maeve, the only Murphy girl that no man ever looked at twice, had also adored – and spoiled – the little sister who looked on her as the only mother she had ever known, and now she adored that little sister's children. Especially Lucy. There was no getting away from it, Lucy's pale little face and wistful blue eyes had wound their way firmly into Maeve's susceptible heart. Perhaps, Maeve thought, tiptoeing into Evie's bedroom and over to the stout wooden cradle in which young Murphys had slumbered for generations, perhaps I'm the sort of person who needs to be needed even more than I need to be loved. Or perhaps someone who needs you automatically loves you. Whatever the reason, though, I couldn't have borne it if Evie had taken Lucy.

She leaned over the cot. Lucy was awake, her thumb wedged into her small mouth, her eyes fixed on the ceiling above her head. She was bald but for a quiff of lint-white hair and she had lately developed a rash around her mouth and chin, but to Maeve she was the most beautiful thing on this earth. She smiled at the baby, a smile full of all the stored up, imprisoned love in her heart and the baby smiled back, her eyes lighting up with pleasure, her mouth curving into that most trustful of expressions, a beam of pure, unselfish love.

'Oh, Lucy, you're going to be my little girl until your mammy comes home,' Maeve whispered, picking the child out of the cot and cuddling her against her breast. 'No man'll ever want me – why should they, indeed? – but you do don't you, me darlin'? You'll want your Maeve for – oh, for years and years and years!'

And the baby sighed and nuzzled against her, seeming to listen when Maeve told her that it was not time for a feed yet, not for a couple of hours at least, but that there was plenty of time for a cuddle.

She climbed carefully into Evie's little bed with the child still held against her breast, and presently she had the satisfaction of seeing Lucy's lids droop, of hearing her breathing become slow and regular.

She's always been dear to me, but she's dearer than ever now, because she's as good as me own, Maeve thought, letting her cheek rest gently against the baby's silky hair. Oh Evie, Evie, I'll miss you sore every day that I live . . . but I'll be a good mammy to your little one. You can trust old Maeve to take as much care of her as you would yourself. No, I'll take more care of her, she added, letting her lips caress the child's soft crown. She'll be my little princess for she's all I've got, until you come home and take her from me. And then there'll be the four of us, in your grand big house, all happy as – as queens!

And on the thought, Maeve Murphy slid into dreams and slept soundly, with Lucy in her arms, until the new day dawned.

There was no waiting room at the small station in the

town, so Evie sat on a wooden bench in a sheltered corner and watched the stars pale in the sky and breast-fed a sleepy but compliant Linnet. She had weaned Lucy off the breast but had continued to feed Linnet, though secretly, knowing that if Maeve knew she would put two-and-two together and make four. Because Evie's plan, to leave the farm and her family far behind her and seek fame and fortune in the big city, had been in her head for two long years. She would have gone before had it not been for Jan.

Jan was the son of a neighbouring farmer, a dark, handsome young man in his early twenties, much sought after by local girls. But he had ignored them all until he came across Evie one bright April day, with her hands tangled in the mane of the new colt their father had bought from Killarney market, being pulled off her feet.

He had rescued her, talked to her – kissed her. Evie, white and gold, sixteen years old, on the threshold of womanhood, had needed little persuading to go with him into the nearby haybarn, where they had fallen on each other like love-starved animals and conceived the twins.

'I'll marry you,' he said when she told him she was going to have a baby, but Evie had shaken her head, feeling the bars of the cage close round her on the words. She had enjoyed making love, feeling his strong arms round her, she regretted that she would have to forgo it, once her child was born. But she wanted more freedom, a life of her own, fame and fortune, and she would not get any of those things once Jan had roped and tied her to his smallholding. Not even the pleasure of making love in a soft bed every night could make up for the loss of her dreams.

The baby finished, burped, was returned to her place in the sling, and very soon afterwards the train came chuffing lazily into the station. I've done all right for myself so far, Evie thought as she climbed into the carriage of the small train which would take her right across Ireland to the magic city of Dublin. She had managed to let everyone assume that the Englishman had been her lover, so that Jan had not lost face over the affair. And there was no ill-feeling between herself and Maeve, for if she had succeeded in her attempt to run away without a word to anyone, leaving Lucy behind, Maeve might well have felt some justifiable annoyance. As it was, Evie had got just what she wanted – escape from the farm – and had remained on good terms with her sister.

The train, which had waited for several moments in the station while goods and a few passengers were put aboard, sounded its whistle, but mutedly because of the early hour, and pulled out of the station. Evie settled herself comfortably in her window seat and looked down at her sleeping child. Dear little, good little Linnet, she would be no trouble, Evie was bound to find someone who wanted to look after her during the day while she sought her fortune. And the child was company, in an odd sort of way. I won't feel lonely whilst I've got Linnet, Evie thought contentedly, letting her gaze wander over the rich green of Ireland as the train chugged along. She was sure Linnet would be beautiful and would have a lovely singing voice, so perhaps they could do an act together when the child was a little older. Evie sat back in her seat and dreamed out of the window, and went back in her mind over what had happened at Ivy Farm that morning.

It was very good of Maeve to let me take the housekeeping money out of the pewter teapot, she reminded herself, because it means I shall be able to live quite well for the first month or so. And I'm sure Daddy won't give Maeve any cash to replace what I've taken until the month's end because he's tight-fisted and mean. A shame it is that he doesn't like me any more just because I fell for the twins, but when he sees I'm gone he'll probably be nicer to the others. He might even be nicer to Maeve, because although she's not pretty, she works harder than most.

The train chugged on and a plume of smoke swept by the window. There was grit on the surfaces and, although the sun was well up now bathing the countryside in gold, it was chilly in the half-empty carriage. A woman with two children, who had got aboard at Killarney, got out a bag of sandwiches and some apples. The woman offered Evie a ham sandwich and Evie accepted graciously and when it was eaten, leaned her head on the window and snoozed.

The children told each other stores in loud voices but the sound scarcely entered Evie's dreams, certainly did not wake her. With the baby snug against her breast, Evie slumbered on.

'She'll come back, Da, when she discovers that life isn't as easy as she thinks,' Maeve said next morning, expertly frying bacon and eggs in the big black pan whilst her father and the farmhands, Tom Flanagan and his son Kellach, sat with their big mugs of dark tea at the breakfast table. 'Inside six months she'll be back home, I'm sure.'

'She'll not be welcome here,' Padraig said at once. 'A wicked girl she is, and a bad example to her sisters. She's gone, now she can stay away.'

Clodagh, cutting bread at one end of the table, smiled at her sister, Éanna, who was making the bread into sandwiches and packing them into two lunch-tins. Both girls were tall, buxom and blonde. Clodagh taught at the local school and Éanna worked behind the counter in the town's only drapery shop, so they usually walked into town together, though Clodagh finished at four while Éanna was not finished until six or later. They were good friends, only a year separating them in age, and Maeve used to wonder whether the twins would be like them when they were older, for the twins, too, were fair-haired.

'If little Evie does come home she can come to my place, alanna, when Niall and I are wed,' Clodagh said, cutting a thick slice and handing it to Maeve for frying. 'Will she come back for the weddin', I wonder? She could be me attendant and welcome.'

'She'll not be welcome here,' Padraig repeated obstinately. 'At your own house, Clodagh, I shall have no say, but I won't have her here.'

'That's all right, Father,' Clodagh said peaceably. She smiled across at Éanna and her sister smiled back. They were placid, pleasant girls, much sought after by the young men of Cahersiveen. Whilst neither was strictly beautiful, as Evie was, the two girls nearest to Maeve in age were acknowledged to be pretty and sweet-natured, and both were engaged to be married to neighbouring farmers' sons.

'If she writes with her address, you must tell her to come back for our weddings, Maeve,' Éanna said comfortably. 'Sure and I wouldn't have little Evie missed out for the world.'

Padraig ground his teeth and Tom, drinking tea, looked from one girl to the other over the top of his mug and grinned.

'Sure an' you'll never get the better of a woman, Paddy,' he said, eyes twinkling. 'Your Evie'll be back home in a twelvemonth, mark me words.'

Kellach was a big, quiet young man of about Maeve's age. He had admired her once, walking her home from school, stopping to chat with her as she worked around the house, but her steadfast refusal to go out with him whilst her sisters needed her had resulted in his looking elsewhere and now it was commonly believed that he had an understanding with a widow who lived six miles away, on the other side of the town. She was ten years older than Kellach if she was a day, but she had a decent farm and at thirty-eight she probably still needed a man. Maeve knew one day she would be sorry that she had not snapped Kellach up whilst she had the chance, but that day was not yet. First it was Clodagh and Éanna who needed her, then Nora and Evie; now she had Lucy to think of. There was simply no time in her busy life to worry about men.

Maeve dished up the breakfasts and watched her father eating with the speed he always showed. He shovelled the food in, packing his mouth with bacon until the grease ran down his chin, wiping spilt yolk with a slice of bread, drinking his tea in big gulps between mouthfuls. The pity of it was, she reflected, that though he was a good farmer, none better, he was always rushing, hurrying to get on. So he seldom praised her meals, though perhaps as the bacon came from the pigs he reared, the eggs from the poultry strutting in the yard outside, even the bread from their own wheat, he might think that to say that the food was good was a form of self-appreciation.

It would have been nice to have been appreciated by her father, but to Padraig Murphy, Maeve was simply a work-horse. A good one, yes, but not valued as she ought to be. It isn't really fair, because if I were pretty then I'd marry and leave and he wouldn't like that, Maeve told herself, putting a piece of fried bread and an egg onto her own plate and taking it to her place at the end of the table. Her father was ashamed of her because she had no man sniffing after her, yet he resented the men who came calling after Clodagh, Éanna and Nora, was continually critical of them and obviously more than a little jealous.

'More tea, Maeve.'

She had only just sat down; Kellach made a half-move, but Clodagh was quicker. She took her father's mug without a word, refilled it, put it down before him. Once again, Padraig showed by neither word nor gesture that he had been given the tea he had demanded.

'Get the honey.'

This time Maeve reached the jar down from the dresser without having to move from her chair and stood it with a crack on the table before him. He reached for it, dug his knife into the smooth, amber sweetness, spread it thickly on a round of buttered bread.

'Lovely manners, Daddy,' Nora said. She had come into the kitchen softly and reached round her sister for the teapot. 'Don't worry, Maeve, I'm not eating breakfast this morning, I'll just have me a nice, hot cup of tea. Oh, and some bread and honey because I mustn't be fainting behind the till.'

Nora worked in the town's only dining rooms and was already clad in her working uniform – a black dress with white collar and cuffs, a rustling white apron and neat low-heeled black shoes. She was golden-haired, like three of her four sisters, and was currently walking out with the schoolmaster, a pleasant, scholarly man in his forties who had never been married and who probably never would be, unless Nora nudged him a little.

Padraig looked up and gave Nora a half-grin; she was his favourite daughter, now that Evie had fallen from favour with such a crash. I was never a favourite, nor ever will be, Maeve thought sadly, though I'm the only one that works at home, slaving to keep the place halfway decent. Still, I've no charm, no pretty ways. How can I expect to be anyone's favourite?

But then she remembered Lucy, sleeping in the cradle upstairs, and a smile curved her lips. Her sisters were lovely and beloved, but she – she had a baby who was as good as her own. She would see that Lucy got the best of everything and when Evie came back, or grew famous, there would be the four of them, closer than friends, staying together for the rest of their lives.

Me Da can be as grumpy as he pleases, and Kellach can court his old widow and go and live in her rich little farm, she told herself, eating her fried bread. The girls can marry their young men and Nora can flirt with the schoolmaster and get prettier and more sought-after by the day together. But what does it matter to us Murphy girls, Maeve and Evie, Lucy and Linnet? We'll manage fine so we shall, Maeve told herself blissfully. And did not even hear her father's voice as it ordered her to cut more bread and look lively, woman, we men have got work to do even if you haven't!

Chapter Two

1924

'Hey, watch out, watch out! Gerrout me wa-a-a-ay!'

Linnet, who had been walking carefully down the snowy pavement on Havelock Street, clutching her messages and thinking wistfully of the hot cup of tea which would await her on her return home, was unwise enough to turn round to see who was shouting, which was how she came to find herself travelling, very fast, along the pavement with a pair of arms clutching her and her bum slithering at incredible speed along the steeply sloping snow-covered flagstones.

The unexpected trip finished with equal suddenness. One moment she and her assailant and a small tin tea-tray were hurtling down Havelock Street, the next they had burst into Netherfield Road and were trying to untangle themselves from a lamp-post whilst a small boy sat on the pavement howling and clutching his knees and a very fat woman belaboured them indiscriminately with a large umbrella.

'Bleedin' gipsies!' the woman shouted, swishing the umbrella in a half-circle and catching Linnet and the would-be tobogganer around their unprotected shoulders. ''Ow dare youse ruffians come into a decent neighbourhood like this, a-playin' your wicked games! As if it ain't bad enough living 'alfway up Havelock Street, which is a rare danger in this sorta weather, without bein' knocked off our feet by kids on bleedin' tea-trays!'

'Sorry, missus,' the boy said, trying to get away from

the flailing umbrella. 'We din't do it on purpose, it were an accident, we're hurt, too, me and the little gal, we din't mean to . . . ouch!'

Linnet struggled to her feet as the woman gave her companion one last, valedictory thump with the umbrella and began to cluck over her small son, leading him up the steep street which she and her companion had just left. Bleakly, Linnet surveyed her string bag and its mangled contents. She had come all this way because Mammy had told her to fetch the new frock Miss Spelman, the dressmaker, had just completed for her, and now look at it! The brown paper was torn and beneath it, the tissue which Miss Spelman had carefully wrapped around it was torn, too, and wet. And she had visited Mammy's favourite confectionery shop first because the owner had promised to obtain for them some rather special crystallised fruit – Mammy loved crystallised fruit – and now the pretty white package tied with pink ribbon was looking decidedly the worse for wear.

'Oh me darling, whatever has happened to my parcels?' Mammy would say, examining the dirty wrapping paper. 'Did you fall over now in all this miserable snow and slush? I scarcely know how to bear the weather we've been having lately, I'm truly tempted to take my friend up on his invitation and go to Paris in the spring, just to get away from Liverpool snow and fogs.'

Mammy never shouted when it wasn't your fault, that was one good thing. And they were really flush at the moment because Mammy had a good part in the pantomime and her latest admirer, Mr Jackie Osborne, liked to buy special treats and to take Mammy out to dinner after the show. So perhaps it wasn't terribly serious that the messages had got a little snow and slush on them – by the time she got home the wrapping paper would, in all probability, have dried out and be as good as ever.

So there was no point in standing here wondering what Mammy would say. The fat woman and her son were labouring up Havelock Street now, the woman heaving herself along by clutching at the house-walls whilst the child's howls had turned to hiccups, but the boy with the tea-tray stood there still, rubbing a scarlet ear and scowling after his attacker.

'Well, as if I meant to do it!' he muttered crossly, turning to Linnet. 'As for you, you wasn't even on the bloody tray, was you? I should think your knickers is probably ripped to shreds though, comin' down Havey at that speed.'

Linnet frowned at him. It was rude to talk about knickers, a boy his age should know better. He looked quite a bit older than she, he must be twelve or thirteen she supposed, so he could not pretend that knickers were a suitable subject of conversation between them.

'I was just walking down the road with my messages,' she pointed out coldly, 'when you knocked me off my feet. You could have spoiled my Mammy's new dress and squashed her crystallised fruit. I think I'd better go now, before anything else happens.'

'Where d'you live?' The boy said, falling companionably into step beside her and ignoring her critical tone. 'I think I might have seen you before somewhere . . . live round these parts, do you?'

Linnet turned her head and surveyed him carefully. Mammy had said not to fall into conversation with strangers, but she had not meant *boys*, surely? Linnet went to a small private school run by the nuns, but boys were everywhere, as common and numerous as the raindrops which spotted the flagstones or the snowflakes which had made all this nasty slush. You could no more avoid boys than you could the rain or the snow, and when one actually spoke to you, you could scarcely pretend not to have heard. That would be rude and Mammy did not like rudeness.

'Well, will you know me again?' the boy said, but not nastily, because he was grinning at her as he spoke. He had a nice face, not clean or handsome or anything like that, just nice. He was thin and brown, with a wide grin and grey eyes and there was something about him, some quality of friendliness and concern for others – he had apologised to the woman and had not tried to blame Linnet for the accident, something a less honest boy might well have done – which made Linnet decide to forgive him for knocking her down and muddying her messages.

'Yes, I'll know you again,' she said seriously. 'I don't live round here, though. I live on Juvenal Street, in rooms over a shop opposite the back of the fruit market. My name's Linnet Murphy, what's yours?'

'I'm Roddy Sullivan,' the boy said readily. He stuck out a grimy hand. 'Well, we're neighbours, Linnet, 'cos I live in Peel Square; that's off Cazneau and right near Juvenal. So we'll walk back together, shall us? Come on, lemme give you a hand with them messages.'

'It's all right, I can manage,' Linnet said, clutching her string bag defensively close. He seemed nice, but you never let a stranger get his hands on your possessions, no matter how friendly he was; she already knew *that* much. 'Where did you get that tray from, though, and what were you doing coming down Havey like that?'

Havelock Street was famous for its steep slope; the elderly and infirm heaved themselves up it with great difficulty, clutching the walls as they went, but Linnet always felt sorry for coalmen's horses, who had no hands to help them along and had to risk a tumble and broken knees every time they delivered on Havelock Street.

'I were sledging, of course, and the tray's me mam's
. . . well, she works for James Blackledge, on Derby Road,
and the tray comes from there . . . an' Havey's steeper'n
it oughter be when you're on a tray,' Roddy explained a
trifle defensively. 'Good thing you and the old woman
was there, come to think, or I'd ha' charged straight out
into the middle of the carriageway. Why, I could of been
killed stone dead!'

'It was a mad thing to do,' Linnet pointed out primly.
'I daresay you might have been killed, but you might
have killed us and all – me, the old lady and the little lad.
What'ud you have done then, eh?'

'I'd've run like the divil,' Roddy said cheerfully. He
delved into the pocket of his ragged trousers. 'Here, want
a licky stick?'

He produced two liquorice sticks. They were shaped
like tiny walking sticks and were liberally covered in fluff
but Linnet accepted one graciously and bit off the curved
end.

'Thanks,' she said. 'Where d'you nick 'em?'

Roddy grinned, not taking offence at the question
though her mam, Linnet knew, would have been shocked
at her rudeness. The trouble with Mammy is that she
thinks Liverpool's just like Cahersiveen, and it isn't, Linnet thought defensively. In Cahersiveen, when Mammy
was a little girl, you never stole anything, 'cos there
wasn't no need. But when you lived in rooms over a
chandler's shop three doors down from the Clock public
house, you soon realised that a great many people had
little choice but to take what they could when they could
– and that included the kids.

I'm lucky, though, Linnet reminded herself, blissfully
sucking liquorice. My mam's got her lovely job in the
theatre so she's hardly ever out of work, she earns good
money and doesn't blue it on drink, so I get all the food

I want and decent togs, not like some. Roddy's thin grey jersey had huge holes all over and his shirt was torn as well so you could see his bare skin in places. As for his trousers – oh well, they cover most of him, Linnet thought charitably. And he had boots, though they were pretty ancient ones, with cracked uppers and almost certainly holes in the soles. Probably, Roddy was one of a big family, whereas Linnet, as her mam often told her, was a lucky only child.

'Got it legal, like,' Roddy said in reply to her question, speaking through a mouthful of his own liquorice stick. 'Payment for takin' a tray of iced cakes from Peely to Havey. Me mam made 'em for a party . . . made 'em in her own time, like. So she give me a penny for delivery an' the old gal on Havey give me the licky sticks. So it's all square, honest to God.'

'Good,' Linnet said politely. Not that she cared. Mammy would be horrified, but Linnet knew that it was a lot easier to be honest if you had a good job and no brothers and sisters. Mammy had told her to steer clear of street kids, but that didn't mean don't watch them. Linnet watched, and had seen with wonder tinged with envy, that the poor kids stuck by one another even in their thieving. One kid would hoist another over the wall and into the back of the market when the stallholders had gone home, then they would share whatever spoils came their way. Another would keep cavey when a friend was after a few toffees and the resultant booty would be religiously divided. What was more, she knew that some kids would never see an orange or a liquorice stick if they didn't prig one now and then. No point in sticking your nose in the air and coming all Holy Joe about it; so far as Linnet could see, it was all right for her to be honest, because she ate well anyway. Others were not so fortunate.

'When you play out, Linnet, where d'you play?' Roddy asked presently, as they trudged through the filthy slush which, two days ago, had been great heaps of white snow. 'I ain't never seen you up our way.'

'No, you wouldn't. I'm not allowed to play in the street,' Linnet said. 'My mam's an actress, though, so when it's school holidays I go to the Playhouse with her, mostly.'

Roddy's eyes rounded. 'An actress! Is she famous?'

'She's Miss Evaline Murphy,' Linnet said cautiously. She had been told to keep her mother's identity a secret – but surely not from this friendly boy? 'I dunno if she's famous, but she does lovely acting, honest to God.'

'Not the one wi' the long yaller curls, the one they calls little Evie?' Roddy said incredulously. 'Cor, my mam saw her in a play last summer, she thought little Evie were a cracker! Blackledge's took their workers to the theaytre instead of on a seaside trip. Ooh, she can't be that Evie, can she?'

'Yes, she's that one,' Linnet said proudly. 'She's ever so beautiful and a very good actress, too, your mam was right. She's played all sorts . . . she's in the panto now, you know . . . she's the lady who gets sawed in half in the Giant's castle.'

'Cor,' Roddy said again, suitably impressed. 'My mam said little Evie come on the stage wi' a white, floaty gown you could see right through, she said there weren't nothing left to . . .'

'Oh well, you have to do all sorts of things if you want to be a star,' Linnet said. Her cheeks felt hot and she wished – not for the first time – that she hadn't started boasting. Not everyone understood that Mammy, who was so strict at home, sometimes had to do things which weren't quite . . . quite nice. 'Mammy sings lovely, too. She sings to me when she puts me to bed.'

25

'Puts you . . . how old are you, Linnie?' Roddy said. 'You looks about twelve, same's me.'

'I'm eleven,' Linnet told him. 'Eleven years and ten days, 'cos I was born on New Year's Day. Why?'

'Well, me mam puts the baby an' Freddy to bed, an' me brother Matt gives little Bert an 'and, but the rest of us gets ourselves there, some'ow,' Roddy said. 'Can't you git to your buttons, eh?'

'I only meant that I get into bed and then Mam comes along an' tucks me in,' Linnet explained hastily. 'Then she sits on the side of my bed and sings a song or tells me stories about the old days in Ireland. That's what I meant, I didn't mean she undressed me or put my nightgown on – I do that for myself, of course.'

'You're a right 'un. A nightgown!' Roddy said. 'What's wrong wi' your shirt, or knickers or whatever gals wear?'

'Well, you see . . . but let's not talk about it, it's just Mammy's ways are different,' Linnet said. She could just imagine how involved the conversation would become if they started talking about the dangers of catching fleas or lice if you wore the same garments day and night for a week. 'You've got quite a lot of brothers and sisters, haven't you? There's only me and Mam in our rooms.'

'What about your da?' Roddy said. Linnet tried not to glower at him. She was already realising that Roddy would always pick on the difficult subjects, ask the awkward questions, unless he was carefully guided away from them.

'My da's back in Ireland,' Linnet told him, mentally crossing her fingers though not doing so in fact, since he would undoubtedly notice. 'Mam left him there. He – he wasn't the sort of man she wanted to live with, you see.'

Roddy nodded knowingly. 'Aye, I know what you mean. Me mam's sister, Auntie Prue, she lives not far from Peely. She's got two brats, Simmy an' Sukey. She din't like either one o' the fellers she went with, she told me mam so.'

'Well, there you are then,' Linnet said bracingly, thanking God for Prue and her brats. 'Tell you what, Roddy, it'll be dark quite soon. If you come home wi' me, Mammy'll give us buttered toast an' fruit cake. We could play Snap, or Beggar your Neighbour if you'd like to.'

'But she don't know me,' Roddy said doubtfully. 'She won't want a kid she don't know in her place.'

'Yes she will, she likes me to have friends,' Linnet said.

The remark was not strictly truthful but Linnet had noticed lately that Mammy, who at one time had frequently told her to steer clear of what she called 'street kids' and had made it plain that she did not want Linnet to bring school friends home, was beginning to change her tune. A year ago, when Linnet was nine, she had decided that her daughter was now old enough to have friends back to their rooms or to visit their homes, when she was invited. And on Linnet's tenth birthday, when Mammy had come, pale-faced and heavy-eyed, into the living room, complaining bitterly that she had a champagne headache, she had reminded Linnet that she still had not brought any friends home, nor visited her classmates.

'You're old enough to find your own friends now,' she had said, accepting the cup of tea her daughter had poured her and using both hands to lift it to her mouth. 'Dear God, my head's about to take off and float round the room! You're to bring a couple of girls home to tea when you start school next week; do you hear me, now?'

But after holding aloof from them for so long, it was strangely difficult to infiltrate the little groups of girls, all in similar circumstances, who went to the small private school in Rodney Street. They had fathers as well as mothers and they lived in the smart houses surrounding

27

the school, whereas Linnet caught the tram morning and evening and seldom talked about her home circumstances. Mammy had impressed upon her that she should not mention that her parent was little Evie, the actress, not to her schoolmates nor to the nuns who taught them. And Linnet had speedily seen that not talking about one's mother also made friendships difficult.

But today Linnet knew at once that this boy, this Roddy Sullivan, was different. He was from their own neighbourhood and despite her mother's dismissive remarks about 'street kids' Linnet felt sure that he would be a friend worth having, if friendship were on offer. And if she had someone tough enough to take care of her and befriend her, someone who could take her round to Peel Square occasionally, then Mammy would be able to go off with her gentleman friend without a qualm.

Because that, of course, was what it was all about. Linnet loved her mother dearly but she was quite shrewd enough to realise that there were times when she was a drag on her mother's career. And Evie's career was tremendously important to her. Linnet knew that it was her fault that her mother had not already reached stardom, and always felt guilty when she found Mammy in tears, staring at her face in the mirror, lamenting an imaginary line or a tiny wrinkle, reminding herself that she was not getting any younger, that the years were passing.

I hold her back, Linnet told herself sorrowfully now, as Roddy considered her invitation. If it hadn't been for me she'd have been a star by now, but having a big daughter of eleven puts a lot of people off. So if this latest gentleman friend means what he says and helps Mammy's career, I must keep out of the way a bit more, learn to amuse myself. And with Roddy as my friend that will be very much easier.

'Finished the licky? Well, if you means it, if you're really a-going to take me back to meet your mam, we'd best clean ourselves up a bit,' Roddy said as they crossed Homer Street and waited on the pavement's edge at Juvenal whilst a huge dray dragged by two immense carthorses thundered past. 'There's a tap in Peely – want to go there first?'

'There's taps in our rooms,' Linnet said, puzzled. 'We can wash there.'

'Ye-es, but your mam . . .'

'Oh, yes, we're a bit lickyish round the mouths,' Linnet said, light dawning. Truth to tell, both their faces were now dirty and sticky, she guessed. Roddy's certainly was and she knew it would be best if her new friend was at least clean. 'But won't your mam mind us going in?'

'Where was you born?' Roddy exclaimed. 'The tap's at one end of the bleedin' square, gal! We can clean up wi'out anyone being any the wiser. Well, 'cept for the kids,' he amended. 'They're everywhere, but they won't care what we does, they'll be playing some game or other.'

'All right, we'll go to your place first, then,' Linnet said. 'I – I don't know where Peel Square is, though. It's not far, is it?'

'No, nobbut a step,' Roddy said reassuringly. 'It's right instead of left, though – you get to Peely down Cazneau.'

'Oh, I see,' Linnet said, following close behind Roddy. Trams thundered along Cazneau Street with the horsedrawn traffic keeping well clear of them, and despite the snow and the cold there was considerable bustle as shoppers made their way along the pavements, trying to get back home before darkness fell. 'We don't often come down this way, me and Mam.'

'No need, I don't 'spect,' Roddy said cheerfully. 'Here we are . . . come on in.'

He dived under a shabby brick archway and abruptly, as though it was the transformation scene in a panto-mime, the street noises were muted, even the light seemed dimmer, softer. It was as though, in walking under the archway, the two children had entered a different world.

It did not seem, Linnet thought rather apprehensively, a very nice world. The oblong which was Peel Square was completely surrounded by sooty houses, each one at-tached to the next so that the only glimmer of daylight came from the sky above and from the archway under which they had just passed. The square was paved with large, uneven flagstones, each narrow house had a set of three steep steps which ended on the flags, and there was one gas lamp, as yet unlit, though in the enclosed space it seemed as though dusk had already fallen.

But the space was not quiet, because it was crowded with children. Small girls played hopscotch on the pav-ing stones, shouting out to one another, small boys kicked a ball about or squatted on the ground, playing fives. Bigger girls and boys were moving purposefully about, filling enamel jugs and buckets at the tap or com-ing and going on messages, Linnet supposed, since they mostly carried bags or bundles of some description.

'Roddy!' A small, tow-headed boy carrying a blue-and-white enamel bucket with a lid came bounding down the step of the nearest house and caught Linnet's companion by the sleeve. 'We're havin' a treat – our mam was goin' to make blind scouse but Aunty Prue got some scrag-end cheap off o' Mr Perkins in the Scottie so we'll have a good supper tonight. Where you been?'

'Deliverin' for Mam,' Roddy said briefly. 'All you ever think about is grub, our Freddy! Now gi's the bucket a mo, we'll have a splash an' then bring it over for you. That's me little brother,' he added in a quiet aside to

Linnet as the small boy nodded his agreement and went back into the house from which he had just emerged. 'He ain't a bad kid.' He jangled the lidded enamel bucket at her. 'Let's stand in line for the tap, then.'

Most of the people queueing for the tap were children, but one or two were much older women. Linnet eyed them curiously. Seldom had she seen such weary, de-feated looking faces, and why were they waiting here? She whispered the query to Roddy, who answered equally quietly.

'Their kids is all working, so there's no one to get water in but them. Most of the old gals will pay a kid a farthing or so to fetch 'em water and that, but some just ain't got the gelt. Ah, us is next.'

They reached the tap, ran it until their bucket was full, then Roddy, disdaining Linnet's offered help, carried it across the yard once more and stood it down near the stained doorstep of No 16.

'The water won't be very nice for your mam, though, after we've washed our hands and faces in it,' Linnet said as Roddy began washing with a good deal of un-necessary splashing. 'What's she going to use it for, anyway?'

Roddy finished splashing water on his face and the front of his hair and wiped himself dry with a grimy sleeve. He shrugged. 'Dunno, everything, I guess. She'll boil the spuds with it, mash the tea, wash up the pots . . .'

'But we've washed in it,' Linnet protested again. She wet her hanky and wiped round her face, then washed her hands, patting herself dry on her warm little jacket. 'You can't drink water you've washed in, we'd better get her another bucketful.'

'Don't be daft, look at that line o' kids,' Roddy said with the sort of affectionate tolerance for her odd ways which Linnet was beginning to expect from him. 'Me mam wants the bucket now, norrin a week's time. Come on.'

He lugged the bucket to the top of the steps, waving Linnet away in a lordly fashion once again when she tried to help, hollered through the door for 'Freddy!' and then came down the steps towards Linnet, grinning brightly.

'All right, are you? Off we goes, then, to your mam's! Now what did you say your name was?'

'Linnet Murphy,' Linnet said patiently. 'You should be able to remember that; I can remember you're Roddy Sullivan!'

'I couldn't forget a name like Linnet, could I?' Roddy said, chuckling. 'It's the Murphy bit – I gorra remember to say, "Evenin', Mrs Murphy, ma'am, how are you today?" ' Roddy laughed at his own words and caught Linnet's elbow as they emerged from under the arch. 'Careful, there's a lorra traffic at this time o' night. We *are* late, here comes Jimmy Winkup to light the street lamps. We'd best hurry.'

'Yes, I don't want my mother worrying,' Linnet said seriously. 'I usually go straight home with my messages. Still, she'll be so pleased I've brought a fr – I mean another friend home that she won't mind me being a bit late, I daresay.'

Chapter Three

1925

It had been a brilliantly hot and sunny day but now the sun was sinking in the west and long shadows striped the dusty road. A small group of schoolchildren, with Lucy Murphy in their midst, were making their way home across Barry's Bridge. They had passed the burnt-out barracks and had stopped for a moment by the big willow near the water so that the boys, Daniel, Peder and Garvan, might cut themselves willow wands, though what they wanted with them no girl, Lucy thought disdainfully, would ever understand. As they walked now, the three boys belaboured the hedges, talking in loud and boastful tones of how they would spend the coming holiday, for it was the last day of the summer term which meant – Lucy hugged herself – two whole months at home, with neither school nor teachers to bother them.

'What'll we do tomorrow, Caitlin?' Lucy asked as they began to cross the river. She paused for a moment when they were a few yards out from the bank and looked down into the water; sinuous silver-bodied fish could sometimes be seen gliding in the depths and Lucy always secretly hoped that, because this was one of those strange and magical spots where the River Fertha and the sea lough joined, she might one day spy the shadowy form of a small mermaid, combing her hair with a golden comb, moving easily with the swirl and sway of the sparkling water. And anyway, she reassured herself, looking never did anyone any harm. 'What'll we do after we've done our messages, I mean?'

Caitlin Kelly was thirteen years old and lived in the cottage nearest to the Murphys' farm. Her father worked on Murphy land and her mother gave a hand in the farmhouse, doing the washing on a Monday and what she called 'cleaning through' on a Wednesday, whilst on a Friday she and Maeve baked and baked until the house roared with heat and the sweet smell of cooking. Though there were large families of children on surrounding farms they were all much further off, so Lucy and Caitlin had been friends ever since Lucy was old enough to toddle and Caitlin's attitude, at first protective since she was the elder, had subtly changed over the years until now they were simply best friends and almost always together.

Fortunately, furthermore, Maeve, who was the most important person in Lucy's life, approved of Caitlin.

'She's a clever girl, that one; she'll go far I wouldn't wonder,' she would say when Caitlin's name came up. 'She'll do our Lucy nothing but good. Big families are all very well, but with only the one to worry over the Kellys can give her the best and make sure she minds them.'

'Tomorrow?' Caitlin said thoughtfully, now. 'Well, we'll be busy till dinner time, that's for sure, but when I've done me chores an' fettled me room I t'ought we'd go on a picnic. We could start out by two o'clock I daresay. Will your Maeve put us up a bite o' tea?'

'Course she will.' Lucy did a little jig, bouncing her bulging satchel up and down in the dusty road and doing it no good at all. But it's time I had a new one, she told herself virtuously, seeing that a red arithmetic book was poking out of a hole in the corner which she did not remember seeing before.

'You were twelve last January; it's time you saw life,' Caitlin was saying thoughtfully. 'And seeing life isn't much good unless it's a bit frightening, wouldn't you say?'

Lucy agreed with enthusiasm. She and Caitlin were great believers in magic as a whole and witches and the little folk in particular and Kerry was a great place to live for all those things. She said as much to Caitlin, dancing along beside her whilst the boys strolled on ahead.

'Sure and wouldn't we be after findin' a mermaid, if we went right down to the shore? We could fish for tiddlers and we'd mebbe find a mermaid – just a little one, you understand – in our bucket by the end of the day. You can't keep sea-folk,' she added righteously, 'Maeve says so. But we could put her back when we'd had a wish or two.'

'Oh, you! There's nothing frightening about mermaids,' Caitlin said with some scorn. 'No, I'd more witches in mind.'

'Oh, I see,' Lucy said rather more doubtfully. There were Irish witches, everyone knew that, and several doubtful characters lived in the area who might fit the bill. There was old Mrs O'Rourke, who lived in the tiny, teeny squeezed up house between two quite ordinary ones in the town, and there was Liam's gran, who was over one hundred years old, bald as a coot, and managed to eat frogs, toads and raw rabbits which she caught with her hands, though they only had Liam's word for that, of course. 'Were you thinkin' of Liam's grandmother, Cait?'

But at this point the boys dropped back to walk with them, mostly in order to tease, and both girls had more sense than to continue the conversation. Instead, they kicked a stone along from one to the other so that the boys could rush at them and try to tackle it away, then they made up riddles, discussed their holiday tasks and, at the end of the deep little lane with its high banks and arching hazel trees, they told each other to enjoy their holidays and promised to meet up some time.

'I dunno why we bother to say all that when we'll see them in church every Sunday and at the Stations, wherever they're held,' Caitlin said as the boys shouted and jostled off down the road. 'I wonder what Mammy's got for my tea?'

'I'm going to start my holiday task this very evening,' Lucy said. 'Why don't you come round later, Cait, then we could do them together. We could work in my room – or in the hayloft, come to that. It's nice up there, all quiet and dusty and the hay smells so sweet.'

Lucy had slept with Maeve until the previous January, when she had qualified for a room of her own because all her aunties were married now, even Nora.

'I might come round,' Caitlin said cautiously. 'What'll you do first? Your arithmetic or the English essay or the history one? I thought I'd do arithmetic, get it out of the way.'

'I shan't, I'll leave my sums till last, in the hopes my brain'll have grown bigger by the end of the holidays,' Lucy said, earning a crow of laughter from Caitlin. 'You may mock, girl, but I'm growing all the time, Maeve keeps grumbling about it, so surely my brain's growing, too? Oh, I do hate sums and I do wish I was like my Auntie Nora who can do a sum without even a wrinkle coming on her forehead – and she doesn't add on her fingers, either,' she finished triumphantly.

'Brains don't grow so's you'd notice, though,' Caitlin pointed out as they turned into the even narrower lane which led directly into the farmyard. 'And they're slow doers, Lu, rare slow doers. You'll do the sums by thinking about 'em and working them out in your head when you're sitting quiet, not by waiting for your brain to expand.'

Lucy sighed deeply and broke into a trot; from here she could see the small kitchen window and Maeve, standing before it, cleaning something in the low stone sink. If she hurried she might persuade Maeve to hand out a bite of bread and cheese and a drink of milk before she began laying up for the family's tea, because Lucy was starving hungry, she realised, almost dead with it.

'All right, I'll do a bit of each,' she called as Caitlin continued past the end of the yard, heading for the Kelly cottage. 'And I'll see you later, shall I?'

'Maybe,' Caitlin called back. 'Ask Maeve for some carry-out, will you?'

'I said I would, didn't I?' Lucy shrieked. 'Where are you now, Caitlin?'

'Passing the cabbage patch,' Caitlin yelled. 'Where's you, Lu?'

'Halfway across the haggard,' Lucy bellowed. This was a nightly ritual which drove the other members of both families mad, but she and Caitlin loved it. 'I've got me foot on the back doorstep now – where's you?'

'Ducking under the lintel . . .'

The slam of the Kellys' door told the rest of the story. Lucy threw open her own back door and hurled her satchel across the kitchen, watching it collide with the sturdy legs of the big kitchen table with a certain satisfaction. 'No more school for two months!' she shouted.

Maeve, scrubbing a sinkful of potatoes which she would bake presently in the ashes, said automatically, 'Shut the door, don't slam it, and pick up that satchel for goodness sake, we aren't made o' money, Lucy Murphy. What do you think your grandad would say if he saw you wearing out your good bag on the old earth floor? He'd want to know why in the name of God you have to hurl your books about, that's what, and by the same token I'd like to know why you have to tell the whole of Kerry your whereabouts each afternoon?'

'Shan't have to for another eight weeks,' Lucy said, begging the question since Maeve knew the answer as well as she herself did. 'As for me satchel, it's full of holiday tasks and they ought to be slung in the river, not just across the floor. It isn't fair is it, Maeve, to give you a holiday with one hand and take it back with the other? That's what holiday tasks are, they're trying to make you be at school even when you aren't.'

'They're to make sure you use your brain during the summer and don't just leave it lie and rust,' Maeve said. She put the last potato on the draining board and turned away from the sink, beginning to dry her hands on a scrap of blue and white striped towelling. 'Well? How did today go, and aren't you going to give me a kiss?'

Lucy struggled out of her school jacket, not without difficulty for it was shrunk from many washes, and slung it across the kitchen table, then hurled herself at Maeve and gave her a squeeze, burrowing her face into Maeve's flowered wrap-around pinny as she did so.

'Today went great . . . oh, I do love you, Maeve! Do you know you smell of new-baked bread? I love that smell – is there a wee bit to spare? I'm so hungry me belly's flapping against me backbone, I could murder a slice of bread and some cheese so I could!'

'You've a clever nose on you to smell fresh bread when the larder door's shut and the loaves came out of the bake-oven first thing this morning, I'll say that for you,' Maeve said with a chuckle. She dropped a kiss on the top of Lucy's head and gave her a hug. 'But since you're starving to death there's a loaf cooling on the marble slab in the larder and some cheese in the meat safe. Can you help yourself while I get these potatoes on to cook?'

'Helping meself is what I'm best at,' Lucy said eagerly.

'Shall I cut you a slice an' all, alanna? Can I have some milk, too?'

'It's a surprise to me you can still do up your school jacket,' Maeve said. 'Go on, then, there's a jug of milk in the safe, you won't want to go trudging over to the dairy when you're worn out from hollerin' at young Caitlin and sweating over your school books. And close the safe door properly,' she added as Lucy danced across to the larder, emerging presently with a large hunk of bread and cheese and a mug of creamy milk.

Maeve was kneeling in front of the oven, pushing her clean potatoes down its hot black throat. 'And now, young woman, where's your report?'

The air immediately became electric. Lucy had no idea what Miss Carruthers had said about her this year, but it was bound to be something horrible, or at least critical. Miss Carruthers had sharp eyes, a sharp voice and an extremely sharp tongue – her pen would no doubt resemble the rest of her. But it would not do to say so; Lucy affected extreme nonchalance.

'Oh, that. It's in the bottom of me satchel, under the red arithmetic book. And I haven't opened the envelope, either. Want it now?'

'Yes, I think so. Get it out of the way before Grandad comes in, shall we? He'll remember it later and probably read it, but we don't want to spoil his tea!'

Maeve was smiling as she spoke and Lucy stooped and picked up her satchel, rummaged her way through the books and produced the long white envelope. If Miss Carruthers has given me a hard time I'll put a live mouse in her desk and a dead one in her outdoor shoes next year, Lucy vowed grimly. Or she can have the plague of frogs next spring; take your choice, Miss C.

Maeve slit the envelope open and pulled out the report form. She sat in a chair and began to read, one finger

following the line across. 'Hmm . . . hmm . . . hmm . . .'
She looked up at Lucy, anxiously hovering, still trying to
pretend indifference but not making such a good job of
it now the moment had come. 'Well, she's given you top
marks for English, both language and literature, anyway.
Which isn't surprising, considering you came top of the
class in the English exam.'

'Good,' Lucy said. Even to herself her voice sounded
somewhat strained. English was no problem . . . but what
about history, geography and the hated arithmetic? And
then there was conduct, and the strangely named
attitude. She'll say something horrid, Lucy thought, and
Maeve will be upset and she'll keep me in tomorrow to
think about things and . . . and . . .

Maeve was laying the sheet down on the table, pushing it across to Lucy. 'You have done well, alanna! I
t'ought you said Miss Carruthers didn't like you – if she
doesn't, she certainly likes your work. She says you try
hard at everything, even your sums, and she says a bit of
after-class tutoring would bring you up to date with
arithmetic, even. Now that's what I call a good report, a
real little beauty! When your grandaddy sees it he'll be
pleased, he couldn't fail to be.'

'What about conduct? And attitude?' Lucy whispered,
staring at the sheet of paper.

'She says you've behaved pretty well on the whole and
have the right attitude to work and to your fellow pupils,'
Maeve said. 'Go on, take a look for yourself.'

Lucy looked and decided that Miss Carruthers was a
saint so she was and she, Lucy, would make sure that no
one ever tried the dead mouse trick on her, or the tadpole
soup torture.

'I'll take on the after-class tutoring,' Lucy said, dazed
by the A grades which marched neatly alongside each
subject on the report sheet, scarcely marred at all by the

B for arithmetic. No one can be perfect, she told herself, beginning to smile. Well and haven't I misjudged the woman after all? I almost wish I hadn't tied her stockings into a knot the day she came and played hockey with us – though she couldn't have known it was me or that conduct mark would have been a bit different!

'Well, alanna, so you're not wasting your time at school after all.' Maeve pushed back her chair and smiled across at Lucy. 'Now how about laying the table for me, if you've finished your bread and cheese?'

Because of the good report Lucy had no difficulty in abandoning the rest of her tasks once she had helped to clear away the tea things. Hurrying round to the Kellys' cottage she found Mrs Kelly scrubbing the kitchen floor whilst Mr Kelly dozed in a chair.

'Caitlin's out the back,' Mrs Kelly said before Lucy could so much as open her mouth. 'Give her a shout, alanna, she's givin' me a bit of a hand cuttin' mint, that's all.' Mrs Kelly was a great one for bottling and preserving, drying and jellying, and Lucy quite envied Caitlin, who would be somewhere out in the garden cutting the mint which would be hung in bunches from the kitchen ceiling beams throughout the summer and allowed to dry. Once it was like tinder it would be crushed, sugared, vinegared and packed into small jars which would last for the whole of next winter, enlivening mutton dishes and giving an added piquancy to vegetable stews.

'Caitlin, is that you?' Lucy said to a patch of vigorously shaking cabbage plants, but it was only Mrs Kelly's one-eyed cat, who was sharpening his claws on a woody cabbage stalk. He gave her a mean look out of his one eye and stalked away from her, tail straight up, feet turned out, fur well fluffed, outrage in every line of his body.

'Lucy?' Caitlin's head appeared from the middle of

what looked like currant bushes. 'Want to give me a hand?'

'I don't mind,' Lucy said, pushing her way through the vegetables until she reached her friend's side. 'Your mammy said you were cutting mint. Shall I bunch them for you?'

'Sure,' Caitlin said, cutting another stalk and handing it to Lucy. 'You're early, aren't you?'

'It was me report,' Lucy told her. 'Me knees fair shook – 'member the stockings? And the bits of chalk I nicked to make indigestion medicine? But she was really nice, she gave me all A grades except for sums, and she couldn't have give me higher than a B for that, not without perjuring her soul, as the priest would say.'

Caitlin sat back on her heels and pushed her lank brown hair out of her eyes. She grinned up at Lucy. 'Told you she wasn't a bad woman,' she said righteously. 'I got mostly A grades as well, Mammy's ever so pleased and Daddy, too. So d'you want to ask if we can go off for the whole day, tomorrow, instead of waiting until after our dinners? We could really cover some distance in a whole day.'

'That's why I came round,' Lucy admitted. 'I've already asked; Maeve said she was sure it would be all right. Go on, if Mrs Kelly's in a good mood she'll likely say yes as well.'

And so it proved. 'But no drownin' yourselves in the lough or gettin' into bad company,' Mrs Kelly warned. 'Is Miss Maeve puttin' up enough dinner for the both of you? Right, then you can have a bag of me dried apple pieces and a bottle of me lemon barley water.'

Polite thanks were chorused and then, as the sun was setting, Caitlin, as the elder, offered to see Lucy home.

'It's funny how your mammy always tells us not to drown ourselves or get into bad company, and Maeve

42

always says to take care of each other and not to play with fire, isn't it?' Lucy said as they ambled across the farmyard in the dying sunset. 'Yet it's my mammy who got into bad company, and my daddy who was drowned. I don't really understand grownups at all, do you?'

'I don't want to understand 'em; we'll be grownup ourselves quite soon enough – too soon,' Caitlin said promptly. 'There's your back door, alanna; get indoors, then I'll run home and we can light our lamps and wave.'

This was another tried and true activity. Lucy had a little room up under the eaves of the old stone farmhouse with ivy constantly trying to block out her light. Caitlin was in an even smaller room in her parents' cottage with a tiny window cut into the thatch. But when they lit their lamps the glow could be seen from both homes, and if Caitlin leaned out of her window and looked very hard to the left and Lucy leaned out of hers and looked downwards and to the right they could each see the lit-up square and the head and shoulders of the other.

Signals were many, including ones which needed a bit of curtain, some cardboard and a lamp held close to the window, but shouting beat them as a means of communication which could be immediately understood.

'Night, Cait!'

'Night, Lu!'

'Where's your cat, Cait?'

'On the bottom of me bed, Lu . . . why?'

'He pulled a rude face at me in the cabbages this evening. He's a funny old devil, your cat.'

'I know. As funny as your old Shep.'

'My old Shep's all right, but they won't let him sleep on my bed, worse luck. Wish I had a cat, Cait. If I could have a kitten . . .' there was a short scuffle and then a wail.

'Oh, Maeve, you are mean to me! Don't you love me? There's something real urgent I've got to tell Caitlin before I close me window and get into bed!'

Caitlin heard mutterings which she guessed were being made by Maeve, then the slam of a window shutting. Presently, it opened again, with extreme caution, as she had known it would.

'Sorry about that – see you in the morning, Cait!'

'Aye, see you in the morning, Lu!'

It isn't unknown for it to rain in Kerry in July and when Lucy woke at daybreak the following day, with the birds kicking up enough row to deafen you, especially in a room right under the eaves, she opened her eyes on the soft and misty rain which so often continues all day and ruins the best laid plans of mice and men.

'Oh, not rain!' Lucy muttered to herself. 'It's the first day of me summer holidays, God, you can't mean to ruin it all with rain!' She sat up on her elbow and peered out through the window once more. Rain was pattering against the window panes and a row of fat raindrops clung to the slate roof-edge, just waiting to drop. Outside, the big red cockerel, who was not above giving you a nip if you went near his harem of hens, cleared his throat and cock-a-doodle-doed; he sounded uncertain, as though he wasn't perfectly sure whether day was really breaking, but was prepared to give it a go anyhow.

'We were going to have a picnic,' Lucy reminded her Maker, snuggling down the bed again. 'It's the first day of everyone's summer holidays, Lord, so you're punishing everyone by sending rain! I do wish you'd think again and give us some blue sky instead.'

With that she fell asleep once more and when she woke because Maeve was slamming about in the kitchen and Grandad was shouting to one of the men and Shep was barking, the sun was streaming in through her window and the sky was so blue it hurt her sleepy eyes.

'Thank you, dear Lord, thank you,' Lucy burbled, jumping out of bed. Ah, it wouldn't do to leap into her clothes without a wash, not when God had been so obliging as to change the rain to sun just for her! She said a couple of Hail Marys under her breath as she washed and dressed, then ran downstairs, humming beneath her breath.

In the kitchen, Maeve had made Lucy's breakfast; two fried eggs, a round of fried bread and a rasher of bacon, crisped just as she liked it. The tea in the pot steamed merrily and on the dresser were two greaseproof packets and a blue cloth bag which bulged in a satisfactory sort of way.

'There's your dinners,' Maeve said, dishing up the food and jerking her head towards the bag and the greaseproof wrapped packets. 'I've done your sandwiches in the greaseproof and you can get some water to drink, and there's apples and some of my rich fruit cake in the bag.'

'Oh, Maeve, you are kind to me,' Lucy said rapturously. 'This is the best breakfast in the world!'

She ate fast and very soon was poised in the doorway, bag in hand, looking rather guiltily back at Maeve.

'Are you sure I can go? That you can manage without me?'

'I'm sure; don't I manage every day of the week and you in school?' Maeve demanded. 'Just go out and enjoy yourself, alanna, tomorrow we'll talk about your house-jobs.'

It was a glorious day. Lucy and Caitlin strolled down the lane, wondering aloud which way to go.

'I vote for the shore,' Lucy said, but Caitlin shook her head.

'No, not the shore, exactly. I've a better idea. How brave are you feeling, Lucy?'

'Very brave,' Lucy said stoutly, though a little shiver of unease ran along her backbone at the words. Hadn't Caitlin said something the previous day about witches? But it was hard to believe in anything evil under a cloudless blue sky with the sun warm on your back so she smiled across at her friend with a fair degree of confidence. 'Why? What'll we do, Cait?'

'We're going to the castle,' Caitlin said at once. 'There's a boat pulled up on the shingle, which means someone's home. What do you say?'

The castle had long been an object of great curiosity not just for the two girls but for most of the children in the area. It stood in a commanding position beside a creek which ran into the lough, and from a distance it still looked impressive. To the left of it was a stand of trees, old and crabbed now and bent all one way by the prevailing wind, and all round it stretched that mixture of meadow and marsh which prevailed near the sea lough. Once, it had been a real castle, no doubt the towers had been manned by archers and men-at-arms had guarded the battlements against pirates and other invaders, but now it was a ruin and almost all that was left was a tower, part of the keep and a peat hut which crouched against the tower like a lamb against a ewe, as though seeking shelter from the old, old stones. Now it looked lonely and sad rather than sinister, Lucy told herself, so there was no need to feel afraid of it. Only it was a well-known fact that it was haunted, probably by the spirits of its one-time occupants, and not even the big boys went near if they could help it.

And there was the boat. If no one lived in the black hut or the old ruin, then why was the boat so often drawn up on the shingly strand of the creek? It was a curragh, made of willow wands and canvas and tarred to keep out the sea, not a proper, modern boat, but even so, who would leave it there, far from any proper habitation? No, the boys were right; someone was living in the tower – someone who did not want to meet his neighbours or want them to meet him.

'Well, Lu?' Caitlin said impatiently now, as Lucy did not immediately answer her query. 'What do you say to visiting the castle?'

'No one else does,' Lucy said. 'Not even the big boys. Not even Kellach has been to the castle.'

'That's why we ought to go, wouldn't you say? Perhaps there's a witch living in the peat hut,' Caitlin said in her spookiest tone. 'But if you're afraid . . .'

'On a day like today? I'd go anywhere in sunshine,' Lucy said stoutly, though with fast-beating heart. 'Tis just at night I'd not go near the castle for a thousand pounds.'

'Nor me,' Caitlin said quickly. 'Will we take your Shep with us, then? For company, like,' she added.

At the words, Lucy realised that Caitlin, though a year the older, was as afraid as she and wanted Shep along just in case. Immediately she felt better about the whole thing, though quite determined that Shep should stay at home.

'Shep's working,' she said. 'But never mind, Cait, there's you and me. If anything scares us we can run faster than most. And if one of us is grabbed the other can make off like the wind and bring help.'

'Sure we can,' Caitlin said, looking anything but reassured. 'Will we have our dinners first, though, down by the stream?'

But Lucy, sensing that she had the upper hand, pressed home her advantage. 'No, let's go straight along there now; we can have our dinners later, when we've seen whatever there is to see,' she said decidedly. 'If there's a stair that's safe we can climb up and eat on top of the tower, perhaps. Come on, let's hurry.'

If the look Caitlin gave her was less than friendly she did not care, for she sensed the underlying admiration. So the two of them set off along the winding little lane, dreaming along in the sunshine, with their eyes every now and then unwillingly drawn to the tower ahead whilst Lucy, at least, kept her imagination firmly under lock and key. But despite their wanderings in the soft, summery air, the castle got nearer and nearer, until at last only the marsh separated them from it.

'We'll go down to the creek first and have a good look at the boat,' Caitlin said at this point. 'Suppose it was a fairy boat, fancy missing it!'

'Even an ordinary boat would be good,' Lucy panted, following her longer-legged friend down onto the marsh. 'I don't suppose anyone would mind if we just sat in it?'

'We could go to sea,' Caitlin said. 'It's just an old, abandoned boat; nobody would care, probably.'

But when they reached the pebbly beach they could see for themselves that the boat was by no means abandoned. It was a curragh as they had guessed and it had been tarred fairly recently judging by the sharp smell of it and the gleam of the fresh tar. It was lying bottom up and the girls prowled round it, trying to assess just when it had last been used.

'The tar may be shining because of the sun,' Caitlin said at length. 'Give me a hand, we'll turn it over.'

It didn't take much strength for it was a light, handy little craft.

'Just right for two girls,' Lucy said wistfully. 'The inside isn't too clean, but it's a dear little boat. No oars, though.'

Caitlin wrinkled her nose. 'It smells fishy, but who cares for that? We could paddle up the creek using our hands, I should think. And further up, where there's trees, we'd probably find something we could use for oars.'

'Shall we just push it on the water a little way?' Lucy suggested, rocking the boat on its shingly bed with one wistful finger. 'Sure and no one would want to keep it on land all the while, the poor little curragh; it's longing for a dip, I can tell.'

'Well, I suppose we could . . . but let's take a look at the castle first. We might even find the oars there – who knows?'

The girls turned and surveyed the castle once more. It looked a lot bigger from here, but still not too dangerous; not with the sun shining.

'It's on a little hill; I don't think I've ever noticed that before,' Lucy said at last. 'It's well above the marsh now, but in winter, when the sea backs up, I've seen it surrounded by water more than once.'

'Who owns it, I wonder?' Caitlin said as they began to jump from tussock to tussock, carefully avoiding the brackish pools. 'Your grandad's beasts graze on the marsh but I don't think he's got anything to do with the castle, has he?'

'Our cattle graze all over,' Lucy pointed out. 'But they're not fools and it's much wetter here than it is to either side because of the creek, I suppose.'

'We're almost there,' Caitlin panted.

'True,' Lucy said. She reached the little hillock and hauled herself up on it, sitting down and breathing hard.

Caitlin came up out of the marsh dragging the bottle of lemon barley water. She sank onto the grass beside Lucy.

'I wonder if this castle ever had a moat and if that's why the marsh is marshier around it?'

'I wouldn't be surprised,' Lucy said. She found that

she did not much want to go on sitting here, talking about the castle, with her back towards it, though. Just supposed there was someone . . . She turned and stared up at it. Close to, like this, what you noticed most was the dilapidation, the air of quiet but lengthy neglect. It must have been lived in once, but if so it was a long time ago. Lucy got to her feet and dumped her bag of food unceremoniously on the grass.

'Sure and we've come all this way so I'm not going home wit'out taking a look,' she announced firmly. 'You coming, Cait?'

'Of course I'm coming,' Caitlin said, getting to her feet in her turn. 'Castle or hut first?'

'Oh, hut, because it'll probably be easier to get in.'

It was true that, now they were so close to the castle, they could see all manner of rubbish piled up in the entrance. It would be the floods, Lucy thought wisely. Bits of branches, what looked horribly like a dead sheep, half a hen coop, there were all sorts in the wide stone archway, but the hut, because its doorway faced a different direction, might well be easier of access.

The two girls climbed the short distance to the turf hut and bent to peer inside. It was very dark in there, but reassuringly empty. There was a fireplace thick with ashes opposite the low entrance, a couple of what looked like bracken couches and a lopsided, short-legged wooden table, so old that it had actually sunk into the earth floor, and nothing else, unless you counted the smell which was almost thick enough to touch.

'Someone's eaten a lot of fish in here,' Caitlin said. 'Doesn't it stink?'

'Yes, it does. And they've kept hens, too,' Lucy decided. 'That's chicken dirt by the bracken. Phew, let's go before we're gassed!'

Giggling, the two of them abandoned the hut and

made for the castle entrance. Working briskly, they cleared it in ten minutes, then peered cautiously in – and were pleasantly surprised.

The small part of the castle which still stood and was referred to locally as the 'keep' had no roof of any description, so it wasn't dark. The walls towered up and up on three sides but the wall facing the lough was no more than six feet high. And despite the fact that the walls were patently inside walls, they had, over the passage of time, taken on many of the attributes of outside walls. Little ferns and wild flowers grew on them, a honeysuckle had seeded itself in the shelter and had climbed the ten feet necessary and now it let its sprays of pink and gold sweetness cascade over the grey stones. To their right an enormous stone fireplace was crammed and crowded with wild roses which fought for space with tall foxgloves and with more honeysuckle, all anxious to seed themselves in this strangely sheltered spot.

'It's beautiful,' Caitlin said slowly. 'It's like the secret garden in that book your Maeve read us when we had measles last winter. Where's the door to the tower, then?'

They knew from their observation of the castle that the tower had no outside door and for a moment they thought it had no inside one either, then Lucy spotted it. In the near corner was a narrow wooden door, tightly closed, in silvery grey wood. Oddly, it looked in quite good repair. She pointed.

'There's the door. Shall we go up?'

'Might as well,' Caitlin said with a nonchalance which, this time, was only partly assumed. The sheer beauty of the castle keep and its wonderful collection of sheltered wild flowers had made the entire expedition suddenly less frightening. Witches, Lucy was sure, did not live in bowers!

'I wonder if it's locked?' Lucy said, and gave the door

a shove. It opened immediately, and the pair of them almost tumbled into a small, round room with a narrow slit window in the wall far higher than their heads and a set of curling stone steps which led up, and up, and up . . .

'Come on, we might as well take a look,' Lucy said. She led the way up the stairs and when she reached the slit window, stopped for a moment to peer out. 'It's a lovely view,' she said. 'Take a look, Caitlin. You can see the sea!'

'I will,' Caitlin said, following her. 'Why does the staircase just stop? I always thought you could get out at the top, I don't know why.'

'You can, there's a door,' Lucy said, following the stairs round. She pushed and, like the door downstairs, it opened at once, though it gave a rather horrid creak. She found herself in a small, round room with four window slits, all giving views over different parts of the countryside. It was, she decided, a nice little room, with wooden boarding on the floor, the stone walls clean and dry . . . and a short wooden ladder which led up to what looked like a trapdoor in the ceiling. Someone at some time had dumped a good deal of hay here, it was piled up high to her right, but it neither smelled unpleasant nor straggled about; unlike the turf hut this seemed simply a pleasant, dry little room which nobody knew about but them. She was standing directly beneath the ladder looking curiously up when Caitlin appeared.

'Phew – a secret garden downstairs and a secret room up,' Caitlin said with considerable satisfaction, coming right into the room and looking curiously around her. 'I don't think witches come here, do you? Now there might be one or two on top of the tower, though – what a place to fly a broomstick from! Just wait till we tell the big boys what we've found! I don't think we need go right up to the tower-top though, do you?'

Lucy already had a foot on the ladder. She turned and stared at her friend 'Not go up? We've got to, and we won't tell the big boys, or it won't be our secret – in fact it won't be ours at all if they ever get their hands on it. Stay if you like, but I'm going!'

She mounted the ladder and shoved hard at the trap-door. It did not give an inch. She was going to shove again when Caitlin, staring up, gave a muffled exclamation.

'Lu, you eejit! There's a bolt – slide it back first.'

Lucy looked, saw the bolt, and complied, then pushed again. The trap door opened easily and she pushed it right back and then hauled herself through the gap, looking round her as she did so.

It was a round roof, of course, surrounded by spiky battlements and because the trapdoor was right in the middle of it, she was able to take a good look in all directions before climbing any further. It looked safe enough so she clambered out and onto a stone roof with some sort of tarry stuff spread on it, and when she looked back at the trapdoor she found that it, too, had been treated with tar, undoubtedly to keep the rain from penetrating the wood and soaking the room beneath. Having satisfied her curiosity on that score she crossed to the battlements, then looked over the edge.

The view was splendid, the best she had ever seen, though she soon found that if she looked down to the ground her stomach turned over in a rather nasty manner and a strange buzzing filled her head. But if she looked straight across she could see to one side of her the sea lough with Cahersiveen beyond it, every detail perfect in the clear summer air. The bridge, the burnt-out barracks, the church and every house, shop and building spread out before her like a living map.

Lucy shuffled round a bit further, still being careful not to lean on the battlements. She could see ferns and tiny plants growing between the stones and she could not help thinking of all the storms and gales the tower must have known, for Grandad said it was as old as time. But when she looked out there was the sea, with what she guessed must be the island of Valentia, looking like a relief map from here. And if she moved round further still she could see, though trees hid the finer detail, both the ivy-covered farm and the Kellys' cottage, whilst above and behind them the hills stretched, golden gorsed, up to the brilliant blue sky.

'What's up there?' Caitlin's voice echoed hollowly round the room below. Lucy walked over and peered down at her, surprised to see that Caitlin's face looked both pale and worried.

'Nothing much, just battlements. But you can see for miles, Cait – want to come up and see Valentia Island? It looks like that map Miss Carruthers showed us when she took us to the museum in Killarney. And I can see your cottage and the farm . . . come on up.'

But this Caitlin refused to do. 'Not today, Lu,' she called. 'We've got to get down yet, and those stone stairs look awful bare when you're going down and it's a long way to fall. Do come back here, then we can have our dinners.'

'I thought we were going to have our dinners on top of the tower?' Lucy said plaintively. She had climbed a long way and now she was hungry – whatever was the matter with Caitlin all of a sudden?

'Our dinners are at the bottom of the stairs,' Caitlin said. 'I couldn't carry the lemon barley water, it's far too heavy, and you dumped your bag. Oh, do come on, Lu, I'm starving so I am!'

And Lucy soon realised that Caitlin had a perfectly valid point; going up the spiral stone steps had been easy, because you were looking up. But going down! It was a nightmare if you weren't too keen on heights and Lucy suddenly discovered that heights, in fact, were not her favourite thing. She clung to the wall and tried not to look down, but she was in a sweat of fear until her feet touched solid ground once more and even then she felt, suddenly, that she wanted to eat her dinner in the bright, clean sunshine and not in this weirdly beautiful place.

'Let's go back to the curragh,' she said as soon as they were in the fresh air once more. 'We've conquered the castle, now let us be rowing off a way in the boat – we'll use two bits of planks as oars.' She seized two short lengths of plank and tucked them under her arm and in five minutes they were across the marsh and making their way over the sandy, gravelly strand to where the boat waited.

Had waited.

'It's gone!' Caitlin's shrill cry was disbelieving. 'Sure and it was a fairy boat, Lucy Murphy, for hasn't it gone entirely?'

'It can't have gone,' Lucy said, though she had the evidence of her own eyes to give the lie to the statement. The little strand was empty, there wasn't a sign of their small craft. 'Wasn't it further down the creek, Cait – or further up?'

'No indeed, it was right here,' Caitlin said. She gave an exaggerated shiver. 'Oh, Lu, it was magic, and we touched it – turned it over! Oh, what'll become of us?'

'We'll have to have our picnic on dry land,' Lucy said prosaically. 'Well, I never would have believed it – who can have come and taken it in the little while we were exploring the castle and climbing the tower?'

'Only someone who was magic,' Caitlin said. 'A good thing they didn't come back for it when we'd got it out in five fathoms of water, that's all I can say.'

'I don't *think* it was anyone particularly magic,' Lucy

said cautiously. She had no urge to upset the little people, particularly if one was hovering nearby, eager to sink his sharp little teeth into someone's unprotected calf. But she was a practical child in her way. 'There's footprints.'

'Where?' Caitlin said, having given the beach a quick glance. 'I can't see any footprints.'

'There, right on the very edge of the sandy bit just where the tide's coming over ... look, quick, or it'll be too late, the water'll cover it.'

Caitlin looked in the right direction but even as she did so the tide gave a triumphant little hiss and water lapped where, a moment earlier, Lucy had distinctly seen the print of a bare foot, with the toes well splayed ... no doubt the owner of the foot which made the print had been pulling his curragh into the water, Lucy told herself, whilst her friend triumphantly asserted that there was no footprint.

'Oh well, the curragh's gone anyway and I'm still hungry,' Lucy said soothingly. 'Whoever took it, it's still not here. Do you want to share dinners? Only I guess Maeve will have put the same in for both.'

'You're not thinking of eating here, on this enchanted beach, are you?' Caitlin said incredulously. 'Why *she* might suddenly appear and magic the sandwiches from our very hands so she might.'

'She'll have her work cut out to get a sandwich off me, I'm so hungry I could eat grass,' Lucy said. 'And if she tried I'd kick her straight back into the water ... suppose it was mermaids? Suppose they swam up the creek and fancied the boat and pulled it into the water ...' But her tone lacked conviction; she had, after all, seen the footprint.

'Or the sea-king, as big as the tower and lying on his belly to get up the creek, and opening his mouth and crunching the curragh down,' Caitlin suggested cheerfully. 'He probably t'ought it was a stranded whale.'

'Small whale,' Lucy pointed out through a mouthful of sandwich. Despite Caitlin's strictures she had un-wrapped the greaseproof to disclose ham sandwiches – her favourite – with Maeve's own mustard pickle. 'He could've thought it was a seal, or a walrus, I suppose.'

'Oh, you!' Caitlin sat down on the grass at the edge of the creek with her feet dangling over the beach and opened her own packet. 'When we've eaten our dinners and drunk me mammy's barley water we must be sure not to sleep, though. It doesn't do to sleep in enchanted places.'

'Whenever do we sleep except in our beds of a night?' Lucy scoffed. 'But I think you were right, we ought to explore the creek now we're here. We can follow it up as far as it goes.'

She did not want to say so to her friend, but she thought that if they went up the creek they might well come upon the curragh and whoever had taken it away. Because the view of the lough from here was a good one, and we'd have noticed a boat, I'm sure we would, she told herself, tucking into ham sandwiches. But if I say that to Caitlin she'll go on about witches and the sea-king until I'm afraid to look round the next bend . . . better just pretend it's to explore.

'I wonder what the time is?' Caitlin said presently, as they passed the lemon barley water from one to the other. They had decided to save the fruit cake for later.

'Dunno; mid afternoon, I guess,' Lucy said. 'We've got plenty of time to explore the creek, especially if we go now.'

'Right.' Caitlin corked the empty bottle and put it into the blue cloth bag. 'Off we go, then.'

It was great exploring the creek. The sun continued to shine and when they got further inland, to where trees leaned over the water, they moved slowly and dreamily along in the dappled shade, watching their feet and legs made green by the ripples, scarcely talking at all save to draw each other's attention to a fish, a particularly fine shell, an unusual wild flower on the bank.

It took them longer than they had thought to reach the head of the creek and both girls were secretly glad to turn back; it had been a long day.

'I'm starved,' Caitlin said, pushing damp hair out of her eyes. 'Let's go back to the castle now and eat your Maeve's fruit cake!'

Oddly enough it did not take them very long to go down the creek, nowhere near as long as it had taken them in the opposite direction. But even so the sun was low in the sky when they reached the little beach, with the castle very black against the red-streaked heavens.

The first thing they noticed was the curragh, of course. Drawn up precisely where they had seen it earlier, lying innocently upon the shingle.

'I don't believe it!' Caitlin gasped. 'Oh Lucy, it *is* a fairy boat – can you see any footprints now?'

Lucy went over the beach with a fine-tooth comb, but this time could see no signs of human interference. She looked uneasily across at Caitlin who was standing on the grassy bank looking smug. 'I don't think there are any footprints this time,' she admitted. 'Suppose – suppose there *is* a witch up there, looking down at us?'

'Do you not want to go back to the castle, then, fraidy cat?'

'We-ell . . .'

'We won't if you'd rather not,' Caitlin said, suddenly all concern. 'It's been quite a long day . . . we can go straight home across the marsh if you'd rather.'

But past experience told Lucy that if she agreed to go straight home, Caitlin would never let her forget it, so she shook her head until her sun-bleached curls bounced on her shoulders.

'No, we'll go back to the castle. Come on, because I want to be home before dark.'

They set off at once, though their leaps from tuft to tuft certainly lacked the enthusiasm of earlier in the day, and reached the castle breathless but on Lucy's part, at least, determined to scotch any idea that she was afraid.

'Come on then, let's take a look round,' she said. 'Are you coming up to the roof this time?'

It was a below-the-belt remark and Caitlin didn't bother to answer. Instead, she said, 'Tell you what; let's hide in the secret room and watch through the window-slits, see if anything out there moves.'

It was, Lucy decided, a good idea. Agreeing, she dumped her blue bag on the ground outside the keep entrance and the two of them went in, far more cautiously this time. Even if Caitlin pretended to believe that a witch or a leprechaun had moved the curragh, she must realise, as Lucy did, that it was far likelier to have been moved by human intervention and, since the boat was now back on its beach, that must surely mean that someone was lurking in or around the castle?

So up the horrible steps they toiled, neither keen if the truth were known, Lucy decided, but both determined not to be the one who said so.

They reached the top of the stair and the blandly empty little room met their gaze. Was the hay more rumpled, as though a body had been lying on it? She didn't really think so, but put the question anyway. Caitlin sniffed.

'Course not, it's just the same. You go to that slit and I'll keep guard on this one.'

'It'll be sunset soon,' Lucy said when they'd been watching – and mildly squabbling – for what seemed like hours but was probably only ten minutes. 'We've got a good walk, Cait. And we've not eaten the fruit cake yet.'

'Oh well, if you're fed up . . . no, don't start, I'm fed up, too,' Caitlin said at once. 'You go down first, though . . . I really hate those stairs.'

'Oh . . . perhaps I should've gone up to the top of the tower, in case there was someone hiding there,' Lucy said belatedly, halfway down the stone steps. She was descending with her eyes shut and one hand clutching grimly at the stone wall. 'Don't you fall on me, Caitlin Kelly, or you'll kill the both of us for sure.'

But no one fell on anyone and within six feet of the ground Lucy opened her eyes and found that she wasn't quite so scared this time. She finished the steps at a gallop, just to prove it, and then turned and told Caitlin to jump, holding out her arms to catch her.

'No, I'm too heavy for you,' Caitlin said. 'Get out of the way, I'm coming down like a ton of bricks!'

She hurtled down the last few steps, cannoned into Lucy, and the pair of them, winded and giggling, rolled around on the floor, clutching their stomachs, until they could breathe properly again.

'Come on, then,' Caitlin said, struggling to her feet. 'Let's have that cake.'

They galloped good-naturedly out of the castle and Caitlin grabbed the blue bag and swung it at Lucy, who promptly tried to wrestle it away from her. They fought amicably over the bag for five minutes, then there was an ominous tearing noise.

'It's all right, it's only a bit of stitching,' Lucy said, having anxiously examined the bag. 'Phew, and isn't that a relief? Maeve wouldn't have taken kindly to another bag going west. My satchel sprang a hole when I tossed it across the floor as I got back from school yesterday afternoon.'

'I'll mend it for you,' Caitlin said. She was good with

her needle, Lucy was hopeless. 'Give it here, you can have it back before bedtime.'

'Thanks, Cait,' Lucy said gratefully. 'Now let's eat the fruit cake.' She opened the bag, rummaged around for a moment, then stared at her friend, her eyes rounding.

'Cait, the cake's gone,' she said in a whisper. 'I swear to God it was there when we came in but it's gone now – there isn't a crumb of it left!'

Later that night, when the hens, pigs and ducks had been fed, tea had been eaten, and the washing up and clearing away done, Maeve sat down by the hearth with her knitting whilst her father settled himself in his chair opposite her and got out his favourite pipe and the farming quarterly which he favoured. When they were all settled, Lucy with her English books spread around her, Lucy cleared her throat and looked up at her aunt.

'Maeve, do witches eat fruit cake?'

Maeve put her knitting down and stared, plainly astonished. 'What a question! There's no such t'ing as witches and well you know it, young lady. But most people like fruit cake I'm thinking, so if there were such things as witches, and they were offered fruit cake, I daresay they'd eat it and enjoy it.'

'Umm ... would they steal it, though? Would they take it from – from a person's box, or bag, or whatever?'

'Now where's all this leading, alanna? No more answers unless I get some questions in, first. Who stole your fruit cake? And what makes you think it was a witch when it was far more likely to have been a wandering child, or a dog even, if you put it down somewhere.'

Lucy looked thoughtfully around the room. She did not intend to tell Maeve any lies, but she had no intention of admitting they had been playing at the castle, either.

As she had told Caitlin, a secret place of your own was only a secret so long as you told nobody, especially an adult who would feel bound to check out that you were safe and the play-place suitable. And if Maeve ever saw those stone steps – well, Lucy could almost hear the words: *You'll not go there again, alanna, tis far too dangerous. There's a million places you can play so stay away from the castle, and that's an order.*

'We did lay the bag down for a moment,' she admitted, therefore. 'And when we got back the cake had gone, clean disappeared, and Caitlin said probably a witch had taken it. I expect it was a dog or perhaps even the cattle, because they like sweet things, don't they? I didn't really think it was a witch, but I just wondered whether they had a fondness for sweet things, that's all.'

'Hmm,' Maeve said. She looked rather piercingly at Lucy, then picked up her knitting once again. 'Well, don't go handing me good fruit cake to a cow another time, ástor.'

'I won't, don't you worry,' Lucy said fervently. 'I'll keep me bag fastened tight.' As she said the words she was remembering the fastening – tied tight. She sighed and opened her English book. It was a mystery and no mistake, not that they'd tried to solve it, mind. The truth was they had taken one quick look behind them to where the castle loomed, and they had run as if their lives depended on it, bounding from tussock to tussock, letting the lemon barley water bottle fall and not stopping to pick it up, whilst behind them they seemed to hear a cackle of mocking laughter.

Once safely in the sloping meadow where the Murphy sheep grazed, however, they had thrown themselves down on the soft grass and looked at one another a trifle shamefacedly.

'Someone played a trick on us,' Lucy said. 'There *is*

someone in that old castle no matter what anyone says. After all, we know the boat was moved, don't we? And we know the cake was eaten. Someone had to do both those things and don't you say "witches" again, Caitlin Kelly, or I'll scream and hit you, so I will!'

'Witches, undoubtedly witches,' Caitlin said with great promptitude, and ducked Lucy's half-hearted swipe with ease. 'Well, that settles it; we'll go back as soon as we finish our work tomorrow and search the place from top to bottom. Or we'll hide in the nice little room and watch the curragh through the window-slits and see who moves it. And if it's an old woman with a pointy hat, or a little feller in green, about so high . . .' she held a hand six inches from the ground on which they lay, 'then you may tell me how sorry you are you called me a liar.'

'I never did!'

'You did so! Well, not in so many words, but you meant it, you t'ought I'd imagined the witches, did you not?'

'Well, you certainly did not see them,' Lucy pointed out. 'Look, let's not argue, alanna. Tomorrow we'll find out, hey?'

'Tomorrow. Give me your hand on it, then.'

Solemnly, they spat in their palms, then shook hands. The handshake started out as a pact and speedily became a trial of strength, then went to the sort of wrestling which Maeve disapproved of because she said girls didn't need to fight and besides, it was unfeminine.

'So's planting spuds and carting manure,' Lucy had said and Maeve laughed and tutted and said that work was a different matter altogether, bless the child, and when a farmer didn't have sons his daughters – and granddaughters – have to do all sorts.

But now, sitting by the fire and knitting, Maeve was a

picture of feminine domesticity, and indeed, these past couple of years, with Mr Murphy taking on extra help outside, she worked mostly in the house, apart from those times of year when all hands were needed outside. When the sheep lambed, the cows calved and the pigs had their litters, then both Maeve and Lucy were needed to help. And when potatoes, wheat or barley were being sown then again it was all hands to the fields, as it was when the crops were harvested.

And the housework, come to that, was no sinecure; the Murphy home was a big, old-fashioned farmhouse with four bedrooms on the first floor and two attic rooms above, and Maeve, her father and Lucy rattled round in it like peas in a half-empty pod.

'What are you studying, alanna? You look more as though you're dreaming, again. As I said, the sooner you get your holiday tasks out of the way the sooner you'll be able to enjoy some freedom.'

'It's holiday reading, this,' Lucy said, flourishing the book. 'It's quite good . . . I thought if I read a chapter a night . . .'

'Then read, girl,' her grandfather growled. 'And stop this chatterin' before you drive me mad as you are yourself.'

Lucy sighed, then got up and dropped a kiss on her grandfather's brow. He pretended to rub it off and scowled at her, but she could see he was pleased, really.

'Sorry, Grandad; I'll stop chattering now, I promise.'

'You'd better, or you'll find yourself weedin' the vegetable garden tomorrow afternoon instead of jauntin' off wit' young Caitlin.'

'I like weeding,' Lucy said. 'I'll do some tomorrow evening, so I will.' She read for a while in silence, then closed her book. 'I'm off to bed now; goodnight, Maeve me love, goodnight Grandad.'

Her grandfather grunted and Maeve glanced up at

the clock above the mantel. 'You'll be wanting to holler to Caitlin I suppose,' she said drily. 'Well, try not to crack all the eggs before the hens have laid 'em.'

'I'll try,' Lucy said blithely. 'Can I take a candle?'

'God have patience, it's as light as midday so it is,' her grandfather exploded, putting down his paper. 'Why the candle?'

'Because if Maeve doesn't want me to holler then I could signal to Caitlin if I had a candle and a bit of cardboard . . .'

'Dear God, will you go to bed and stop your chatterin'?' her grandfather said. 'Oh go on, go on, take a candle, pauperise me before me time, don't you worry about your poor grandad's purse, always more where that came from . . .'

'Thanks, Grandad,' said the unrepentant Lucy, kissing his head as she passed him. 'See you in the morning!'

But later, in her own bed, Lucy fell to wondering once more about the cake. *Someone* had taken it, either an animal or a person, and there weren't many animals, in Lucy's experience, which could extract cake from a person's bag, and devour it without leaving so much as a crumb.

Unless it was a rat? Rats are cunning, and ingenious with their paws and teeth . . . I suppose it must have been a rat, Lucy concluded, and began to drift towards sleep, but in her heart, she was not convinced. Someone had taken the cake, someone had moved the curragh . . . but it had been a long day. Soon, she slept.

Maeve sat on for a while, finishing her row, then she rolled up her work and put it up on the mantelpiece and yawned.

'Want a cup of cocoa before you go to bed, Father?'

'Might as well. Got any soda bread?'

'I'll butter you a piece.'

Maeve went through to the kitchen, reflecting how Lucy had mellowed her grandfather these past few years. He had begun by resenting the child and had ended up doting on her – not that he would ever admit it, mind. It was strange, really, that he seemed only able to love one person at a time, unlike the rest of humanity, who had affection and to spare. First, years ago, it had been his wife, then his daughter Evie. When Evie had gone Nora had become his favourite and reigned supreme for a couple of years . . . but gradually, even before Nora's marriage, Lucy's star had begun to be in the ascendant and by the time Nora left her father had scarcely missed her at all.

'Time they were gone,' he had said gruffly to Maeve. 'The three of us will do very nicely, very nicely.'

He still doesn't love me, Maeve told herself now, bustling round the kitchen and making the cocoa, buttering the soda bread. But he tolerates me much better than he did – and he dotes on Lucy, so he does. And he's a good farmer, very much better than most in these parts, so whatever he may say the money's there to keep the child in comfort when he's gone.

And there was Evie. Not that they heard from her much, especially lately. But she sent money regularly, and Maeve put it all away in the post office so that Lucy would have something of her own one day.

Maeve wrote, though always to a theatre or a post restante address since Evie assured her sister she was always moving around. Maeve asked about the other baby, Lucy's twin sister, in every letter, but apart from saying that Linnet was well, growing out of her clothes and eating her out of house and home, Evie never really gave details.

Still, if Evie was really doing well, and it seemed that

she was, then it surely could be only a matter of time before she came back for a visit? England isn't the ends of the earth, Maeve told herself sometimes. It was more than twelve years since Evie had left Ireland, so wasn't it about time that she came back, if only for a visit? And how lovely it would be for Lucy and Linnet to meet! Lucy knew all about her sister, of course, but had long ago stopped asking about her. She was more bound up with Caitlin and her life on the farm than with a mother who had abandoned her at four months old and a sister she had never seen. It was all right for Maeve, because she only had to close her eyes to see Linnet, who would be the spitting image of Lucy, only a bit bigger since she had been the stronger, stouter baby. But because she had not liked to tell Lucy that she had a double, she had never mentioned the likeness, nor even the fact that they were twins. Lucy had somehow got the impression that Linnet was older than she, which was why Evie had taken her sister and left Lucy, and Maeve thought it was better that way. To explain why a mother would abandon one twin and take the other was too complex for Maeve, and besides such an explanation might not show Evie in a good light, and Maeve loved Evie still and always thought and spoke of her with affection.

Maeve had a vague idea that Lucy might sometimes hear her mother talked of – possibly even slightingly – by other children whose parents were in no doubt that Evie Murphy had been no better than she should be, but she continued to believe that Lucy regarded her absent mother with fondness and her sister with interest. In fact, though, it was far simpler than that. Lucy simply never thought of her mother or sister at all.

Chapter Four

When Linnet was thirteen, she was asked to make a big decision: to go or to stay? She came home from school on a bright but windy October day to find Mammy in a state, sitting on the green silk sofa she was so proud of and weeping buckets into a small, lace-edged hanky.

'What's the matter, Mammy? Are you ill?' she had asked, very dismayed at this sudden change of tack, for her mother had been on top of the world for the best part of a week, singing around the flat, taking Linnet out for fish and chip dinners, buying herself pretty hats and elegant shoes.

Her mother looked up. Her face was quite swollen with tears and her eyes were red-rimmed from weeping. 'Oh, Linnet, my little darling, the most distressing thing! Th-they don't want me to take you with me when I go off in a month's time!'

Mammy had been touring several times, ever since Linnet was eight, in fact. 'You can take care of yourself, a big girl of eight,' Mammy had said persuasively, and though at first Linnet hadn't liked it much she had soon grown accustomed. It wasn't nearly as hard as it sounded since Mrs Roberts in the flat downstairs had Linnet in for her tea each day and saw to her washing and came up and did any big housework that Linnet could not tackle. And later Mrs Sullivan, Roddy's mam, had been equally eager to help out – for a price, of course. So Roddy and Linnet had roamed the city to their hearts' content all through the long summer holidays and Linnet had helped Roddy to sell wood-chips, to run errands, to hang round the people coming off the ships at the docks, offering to carry their cases for tuppence and, alas, to prig vegetables from St Martin's market when Mrs Sullivan fancied blind scouse but had somehow run out of money.

So what was different this time? Linnet said as much, taking the sopping wet hanky from her mother's hands and replacing it with a dry one.

'This time it-it's further, and for l-l-longer,' her mother had wailed. 'This time it's Am-Am-America, alanna. And it's my b-big chance!'

'Then you must go,' Linnet said stoutly, though her heart failed her a little. America! That was a long way off, further even than the Glasgow Empire, she believed, where Mammy had played to packed houses only a few short months ago. 'It's your career, after all,' she added. 'Your whole future, Mammy!'

She was well-trained; she had said the words a dozen times before, but had never meant them less, because she would have been a fool had she not realised that Mr Terence Beatty, her mother's latest impresario, did not like her, resented her in fact.

Other impresarios had come and gone, and there had been one or two who found her a nuisance, but never had there been one who showed it more constantly than Terence Beatty. He wasn't elderly, for a start, which she thought a great shame; elderly admirers were usually very generous, both to the object of their admiration and to her small daughter. Younger men, though they might lavish gifts on little Evie, were more inclined to give Linnet a sixpence and tell her to go and see a film-show and then grumble when she came home.

The odd thing was that Terence was beautiful by anyone's standards. He had richly curling black hair, dark, flashing eyes and a mobile mouth which smiled easily and often. Women adored him, and Linnet had been totally taken in by his beauty and willing to fall at his feet, but he had not wanted her. From the outset he had made it clear that Linnet was nothing but a nuisance, though he had fallen head over heels in love with little Evie the very first time he had seen her on stage.

'In the raw?' Roddy asked with interest when Linnet told him this tale, and got a clip round the ear for his pains. Linnet might occasionally dislike an impresario – she very soon hated Terence – but she was too loyal to her mother to let it show. Roddy, as her dearest friend, was allowed a good deal of licence, but he should know better than to make a remark critical of little Evie!

'Why should it matter what she was wearing?' Linnet had said when the subsequent insults – and a few rapid blows – had been exchanged. 'Me mam's ever so lovely, and you know it, Roddy Sullivan!'

'Oh aye, she's pretty,' Roddy agreed. 'But you don't much like Mr Beatty, do you, chuck?'

Linnet had never lied to Roddy and she was not about to start now, especially over Terence Beatty.

'No,' she said shortly. 'But he's a big impresario in the United States of America; Mammy says he may ask her to star on Broadway!'

Every small cinema-goer knew about Broadway, where unknown girls became stars overnight. And then there was Hollywood, where even little girls and boys could become stars – look at Jackie Coogan! At her words even Roddy looked impressed.

'Cor! But would you like that, our Linnet? All them traffic cops an' cowboys an' Injun braves? Suppose 'e *marries* your mam? Then you'd be 'is kid and you'd live over there for always!'

'Oh, I'd get used to it, I suppose,' Linnet had said airily. 'I've never tasted an ice-cream soda.'

And now the crunch had come and Terence Beatty, it appeared, had put his foot down. He wanted, needed, adored Evie, but he neither wanted nor needed, far less adored, her daughter.

'I *told* him I couldn't think of leaving you,' her mother sobbed now, sitting on the little green sofa and filling yet another hanky with her tears. 'What'll I do, oh, what'll I do? Me big chance . . . if only you'd been a little sweeter to him, alanna, if only you'd tried a little harder!'

'I *did*,' Linnet said, stung for once by her mother's blatant unfairness. 'I've done everything, Mammy, run his errands, polished his shoes, made that beastly, sickly pudding he's so fond of . . .'

'There you are!' Evie said triumphantly through her tears. 'You resented him from the first or you wouldn't call Italian trifle a beastly, sickly pudding! And now look what's happened. He simply won't get you a ticket and when I said I'd buy it he looked at me with flashing eyes and said if I did he'd see I lived to regret it. Oh, Linnet, I'm so very, very unhappy.'

Even at thirteen, Linnet was quite old enough to see that if her mother turned down this opportunity she would blame Linnet for it for the rest of her days. And she would be right, Linnet told herself stoutly, putting the kettle on to make a cup of tea and assuring Evie, in motherly tones, that she must not think of losing the chance of stardom. She, Linnet, would manage just as well with her in America as she had managed when Evie was starring at the Glasgow Empire, or in the summer show on the pier at Scarborough, or up in Blackpool at the wonderful Winter Garden Theatre.

'But what will people *say*?' Evie wailed at last, taking the cup of tea Linnet held out to her with a trembling hand. 'They'll think I'm a monster of selfishness to leave my little girl and go off to New York with Mr Beatty! I can't bear that folk will think ill of me, and I'd sooner die than let you down, ástor.'

'Mam, what else can I say?' Linnet said at last, when Evie had poured out her feelings ten times over, interlacing them, unfortunately, with reproaches to Linnet for not being nicer to Mr Beatty. 'I'm happy to stay here – I don't want to go to New York – so why shouldn't everyone accept that? My schooling's important,' she added cunningly. 'You've said so over and over indeed, so why not simply say I'm staying in Liverpool until I leave the convent?'

'We-ell now . . . d'you think folk would believe me if I said that, alanna? Every word is true as I stand here, mind, for 'tis an excellent school and I'd not be happy taking you away from the good nuns over to a land where for all I know they may have shockingly bad schools.' Even as she said the words, a little smile spread across her face and her cheeks began to glow again. Evie was about to convince herself she was doing the right thing and that will at least mean some peace until she goes, Linnet told herself. So be happy with that – and anyway, it'll stop her remembering she's thirty years old now. And when she starts crying in front of the mirror because she's seen a wrinkle and demanding asses' milk for her skin, at least it'll be darling Terence who gets sent out for it and not me . . . asses' milk indeed! How Roddy had laughed when she told him, and how she had jumped at his suggestion that they went round to Ward's dairy on Limekiln Lane and bought a gallon or so of skim.

'She won't know whether it's from an ass or an ox, just so's it's fresh milk,' he said cheerfully, dragging Linnet through the streets with a clanking bucket in both hands. 'What did she give you?'

'Four whole shillings,' Linnet had said, cheering up.

'What'll they charge us for two buckets o' skim, d'you suppose?'

' 'Bout tenpence, probably. And this time, young Linnet, don't you go handin' the change over, meek as – as milk. You hold onto it for the next time she buggers off.'

She had felt mean, but she saw the point of Roddy's advice, because though her mother always did send money, it was often very late indeed and harsh words were apt to be said before the money orders turned up. With some savings of her own tucked away, therefore, she could appease Mrs Roberts' strident demands with the odd bob or two.

'You really mean it, then, Linnet acushla? You truly don't want to come to New York? You'd really rather stay here, with your school friends and Roddy?'

'I truly would,' Linnet said steadily. And then decided that, if she was to be left, she might as well say a word or two of warning. 'But I really don't like Mr Beatty, Mammy, and I just hope he means well by you.'

Evie, sipping tea, laughed and leaned over to stroke her daughter's cheek. 'Darling, of course he means well by me,' she said indulgently. 'He's going to make me a star – I *told* you.'

'Yes, but . . . other impresarios have said that, and it hasn't quite come off, has it?'

It was extremely brave of Linnet to say this since it was a forbidden subject, but though her mother frowned and looked reproachful, she did not start to cry, or tell Linnet that she was cruel and unjust and simply did not understand show business.

'Ah, but Terence is rather special, alanna. He has connections with the highest in the land, he's going to introduce me to everyone . . . he could've been a star himself with his looks, but he's chosen to scout for talent all over Europe instead, because he so loves to travel.'

'But, Mam, suppose something goes wrong and you don't – don't *take*? What'll he do then?'

Evie gave a soft, triumphant laugh and set down her cup of tea; then she jumped to her feet and began to dance, whirling and twirling, with her arms round herself in an ecstasy of excitement.

'Ah, then, what do you think? You'll never, ever guess!'

'He'll bring you home?' Linnet suggested, and saw her mother's brow momentarily marred by a frown.

'No, alanna, what a dreary thing to say – he'll marry me, of course!'

Evie left for New York in November and although Linnet wept and at times felt both lonely and vulnerable, she very soon settled into a routine. It was no different really from her pantomime routine – except that when January and February, both miserably cold and snowy months, had passed, there was still no sign of her mother's return. Her letters had been few and somehow guarded, as though she did not want to talk about her life, and this worried Linnet, but Roddy cheered her up by reminding her that it was early days, that her mother had already been in some famous revue on Broadway and that the money, at least, came regular.

'Which it didn't always do when she were in panto, as we both know,' he reminded her. 'I reckon your mam's doin' all right. She'll send for you one of these days, just you see.'

'I don't want her to send for me,' Linnet pointed out. 'I want her to come home!'

'Oh, well, send for you or come home, what difference does it make, so long as you's together? And anyway, you're with friends and old Ma Roberts is all right to you, ain't she?'

Mrs Roberts was all right and continued all right until just after Easter, when she came up to 'have a chat' as she phrased it. It was just after they had finished the hot meal she had served downstairs for herself, Linnet and her elderly and apologetic husband and Linnet, answering the door to her, had to hastily shove out of sight the large bar of Nestlés chocolate which she was using to fill the chinks left by Mrs Roberts' rather uninspired cooking.

'Come in, Mrs R,' she said, however. 'Make yourself at home.'

Mrs Roberts settled herself on the little sofa with its pale green silk upholstery, looking very out of place, Linnet thought privately, and cleared her throat a couple of times before she spoke. And when she did speak, she did not once look at Linnet but allowed her eyes to rove around the living room, now alighting on the little walnut wood piano, now on the fancy what-nots with their burden of pretty china ladies and gentlemen, now on the tasteful watercolours in their gilded frames which hung on the walls.

'Well, queen, this is a snug little place an' no error,' she said at last. 'And your mam sends the rent regular, I'll give 'er that.'

'Yes, I know she does,' Linnet said politely. 'I bring it round, don't I, Mrs Roberts?'

'Oh aye, indeed you does. Yes, indeed. The only trouble is, queen, that prices 'ave riz. Oh aye, they've riz somethin' shockin'.'

'Butter is a little dear,' Linnet said cautiously. She had not actually noticed much change in prices, but it was usually politic to agree with grownups. 'Margarine is nearly as nice, though.'

Mrs Roberts began to bridle and Linnet realised that she had been a bit tactless. Mrs Roberts had indeed begun to make Linnet's butties for school with margarine, but perhaps she should have gone on pretending that it was butter? Grownups are so weird, Linnet thought despairingly, how was one ever to learn how to treat them?

'I wouldn't know about that, being as 'ow I allus buys butter,' Mrs Roberts said untruthfully but with such conviction that Linnet wondered if she could have been mistaken. 'But things *is* a price, chuck, so I wondered whether . . .'

'Whether what, Mrs Roberts?' Linnet asked when the silence began to stretch uncomfortably. 'Do you want an errand running?'

'No, norran errand. I was wonderin', queen, whether it wouldn't be a good scheme for you to share this flat, which is plenty big enough for two. Then I wouldn't 'ave to write to your mam askin' for more money, you see.'

'I could eat less,' Linnet offered after a moment's thought. 'I don't need butties for school, I'll wait for me tea. Mrs Sullivan usually gets me a hot meal.'

'But sharin' would be company, like,' Mrs Roberts wheedled. 'You're only a child, if the authorities knew you lived 'ere alone . . .'

Danger, said a little voice in Linnet's head. She's right, they wouldn't like it, people like schoolteachers and attendance officers and doctors. Mam meant them when she said 'People won't like it,' and now this old terror is going to tell on me just so's she can get more money out of Mam!

'I'll write to my mother, Mrs Roberts,' Linnet said, suddenly seeing that in prevarication lay her salvation. The longer she made Mrs Roberts wait for a reply the more likely the old girl was to forget the whole business. 'It's for her to decide, but I don't think she'd like someone else living here when she's gone to such trouble to keep the place nice, do you? I mean there's all the ornaments and the knick-knacks, to say nothing of the pictures. Some of them are valuable, you know.'

'Oh aye, but if it were another gairl from 'er very own theaytre?' Mrs Roberts said, almost pleadingly, Linnet thought. 'Norra rough type o' woman but a nice little actress, say? A decent gairl what 'ud tek good care o' you, for your mam?'

Oddly enough, the thought of company made Linnet hesitate before reiterating firmly, 'I'll have to write to my mother, Mrs Roberts.' She had sat herself down on the little round chair with the tassels, now she stood up as she had seen her mother do when she wanted to end an interview. 'Thank you for calling,' she said with great formality. 'As soon as I hear from my mother I'll let you know.'

She watched Mrs Roberts out of the door and down the stairs, then she settled herself at the table with a pot of ink, a scratchy pen, and a pad of paper. She would write to her mother immediately, and then she would nip round and see Roddy. He would have an opinion on the matter, she was sure of it – and Mrs Sullivan, though her home was threadbare and money tight, had her head screwed on right in certain directions. She would soon tell Linnet whether she was being taken advantage of or not!

Roddy was having his tea when Linnet knocked on the door and then entered, as she always did. The whole family were there, with Mrs Sullivan presiding over them all in her wrap-around apron and scuffed, down-at-heel shoes. When she saw who their visitor was she grinned at Linnet, revealing bare pink gums save for one defiant front tooth.

'Well, if it ain't our Linnet! Want some grub, chuck?'

'Please, Miz Sullivan. And some advice, if you don't mind.'

The arrangement was that Mrs Sullivan would feed Linnet during the school holidays and at weekends and Mrs Roberts would do so the rest of the time, so since this was a holiday Linnet felt entitled to slip onto one of the broken wooden chairs, square her elbows, and begin to eat, whilst explaining, rather thickly, that she was having a problem with her landlady.

Mrs Sullivan was a first-rate cook and could, as she was fond of saying, make a meal fit for a prince out of what others threw away. Her dumplings swimming in a rich mutton gravy had to be tasted to be believed and Linnet wished her present hostess might teach Mrs Roberts how to cook cabbage so that there was still flavour left in it, and potatoes so they didn't just mysteriously disappear into the water. But of course she could not possibly say so, or not to Mrs Roberts at any rate.

'More spuds?' Mrs Sullivan said when Linnet's plate was mysteriously cleared – it was mysterious, Linnet thought guiltily, when you considered that she had eaten what Mrs Roberts would no doubt think of as 'a good, hot dinner', not half an hour ago. 'Eh, you're one for your vittles, our Linnie, an' no mistake.'

Liverpudlians dearly liked to shorten names and Mrs Sullivan was no exception. Roddy's real name was Roderick, Freddy's Frederick, Bert was Albert and Matt was Matthew. So Linnet did not object to being called Linnie but regarded it as a love-word, like alanna or acushla on Mam's lips.

'You mean I'm greedy, Mrs Sullivan,' she said now, holding out her plate. 'Just a couple then, if you can spare 'em. And now, what do you think? Mrs Roberts says prices have riz . . . risen, I mean, and she wants me to share my flat with someone else!'

'Ow much rent'll you get?' Mrs Sullivan said at once. 'If you're short of a bob it ain't a bad idea. There's always someone wantin' a roof over their 'ead in the city an' Roddy says you've gorra nice little place there.'

'Oh! Well, I think Mrs Roberts means to keep the rent,' Linnet said doubtfully. 'I'm pretty sure that's what she meant. She said if I'd share it would mean she wouldn't have to ask Mammy for more money.'

Mrs Sullivan shook her head decisively. She was a small woman, flat-bosomed but blessed with a large bottom and very large grey eyes which twinkled across at Linnet now with a touch of reproach in their gaze. 'She can't do that, you pay a fair rent an' I'll tell anyone who asks it's norra penny too little. If you rents out, that's one thing. If she's tryin' to do you outer your place, that's another. What did you say to 'er?'

'I said I'd write to my mam,' Linnet said. She popped the last piece of potato into her mouth, chewed and swallowed. 'Eh, that was great, Mrs Sullivan; I wish old Ma Roberts could cook like you can.'

'It's nice as someone appreciates me,' Mrs Sullivan said. She winked at Roddy. 'Don't you lerrer push you around, chuck. She's doin' very well out o' you, let's make no mistake.'

'Right. I'll tell her my mam says I'm not to share, then,' Linnet said. Mrs Sullivan shook her head at her.

'Don't say that, say your mam might think of sub-lettin', but you'll lerrer know when,' Mrs Sullivan said. 'If you need a bit o' extry money one day, chuck, that's a better way 'n most to earn it. I'm not sayin' Mrs Roberts might not get 'er claws on some of it,' she added gener-ously. 'But not all, by no means. Lerrer put tharrin 'er pipe an' smoke it.'

'You comin' out, queen?' Roddy said presently, when Linnet had helped his mother wash up and clear away.

The boys usually gave a hand but Linnet enjoyed it and the boys, who often lamented their lack of a sister, enjoyed a break from housework. 'We could go down to the pier'ead.'

'Don't mind if I do,' Linnet said cheerfully. 'Will you come back with me, afterwards, Roddy? I'll read you me letter.'

'Sure,' Roddy said easily. 'And me mam's right; you don't wanna let that old crow do you down.'

'No-oo. Except that sometimes I do get scared, by myself at nights,' Linnet admitted as they strolled along Byrom Street, looking in shop windows as they passed. 'To tell you the truth I've always been a bit scared, like, at nights when me mam's away. It's no worse now, so I can put up with it, but in a way I wouldn't mind someone living with me. If it was someone nice, that is,' she added hastily.

'You've never told me that before,' Roddy said, staring at her. 'You've always said you liked it fine, bein' alone.'

'Yes, well, it's never gone on for so long before,' Linnet said lamely. 'It's better in the summer, with the lighter evenings. Are we catching a tram or not?'

'Not,' Roddy decided, turning out his pockets. 'Let's go down to the docks, instead, eh? 'Tain't so far.'

'Right,' Linnet said cheerfully. 'Race you to the next tram stop!'

The letter to Evie had been finished off when Linnet and Roddy got back from their stroll by the river and Linnet had finally gone off to bed quite satisfied with what she should do. She did not hold out much hope of her mother replying quickly – it took weeks for a letter to get to New York and if Mammy was off touring, as she said she might be, then it would be some while before she actually read it, let alone got round to answering. But Mrs Sullivan was a sensible woman, and she had undoubtedly given the same advice that Linnet's mother would give, particularly as, under Roddy's instructions, Linnet had assured her mother that Mrs Roberts would take the extra money for herself.

'No point in your mam thinkin' she could send you less rent money,' Roddy said, ignoring Linnet's objections that her mam would not do anything so unkind. 'That would put the cat amongst the bleedin' pigeons, 'specially if old Ma Roberts couldn't find no one to take it on. No, chuck, play it safe an' just mention it, like.'

So Linnet had heeded the advice and gone off to bed satisfied that she had done her best to keep herself – and her mam's beautiful rooms – safe until Evie's return. But in the very back of her mind there was a warmness, a security, which had not been there before; if Mammy really did not come back, if she intended to stay in America and did not send Linnet the ticket which, at first, she had promised in every letter, then at least her daughter did have a means to make a living, of sorts. Whilst the rent continued to come regularly she would live in the flat alone, but if prices really did rise, and Mam found herself unable to send more, than she could always sublet, as Mrs Sullivan had called it.

And in the very very back of her mind, where nightmares lurked, Linnet also told herself that if she was ever threatened for living alone, then she would take a lodger, a nice young woman not many years older than herself, who would provide her with the respectability which, she knew, she would lack in the eyes of authority if they knew her mother was away.

Happier in her mind than she had been since her mother's departure, Linnet slept well that night.

*

It was about the same time – the Easter holidays after the twins' fourteenth birthday – Lucy and Caitlin finally discovered who had stolen their fruit cake the previous summer.

After that first visit to the castle, and the mysterious theft, they had decided they would make a point of visiting the old castle at least once a week, and at first they actually did so. But after a couple of visits the curragh wasn't there, and it did not appear again. After that they went because they enjoyed having a place of their own, one which nobody else knew about, but it gradually palled because it was a long walk, because the marsh grew next to impassable as the summer rains swelled its puddles into small ponds, and because nothing much happened when they went over there.

'We ought to have gone over in winter, because whoever was living there likely wouldn't be watching for visitors in winter,' Lucy remarked on Easter Sunday as they stopped by the gate to the meadows and the marsh. They leaned on the mossy top bar, looking across at the black finger of the tower pointing up at the pale blue sky. 'What's more, whoever lives there would have needed a fire, and newly dead fires leave traces . . . oh, why didn't we go over in the winter?'

But they had not gone because they were busy with other, indoor activities and also because as the weather worsened so the lure of the castle had palled. It no longer seemed mysterious when the rain sheeted across the marsh but just lonely and dilapidated, and when the snow came, and the howling gales, both girls found plenty to occupy them in the old farmhouse with its empty rooms and crowded attics, or in the sheds and barns which abounded around the farmyard.

'But this holiday, now that we're fourteen and past, we'll go back again and do all sorts,' Caitlin announced.

'This year, we'll do all the things we didn't do last year, starting off by nagging our daddies to make us a curragh of our own.'

'I don't have a daddy,' Lucy reminded her. 'Is it my grandad you're meaning?'

'Yes, of course. I do forget,' apologised Caitlin. 'Your grandad will help my daddy to build us a curragh, won't he?'

'I doubt it; he'll say there's easier ways of gettin' rid o' the pair of us than be drowning,' Lucy said placidly. 'They're against boats, the Murphys. They say they're farmers, not fishermen.'

'Oh well, we'll have to find the magic curragh, then,' Caitlin said. It was a fine day and she was in a good mood and besides, school had broken up which meant that though they would be busy about the farm they would not have to go off to school each day. 'Are we plantin' spuds tomorrow?'

'We are. I'm going to get the thickest sack out of the barn for me poor knees, you'd better do likewise.'

On Easter Sunday itself, of course, they had been too busy with church services, visiting the graves and being lugged here and there by their respective families to go anywhere or do anything, but finally, after tea, Caitlin came over and the two of them agreed to plant potatoes all the following day in return for a picnic the day after that.

'Fair enough, though if the rain holds off your grandad will expect you to finish the big field,' Maeve warned Lucy. 'It's half done; mind, but there's still a power of plantin' left to do.'

As it happened, the next day started off chilly and overcast and it seemed that it had rained most of the night – at any rate, as the children, Maeve and the farmhands squelched across the half-sown field every step was a battle.

'If it had rained *now* then they'd likely have put the plantin' off till tomorrow,' Caitlin moaned, as they reached the end of the rows and dumped their sacks on the cold, wet ploughland. 'As it is, we've got to put a good face on it and start, at least.'

Lucy said nothing but threw her own sack down and knelt on it. Oh, the pain of the sharp little pebbles digging into her kneecaps, the discomfort of hands gone numb from the cold and wet, trying to delve into the claggy soil, oh the misery when, presently, the nippy wind brought a gust of cold rain with it, not enough rain so that they might give up, just enough to fur their lashes with wet and to soak their hair into rats' tails.

'At least the best part of the field's done,' Maeve called over her shoulder at one point. 'And Kellach's such a worker, look at the rate of him, shootin' up his furrow like a racin' greyhound!'

The simile made Lucy smile – her first that morning. Kellach was a beefy young man and his broad behind, moving stolidly along his furrow, resembled a greyhound about as much as Clara Bow, the mournful old mule who had done the ploughing, resembled a race-horse.

'Sure an' it's nice to see you smile,' Maeve said encouragingly. 'Let's see if we can keep pace wi' one another, shall we? Then at least we can talk.'

'I don't feel like talkin',' Caitlin grumbled. 'Sure an' isn't the inside of me mouth the only warm bit of me? I'm not after gettin' that cold by openin' me gob more'n I have to.'

That made Maeve and Lucy laugh and Maeve said that since they were all working like Trojans now, she'd offer them a bit of a prize . . . Kellach would undoubtedly finish his row first, and probably be halfway down his second before any of the females had reached the hedge, but whoever came second to Kellach at the end of the field would get a bag of Maeve's cinder toffee and a three-penny piece to spend.

It definitely gave a point to the work, Lucy thought, seizing her bag of spuds and heaving herself further along the row. She planted two likely looking potatoes, eyes up, and entombed them, banged the earth flat, moved on. Maeve was a little ahead of her still, Caitlin a long way behind. But Caitlin had heard, and was rapidly brightening up despite the rain which was starting in earnest now.

'We should've started off evens, though,' she panted at Lucy's heels 'What's the prize for whoever comes in third?'

'A clip round the ear,' Kellach shouted from way up front. 'Delivered be the all-time winner, Kellach Flanagan, and am't I the best spud-planter in all of Ireland, now?'

'First isn't important today, Kellach,' Lucy shouted. 'The race is a ladies' race with just me an' Cait competin', and I'm in the lead as they round the bend!'

'Neck and neck!' Caitlin screamed, drawing level with Lucy. 'Put your money on the Kelly filly, ladies an' gentlemen, sure an' she's got the stamina an' the speed, what more can you ask?'

'The Murphy mare's drawin' ahead,' countered Lucy, planting like mad. 'The Murphy mare's got the legs on the filly, she's used to heavy going, she's got a light foot on her so she has!'

Maeve was laughing so hard that they caught her up, both now ignoring the dreadful weather conditions, not even bothering to lift up their kneeling sacks but bending and straightening, slamming the seed potatoes into place, covering them up, stamping them down and dragging their equipment on to the next bit of trench.

'Sure and if old Tom was out here he'd be puttin' a bob each way on the pair of ye,' she called after them. 'Mind them spuds don't get planted upside down, we don't want to have to dig six foot down to get 'em when they're ready.'

'Australians would get them,' Lucy said, pushing her hair back from her forehead with a muddy hand. 'Good Irish potatoes, gone all that way ... oh, oh, you distracted me, Maeve, now the poor Murphy mare's handicapped!'

By evening the race was won and the field finished. Mud to their eyebrows, the children went to their own homes, almost too tired to shout a goodnight; almost, but not quite. Lucy reached the haven of her little room under the eaves, opened the window into the downpour, and leaned out, but only a little way, out of deference to her clean white nightgown.

'Caitlin, are you in your room?' She shouted needlessly, since she could see both Caitlin's candle and her head and shoulders against the light. 'Have you had a bath? Maeve said when she emptied my bathwater she might as well have taken it straight along to the nine acre, for 'twas all good, rich loam. I washed me hair, though I didn't see the point; it 'ud been rinsed in rainwater all day so it had.'

'I'm bathed,' Caitlin answered. 'And I'm dog-tired, so I am. If I live the night out shall we go over to the castle tomorrow? For I'm damned if I'll set another potato until next year.'

'There aren't any more to set, thank the good Lord,' Lucy said piously. 'If the sun shines I want to go a picnic tomorrow. If it's rainy again we might go into Cahersiveen with Maeve in the donkey-cart. She's got shoppin' to do, she says.'

'We could go to the cinema,' Caitlin said eagerly. 'Honest to God, Lu, your Maeve knows a t'ing or two –

we earned those threepenny bits twice over so we did.'

'Aye, you're right there, she's a psychia . . . whatsit, isn't she just?'

'A cunning old mavoureen, you mean,' Caitlin called. 'See you in the morning then, alanna. Goodniiiiiiight!'

'See you in the morning,' Lucy shouted back. 'Goodniiiiiiight!'

She shut the window, causing drops to fly into the room and speckle the floorboards, and took a flying jump into her bed. The bed cannoned into the wall and the metal head rail squealed and scattered flakes as it rammed against the whitewash.

Lucy cuddled down the bed and dragged the blankets up over her shoulders. Tomorrow they would . . . they would . . .

She slept.

'Well, me prayers were answered,' Caitlin said with a good deal of satisfaction next afternoon as they set out for their picnic. 'Didn't we work like a couple of Irish navvies all morning so as to get our legs loose this afternoon, and aren't we rewarded? Isn't it just the sort of day we wanted, alanna? A bit windy, I'll grant you, and wit' the odd cloud floating along, but it's sunny, that you cannot deny.'

Lucy looked dubiously up at the sky above them. It was sunny, that was certainly true, but there was a great deal of cloud above and there was an oddness in the weather, something she described to herself as a sort of brassiness, which she did not much like.

'Well, I don't know,' she said heavily. 'The air tastes odd, don't you think? Perhaps we'd better stick close to home, eh, Cait?'

But Caitlin was having none of it. 'For a start off, if we stick close to home then your Maeve and my mammy will see us and hand out jobs, sure as me name's Kelly,' she said. 'And for another start off, it's sunny and you can't be too sure of sunshine in April. And for *another* start . . .'

'You can only have one start, the rest isn't,' Lucy said pedantically. And then, when Caitlin pulled a face and fell silent, 'Well then? What's the next start?'

'How can air taste funny?'

'It can,' Lucy said, after a short pause to consider. 'It tastes of metal polish.'

'Smells of it, d'you mean? Because sure I can understand a smell of metal polish, but a taste of the stuff? Air can't taste, it's not water!'

By now they were across the long meadow and climbing the gate onto the marsh so Lucy just shrugged and wrinkled her nose.

'I don't know how it can taste, I just know it does. I can taste it in my mouth. Are you saying you cannot?'

They crossed some more marsh, leaping from tussock to tussock and avoiding the brackish, sky-reflecting pools.

'I know what you mean,' Caitlin said at last. 'Only I don't think it tastes so much of metal polish as torch batteries. D'you want to turn back, then?'

It was a good question since, as Caitlin spoke, they could see blowing across the lough towards them a rain-shower, fine as cobweb, colourful as a rainbow as it caught the sunshine. And looking across at it, Lucy could feel the tingle in the air, the strange stillness, which presages exceptionally bad weather.

'Too late,' she said, however. 'We'll never get home before the rain reaches us; let's make for the castle.'

They ran on, but very soon the rain was upon them, misty and cool on their skins, not at all unpleasant. They reached the edge of the mound in good order and were about to pull themselves up when from the rapidly gathering clouds overhead came an ominous rumble and almost at the same moment, a vivid fork of lightning arrowed down into the lough.

'God help us!' Caitlin gasped.

Lucy, fervently echoing her friend's words, bounded the last couple of yards, hit the grass running, and made straight for the castle, Caitlin close on her heels.

'It's an electric storm,' she gasped as they ran in under the arch. 'I'm scared, Cait, we shouldn't be out, we should be indoors . . . aargh!'

She had shrieked because at that moment the thunder cracked overhead so loud that it pained the ears, and the narrow space in the castle keep was lit up by a brilliant flash which completely swamped the afternoon light.

'Oh, oh, *oh*!' Caitlin squeaked as the thunder cracked a second time. 'It's right overhead, we'll be killed stone dead! The bloody castle will fall on us and Mammy and Maeve will skin us alive!'

'It's stood for a thousand years, so no reason why it should keel over now,' Lucy said stoutly, but perspiration was trickling down the sides of her face and her heart was thumping like a trip-hammer. 'You made a poem just now, Cait – *It's right overhead, we'll be killed stone dead*! That's a p . . . oh, oh!'

Even as she spoke a tongue of lightning struck the sapling growing out of the highest wall and licked down the stones towards them, causing both girls to shriek and Caitlin to cover her head with both hands in a gesture as instinctive as it was futile.

'Get through the door, for divil a hope have we got here,' Lucy said briskly, giving her friend a shove. 'Go on . . . at least there'll be a roof over our heads.'

They dived through the door just as another great, hollow clang of thunder echoed around them so that the slam of the door was noiseless. And just before it closed they saw more lightning flicker horribly around the keep.

'Phew,' panted Lucy, leaning against the door. 'That was the most frightening thing ever! But what a storm, Cait! Shall we go up to the secret room?'

'Climb those terrible stairs in a storm I will not, and you would be mad to do so, Luceen, with the place liable to tumble around your ears any second,' Caitlin said roundly. 'Let's sit on the floor under the table and say a Hail Mary.'

'I'm going up; think of the *view*, Cait,' Lucy said, though she did not much fancy climbing the stone steps whilst the thunder continued to crash right overhead. 'If the stairs shake though, divil a bit further will I climb, you may be sure of that.'

'Don't leave me down here alone,' Caitlin said, clutching her friend's sleeve. 'Oh stay, Luceen, your Maeve will kill me if I let you get into mischief.'

'Come with me, then,' Lucy said stoutly, heading for the stairs. 'I need to be doing, Cait, I can't stay here shaking like a lily leaf, I'm better doing.'

So when Lucy started to climb Caitlin was close on her heels and presently both girls realised something which made them feel a good deal safer.

'The stairs don't shake, not even a tiddy bit,' Lucy said. 'I told you these old stones had lasted a thousand years and would go on for a bit yet.'

'Aye, they're steady so they are,' Caitlin agreed. 'Are we nearly at the door, alanna?'

Glancing back, Lucy discovered that Caitlin was climbing with both eyes squeezed tightly closed and that her own brief skirt was clutched in Caitlin's paw. For the first time ever she was the leader and she liked it. She gave her friend's shoulder a reassuring pat.

'We're there,' she said, stopping in front of the door. 'And I think the storm's moving away at last. Let's hope the door doesn't stick or we won't get a good view at all at all.'

As if the thunder had heard and wanted to make a liar of her it crashed again, sharply, right overhead, just as Lucy pushed the door and it swung obediently open. She and Caitlin stepped into the secret room – and stopped short.

They were not alone. Leaning half out of the window was a small and shabby figure with a shock of white hair. Dressed in an ankle length black skirt, cracked black boots and a tattered shawl which was more hole than pattern, the person – a woman, presumably – had not heard them for the sounds of the storm, or possibly for the sounds that she herself was uttering, for she was shrieking like a banshee and cackling first with laughter and then with what sounded like annoyance, though it was difficult to tell without being able to see her face.

'Who is it?' Caitlin whispered. She had obviously opened her eyes, the journey up the stairs having been accomplished. 'What's she doing?'

'Watching the storm,' Lucy whispered back. 'I don't want to startle her in case she falls out . . . we'd better just stand still until she turns back into the room.'

But Caitlin had not suffered the terrors of the stairs for nothing. She shook her head obstinately. 'I want to look out,' she hissed. 'Come on, the old woman won't notice us moving round.'

And Caitlin was right. The small female continued to shriek, to swear, and to laugh whilst the two girls moved round to the nearest window-slit and peered out.

And it was worth doing so. Lucy watched, awed, as first the rain came sheeting across the lough like a veil, then the sun would peep out from behind a black cloud making rainbows, then the thunder, rumbling sullenly, would crack and the lightning would flicker across the blackness, looking not gold or silver, but a sort of electric lavender blue.

'It is moving off,' Caitlin breathed against Lucy's ear. 'I never did see such a storm, me. Oh, look at the rainbows!'

'Look at the big one will you, stretching right across the lough . . . ah, here comes the rain in earnest.'

They stood back from the window as the wind, which had dropped whilst the storm raged, drove the rain straight at them, or so it seemed, and at the same moment the little creature gave one last squawk and turned towards them.

She was very old and very, very dirty. Her snow white hair was laced liberally with dirt and bits of hay, and her skin was soft and dark, crumpled and cobwebbed with tiny lines. She was thin as a thread, and bent like the moorland trees, and she was no bigger than a child of six or seven. But, astonishingly, Lucy saw that she was still pretty, with eyes as black and sparkling as a young girl's, a haughty little nose and a firm and pointed chin beneath a mouth sunken through age and toothlessness.

They didn't get much chance to look at her though. She shrieked again, revealing that she didn't have so much as a tooth in her head, and dived head-first into the piled up hay, disappearing so fast that the girls did not have a chance to stop her.

'Well, did you see that?' Caitlin gasped. 'Why did she go in there?'

'Scared,' Lucy said briefly. 'She didn't know we were here, so we frightened her, I suppose.' She leaned down over the pile of hay. 'Come out do, alanna,' she said coaxingly. 'Sure and we'd never hurt you, this is your own little room, I daresay? Come out and say good afternoon like a Christian.'

The hay remained unmoving.

'Who were you shouting at?' Lucy wheedled. 'Wasn't the storm great, then? Ah, come on, we're only a couple o' kids, we wouldn't hurt you, grandma.'

Several more remarks failed to get the hay to stir and Lucy was about to give up when Caitlin sat down on the floor with a thump and addressed her friend, whilst keeping a wary eye on the hay-tump.

'Amn't I glad we brought so many delicious hard-boiled eggs and so much of your Maeve's new-baked bread, Lu?' she said innocently. 'Enough there is for an army and we'd share willingly, wouldn't we, Luceen? And the chocolate cake with the butter icing that melts in the mouth – enough for five or six my mammy did pack in our old blue bag. And it isn't everyone who can make lemon barley like Mammy, to quench your thirst and make you want more at one and the same time.'

The hay definitely stirred. Both girls held their breath.

'It's the drink I'm longing for,' Lucy said, her eyes on the hay. 'Sure it'll slide down me dry t'roat like a trout slipping along the stream bed. Why, if there's a drink I do love it's your mammy's lemon barley.'

A small and dirty face could be dimly seen through the hay, whilst two large, dark eyes burned out at them. Caitlin opened the blue bag and peered inside as though unaware she had an audience. She brought forth rustling parcels and laid them tenderly on the dusty boards between herself and Lucy. The watching face emerged altogether from the hay and the owner heaved herself right out and crouched there, staring at them, half hopeful, half wary.

Lucy leaned forward and picked up a slice of chocolate cake.

'Would you like some of this, missus?' she asked politely. 'Or would you rather start with a sandwich or two, and a drink?'

'Sure an' we've not been interduced,' the old lady said

in a voice creaky with age and lack of use. 'Will ye not give me your names before we share a crust?'

But her bright eyes did not seem able to move from the cake and when Lucy held it out a grimy paw with blackened nails reached out and grabbed it, though she did not immediately carry it to her mouth.

'Sorry, missus,' Caitlin said humbly. 'I'm Caitlin Kelly and me friend's Lucy Murphy. And your name?'

'Moggy, Granny Mogg,' the old woman said thickly; the cake had at last reached her mouth, crammed in by an impatient hand. 'I'm Granny Mogg so I am, Moggy to me pals.' She cackled briefly, spraying crumbs. ''Tis good cake,' she added, swallowing the last mouthful. ''Tis rare tasty, Caitlin. Ah, wouldn't it be grand if I had cake like t'at every day, now?'

'We don't get chocolate cake every day, Granny Mogg,' Lucy said hastily. 'Only for a special picnic. Would you be having a drink of the barley water now?'

The old woman looked curiously at the bottle, but shook her head. 'I'm thinkin' I'd best stick wit' tay,' she said. 'A cup o' tay goes down well wi' cake.'

Silently, Lucy leaned forward and picked up the remaining piece of cake; it was taken from her hand – almost snatched – at once and despite her toothlessness the old lady made short work of it. Then she sat back on her heels and gazed expectantly at the girls. Lucy broke the silence.

'The storm's moving away, thank the Lord,' she said. 'But would you look at that rain? We'll be here for a while yet.'

It was true that the rain was falling steadily but Lucy did not think it would last all that long, she had merely made the remark for something to say, and now she sat down and began to unwrap the rest of their picnic.

'A sandwich, Mrs Mogg?' she said presently and, after

some rather unconvincing remarks that 'I shouldn't take your food, indeed indeed,' the sandwich disappeared inside Granny Mogg, who smacked her lips and said it was 'a fair treat, so it was'.

'Have you lived here long?' Lucy asked presently, when the first edge of their hunger was dulled. 'Where do you do your shopping? I can't remember seeing you in Cahersiveen.'

Granny Mogg stared reflectively out at the steadily falling rain. 'I've lived 'ere a whiles,' she said after a moment. 'I doesn't do no shoppin', though, child. How would I pay for shoppin' eh? I lives off the land, I does.'

'Do you eat rabbits? And raw corn, and blackberries, and nuts?' Caitlin asked, letting her incredulity show. 'We've got a friend at school, his gran's a hundred years old and she eats rabbits wit' their fur and all still on.'

'I skins 'em,' Granny Mogg said with disdain. 'Eatin' fur's mortal dirty, an' bad for ye. I dunna tek to raw flesh, either. Why, your friend's gran must have a set o' teeth on 'er like a farmer's dog if she kin eat raw flesh.'

'Oh, it's only what they say,' Lucy said comfortably, taking a pull out of the bottle. She swallowed, then handed the drink on to Caitlin. 'Do you eat fish, cooked over a fire?'

Granny Mogg thought for a moment, giving Lucy quick, bright little glances out of her shrewd and sparkling eyes, then nodded. 'Aye; I'm fond of a nice piece of fish.'

'The trout in the lough are good,' Lucy said, nodding, too. 'Do you fish from the curragh beside the creek?'

This time there was a distinct pause whilst Granny Mogg's brow wrinkled in cogitation. Then, with some reluctance, she shook her head. 'No indeed, for if I got into t'at tippery shell wouldn't I be drownded dead in a moment? Girls can't swim, childer, it ain't for females, not swimmin' ain't. No, I gets fish give be – be a friend.'

'He's a very shy friend, the one who fishes from the curragh, for never have we set eyes on him,' Caitlin remarked. 'What does he use for oars, Granny?'

The old woman shook her head. 'Ne'er mind,' she said. 'If it hadn't been for the young devil I'd not be here. And you'd best forget you met me,' she added. 'We're hidin' up, see? Not hurtin' no one, just hidin' up.' She dropped her voice and made the sign of the cross, first to her left, then to her right, then on the bony ridge of her breast bone. 'Sure an' they t'ought I was dead,' she whispered. 'They meant me to die, they put me out on a turble night, with the snow sweepin' in across the mountains . . . if it hadn't been for the young devil . . .'

The girls leaned closer to catch her words, Lucy uneasily aware of a thrill of fear running through her. Was the old woman mad, or had someone really tried to kill her? And if so, was that person even now approaching the castle with evil in his heart – evil which might spread to encompass two defenceless girls as well as the old woman?

'Who did it, Granny?' Lucy asked, unconsciously whispering in her turn. 'Who tried to kill you? And why?'

But before Granny Mogg could say a word the door to their retreat shot open, causing all three of them to give a shriek of sheer shock and terror, before Granny Mogg dived into the tump of hay and Caitlin and Lucy, hearts thumping, turned to face the doorway.

A boy stood there, framed by the silvery wood. His mouth was opened on an 'o' of surprise and his eyes, black as night, rounded with disbelief when they met Lucy's before narrowing again to slide quickly round the room. Then he stepped in and Lucy noticed the string of trout in one hand and the spoon-shaped oar in the other. It was undoubtedly the curragh owner, the giver of fish . . . the young devil himself!

Chapter Five

For a moment no one said a word; the hay stopped quivering, the boy's stare ceased to roam the room and fixed itself with unnerving steadiness on Lucy, and outside the rain seemed to give a little sigh before continuing to fall whilst the thunder rumbled away into the distance and a long finger of golden sunlight slid through the western window-slit and fell across the dusty floor.

'And just what've you done wi' the old woman?'

The accent was strange – Lucy found herself wondering what part of Kerry the boy hailed from – but the meaning perfectly clear. Lucy pointed to the hay. The boy nodded.

'Sure and she's the nervous one, isn't she? No wonder, either, after last summer – and now tell me, will you, just where you two beauties sprang from?'

Out of the corner of her eye Lucy saw Caitlin bridle and drop her eyes so that she could look up at the boy through her lashes; it made Lucy smile since she was absolutely certain of one thing – that when the 'young devil' used the expression 'two beauties', the last thing on his mind was their looks. And Caitlin suddenly seemed to realise the same thing, for she stopped looking coquettish and looked worried, instead.

The boy sighed, then laid his fish carefully down on the board floor and propped his oddly shaped oar against the wall. Then he took two steps into the room and Lucy shrank back, suddenly aware of menace in his dark-eyed glance. He was older than she and Caitlin, taller, stronger

. . . and he seemed to be angry with them, though why this should be she had not yet worked out.

'Well? You, the little fair one, where d'you come from and what are you doin' in this old castle, where no one comes?'

'We came for a picnic,' Lucy said. She stood her ground but could not help her glance shooting towards the hay-tump. It was moving again, not much but enough to make her realise that Granny Mogg, having realised who the boy was, was definitely considering emerging. This made her feel better, though she could not have said why. 'Only there was the storm . . . so we came into the castle and climbed up here and . . . and there was Mrs Mogg, watching the lightning through the window.'

'Aye; leppin' like a – a leprechaun and swearin' like a trooper and cacklin' like a hen going to lay an egg,' the boy said, suddenly good-humoured. He grinned at Lucy and she saw that he was good to look at when he grinned, with the very dark eyes narrowed into shining slits and a long laughter dimple in one thin brown cheek. 'Scare you, did she?'

'Only for a moment,' Lucy said stoutly. 'It was the shock – we'd got used to thinking there was no one here, you see.'

He nodded, then bent down and picked up his string of fish. He walked over to the pile of hay and swung the fish ruminatively, then bent down and spoke. His voice, which had seemed harsh and rather angry to Lucy, went very soft and deep.

'Come along out wit' you, Gran, tis meself out here, wit' the younglings.'

The hay shook and Granny Mogg emerged. She was grinning, showing her pink gums and her tooth, but there was a wariness about her, as though she secretly doubted her welcome.

'Twaren't my fault they found me,' she squeaked. 'They come on me sudden like, when the thunder was roarin' too loud to hear a scream o' mortal terror. You shouldn't ha' leaved me, you should ha' stayed by me.'

'I've got six trout,' the boy said ruminatively. 'Two each for you an' me, Gran, and one each for these spratleens. Shall we tek 'em down to the fireplace and fry 'em?'

I just hope he means the trout and not us, Lucy thought fervently, whilst the old lady nodded, grinned, and shook the hay off herself, then began to hobble at a fair speed across the floor towards the open door.

Lucy went to follow her, but the boy put an arm across the doorway, barring her.

'Not so fast, girleen; now you can tell me, slow and quiet-like, what you're doing here and how you came to find me gran.'

'We live over there,' Lucy said, waving a vague hand in the direction of the farm. 'My grandad owns all this land, though not the castle, of course. He grazes his cattle on the sea marsh and the meadows leading down to it. We came down here last summer and we thought then that there was someone here, but we couldn't find you. Only the curragh.'

He nodded, thoughtful now, gazing absently past her, his eyes fixed on the window-slit behind her head.

'Aye, last summer . . . there was someone, I remember Gran saying. But she's kept well hid, until now.'

'Why does it matter if anyone sees her?' Caitlin said from behind, giving Lucy quite a surprise. So involved had she become with the boy that she had almost forgotten her friend. 'No one would really hurt an old lady.'

The black eyes left Lucy's face for a moment and fastened on Caitlin's, with a mocking look in their depths.

'Would they not? Have you never met an Irish tinker, girleen? There's good and bad amongst them but Granny Mogg was with the Duveen tribe, and they're rough, real rough. A year gone she sickened and Vorth, the boss, decided she was dying. He left her, wrapped in a soaking wet blanket, under a hedge. She should've been dead by morning but Mogg's a tough old bird. I found her and carried her to where she'd be safe, gave her water to drink, put her deep in the hay and waited. She slept and snored for two days, half-waking to drink, and on the third day she sat up and demanded food. You could say she's never looked back since.'

'But why should the tinkers care whether she's alive or dead?' Lucy demanded. 'She's just an old woman, she can't hurt anyone.'

'True. But she'd make a liar of Vorth, she would indeed, and he'd never stand for that. Told the tribe she was dead, see? So as far as Vorth's concerned Granny Mogg's dead and should stay so. Which is why she dives into the hay and keeps out of sight most of the time, though I tell her the tinkers may not come this way again for many a long year.'

'Or they may come back tomorrow,' Lucy said in a hollow tone. 'Scared I am at the thought – they might kill us all!'

'Not me,' the youth said. 'Nor the old'un whilst I've breath in me body to defend her. She's a good old gal, no one shall hurt her. But the Duveen tribe's a bad lot, I don't mind tellin' you, and Vorth – he'd murther the lot of yez if he took it into his head so he would. And come to that, if either of you say a word about Granny Mogg to your mammies and daddies, sure and won't Finn Delaney slit your little t'roatsies for you from ear to ear?'

'Are you Finn Delaney?' That was Caitlin again, peering out from behind Lucy's shoulder. The boy nodded.

'That's me. And who are you two? Not sisters – friends? In the same class at school, mebbe?'

'That's right,' Lucy said since Caitlin simply mumbled something beneath her breath. 'I'm Lucy Murphy and me friend's Caitlin Kelly. So now we all know each other can we go down to your gran? I'm longing to see where she puts the fire, so I am, for divil a sign of new ash did we see.'

The boy chuckled but stopped barring the door and went ahead of them to the top of the stone stair. 'And see you shall. Now I'll go first so's if you fall you'll have a soft landin' on me back, though I hope you won't fall – you're neither of you feather-weights by the looks.'

'You're heavier than the both of us,' Lucy said stoutly, eyeing the broad back and shoulders before her as they began to descend the stairs. 'A nice dint in the ground you'd make if you fell.'

He turned to grin at her. 'Aye, but Finn Delaney's never been known to fall – I climb like a goat, run like a racehorse and fight like a tiger, so show me respect and you won't go far wrong.' He glanced past Lucy to Caitlin, clinging once more to her friend's skirt. 'What's wrong wi' you, Caitlin? Open your eyes, woman, or you could kill the t'ree of us.'

'She doesn't like heights,' Lucy said calmly. 'If she looks she freezes and divil a down will she go. And if you keep turning round . . .'

She said nothing more since Finn, still staring at Caitlin, bounced a shoulder on the wall, staggered and fell off the step five but one from the ground. Being a feller he pretended he'd done it on purpose, of course, and held out both hands to Lucy to jump as well, but Lucy knew it had startled him and gave him a told-you-so smirk before ignoring his outstretched hands and going demurely down the rest of the flight.

'We're there,' she told Caitlin, preventing her friend from continuing to grope for the next step with one foot, and Caitlin opened her eyes and gazed round in a dazed sort of way.

'So we are indeed; where's Granny Mogg, though?'

'In the sod hut,' Finn said briefly. 'Come on.'

He led the way out into the now tenderly falling spring rain and dived into the turf hut. Sure enough, there was Granny Mogg lighting her fire which she had set right in the middle of the long-dead ashes. She blew on it, and ash floated into the air, making her sneeze, but even as the girls watched a steady red glow began to invade the peat and Granny Mogg reached into the pile of dead bracken and produced a frying pan, blackened and heavy but obviously still very much in use, an ancient iron trivet and a kettle.

'Never saw 'em, did you?' she cackled, turning to grin at the girls. 'Ah, younglings never look beyond their little noses, never!' She picked up the kettle and began to fill it with water from an old milk churn pushed well into a corner and disguised by a pile of ancient turves, then she hung it over the fire. 'We'll eat an' drink when the kettle boils,' she stated calmly. 'I'll make us a wet o' tay.'

'Where do you get the tea from?' Lucy asked as Finn, hunkering down, began to gut the fish and throw them into the blackened pan. 'You can't find tea, you have to buy it!'

'I get it for her, sometimes from O'Rorke's in Cahersiveen or from a nice little shop I know in Caherdaniel village,' Finn put in. 'Granny Mogg stays here when I'm away, so she has to have supplies to keep her goin'.' He looked speculatively at the two girls, but his eyes rested longest on Lucy. 'Ye wouldn't like to look in on her from time to time?' he wheedled. 'She hates to be left so she does, but I've our livings to make.'

'What do you do?' Caitlin asked inquisitively. 'You don't work on any of the farms round here or we'd have recognised you. And you don't work in the shops in Caher, either, I'm sure. Well, it isn't everybody who would . . .'

She stopped short. Finn finished the sentence for her. 'It isn't everybody who would employ a tinker, Caitlin, is that what you were goin' to say?' he asked softly. 'Sure and you're right, but they'd take a one-legged Protestant negro on the fishing boats if he could haul a line and trim a sail and pull an oar. And I can look as respectable as – as a farmer when the harvest needs all hands.'

'But not round here,' Caitlin persisted. 'You don't work round here, do you, Finn? Because Lu and me, we go round the other farms when they have the Stations, or when they need help with the harvest, and we've never seen you, have we, Luceen?'

'Divil a once,' Lucy said cheerfully. She picked up the panful of fish and pushed it into the heart of the red-hot turves. 'I'll see to the fish, Finn, whilst you find us something to drink out of – you don't take your tay from the kettle, do you?'

Finn laughed. 'We've two tin billies which do duty for all,' he said cheerfully. 'But you'll have to sup hot tay from your cupped hands and eat fried fish with your finger-ends. Unless there's something in the blue bag?'

'Of course!' Caitlin said. They had left the bag in the castle and she turned and went out of the hut. 'I'll fetch our bottle, Lu, that should do for us.'

As soon as she had gone Finn turned to Lucy. He put a strong brown hand on her upper arm and gripped it, urgently but with care and gentleness. 'Lucy, I want speech apart. Where can we meet where Caitlin won't follow?'

Lucy stared at him, a frown knitting her brow. 'You

could come to my house,' she said slowly. 'When it's evening time. But whether Maeve or Grandad would let you in I can't say.'

He laughed with a trace of bitterness. 'Let a tinker into a farmhouse for to visit the farmer's daughter? Is it likely, alanna? Can you not come out, say you want to be private? Pay a visit?'

'Oh, I don't know,' Lucy said doubtfully. 'For why don't you want to see Caitlin at the same time, Finn? She's me best friend.'

'I've got something for you,' Finn said after a short pause. 'Only one I do have, Luceen, so none for Caitlin there is. And soon I'll be gone from here. Where shall we meet?'

'Tonight, do you mean? After it's dark?' She was tempted to say she did not dare, did not know him well enough, but then she heard Caitlin's step returning. He seized her hand, his fingers hard now, and urgent.

'Your home?'

'The big farm built of pale stones with the ivy round the front,' Lucy whispered rapidly.

He nodded, the dark eyes still fixed on her face. 'I know it. In the big barn just inside the gate . . . tonight.'

He moved away from her but she followed, anxious. 'What time, Finn?'

He shrugged. 'I don't go by clocks. When the moon is high . . . when all the eyes in your house are closed and the windows of your farm are in darkness. I'll wait for you.'

She barely had time to nod, to say she would do her best to be there, before Caitlin was back, the blue bag in her hand. They shared out the sandwiches, drank the lemonade between them, then had the fish, so hot that Lucy and Caitlin wrapped theirs in their sandwich paper and even then squealed whenever they took a

bite. Granny Mogg and Finn ate theirs unconcernedly
with their fingers, and drank the tay from their tin billy
cans, so hot that it hurt Lucy to watch them. And presently Finn took them down to the lough to see the
curragh whilst Granny Mogg had a snooze in the sun
and then it was time to go, because though the soft rain
had not ceased to fall all day, it came down from a
darkening sky.

'Shall we see you tomorrow, Finn?' Caitlin asked, as
he waved them off.

He shrugged. 'Mebbe. But I'll be gone before long;
you'll visit the old 'un for me? And say no word, for fear
of Vorth comin' to know she's alive?'

Both girls promised they would, then began to cross
the marsh, scampering through the puddles and pools,
intent now on getting back home before they were late
for their tea. But Lucy, at least, did not forget Finn for a
moment; whether he was good or bad she did not yet
know, but he fascinated her. She knew she would meet
him tonight, if it was humanly possible, even if it meant
lying to Grandad and deceiving Maeve. After all, there's
the old 'un to consider, she told herself righteously. You
can't let an old lady down. But inside her head it was
Finn's dark eyes which danced, Finn's curving mouth
which smiled . . . and the recollection of the feel of Finn's
hard brown hand on her arm which brought that
shivering pang of excitement darting through her.

Finn stared after them until they were just dots crossing
the lushness of the distant meadows. What luck that they
should have come today, when he was beginning to think
that he must leave Granny Mogg alone here whilst he
went foraging for food! They would look out for the old
'un, he had no doubt of that, and because they were now
thoroughly frightened of Vorth, whatever they might

pretend, they would give neither Granny nor himself away.

Not that they had any idea that he, too, was in hiding of a sort. But when all was said and done they were only a couple of children, and you couldn't tell children too much or they would get in a panic and tell their parents and then where would he be?

He liked the little fair one, though. There was something about her, he did not know what it was, which made him want to look at her and go on looking. It was strange really, because she had fair hair and he liked dark women, and she had grey-blue eyes and he admired a passionate, dark-brown gaze. What was more she was a child, no more than thirteen or fourteen, and he was a man – sixteen at least and not interested in children.

Finn had had his first woman over a year earlier, after his mother had died and his father had remarried, choosing Eilis of the Duveen tribe, a woman as voluptuous as his mother had been slender, as bawdy as his mother had been gentle.

The marriage had been a success in that Eilis had made Paddy happy, but she resented having a stepson only half a dozen years younger than she and made no secret of it. And the Tuam people did not take to Eilis and did not trouble to hide their feelings, which was why the Delaneys had moved in with the Duveen tribe and why Finn had come across Brónach one fine April morning just after Easter. The two young people had seen each other often enough before, but had never so much as spoken until they had chanced to meet on Church Island, in Caherdaniel Bay. It was a small island almost completely taken over by the local churchyard and Finn had been digging cockles on the long sea strand and had come up to the island to sit on the grass and drink from his bottle of cold tea. He came over the ridge, his cockles in a bucket, sweat beading his brow, and the first thing he saw was Brónach, with a mass of flowers by her side, sitting on the green spring grass between the graves. He could see she had been stealing the Easter flowers to sell in the nearby town, an activity of which he disapproved, but she smiled at him so he walked over to her and, as he felt courtesy demanded, wished her top of the morning.

One reason that Finn had not mixed much with the Duveen young was that they were very different from the Tuam tribe, who were horse dealers, donkey barterers and lace-makers. In fact, the Tuams worked for their living in every possible way. Children cut hazel-wands and the women wove them into baskets which the men sold to the villagers and townsfolk. Old men cut rushes and mended chair seats. Others searched for the lucky white heather and wheedled pennies out of superstitious housewives. They lived, by their own standards, fairly enough. The Duveens, however, lived not on the country, but on the people. They preyed on villagers and townsfolk alike. They were thieves for a living and stole hens, eggs and farm stock without compunction. They took the flowers from the graves, the butter from the churn, the milk from cows in the meadows, and seemed to believe they had a God-given right to do so. They would pull down an isolated cattle shelter and burn it on their fires, or untie the dog from his kennel and demand a ransom for his return, or steal the washing from the line or the bicycle from the shed. They were able-bodied but idle and feckless in the extreme, with a streak of real viciousness if things did not seem to be going their way.

So Finn's feelings upon seeing Brónach were not exactly of unalloyed joy but were laced with considerable caution. She was a year older than he and a naughty girl, even his stepmam said so. However, one could not be rude, particularly to a member of the opposite sex, his real mother had taught him that.

So after cautious greetings had been exchanged he had sat down next to her and, after a quick glance at him, she had pushed her skirt back so that her long, slender brown legs could enjoy the warmth of a rare day's sunshine. Finn had looked at the legs – he swallowed now at the recollection – and then at Brón, looked at her properly for the first time. She had a small face, almond-shaped dark eyes and ripe red lips, the lower one bee-stung, fat and tempting, reminding him of some exotic fruit. And when she laughed she showed teeth which were small and perfectly white, and the tip of a scarlet-strawberry tongue.

He had never felt the urge to touch a girl before but suddenly it was upon him, hot and strong and irresistible. He glanced sideways at her and she was laughing at him, eyeing him coquettishly through the long, curly lashes which fringed her big brown eyes. Though a year younger, he was both taller and broader than she, and suddenly the surge of desire in him peaked, could no longer be denied. He took hold of her shoulders and pushed her back onto the sweet spring grass.

'Brónach, you're a beautiful crathur.'

She smiled sleepily up at him and her tongue flickered out and ran across her lower lip. 'Sure, sure,' she murmured. 'And what are you goin' to do about it, Finn Delaney?'

He smiled, too, suddenly sure of himself, suddenly seeing where the conversation was heading – if you could call it a conversation, that was. He had been born in a tinker's tent and bred in the sod huts they built to over-winter, and in the wooden caravans which were the palaces of his tribe. No child could be brought up in such circumstances ignorant of the facts of life. Many a night when he was very small he had lain awake wondering what made his mother cry out softly and his father groan with pleasure, and as he grew so did his understanding of such nightly activities. So now, in the quiet graveyard with the water lapping at the little strip of golden sand which would presently be covered as the tide rose, he put his hands on beautiful Brónach's beautiful body and gently pulled the dress down over her rounded shoulders and began to stroke her smooth skin and make much of her. And in a little while he had made love to her and laughed at her when she screamed like a vixen in spring and clung to him and vowed she would love him for ever.

By then he had heard it all before, knew it was the way of a tinker's woman to scream when she was aroused, though his mother had been a gentle soul who took her pleasures gently, too. But Eilis was uninhibited in bed and he had lived in the same small wooden caravan as she and his father for six months.

Parting company with his father had happened easily in the end, almost painlessly. Finn had been eating his share of a pan of sausages when his father had come up to him, cleared his throat and delivered what was, in effect, an ultimatum.

'We're goin' across the water, Finn me boyo, to feed on the fat lands of the English,' Paddy Delaney had said. 'The Tuams didn't like me beautiful Eilis and to be frank, boy, the Duveens are trouble. So we're gettin' right away from the both of 'em. Are you with us?'

Finn had looked at his father and had read in the older man's face enough to realise that it would be a mistake to accompany them. His father loved him, but his loyalty, now, lay with Eilis and his new marriage, the babe which would come to Eilis when autumn coloured the trees. Finn had been fifteen, near enough a man in his own right, so he shook his head and tried not to be hurt by the relief in his father's dark eyes.

'No, I'm for stayin',' he had said simply. 'I'll move out from here and I'll work for meself, so I will.'

He had meant to do so, meant to search out the Tuams and move back in with the tribe. Finn would have been happy with them and might have gone back indeed, but he stayed partly from laziness, partly because of Brónach. He took his shabby little tent and parked it near Granny Mogg's old wooden van and told anyone who would listen that he would be gone by winter. And though he had held aloof from the stealing and general wickedness of the other lads his age, he had not got himself a job but had idled the summer away, meaning to move away but doing nothing about it. And he had thought himself a man, pleasuring Brónach and being pleasured by her whenever they could sneak away from the others, and had swaggered around the camp like the man he so nearly was, looking down on the lads who stole and boasted because they didn't know how good it was, to lie in the heather with a beautiful woman and make love to her.

Granny Mogg wasn't a true Duveen, though, and looked down on those who were. She was Vorth's mother-in-law, the mother of his first wife, who had been older than he and very beautiful, and she told Finn she would never have moved back in with the Duveens except that she was too old, any longer, to keep herself, and the tribe to which she had belonged were all old too.

'An old 'oman waren't good for nothin', an' Vorth's the nearest t'ing I've got to kin,' she told Finn. 'But he's a bad'un, so don't you take him as a sample of how to live. Work for what ye want, me laddo, because tinkers don't have to steal, there's good work on the land for the likes of us. I'd not have brought my old nag and my old shack over to the Duveens if I'd known how low they'd fallen since my darter died.'

But then she had got ill and one night Vorth had come quietly past Finn's sacking tent and stolen into the creaking wooden caravan. Finn thought he was just looking in to see the old lady but next day he guessed, when he found the caravan empty, that Vorth had picked her up like the bag of dry old sticks which she so closely resembled and carried her off for reasons of his own. Not good reasons, he was sure of that. If someone died in a van no self-respecting tinker would live there for fear of the ghost of the departed; instead they would set fire to the caravan or tent or sod hut, turning it into a funeral pyre, and Finn knew that Vorth wanted the old wooden van for his sullen, mean-eyed eldest daughter and her new husband. Vorth was sick of sharing space with newly weds who made sheep's eyes at each other and never helped with the cooking, he'd been saying so for a month. Granny Mogg's caravan was clean and relatively spacious, and fully furnished with all that was necessary for life on the road – what more could a daughter ask?

So Vorth had gone off in the dead of night and next day, when Finn asked where the old lady was, he told the tribe that Granny Mogg had known she was going to die and had begged him to take her some distance away for her final moments so that he might take over her caravan when her soul had departed this life. He said he had put her in a curragh and set fire to it, pushing it out to sea so that her bones might rest in the deep, as she had requested. Whether the tribe believed or not Finn did not know, he just knew they accepted it. Easier, they would think, than questioning their leader who, in a rage, could kill a man with a single blow – not only could, but had done.

So Finn had pretended to believe, too, and had left the camp as soon as he could and tracked Vorth's passage of the previous night with all the skill and persistence which had been born in him. He had followed Vorth's footsteps across the wet field, through the mud at the gate where the cattle had poached the ground, along the lane, through a copse. And his eyes on the ground had seen every step, noted the deeper marks of the heels because of the burden the man carried, seen where he paused, how he laid the old woman down to open a gate, saw in his head a picture of Vorth's doings of the previous night as clear as though he was seeing it all in a crystal ball.

He had guessed what he would find in the ditch before he reached it, because the footsteps going out were deep still but here they crossed with footsteps coming away which were shallower and with the gaps between them longer, too. An unburdened man had made those prints. Finn ran, then, suddenly afraid. If she was in truth dead why leave her in the ditch, why not build her a funeral pyre from dry branches, or turves, and send her body cleanly on its way? Vorth had told everyone she'd wanted her mortal remains to be carried out to sea in a curragh and there burnt, but the footsteps stopped by the ditch . . . if her body lay there still, then Vorth was the liar and the murderer Finn had always thought him.

He dived into the ditch and there she was – his heart jumped when he bent over her though; her breathing was stertorous, her face blotched white and purple. She was alive still despite Vorth's treatment; he must have hesitated to deliver the *coup de grâce*, believing she would die anyway if abandoned in the ditch. Finn said her name softly, then picked her gently up in his arms. The blanket in which she was wrapped was soaking wet and as he held her he realised she was shuddering and shaking as though with an ague. But she was still alive and would remain so if he moved swiftly. Granny Mogg, who had been kind to him when his father had left him with the Duveens, was in his charge now, and needing him. And Finn Delaney, Finn told himself as he walked steadily away from the ditch, was not the man to let her down.

He carried her, still wrapped in the stinking wet blanket, to the only dry spot he could find – a haystack. He buried her deep in the heart of it and stayed with her, feeding her water from a cracked old cup when she stirred and cried out for a drink, stealing eggs from the birds' nests and feeding her with them, too. For three days she had not known him, had burned with fever, had cried out and cackled, putting him in mortal fear that she would bring the Duveen tribe, or at least Vorth, down upon them. But she was a strong and wiry old bird, and she had recovered. Her mind was not as sharp and quick as it had been, but her body was healthy once more and she remembered Vorth and what he had tried to do to her.

She had woken that night to find him bending over her, a look of such evil on his fat, dirty face that she had thought her last moment had come. So when Finn told her that they must lie low for a while she had nodded anxiously, understanding the necessity, and had followed him trustingly to the castle, which he had found when she had been so ill that she had not known whether he was with her or away.

For a whole year they had lived there, hiding away. He had found the curragh washed ashore with a hole in its outer canvas and made it his own. He had fashioned the oar, patched and tarred the little craft to make it watertight, and then he had gone into Cahersiveen and bartered for a net so that he might catch fish in quantity. He dared not work on any of the nearby farms, however, for fear a Duveen might come there and guess what he had done, might let it be known that the old 'un lived and that he, Finn, was taking care of her. So he left the old 'un for as much as a month at a time in the summer and tramped until he found work on a distant farm. He went out with the fishing boats further along the lough in winter and earned money to see them through . . . and sometimes, he fretted a little for the feel of a strong, supple girl like Brónach in his arms, and the soft whicker of a horse as he tacked it up before riding it along the country lanes. But mostly he enjoyed his freedom, Granny Mogg's strangely restful company, and the sensation of being entirely his own master.

Until now. Until a fair-haired, blue-eyed scrap of a girl had looked him in the eye and he had felt his stomach clench, not with any sort of sexual desire but with a sort of *knowingness*, as though he and Lucy Murphy meant something to each other, as though their fates were, in some way, entwined.

And he wanted to see her again, wanted to see her so much that he could not resist making a rendezvous, even though it wasn't wise to mix with buffers, not if you were a tinker born and bred.

But perhaps it was different for him, because his mam had not been a tinker, she had been a respectable girl from a respectable farm just outside Roscrea, and she had fallen in love with the dark-eyed, curly-haired tinker who came to the farm to visit her father, wheeling and dealing, promising his fine grey mare, with a foal at heel, for the farmer's broken-down old plough horse – new lamps for old, his mam had said with a small, secret smile.

So the respectable girl had run away with the handsome tinker, only to find the travelling life was no very wonderful thing – but she had stuck with Paddy Delaney through hell and high water, and she had loved her son and taught him to read and write and given him a love of books and stories, though it was few enough of the first that came his way.

But . . . Lucy Murphy, thrown in his path by chance, too young for him, too innocent, too indifferent, even. She had laughed at him when he fell off the stairs, it was her friend who had slanted looks at him through her lashes, looks which told him that one of the little birds was on the threshold of womanhood – but it wasn't the one he wanted.

'Tis not right nor fair to meet the girleen in her father's barn when she's as unawakened as a day old kitten, he told himself severely. If you're so mad for a woman then go into Caher and find a willing lass – the barmaid from Tom's Tavern on Main Street, or the plump and laughing beauty who gave you a startled, admiring glance as she came out of the O'Connell Memorial Church last Sunday fortnight. Stand Lucy Murphy up, give her the go-by, Finn Delaney, he ordered himself; she'll be disillusioned, sure, but that way she'll be far less hurt than if you let her believe the two of you have a future together. Not that she would believe any such thing, not a child like her. So I won't go, she can wait in the barn until morning comes, but Finn Delaney will be long gone about his own business.

So he fed Granny Mogg and himself and tucked the old 'un up in her bed of hay halfway up the castle tower and went down and stood beside the curragh in the gathering dusk and watched the stars prick out one by one over the lough and the distant sea – and knew he would go to the farm, and stand just inside the barn door, and wait for her to come to him.

'Lucy, where's your appetite? Didn't I make pancakes especially for you, and aren't you pushin' them round and round your plate and scarcely a bite have you taken?

If you're ill, alanna, then it's in bed you should be and not sittin' at the table playin' with your good food.'

Lucy hastily took a mouthful of her pancake and brought her mind back to the job in hand – eating her tea. A pleasant job enough, too, when Maeve had made pancakes with honey over them and a squeeze of lemon.

'Sorry, Maeve. I was thinking so I was,' she said humbly, swallowing her mouthful and giving her aunt a reassuring smile. 'There's nothing wrong with me at all at all, only I was dreaming. When I've had me supper, shall I be after collecting the eggs? I saw the hen with the ragged comb going into the big barn as I come up with Caitlin for me tea, and the speckled hen likes to lay right up against the orchard hedge – I could look there.'

'I got them earlier,' Maeve said, looking surprised, as well she might, Lucy reflected guiltily. Maeve knew too well that Lucy hated being sent out at dusk to search for eggs and right now dusk was rapidly turning into darkness. 'Besides, you've some darning to do, young lady.'

Lucy groaned. She absolutely hated any form of needlework and was dreadfully bad at it, but Maeve was adamant. She must be able to darn and to sew a little because farmers' wives – and she was obviously going to be a farmer's wife – made their children's clothing if not their own.

'Oh, Maeve, I'm ever so careful now about me socks, I hardly ever make a hole in the heel, and . . .'

Grandad was sitting at the head of the table reading a farming journal and eating a round of bread and cheese with a pickled onion. He did not care for pancakes. Now he looked at Lucy over the top of his pince nez and shook his head sadly. 'You'd sooner plant an acre of spuds than darn one,' he said placidly. 'I've said it before and I'll say it again – you should have been a lad, Lucy Murphy.'

'There's a hole in your fawn socks and a rent in your

checkered pinafore,' Maeve said inexorably, ignoring her father's words. 'Might as well get it over, alanna, but first we'll wash up if you've done pushing that pancake round your plate.'

'I'll eat it, I'll eat it,' Lucy squeaked, gobbling pancake. She cleared her plate and pushed it away, then slid her chair back. 'Come on, then, let's get on with the washing up.'

'There's something up with that young lady,' Maeve said to her father when Lucy had done her tasks to the best of her ability – a cobbled up sock and a torn apron now boasted her huge, untidy stitches – and gone off up to bed. 'Never have I known her so vague, nor so willing to go to her bed. No doubt we'll hear her raisin' the echoes presently, bawlin' out to Caitlin how misunderstood she is.' Maeve put her own sewing down in her lap and rubbed at her tired eyes. 'She'll need a new school skirt come the autumn, she's growing so fast. I'll go into Caher tomorrow, see if I can pick up some material, cheap.' She glanced sideways at her father, smoking his pipe now and gazing reflectively at the empty fireplace, for in summer they no longer lit the fire even in the late evening. 'I wouldn't mind catching the train up to Dublin for a nice day out, and there'll be material cheaper there than I can get in Caher. The child might enjoy it, too. I could ask Mrs Kelly if I could take Caitlin along.'

The farmhouse was old, its walls a foot thick, its ceilings substantial, but because it was a warm evening the parlour window was flung wide and the door leading into the hall was open, too, letting the gentle evening breeze freshen the rather stuffy room. Through the window they heard Lucy's window shoot open.

'Caitliiiiiiin!'

'Oh dear God preserve us, here they go,' Padraig Murphy said resignedly, but there was a twinkle in his eye nevertheless: 'One of these days that voice'll crack every pane of glass in the house so it will.'

'I'm here, Luuuuuuuucy!'

'I'm rare tired, Cait. Goodniiiiiiiight.'

'Oh but Lucy, we've not . . .'

Crash. The firm closing of Lucy's window was only just short of a slam. Padraig looked across at Maeve and raised his grizzled brows. 'A row have they had, Maeve? Never have I heard the whores' chorus come to a more abrupt end!'

'Hush Dad, you mustn't talk like that,' Maeve admonished. 'Now I wonder what's up with those young devils tonight? I *knew* something had upset Lucy earlier, when she wasn't eating her tea. I wonder, should I go up?'

Padraig yawned, stretched, and tapped his pipe out on the empty fire grate. 'It's time we both went up, but not to interfere with the childer,' he said decisively. 'If they've had a fight they'll make up, if the child's ill we shall fetch the doctor in the morning. But right now, Maeveen, you and I need all the sleep we can get, for tomorrow, all being well, we've got those young heifers to drive down to the market.'

Lucy thought it would never get dark, or not dark enough, and then she thought Grandad and Maeve would never douse the lamp and come up to bed. And then, of course, after her vigorous and exciting day, she began to fear she would simply fall asleep and slumber straight through the night until Maeve woke her for her breakfast next morning.

But she was in luck. She was down the covers with her window closed and her lamp out when her bedroom door creaked open; it was Maeve, looking in on her to give her a goodnight kiss. She tiptoed over to the bed and Lucy felt gentle fingers caress her cheek and then land, featherlight, on her brow for an instant. She thinks I'm maybe not well, Lucy thought, instantly remorseful. She knows me so well, she could read my troubled mind. But with a bit of luck she would put it down to a tiff with Caitlin or a slight stomach upset and go to bed now herself and leave Lucy to sleep whatever it was off till morning.

And she was right, for presently Maeve tiptoed over and opened the window, then left the room, closing the door gently behind her.

Lucy lay very still for what felt like an hour but was probably more like five minutes. Then she jumped out of bed and, with infinite care, opened her door a crack. She could see the line of light from Maeve's lamp shining under her aunt's bedroom door. As soon as the light goes out I'm off, she told herself, reaching her dark coat down off the back of the door and pulling on her fawn socks, complete with cobbled heel where her darning had grown slipshod. It's a mild night, I don't need anything but the coat and me socks and wellingtons – and they're in the kitchen, of course.

But the stairs creaked, and Maeve would probably take a few minutes to actually go off to sleep. Maeve had told her so many times about how she had woken in the middle of the night and just kind of known that little Evie, Lucy's mother, had been downstairs, preparing to leave the farm. Suppose such second sight leapt into being again tonight and Maeve turned up just as Lucy was halfway down the stairs, or worse, tiptoeing across to the barn? She'd be mad as fire, Lucy thought fearfully, just as Maeve put out her lamp and, judging by the sighs and creaks, settled down in her bed. Oh mercy, what'll I say if she catches me outside in me nightie, jabbering away to a tinker, when she's always telling me how they kidnap little girls and take them away to work for them?

119

The thought was almost enough to have her climbing back into bed and pulling the covers up over her ears. Almost, but not quite. As it was she tiptoed down the stairs, light as a feather and almost without breathing, and into the kitchen.

It was dark in here, but it smelled nice. Maeve's baking, the pancakes, even the lemon which had been used to flavour them, were all still here, in the warmed kitchen air. And there stood her boots, like a couple of soldiers on parade, right by the back door.

Lucy put the boots on – she was already wearing her coat and socks – and gently turned the key in the back door lock. It squeaked, but only as a mouse might squeak; even to Lucy's senses, heightened by fear, the squeak was a small one. Then the door was unlocked, she turned the knob and opened it and there was the yard, bathed in moonlight, with that air of other-worldliness which comes over any familiar place seen in unfamiliar circumstances.

Out I go, Lucy said to herself, remaining frozen to the spot. Out I go and across the yard and into the comforting shadows of the big barn. I'm not scared, I know who's waiting for me there . . . I'm fourteen and a half years old, almost a woman grown, I'm sensible and I'm good at me schoolwork and I love writing essays and the history of me country and – and I'm scared witless and I don't think I'll walk out into all that enchantment and danger and excitement, I think I'll go back to bed instead, the same as Maeve would want me to do if she knew about all this.

But . . . that would mean letting Finn down. I don't know him, not properly, Lucy argued to herself, all I do know is that he's a tinker and tinkers do dreadful things to little girls, they steal them away and make them work in big houses in Dublin and pinch their bottoms to make them scrub faster. This was the nearest Maeve had ever got to explaining that there were men in the world who exploited young girls for their own ends but it was quite enough to put Lucy off – she thought that having a man pinch your bottom without so much as a by-your-leave was quite the most horrible thing which could happen to a girl, and did not intend that it should happen to her if she could possibly prevent it.

Therefore, her sensible mind told her now, you don't go out to a black-shadowed barn through enchanted silvery moonlight, because that's how they get you. For all you know Finn may be false, she told her shivering, cowardly self, he may have a whole band of tinkers waiting in that barn to carry you off to Dublin, shut you in a blackbeetle-ridden kitchen and pinch your bottom until you've peeled a ton or two of potatoes and scrubbed several miles of filthy floor.

So right then and there, whilst her whole body was shouting at her to turn back, relock the door and make for her warm, safe bed, Lucy marched – but quietly – out of the kitchen, leaving the door gaping open behind her though in case she needed a quick retreat, and across the moonlit yard. She did not know that the moonlight silvered her hair and made her skin shine with a soft pearly glow, or that the moon-shadows made her eyes look huge, enhanced the small curves of her budding breasts beneath her nightgown, turned her, for that short walk, into the woman she would one day become.

But the watcher knew. He saw her coming steadily across the yard, saw the dog in its kennel glance up, then lie down again, secure in the knowledge that his little mistress was in command of the situation.

Lucy came on steadily, then slid into the shadowy barn and there was Finn, smiling at her, taking both her hands in his warm, safe clasp.

'And aren't you a fine, brave girl?' he said softly, and

the touch of his hand excited her less than the warm commendation in his voice. 'Oh little Luceen, I'm glad you weren't scared that the tinker meant you harm, for I swear by Jesus and Mary and by all the holy saints that I wouldn't hurt a hair of your head, nor let anyone else do so. Will you come up with me, into the hay?'

With his hand in hers, all her hesitations and doubts were lost. She nodded and followed him closely as he loped across the barn floor and began to climb the short wooden ladder which led to the hayloft. He was neat and quick, she no less so, and a moment later he made a nest in the hay, using his body, then held out his hands to her.

'Sit down, alanna; then we can talk.'

Afterwards, Lucy could not remember much of what they had talked about; she could remember far more easily the feel of his hand in hers, the smell of his skin, the way he would give a sudden crack of laughter, hastily muffled, over something she said.

At one point they talked about Granny Mogg and he told her he was going away, probably for as long as a month, and would be obliged if she would keep an eye on the old 'un.

'Her mind isn't always her own,' he said carefully. 'Most of the time she's great, but then something seems to slip in her head and she's – she's not so good. But if you can take her a bit of bread and cheese, some milk, make sure she drinks each day, then she ought to be all right until I get back.'

'Where are you going?' Lucy asked. She stroked his arm very gently, as one might stroke a wild cat who might run at your touch. 'Is it far? Can I get in touch with you, Finn?'

'I'm going fishing, then I'll join in the harvest of some crop or other,' Finn said. 'I don't know where I'll be though – anywhere I can get work, I guess.'

'And you'll come back?'

He laughed, then caught at the hand which was stroking his arm and kissed the palm, his lips warm and somehow intimate against her skin, the small gesture sending odd shivers down her spine.

'Of course I'll come back, little eejit,' he teased. 'Would I leave Granny Mogg to your tender mercies? Or you to hers, for the matter of that? I'll come back with me pockets bulgin' with good t'ings, and a host of stories and tales.'

'Good,' Lucy said. She was getting tired but had no desire whatsoever to leave her nest in the hay. She leaned her head against Finn's shoulder. 'I do love a story, Finn. Shall you tell me one now?'

'If I do you'll go to sleep and then where will we be?' Finn said. But he looped an arm round her shoulders and drew her close. 'What tale would you like, then? A story of witches and wizards in old Ireland, or leprechauns and the fairy folk? Or shall I tell you about me travels with the Tuam tribe, before I met up with Vorth and his band?'

'Tell me about your travels,' Lucy begged sleepily. 'I'd love to hear where you've been and what you've done, Finn.'

Finn knew himself to be a fine story-teller and began in time honoured fashion with 'Once upon a time . . .' but he had barely got to the bit where he rode his first horse and got thrown into his first gorse bush when he felt an extra heaviness in the head leaning on his shoulder and glanced down at her, tenderness mixing with something wild and sweet which he had never felt before.

She slept, trusting him totally. And she's right so to do, Finn told himself, for no safer could she ever be than she is this night. Ah, but this girleen will be safe with me for the rest of her life – and special to me, also. One of these days, Lucy Murphy, you'll be all mine, but until that day dawns, I'll not touch a hair of your head, and nor shall any man.

He woke her when the stars were beginning to pale in the sky and Lucy, alarmed, sat up in the rustling hay and apologised for falling asleep and promised, in a flurried whisper, that she would see the old 'un lacked for nothing.

'If she's ill, I'll get Maeve to her, and a doctor,' she hissed. 'But only if she's rare bad, Finn. You – you won't be away longer than a month, will you? I'll miss you sore.'

She saw his teeth flash in the dark as he grinned down at her.

'You scarcely know me, alanna! But I'll miss you more than ever you could miss me. Now you'd best get back to your bed before day dawns. I'll help you down the ladder.'

He scrambled down ahead of her, then turned, hands held out. 'Jump!'

She jumped; he caught her, held her for one breathless moment against his heart before putting her away from him and then, with a suddenness which startled them both, snatching her back and dropping three kisses on her upturned face – one on her brow, one on the tip of her nose, the last on her chin. Featherlight kisses they were, almost casual, almost teasing . . . so why did the touch of his lips burn on her skin for what was left of the night?

'Off you run now, alanna. I'll see you again as soon as I can get my business done.'

He took her to the barn doorway and from its shadows they surveyed the house. All was in darkness, the kitchen door gaped open still, the room behind it black.

They crossed the yard like a couple of shadows and Lucy slipped into the kitchen. She glanced around and was at once reassured: no one had stirred, everything was as she left it.

Finn must have been able to tell that the tension had left her, for he gave her hand a quick squeeze and turned away.

'Goodbye for now, Lucy. Take care, and – and don't forget me.'

'I never could,' Lucy whispered vehemently. 'Oh, Finn, I never could forget you! I like you better than anyone else I know.'

He was gliding away from her when the dog in the kennel looked up again, his muzzle turning from Lucy to Finn and back as though questioning whether he should not, perhaps, bark a bit at this stranger?

'Friend, Shep,' Lucy whispered. 'Best friend, dearest friend. Don't you bark, Shep, or I'll give you a clout, so I will.' And she stood in the doorway and waved until Finn was out of sight and the pre-dawn dark was still again, save for the wind stirring the leaves on the tall old elms and the scuttle of a mouse behind the corn bins.

Only then did she turn and make her way back, unde-tected, to her cold little bed.

Chapter Six

At first, when the money stopped coming, Linnet thought it was just that her mother hadn't remembered, or had had a bad few weeks. Then she thought it must be the post, notoriously unreliable for a long distance letter. She was sure, of course, that Evie would not let her down and besides, she had her savings; so for the first few weeks she continued to pay the rent and keep herself from the money she had salted away during the pantomime season when she had taken in two chorus girls as lodgers. Mrs Roberts had not liked it, but Linnet had given her some of her rent and the landlady had taken the money, though not with a very good grace.

'I'll 'old you responsible if there's any trouble from them gairls,' she had said. 'And tell 'em no fellers or they'll be out on their ears before you can blink.'

So Linnet, though worried by Evie's apparent defection, had at least been able to support herself for the first month, though she had confided to Roddy that her money would not last for ever.

'If only me mam would write,' she said miserably. 'Then at least I'd know what had gone wrong for her.'

'You're fifteen years old, our Linnie,' Roddy reminded her. 'Most gals are workin' be the time they're your age. Perhaps your mam just got fed up wi' feedin' a chick which oughter 'ave flown the bleedin' nest months agone!'

'She knows I'd work if she wanted me to, only she said to stay on at school until she give the word,' Linnet reminded her friend. 'Mammy wouldn't just forget all about me, even though she's been doing awful well – she says so, in her letters. No, something's gone wrong, I can feel it in my heart.'

She clasped her hands to her chest and Roddy jeered at such a theatrical gesture and got a clout round the ear for his cheek.

'You don't know nothing, Roddy Sullivan,' Linnet shouted at him. 'My mammy says education is terrible important – I don't want to work in a match factory and come home all yellow-faced like your Auntie Prue, nor do I want to get all filthy and bloody like you get when you help in that butcher's shop! Mammy will write to me soon, just you see!'

Roddy never got cross with her because he understood that she was upset and worried, but he did scowl. 'You needn't come near me when I've been workin' if you're so high and mighty,' he muttered. 'You're glad enough of a loan of the spondooleys, though.'

It was true that Roddy had lent her money for her various needs when he had the cash to spare and Linnet immediately felt guilty. 'I'm sorry, that was a horrible thing to say,' she said remorsefully. 'Oh, Roddy, if only she'd write!'

But the truth of the matter was that Evie's letters had speedily degenerated from chatty epistles to a couple of lines, and that in the first six months of her absence, too. So now, after nearly two years, Linnet did not expect much in the way of news or information – but she did expect the money.

When the letter came at last, whilst Mrs Roberts was muttering darkly about the selfishness of theatricals, as she called them, in not paying her rent for two months, Linnet was so relieved that she couldn't even open it for a minute. She just held it in her hands and breathed deeply and thanked God, as well as little Evie, that she was about to receive proof that she'd not been forgotten, after all. The writing on the envelope did not look much like Evie's bold and confident hand, but it was her writing, nevertheless. Rosy with relief and anticipation, Linnet opened the letter. And it was just a letter, there was no money, not so much as a penny piece. But the letter would explain, Linnet knew that, so she had best read it immediately.

Dear Linnet, it said in a spidery hand which Linnet could scarcely recognise as her mother's. *I have been very ill and unable to earn money, which is why I'm afraid you've had to go short. I don't know when I shall be able to return to the stage, so I want you to go back to Ireland, to your Auntie Maeve, and ask her to take care of you for me until I'm well again. Don't think too harshly of me, alanna, Mammy.*

Linnet stared down at the blotched page and the thin, wobbly writing. Little Evie must have been very ill indeed to write so for the nicest piece of the letter was missing, the bit where Evie always said, *With much love from your very own Mammy.* And how could Evie expect her daughter to go back to Ireland? Linnet knew her aunt's name was Maeve Murphy and she knew Evie had gone to school in the town of Cahersiveen, but she did not know the name of the farm, nor whereabouts in Ireland Cahersiveen might be . . . and she had no money now, not so much as a penny piece. She could scarcely buy a tram ticket to the docks, far less her passage to Ireland!

She stood in her mother's neat living room whilst black despair washed over her. What on earth was she to do? The month was June, which meant that the next pantomime season was six months away and in any event, though the money her lodgers paid her was a help, it could scarcely keep her and pay the rent, too. Right now she had no money at all, no prospect of money from what her mother said, and no idea what to do next. But one thing she did know – she must run round to Roddy at once and tell him what had happened. She thought now, going back over his attitude these past couple of weeks, that he would not be entirely surprised to hear that little Evie was penniless and far from sending the rent, was actually advising her daughter to go back to Ireland. But Roddy was a realist. He would see at once that this was impossible and would suggest an alternative means of keeping body and soul together. Roddy was resourceful and intelligent, he would advise her on her best course of action.

It was a Saturday morning which meant no school, but when Linnet ran down the stairs, Mrs Roberts popped out of her own quarters.

'When can I 'ave me rent?' she said belligerently. 'Or weren't there no money? It were a skinny sort o' letter, weren't it?'

'The money's following,' Linnet said quickly. 'I've got to go out now, Mrs Roberts, I'm fetching the shopping for Roddy's mam.'

Mrs Roberts started to say something but Linnet just ignored her, flying down the hall and out of the door, turning at once in the direction of Peel Square. She had crammed the letter into the pocket of her jacket and it burned there like a guilty conscience. What on earth was she to do? Even nice Mrs Sullivan had mentioned mildly that times was 'ard and she didn't like to grumble but feedin' one extra every day . . .

Roddy was coming out of the square just as Linnet rounded the corner at a gallop. She must have looked pretty desperate because he stopped short and put a soothing hand on her arm.

'Wharrever's the marrer, chuck? Come on, tell your pal.'

'Mam's written; she's not got any money,' Linnet gabbled, clutching Roddy's hand. 'She says to go back to Ireland, but I can't do that, our Roddy! I dunno where me mam's sisters live, I only know the name of the town, and I haven't got any money at all, honest to God. Oh, Roddy, you should see her writing – she must be real bad, real ill.'

'Show me later,' Roddy said when Linnet tried to press the crumpled page into his hand. 'I've gorra deliver this lot.'

For the first time Linnet realised that her friend was wearing a long blue-and-white striped apron and carrying what looked like a very heavy basket.

'Oh, you're working; I'm sorry,' she said humbly. 'Can I help, Roddy? Only I can't go back to old Ma Roberts, she'll say things . . . I've got to think.'

'You can walk along o' me and tek some o' the parcels into the 'ouses,' Roddy said. 'We're goin' right along to Tenterden Street for the next delivery though, so you'll 'ave plenty of time to talk. Tell you what, you'd best read me the letter as we go.'

This seemed like a good idea so as they plodded along – for the basket was heavy – Linnet read the pitifully brief letter aloud and then looked hopefully at Roddy.

'Well? What d'you think? Will some money come, Roddy?'

Roddy began to shrug, hesitated, then shook his head. 'It's no good lyin' to you, chuck. I reckon your mam's real ill an' I don't see 'ow she can earn if she's ill. You've gorra give up any idea of help from that quarter; you've gorra get yourself out o' this mess.'

'How?' Linnet said bluntly. 'I can't think straight!'

'We'll sell some o' that posh furniture, for a start off,' Roddy said, changing his basket to the other arm. 'You'd gerra pretty penny for that walnut pianny, and there's the oil paintin' over the mantel; that oughter make a bit.'

'I can't take furniture without Mrs Roberts finding out,' Linnet pointed out, trying very hard not to let Roddy see that she was crying. The letter for which she had longed had turned out to be the final straw. She felt completely at the end of her tether and incapable, any longer, of being brave. 'If she finds out there's no money coming then she'll kick me out and take everything for herself.'

'Yeah, I can see that,' Roddy said thoughtfully. 'Wharrabout smaller stuff, though? Some of them ornaments is worth a mint, we'll run 'em down to Uncle's, see what 'e'll cough up.'

'Yes, we could do that,' Linnet said rather reluctantly. She had visited T J Cookson, the pawnbroker on Scotland Road, more than once, accompanying Roddy when he took his mam's hat and his own Sunday suit in on a Monday morning, and thought it an odd way of getting money, particularly as it had to be paid back in time for church so the clothing could be worn once more for Sunday services. 'Some of the little china things are valuable, Mammy said so. But that won't pay everything, you know. There's the rent and what I owe your mam, and soon it'll be school fees . . .'

Roddy looked at her, then stood his basket down alongside the plate glass window of a flower shop with beautiful carnations, roses and lilies pressing close to the glass and buckets full of blooms on either side of the doorway. 'John Tart, Florist', ran the legend over the door, and Linnet sniffed appreciatively as the most wonderful scent came to them from the lavish array of blooms. But Roddy seemed indifferent to their beauty. He took hold of both Linnet's hands and shook them to emphasise his words.

'You've gorra gerra job,' he said forcefully. 'The

money your mam sent covered your school fees, your rent an' your food, but now it's stopped. So you'll 'ave to leave school, chuck. I left school long ago, our Linnie, an' most of me class did the same. You've gorra be practical, gel, you'll 'ave to work.'

'Yes . . . but what can I *do*?' Linnet said, her voice rising to a wail. 'It's awful hard to get a job unless you're trained, and the nuns don't teach you how to be a shop girl or a factory hand. And those are the only jobs I know!'

'You're pretty, clever and well-dressed,' Roddy said, rubbing a dirty hand across his sweaty face. 'You'll gerra job awright, chuck. But I dunno whether it'll run to payin' Mrs Roberts' rent, 'cos she charges your mam a deal o' money, from what you've said. I think you'll have to move, Linnie.'

Linnet stared. 'Move? But what about all me mammy's lovely things?'

'You'll be eatin' them,' Roddy said. 'Linnet Murphy, you've lived amongst us for the past two or three years an' you still 'aven't learned, 'ave you? Folk like us can't afford pretty china wozzits an' nice furniture. Think on, our Linnie.'

Linnet thought. Mrs Sullivan was grand, she worked very hard for her kids and her husband worked hard, too, when he could get the work, that was. But they had almost no furniture save for the big kitchen table and some broken-down chairs, they slept on straw mattresses on the floor, and with six kids to feed Mrs Sullivan thought herself lucky to have fuel for the fire – it never occurred to her that a mantelshelf might have contained ornaments or a clock, so long as there was a bit of coal and some kindling sticks she was well satisfied.

Thinking back now, Linnet remembered that when she'd first known the Sullivans Roddy's mother had worked for Blackledge's, the baker on Derby Road, and

Roddy's father had been at sea. But then he'd had an accident – he'd been below, fastening a couple of loose barrels during a storm when a whole ruck of them had broken loose and crushed both his legs. Now he walked oddly, a bit like one of the little yellowy crabs which lurked in the thick, smooth black mud down by the Pier Head, and they wouldn't let him go to sea any more. Instead, he did bits and pieces of work when he could get someone to employ him, and for the rest they survived on what the kids and Mrs Sullivan could earn and on what Linnet's mother paid for her keep during the school holidays.

'Have you thought, queen?'

That was Roddy, massaging the arm which had been carrying the basket, looking thoughtfully into the window behind them with its brilliant and tempting display of something which, surely, few of the shoppers thronging the street could possibly afford to buy? Flowers, Linnet found herself thinking defensively, are even more useless than china you can't eat them and you can't look at them for long, either, because they die. Was that why Roddy had chosen to stop outside the florist's, to prove something? But if so, she was no nearer understanding, not really. Except that she was a bit like one of those roses or lilies herself – she didn't work, she just looked pretty, and what good was that when the odds were against her? Precious little, it seemed. And poor Mrs Sullivan had scarcely said anything when Linnet had mumbled that the money still hadn't come, she'd gone on feeding one extra. I've been horribly selfish, Linnet thought humbly, but all that's over. I'll do just what Roddy says and at least I'll be able to pay his mam for all the food I've eaten these past couple of months. She turned to Roddy.

'Yes, I've thought. What I'll do, I'll sell some of the little things and pay the last month's rent and your mam as soon as I get enough money. Then I'll sell something like a picture, or that small green velvet chair, and look round for somewhere cheaper.' She hesitated. 'I suppose your mam wouldn't like a lodger, Roddy?'

'She'd like one, but where'd we put you?' Roddy said with all his usual frankness. 'There's too many of us crammed into the 'ouse already and you wouldn't want four inches o' straw mattress an' young Freddy an' little Toddy breathin' into your face all night, would you? 'Cos Mam wouldn't want you sharin' wi' us big lads!'

'There wouldn't be room, not with the four of you all fighting for space,' Linnet said. The thought had given her her first smile that morning and now she seized the handle of the big, heavy basket. 'All right, now let's get this lot delivered, then I'll go home and start taking stuff out – are you sure Uncle's the best one to go to, though?'

'If you think your mam might want to buy the stuff back one day a pawnbroker's the only place what'll hang onto it for 'er,' Roddy said, taking the basket firmly away from her. 'Just keep your tickets somewhere safe. But if you think your mam will just buy new, then you'd get a better price, I guess, from a shop what sells such things. We'll go round and ask when I've done me deliveries. Now let's 'urry, queen, or I'll get into trouble for bein' too late for their Sat'day dinner.'

The plan worked well for the first week. It might have gone on working well, too, but for one of those wretched, silly little accidents which can happen to anyone. Linnet discovered a kind man in a shop on Church Street, a very smart area of the city, who remembered little Evie and was happy to give her daughter a fair price for ornaments which had been lovingly dusted daily and washed in soap and warm water weekly, so that they looked as good as new.

Linnet took sufficient to pay Mrs Roberts the rent owed, pretending to have received a letter whilst her landlady was otherwise engaged. She sold a few more china shepherdesses, goose girls and a child with an apron full of chicks and paid Mrs Sullivan, too. And then she decided to take the picture next.

There were lots of pictures, but the one over the mantelpiece, with its rich, dark colours and the elaborate gilded frame, seemed likeliest to raise a decent sum, so Linnet waited until the Robertses were eating their midday dinner and then stole carefully down the stairs, with the picture none too well concealed in the folds of her winter coat. And halfway down the flight, the door to the basement where the Robertses lived shot open and Mrs Roberts emerged into the small, dark hallway, saying at the top of her voice that she'd heard that dratted boy rattlin' on the front door again and she'd give him sauce.

Linnet dropped the picture. Mrs Roberts looked up. There was a moment of ghastly silence before Linnet said, 'I'm taking it to be cleaned, I do hope dropping it didn't do much damage. You startled me, Mrs Roberts.'

Mrs Roberts said nothing. She simply stared very hard at the picture, and then at Linnet, whilst you could almost see the rusty wheels inside her head start to whirr until the answer she sought finally clicked into place.

'I...see...' she said at last, in a menacing sort of voice. 'Ho, yes, I see indeed!'

Linnet shot down the rest of the stairs, across the hall and out of the door but as she told Roddy later, she feared she'd given the game away. Now the old girl would be watching her all the time.

But she was wrong. Mrs Roberts did not bother to watch her at all. When Linnet got back that night, rather later than usual in the hope of not having to explain anything to Mrs Roberts, she found the lock on her door had been changed. She tried her key again and again, but it would not turn. Finally she had no choice but to go downstairs and confront Mrs Roberts.

'You was goin' to do a moonlight, owin' me a small fortune in unpaid rent,' Mrs Roberts said coldly, her mean eyes gleaming in the gaslight. 'So I've took your stuff in lieu of rent and you're out, madam. Don't you come botherin' me again or I'll 'ave the scuffers round 'ere before you can say knife.'

'But I paid your rent, every penny,' Linnet said indignantly. 'The furniture in the flat belongs to me mam and to me, too. You can't take it, that's stealing!'

At the mention of stealing, Mrs Roberts' face went a dark and ugly shade of red and she shot out a hand, gripped Linnet's shoulder, and shook her vigorously. 'That's done it! I might 'ave felt sorry for you before, let you 'ave a bed for the night, but not any more, not now you've accused me of stealin' your stuff when it's mine by right. Gerrout of this place, you saucy little bleeder, an' don't you never come back no more!'

'I'm going to the police station in the morning,' Linnet said when she went round to Peel Square to tell Roddy and give him a hand with his deliveries. Roddy's job was badly paid but at least the money was regular and Roddy was delighted to be a wage-earner, though it cut down his time with Linnet. 'I'll tell them what's happened and they'll put Mrs Roberts in prison, I'm sure they will.'

'Ye-es . . . but suppose they put you in one of them orphan asylums?' Roddy said uneasily. 'Or even the work-'ouse, chuck? You wouldn't want that, would you?'

'You can kip down on our kitchen floor if you can gerra blanket from the market,' Mrs Sullivan said. 'Just till you get somewhere of your own, like. I'll come wi' you to the cop-shop tomorrow, 'ow's that?'

Linnet was delighted and, the next day, trotted down to the police station beside Mrs Sullivan feeling that at last she was to be vindicated. The policeman was a fatherly man who listened seriously to her story, wrote in his little notebook, and promised her that they would all visit Mrs Roberts together, right now, and find out just what she was playing at.

'When I see you at teatime we'll have sorted it all out, and I'll have me mam's stuff, if not the flat,' Linnet told Roddy joyously. 'I can't wait to see her face.'

Over the teatable, Linnet gnawed on her disappointment like a dog with a bone, scarcely able to eat for her rage against Mrs Roberts.

'She'd cleared the whole place,' she said furiously, whilst the Sullivans listened and ate boiled spuds and scrag end of mutton. Mrs Sullivan, almost as upset as Linnet, was in the kitchen, boiling the kettle for a fresh pot of tea. 'Not a single ornament was left, not a carpet, not a rag of curtain. The sergeant was ever so nice, too, I never knew a scuffer could be so kind. But there weren't anything he could do, only say he was sorry to me and warn Mrs Roberts that if she'd lied to him she'd find herself in big trouble.'

'What did she say, Linnie?' little Freddy piped up, taking a pull at his weak tea and then putting his mug down on the table with a bang. 'She must ha' telled lies, o' course.'

'She did,' Linnet said heavily, fighting back tears. She toyed with the food on her plate, pushing a boiled potato round and round until it collapsed into the gravy. 'She said I'd sold everything in the flat meself and that and she'd got proof . . . she'd found a couple of receipts or whatever they call them under the clock. The sergeant said sure I'd sold a few ornaments, and hadn't I already told him so indeed? And then she produced a receipt for the chair to prove I'd sold it as well as all the other things. She'd only got a bob for it – a bob for me mam's lovely antique chair – and she'd sold it to the little feller in Paddy's market, a black-hearted little bugger the sergeant called him. She said he'd swear he'd bought it from a small, fair-haired girl and the sergeant said Finkel – that's his name, Jeremiah Finkel – would swear black was white if someone paid him, and Mrs Roberts said she wasn't the only one who wanted to watch what they said and that there was a law of libel whether you was a scuffer or just a poor woman trying to make ends meet. Honest to God, I do hate that old woman!'

'So you should,' Roddy said, but he didn't look anywhere near as miserable as Linnet felt. 'So tomorrer, queen, we'll go lookin' for a job for you, right? For tonight you can lend me blanket, it's a warm night, I'll be awright with me coat.'

'She sold all me clothes, too,' Linnet said broodingly. 'Oh, I'll get back on her one of these days, you see if I don't.' She turned to Roddy. 'Your mam's the best person in the world, next to me own mam,' she said. 'That scuffer really liked her, he said she had a heart of gold and I was all right whilst I had Janice on my side. And he give me two lovely thick blankets and another pair of shoes, so at least I'll look respectable enough when I try the shops for work tomorrow.'

'Letter for you, Maeve,' Lucy said, coming into the kitchen and throwing the envelope down on the table. She and Grandad had been taking the milk churns down to the gate for the lorry to collect and she had spotted the postman coming up the lane just as her grandfather had turned the cart round to return to the farm. 'It's probably from *her*; it's a foreign stamp, anyroad.'

'If you mean your mother, you should say so,' Maeve

said mildly, but Lucy didn't bother to answer. What sort of a mother just went off, taking your sister and turning you into an only child, and then scarcely ever wrote? 'No, it isn't from Evie, it's . . .'

'What's the matter, girl?' Grandad said, pausing with a forkful of bacon halfway to his mouth. 'What's happened?'

Maeve looked up at him but Lucy did not think she saw either the old man or indeed the farm kitchen, for her eyes had a dazed, faraway look. But she suddenly gave herself a little shake and spoke.

'Oh, Daddy, it's from a feller in New York – our little Evie . . . she died ten days ago. He – the feller – didn't ever know her, he says, but he took her room over after she – she left, and found a letter for me and guessed we'd not been told. He's enclosed the letter, if you can call it that – it's just a couple of lines. All she says is: *Maeve, love, take care of Linnet, I've been a bad mammy to her* . . .' Maeve's voice broke and she laid the sheets of paper carefully down on the kitchen table and turned her face away from them, looking out across the yard.

'Evie, dead? But she was the youngest of you . . . there must be some mistake, you say the feller didn't know her . . . we must bring her home, Maeve, she can't stay out there! I'd go meself, though I'd be no use, no use at all, but at least we've got the money so's you can go for me, alanna. At least we've got money in the bank.'

Maeve nodded, swallowed, then turned back to the table. 'And there's the child, Linnet, alone in New York . . . you're right, Daddy, I must go to her. I'll fetch Clodagh back before I leave, though, to keep house whilst I'm gone – she has no children, she could manage it – and for the rest, you've grand, reliable workers who'll give an eye to things if you need them.' Maeve turned to Lucy. 'You'll be a good girl whilst I'm gone, Lu? You'll help

Auntie Clo in the house and do your usual work on the farm, won't you? And think how nice it will be for you, to have your sister living back here again.'

'I don't know her,' Lucy said slowly. 'Is she nice? I wish I could come with you, Maeve, and see New York for meself, but of course I'll take care of Grandad for you,' she smiled across at her grandfather. 'We'll take care of each other, won't we, Gramps?'

'We will so,' her grandfather said. 'As for nice – are you not nice yourself, Luceen?'

'People change,' Lucy said quietly, but she said it beneath her breath. She found that she had no desire for an unknown sister to turn up here to boss her about and tell her what she should and should not do – older sisters always bossed you about, she had heard the girls at school say so many a time – and she could not squeeze out a tear for a mother who had abandoned her when she was only a couple of months old. 'When will you leave, Maeve?'

'As soon as I can buy me ticket,' Maeve said distractedly. 'Oh my poor darling, to die so far from home!' She jumped to her feet on the words and ran out of the kitchen and when Lucy would have followed, Grandad caught her arm and held her back.

'You didn't know your mammy, child,' he said gruffly. 'And no doubt you feel you have a good reason not to love her. But Evie was a sweet girl once, and it's that Evie that Maeve and I are after remembering. You must respect our tears, alanna.'

And Lucy, turning to throw her arms round the old man's neck, saw that he was indeed weeping.

In her bed that night, Maeve planned her journey. She would go across to Liverpool and catch a ship to New York from there. She thanked God that there was money saved which could be spared both for the journey and for her keep whilst she was in America. The farm was doing well, her father was a shrewd judge of what would sell and what would not. And her sisters were good, they would take it in turns to keep an eye on the farm and on the child, too.

It was a long way, though, especially for someone who had never left Ireland before. But Maeve had seen too many friends and relatives go off to America – and come back, too – to worry unduly about the journey. It took a couple of weeks, but modern ships were comfortable, the crews kind to bewildered passengers. And when you got there, sure and didn't you meet nearly as many Irish as you did in Ireland, now? Evie had gone when she was a good deal younger than Maeve – so had Maeve's old school friend, a couple of cousins and Maeve's Aunt Maria.

It would have been nice to take Lucy, though, Maeve thought rather wistfully, heaving the sheet up over her shoulders. Nice for Linnet to meet her sister at last, nice for Maeve herself to have the company. But no point in even considering it. Lucy was doing well at school, she was useful on the farm, sensible and helpful. Padraig would do very well with Lucy and with one of his other daughters to keep an eye on things, and the twins would meet up again soon enough, for Maeve was determined to bring Linnet back with her. She hugged herself at the thought of that other fifteen-year-old, waiting in New York, about to get the surprise of her life when her Auntie Maeve turned up to rescue her.

And still smiling at the thought, Maeve fell asleep at last.

'Are you well, Granny Mogg? A pity it is that Finn's gone off to the fishing, because I've news for you both. Me mam, the one I telled you about, has died in America and Maeve's gone off to New York to bring me sister back here to live. Now, what d'you think of that?'

Granny Mogg was sitting in the evening sunshine with a bowl in her lap, gutting fish. Lucy had set her up a line and if she felt in the mood she would pull the line in, detach any fish they had caught from it, and bring them back to the sod hut to be prepared for her evening meal. Now she smiled very sweetly at Lucy and beckoned her over.

'Did you bring me bread an' milk, so? Oh, I do love me bread an' milk warmed over me fire before I go to me bed. What's that you say?'

Lucy squatted down beside her and produced half a loaf and a covered jug full of milk. Maeve had found out about Granny Mogg a long while ago but Maeve was kind and generous; she simply gave the girls food for the old lady and sometimes a soft shawl she did not need, or a blanket, and let them get on with it. So Granny Mogg thought herself undiscovered and was happier so.

Lucy had never once regretted her decision to take on the responsibility for seeing to Granny Mogg . It meant that she saw Finn whenever he could spare time from earning a living to come and see Granny, and as the old woman grew stronger with the good food which Lucy and Caitlin brought over to her so she grew stronger in her mind, too. She told the girls stories of her life with the tinkers, of her love for her husband who had died . . . oh, a lifetime ago . . . and older stories, too, folk tales, legends, stories of the days when dragons roamed the hills of Ireland and knights on horseback fought and conquered them, drove them away from the enchanted hills.

'I said my mammy has died in New York and Maeve, who has been like a mother to me all me life, has gone off to bring home a sister of mine called Linnet, to keep me company,' Lucy repeated. 'Maeve thinks I should be glad, but divil a bit o' gladness can I find in me heart. Mammy took her and left me, why should I be glad she's coming home?'

Granny Mogg considered the question for a moment, head cocked, bright eyes fixed on infinity. Then she put the fish down beside her and heaved herself to her feet. 'I'll take a look,' she muttered. 'Fetch me water, girl, dear.'

'Bossy, bossy, bossy,' Lucy said, smiling. 'Do this, do that – what do I want with a sister when I've a Granny Mogg always on at me?' But she picked up the old bucket and went down to the creek and half-filled it, brought it back to where Granny sat outside the sod hut, and poured it with great care into what Granny called her 'seeing bowl', though Lucy knew perfectly well that it was only a fat glass jar with well-rounded sides and a narrow opening at the top. When it was full she put it down carefully on the grass near the old woman and sat back. She was a complete sceptic so far as Granny's second sight was concerned, but she loved watching the old woman going through her ritual, nevertheless. Once, she knew, Granny had told fortunes on the fairs, and she still went through the same mumbo jumbo even though Lucy, this evening, was her only audience.

Granny took off her darned black shawl first and threw it over the sweetie jar. Then she leaned forward and began to sing; she didn't use any words but just sang in a deep, hypnotic, thrumming hum which, Caitlin had once said, sounded right across the marsh on a still evening.

Lucy sat back on her heels and watched. The sun was sinking in the west, casting a glorious red-gold glow over lough and marsh, meadow and mountain, and as Granny removed the shawl with a quite unnecessary flourish Lucy nearly jumped, for the water was blood-red.

But only for a moment. It was the reflection from the sunset, Lucy told herself, leaning forward to see what would happen next. The water in the jar was clear and dancing again so Granny must have moved it. Not that it looked as though it had been moved, so still it lay, but there had to be an explanation for the water seeming red one minute and clear the next, and Lucy was far too sensible to think that there was anything in Granny Mogg's forecasting of the future.

'She died violently,' Granny Mogg said. She sounded surprised, as indeed Lucy would have been had she believed a word of it. 'But she's at peace now. Pretty t'ing, pretty t'ing, she's leavin' all the noise an' fuss behind an' driftin', like the good white mist of autumn, back to the places she loved an' left.'

'Sure she is,' Lucy murmured wickedly. 'Sure and haven't I seen her, comin' over the marsh towards the house, with her head tucked underneath her arm?'

Granny Mogg had closed her eyes and was rocking herself gently backwards and forwards, but at Lucy's words her eyes flew open and she scowled at her companion. 'Shut your gob, young Morphy,' she said, very rudely Lucy thought. 'And listen whiles I tell ye what is to come.'

'Sorry, Granny. I'm listening,' Lucy said contritely. She produced a chunk of bread from one pocket and the bottle of milk from the other and began to crumble the bread into one of the billy cans whilst Granny Mogg continued to regard her jar of water as though it was doing something a lot more interesting than sitting on the grass and reflecting, in miniature, the world of castle, marsh and lough.

'Ah, here it comes,' Granny said at last, when the bread

and milk were ready for warming. 'Give the fire a poke and blow on the ashes, alanna; there's enough heat left in it to warm me bread an' milk.'

Lucy turned to stare at Granny Mogg's fire, which looked like dead ashes but would, she realised, come to life again with a bit of a stir. She found the stick which Granny used as a poker and then blew life into an ember, then another, until the fire burned up brightly once more.

'Give us the billy can, Granny,' she said at length. 'Have you finished with your seeing bowl?'

'Sure an' didn't I say so?' Granny muttered. She tipped the jar sideways and a flood of water poured out, sank in the grass and vanished. 'I've seen, haven't I?'

'I don't know. You just said me mam died violently which . . . which . . .' she decided, quite suddenly, not to say as she had intended, 'which I do not believe for one minute,' partly because it was rude but also, she realised, because she was not sure at all how her mother had died. 'Which is rather upsetting,' she finished instead, feeling a fraud, because she had no feelings one way or t'other, for her mother. 'Have you got a screw of sugar handy?'

Granny Mogg produced a spoonful of sugar in a screw of blue paper and Lucy shook it into the billy can, then stirred it and waited for the bubbles to start. Granny, meanwhile, hunkered down beside her, staring into the blue and gold flames.

'She won't come back,' she remarked at last, as Lucy brought the can off the fire and stood it on the grass to cool. 'Not this time – no, not this time. Poor gel, poor gel.'

'Who, my sister? But Maeve's gone 'specially to bring her back and she can't be more than sixteen or seventeen, a year or so older than me, so I suppose she'll have to do what Maeve says, won't she?'

'Oh aye, she would . . . only your Maeve won't find her,' Granny Mogg said with a quiet certainty which

Lucy found rather unnerving. Honestly, the old woman really believed she could see all sorts, and in an old sweetie jar full of water at that! 'She'll search and search, she'll come closer'n she knows, but she won't find her.'

What nonsense it all is, Lucy told herself, pretending to agree with Granny Mogg that if she saw it in the seeing bowl of course she must be right. When Maeve comes back with my horrid sister with the silly name which isn't a name at all I'll bring her over here and make Granny Mogg eat her words. Not find her indeed, and Maeve as persistent as any old sheep when she sees a hole in the hedge and decides to cram herself through it. I just hope she's not long away, though; Clodagh will drive me mad before the first week's end with her pernickety ways.

Maeve arrived in New York after a long and trying journey, only to find that the theatre, where she had hoped to get news of Evie's child, was inhabited by a touring company who did not even know Evie's name.

'But you can find up the manager; he's not gone with them,' the girl in the box-office drawled when Maeve explained that she only had a limited time in the United States of America and had hoped to accomplish her mission in that time. 'He lives on West 52nd Street—that's on the West Side, near the docks. If you'll hold on here, I'll find up the number for you.'

She did so and Maeve ventured onto the subway system, terrified of the speed at which the trains moved, the black faces amongst the passengers, and the awful sameness of the dead straight streets and their fringes of identical buildings. And it did her no good. The manager was a nice man, eager to help, but although he had a vague recollection of a girl in the chorus who had been called little Evie, he assured Maeve that she had not worked at the theatre for a long, long time.

'And she's dead, you say? Well, I don't like to upset you, Miss Murphy, but hadn't you better look in a burial ground? There are a great number of them, but if you go to the department of . . .'

'My sister left a child, a girl of fifteen,' Maeve said, when the man paused for breath. 'I'll want a copy of my sister's death certificate but I see little point in searching for an unmarked grave. Why, we didn't even know she was ill until a perfect stranger wrote to me to tell me he had taken over her flat after her death and found a letter, half-written, addressed to me.'

'Flat?'

'Oh, I think you call them apartments,' Maeve said. 'Thank you for your help, but I think I'd better search out Mr Caleb Zowkoughski and see what else he can tell me. You don't remember my niece at all, then?'

'I daresay the girl I thought might be your sister was someone altogether different,' the man said with a weary smile. 'An English accent is rare and therefore memorable, but an Irish one forgive me – is commonplace. Our city is full of such immigrants, some of them of many years' standing.'

Maeve, who had been sitting on a long sofa in the window of the manager's apartment, rose to her feet. 'Thank you for your time,' she said formally. 'But I must not waste any more of it. I have a farm and a family at home who need me.'

Next, Maeve visited Mr Zowkoughski. She rang the doorbell and listened with considerable trepidation to the footsteps approaching the front door. Suppose he had been lying to her? Suppose he had Evie trussed up inside – her heart rose at the thought that her sister might still be alive – what would she do then? But Mr Zowkoughski turned out to be a man of around Maeve's own age with an open, friendly face, tufty, toffee-coloured hair and matching eyes. He guessed who she was before she had opened her mouth and asked her in.

It was a nice apartment, though extremely high, with a view over the masses of shipping in the enormous docks. Maeve accepted his offer of a cup of coffee and a doughnut and sat on a long windowseat, almost afraid to look down at the ant-like figures of people in the street below.

'Miss Murphy, I'm real sorry to have brought you here on a fool's errand, but from what I've managed to discover, your sister didn't have a child here in New York. Most folk think the kid lived in the country round about, since Miss Murphy went away most weekends, probably to visit her. But all my asking has got me nowhere, so far. And – and I do earnestly suggest that too many questions . . . I don't know what sort of a man your sister was mixed up with, but I – I do have reason to believe that – well, she didn't die in her bed, Miss Murphy. '

Maeve was so shocked that she couldn't speak. She just stared at Caleb Zowkoughski whilst all the blood drained out of her face, leaving her feeling sick and lightheaded.

'Didn't you know? I feared you didn't, but I felt I had to write . . . I have acquired a copy of the death certificate, if you would like to see it . . . '

Maeve took hold of the certificate by one corner, and managed to take in what was written without once actually looking straight at it. Little Evie had bled to death as a result of multiple wounds caused by being struck repeatedly by a knife.

'I saw the police,' Caleb murmured, when she had recovered from the dreadful shock and the storm of weeping which had shaken her after reading the certificate. 'She wasn't in this apartment, she'd gone to – to someone's place in Brooklyn Heights. The police think it was a case of – of friends falling out. She had been very

148

ill, it seems, but had felt well enough, on that particular afternoon, to – to visit her friend. I don't know the circumstances, of course, but the police surgeon said your sister would not have lived long, in any case. She was a sick woman, Miss Murphy. Perhaps that was why she decided to try to talk to the man who killed her, instead of steering well clear of him.'

'I don't understand,' poor Maeve said, thoroughly bewildered. 'My sister was on the stage, she was doing very well, she'd said nothing to us of an illness. When she first came over here she spoke of a man called Guiseppe Fuego who was going to make her rich and famous, and I thought, reading between the lines, that he was in love with her and planned to marry her. Did it have anything to do with Mr Fuego, this business?'

Caleb, who had been understanding and kind but perfectly at ease, began to show signs of considerable perturbation at the mention of Mr Fuego's name.

'Yes . . . no . . . I'm not sure,' he stammered. 'You'd do best not to mention Mr Fuego, Miss Murphy, neither to the cops – the police, that is – nor to any of Evie's acquaintance. How old did you say the child was?'

'Only fourteen. You aren't going to tell me . . . '

Caleb moved closer to her. He took both her hands and spoke urgently, his voice low.

'Miss Murphy, this is a dangerous city and your sister mixed with dangerous people, very dangerous people. I don't think for one moment that she would have involved her child with those people but the best thing you can do is go away from here. Leave New York, go back to Ireland, and wait. If your niece needs you she'll get in touch. If she doesn't, if she's living with good people and happy with them, then the best thing she can do is to mourn her mother quietly, and then forget the whole business. Believe me, this is a dangerous city.'

'But my niece . . . I must find her,' stammered Maeve. 'She's got to be here somewhere – her name's Linnet Murphy, surely I can trace her from that?'

Caleb looked doubtful. 'Without an address, ma'am? With no idea where she might be? Well, you can try, I guess, and I'll do my best to help you. But I can't guarantee that we'll get so much as a sniff of her.'

Maeve smiled at him, immensely cheered to hear him say 'we' and not 'you'.

'Thank you, and God bless you,' she said fervently. 'I'd be most grateful for any help, so I would. Can we start looking tomorrow?'

It was that same autumn that Granny Mogg began to show her age. She took longer to climb the long stone stairs to her upper room and scarcely ever ascended the ladder which led out onto the roof. She had always had a healthy appetite but now it gradually shrank as food interested her less and became less important. And she hardly ever looked into her seeing bowl, nor did she cross-question Lucy about her comings and goings. She simply accepted Lucy's absence and rejoiced in her presence and when she was left alone she slept a lot. It was not Lucy who noticed first that something was wrong because she was with Granny, on and off, most of the time, but Finn spotted it the moment he strolled into the upper room at the castle.

'She just smiled at me, so she did, and not a moan about her aching bones nor a question as to where I'd been hidin' meself this time,' he said helplessly. 'So meek and quiet she was that I knew all wasn't well. It's as if she's lost her zest of late, and I'm sure she's shrunk, too, got physically smaller since I was here last.'

'We've had enough rain to shrink a six foot giant down to a two foot pigmy,' Lucy said gloomily. 'She's had a nasty cough, mind, but I gave her honey an' lemon which seemed to help. Only then she got her feet wet going down to pull in our fishing lines, and the cough came back and a headcold with it. She's over both now, but with every cough and sneeze she seems to get a bit weaker, a bit less quick to get over the next one.'

'I wonder should she see a doctor?' Finn said uneasily. 'I've got the money; sure and haven't I had the good season this time? Aye, there's a penny or two to be spent over the hard months.'

'I don't think a doctor would say much except that she was getting old, wearing out,' Lucy said. 'Caitlin's grandaddy's the same age as Granny Mogg and he's wearing out, the doctor says so. But there are things we might do which could help a bit; if it wasn't for the stairs I'd say she should give the old turf hut the go-by and stick to the upper room. It's healthier, I think.'

'But she likes her summer home, as she calls it,' Finn said. 'I can understand it, 'specially now she finds the stairs hurt her poor ole knees. Aw heck, I knew this would come one day, but I didn't know it would be so soon. What'll we do, alanna?'

Lucy felt a lovely warm glow at that 'we', but it didn't solve the problem, of course. The marsh was damp, the lough was downright wet, and the rheumatics were in Granny's bones something cruel. Getting her away from the low-lying ground, she supposed, would probably be best. She voiced the thought aloud and Finn, to her surprise, jumped at the idea.

'You're right, Luceen. Where'll I take her, then?'

'Well, she needs a proper roof over her head,' Lucy said slowly. 'There's turf huts in plenty high in the mountains but when it rains she'd be wetter than she is down here, or at least as wet. I suppose you couldn't build her something?'

'I could,' Finn said with a grin. 'But be the time I finished it I'd be pushin' me own century so I would. What would your grandaddy say to a lodger, eh, just for the winter? With Maeve still gone you must have the room and to spare.'

'Well, we have, and Maeve doesn't look like coming back yet awhile,' Lucy admitted. 'But Finn, if I could persuade me grandad, and Clodagh, because she's still up there standin' in for Maeve, would Granny come with me? A barn she might enjoy, but someone else's house, where she'd have to ask before she fried herself a trout . . . I don't know. And I don't think Grandad would let you live with us as well. I wish he would,' she added with the candour which Finn found so delightful, 'but he'd say it wasn't right to have a young man and a young girl in the house together and them not even relatives.'

'You're probably right and Granny wouldn't stand for it,' Finn said, after some thought. 'She's never had a proper roof over her head, not a house roof which belongs to someone else. I'd think about a caravan, only we've got along fine and no trouble from the Duveens for so long it seems mad to tempt fate. If your Maeve was here you could ask her what best to do; you always say she's sensible.'

'She is, and I wish she'd come back,' Lucy admitted with a sigh. 'She's been gone so long – that wretched sister of mine's disappeared, you know, they can't find her anywhere, but Maeve's stubborn. She won't give up, and America's a huge country.'

'They? Who's they?'

'Oh, didn't I tell you? She's met a feller called Caleb Zowkoughski, he's an att-attorney and I think he's sweet on Maeve, so I do. Her letters are full of him and in the last one she said she might bring him back home when she does come, since his ancestors were from County Kerry and he'd like to see the old country.'

'Well, that 'ud be nice,' Finn said. 'Nice for Maeve, anyway.'

'Yes. And nice for Caleb, too.'

They stared at each other with unrelieved gloom for a moment, both sunk in their own thoughts. Then Lucy spoke.

'We ought to get Granny to get out her seeing bowl; if Maeve's going to marry Caleb I'd like to be prepared.'

'Gran's gettin' too old for seein' things,' Finn said. 'Besides, we'll know for ourselves soon enough. She wouldn't stay away for Christmas, surely?'

'I dunno. She really does like Caleb, Finn, I can tell from her letters. If she does marry him then I don't suppose she'll ever come home.'

If Linnet had expected getting a job would be easy, she was to be disappointed. Day after day she washed carefully, brushed her hair, put on her best winter coat (only just beginning to be a little small) and sallied forth. Every evening she came back to Peel Square with less of a spring in her step as the weeks became months and still she was reliant on the Sullivans.

'It's the weather, chuck,' Mrs Sullivan said in mid-January, when the snow was a couple of feet deep around the sides of the square, though the constant passage of many boots kept it to slush in the middle. 'Folk aren't doin' much shoppin', there ain't much money about . . . you'll do better when the warmer weather comes.'

Linnet said she was sure she would and set off next morning, with great determination, to try the factories.

'I know I said I wouldn't work in one and get a yellow face, but I'll do anything to help your mam out,' Linnet told Roddy as they walked up Scotland Road together in the dark and early morning. 'You work for that beastly butcher and I know you don't like it, our Roddy.'

'Oh, it could be worse,' Roddy said. 'I 'ates the smell o' blood an' the feel o' carcasses on a cold mornin', but it's a job, queen. Look, it's early, come into Cobble's canny house wi' me an' I'll buy you a wet nellie to set you up for the day.'

Linnet squeezed his hand, her mouth watering at the thought of the doughy roll soaked in syrup. She had not eaten any breakfast because she felt so guilty, taking from Mrs Sullivan all the time, when that good lady had her work cut out to feed and clothe her own brood. Trust Roddy to notice, though, and he was always slipping her the odd copper to see her through the day and heaven knew he earned little enough from that old skinflint!

'Oh, you are kind, Roddy! But I shouldn't let you spend your money on me, you don't get much to spare.'

'Wet nellies don't cost a fortune,' Roddy said grandly. 'I'll mug you a cuppa tea an' all if you're good.'

They reached the canny house, which was really only a room which faced onto the pavement, and went inside. Immediately the noise hit them; the porters from the market shouted across to one another, a delivery boy with a box of bread rolls was trying to get someone to take them out of his wooden tray and even at this early hour there were women shoppers, eyeing the food on sale with critical interest, reading the chalk board or peering over the top of the high wooden counter to the shelf at the back which held Mrs Cobble's collection of cakes and prepared sandwiches. There was also a line of would-be customers standing by the counter, none of them looking too happy at being kept waiting.

'Mrs Cobble does a nice cuppa,' Roddy said, catching hold of Linnet's elbow. He raised his voice to a bellow, for there was no sign of Mrs Cobble behind the counter.

'Come on, Ma Cobble, gerra move on or I'll be late. The old feller wants me to clear the snow before I start an' our Linnie 'ere is goin' job-huntin' agin.'

'I can clear the old feller's doorway for free,' Linnet said, delighted to be able to pay Roddy back for once. 'I can, honest, I'm strong, I can shovel snow.'

Roddy laughed and leaned over the counter. 'Two wet nellies an' two cuppas, Mrs Cobble,' he shouted. 'Shift yourself, Auntie!'

Mrs Cobble emerged from her tiny, steamy slit of a kitchen and grinned across at Roddy. She was a fat little woman with thinning grey hair screwed into a tiny bun on top of her head, small grey eyes which twinkled at the world beneath bushy grey brows, and a laugh as raucous as a crow, only a good deal louder.

'Good Lor', it's the butcher's boy, wantin' service,' she announced to the world at large, slapping the tray she held down on the counter. 'Gorrany pennies, Roddy?'

'Enough for two wet nellies an' two cups o' tea, Auntie,' Roddy said promptly. He slapped the coins on the counter. 'Gerron wi' it, queen, or we'll be in trouble, our Linnie an' me. What's gone wrong this mornin', hey? Be this time you're usually servin' like a mad thing!'

'Four cups o' tea an' eight toasts,' Mrs Cobble said, removing tea and toast from her tray and pushing them over to the customers. 'An' you was a breakfuss, weren't you?' The man she addressed said he was indeed and Mrs Cobble piled a plate with fried food, handed it to her customer, and then turned back to Roddy. 'Ain't you got eyes in your 'ead, young feller?' she said, reaching for the wet nellies and sticking them onto a couple of white pot plates. 'Wharrabout your ear'oles, then, eh? Don't you listen to gossip, chuck?'

'Dunno what you're talkin' about,' Roddy said.

'Butchers' lads know everything there is to know; well-known fact.'

A fish porter, smelling strongly of his wares, pushed past Linnet and dumped a box of fish on the counter. He leaned across it and spoke right into Mrs Cobble's flushed face. 'Ere, I can't wait all mornin', gi's me money an' I'll be orf. Ten pun' o' cod you said an' ten pun' o' cod you've gorrin this box.'

'Ta, love,' Mrs Cobble said, fishing money out of the till and pushing it across the counter. 'God ha' mercy on me, where's that bleedin' baker's boy?'

'He's gone, but he left the bread,' Linnet volunteered. 'He's coming back for his money later, he said. And he wants his tray back, too.'

'And two teas,' Mrs Cobble said, pouring tea from a big black pot into two chipped cups. 'I'm short-'anded, Roddy me lad, which is why I'm buyin' bread in instead o' makin' me own. You must ha' heard about Millie, the gal what worked 'ere?'

'Who? No, 'aven't 'eard nothin',' Roddy said, picking up the two cups. 'What's she done, then?'

'Oh, nothin' much, only 'ad a baby, that's all,' Mrs Cobble said heavily. 'I didn't even know she were in the fam'ly way, like. So me right-'and woman's out o' the picture for a bit, 'cos I won't 'ave a squallin' brat in 'ere, upsettin' me customers.'

Roddy was carrying the cups over to the nearest table; he stopped short, put the cups down so hastily that he splashed tea on the table's plain deal top, and turned back to the counter. 'You need someone like our Linnie 'ere,' he said. 'Me mam swears by 'er – she's a dream of a cook, our Linnie, an' that fast on 'er feet . . .'

'Hold 'ard a moment, young Roddy,' Mrs Cobble said. She stared at Linnet across the counter. 'Your mam don't 'ave no gels!'

'No, our Linnie's a – a cousin,' Roddy said quickly.
'She's been livin' with us for a while, ain't you, Linnie?
Real quick, is Linnie – why don't you let 'er give you an
'and just for this mornin', eh?'

Linnet looked from one face to the other. The possibil-
ity of a job loomed suddenly, and this – this was a nice
place! Little Evie would have thought it low, but Linnet
had stopped taking little Evie's word for things like that
long before she left for America. So she smiled hopefully
at Mrs Cobble, and to her pleasure Mrs Cobble smiled
straight back.

'Well, gel? Gorra tongue in your 'ead, 'ave you?'

'Yes, Mrs C-Cobble,' Linnet stammered. 'I'd like to
give you a hand.'

Mrs Cobble nodded slowly. 'Convent schooled?' she
hazarded. 'Mam Irish, father missin'?'

'More or less, Mrs Cobble,' Linnet agreed. 'My mam
died a while ago and I never did meet my dad, but Mrs
Sullivan's been very good to me.'

'Aye, Janice is a good woman,' Mrs Cobble said, still
staring thoughtfully at Linnet whilst leaning her elbows
and a large bosom heavily on the counter. She suddenly
seemed to make up her mind and stood up straight.
'Awright, queen, you're on. Come round 'ere an' get the
overall off of the kitchen door. You can start servin', I'll
explain as we goes on.'

Linnet came out of Cobble's at eight that night, almost
dizzy with tiredness but with a big smile from ear to ear.
It was snowing again and as she left the shelter of the
doorway someone fell into step beside her. It was Roddy,
his striped butcher's overall filthy, his boots clagged with
slush.

'Hello, chuck,' he said, taking her arm and tucking it
through his. 'How did it go?'

'Oh, Roddy, I can't ever thank you enough – she's going to keep me on and it's a grand job, I love it! She's already taught me how to cook scouse for twenty people, to bake a huge flat loaf of bread – she cuts it in pieces to go with the soup – and to make a sandwich so fast you wouldn't believe. And I serve the customers . . . they give you the odd ha'penny, too . . . and get to bring leftovers home . . .'

'What's the money like?' Roddy said. 'Twon't be great, but work's so scarce any job's a good job.'

'It's all right; ten bob a week, and it's only eight till eight because Mr Cobble helps early and late. What d'you think?'

'It's bleedin' good,' Roddy said admiringly. 'I only get twelve an' a kick meself. Well, you're made up, I can see. So'll me mam be when we tell 'er. When does Ma Cobble pay you, eh?'

'Saturday night, but because today was just a trial she gave me two bob in my hand – wasn't that kind? And she gave me half a fruit cake, I've got it in under me coat.'

'Coo,' Roddy said reverently when Linnet showed him the cake, nestling in her apron pocket. 'The kids'll go barmy – it ain't often they get cake mid-week.'

'They're welcome to it,' Linnet said. 'Mrs Cobble gave me a big dinner at noon and a big tea an' all. Me stomach's tight as a drum, you won't see me eating cake.'

'No? All the more for the rest of us, then,' Roddy said. He squeezed her arm. 'I'm that glad for you, queen, because I knowed you was miserable, feelin' you were a charge on me mam.'

'Well, I was,' Linnet pointed out as they turned the corner and plunged under the arch into Peel Square. 'I've helped her in the house of course, and done the ironing when she's washed sheets and stuff, but I couldn't pay for me keep, though I know you handed over extra, often and often. You Sullivans have been very good to me, Roddy.'

'Oh well, you can pay us back some day,' Roddy said obscurely. 'Want to go in first and tell me mam about Cobble's? Or shall I go first an' make trumpet noises for your entrance?'

Linnet laughed delightedly. She thought she had never felt so happy, not even when Mammy had been alive to share her pleasure.

'You go first,' she urged. 'Get 'em all in the kitchen, so's I only have to tell me story once!'

Lying rolled up in her blankets on the floor by the kitchen fire that night, Linnet reviewed her day. It had been the best of days, and she could not imagine ever being more excited by a job than she had been as what Mrs Cobble called 'me gofer'.

'What's that?' Linnet had asked, and Mrs Cobble told her that it meant a sort of dogsbody, a do-everything, called a gofer because she would be told to 'go for this and go for that'.

But the best part had been marching proudly into the kitchen whilst Roddy made a trumpet of his hands and blared triumphant music through them and Bert did wonderful things with a comb and a bit of paper.

'Here comes the conquering 'ero!' Freddy shrilled. 'Wharrever 'ave you done, our Linnie, to make Roddy play 'is trumpets?'

'She's gorra job!' Mrs Sullivan had hazarded. 'Oh, queen, I couldn't be 'appier for you an' it ain't the money, neither. Wharra you doin', eh? Clearin' snow? They pay a bob a week some firms, to 'ave snow cleared away.'

'No, Auntie Sullivan, it's a real job,' Linnet had said, her voice shrill with excitement. 'I'm waiting on at the Cobble's canny house, for ten bob a week and the left-overs.'

The hugs, the kisses, the excitement which followed! Mr Sullivan, who had a bad heart as well as crippled legs, gave her a big hug and told her she was a good girl and deserved some good luck. Mrs Sullivan danced her round the kitchen and promised to make her a nice apron to wear for work just as soon as she could get some sewing done. The younger boys were delighted with the news and enjoyed the cake to the full and Roddy, of course, was more pleased than anyone except Linnet herself.

'You're a good kid, our Linnie,' he said affectionately when the fire had been banked down and everyone was going off to bed. 'Now you won't need to worry that you stayin' 'ere ain't fair on me mam.'

'Well, it isn't,' Linnet said. She was spreading her blankets out preparatory to rolling up in them. All she did when she went to bed at night was to take off her skirt, jumper and shoes. Her neat cotton nightgowns had disappeared with the horrid Mrs Roberts and though Mrs Sullivan had bought her a second skirt and some cheap shoes, she was still very short of clothing. 'I shouldn't expect your mam to let me sleep on her kitchen floor for ever; and though I try ever so hard, I do take up room, Roddy. Your mam used to spread the washing out here at nights so it would dry in the fire's warmth, but now she can't, and that isn't fair either. As soon as I can afford it, I'll have to move out.'

Upstairs, the boys were already asleep and Mr and Mrs Sullivan were settling down, their voices rumbling slower and slower. Roddy caught hold of both of Linnet's hands, then drew her towards him.

'Our Linnie, I want you to stay 'ere for always,' he said hoarsely. 'You're the best thing what ever 'appened to me, honest to God you are! We all love 'avin' you in our 'ouse, me most of all, so don't you talk about movin' out, 'cos we'd miss you somethin' cruel.'

'I won't go far, Roddy,' Linnet promised. She felt rather uneasy as Roddy pulled her hard against his chest. 'Do stop it, you're squashing me!'

'No I ain't, I'm cuddlin' you,' Roddy said and put both arms round her tightly. He gave a sort of moan under his breath and then he began to kiss any bit of her face which he could reach despite Linnet squiggling away like mad – and giggling, as well, for this was not how she thought of Roddy at all, he was usually so sensible. 'Oh Linnet, Linnet, you don't know 'ow I feel about you, you're just the best, the prettiest . . .'

'Roddy, your mam . . .' Linnet was beginning, when the kitchen door opened. Mrs Sullivan stood there.

'Ah, Roddy, I were just about to call down to you to bring me up that bit o' darnin' I were doin' before supper. But I'll fetch it meself, now I'm 'ere.'

Roddy, scarlet as a lobster, had let Linnet go as soon as he saw his mother standing there, and now, shifting from foot to foot, he said loudly, 'I'm sorry, Mam. I were just – just showin' our Linnie 'ow pleased I am she's gorra job.'

'I daresay. But there's other ways of showin' you're pleased about a job, without pullin' the gel about,' Mrs Sullivan said severely. 'You didn't oughter stay down 'ere after we's gone up, Roddy. It ain't decent.'

'But Mam, I weren't doin' nothin' . . .' Roddy began, to be firmly interrupted.

'I should think not, indeed, when Linnie's in your mam's care! Off wit' you, son, we'll talk in the morning.'

She smiled at Linnet, tipped her a wink, and followed her son out of the room and Linnet removed her outer clothing and rolled herself up in her blankets. And now she was thinking over her day and wondering how long it would take her to save a decent sum.

Because no matter what Roddy said she knew she

would have to go. She was sixteen, Roddy eighteen, and when Roddy had squeezed her just now there had only been a part of her complaining and giggling. The other part, the part which was conscious of a burgeoning figure and her increasing interest in young men, had known a strange, guilty excitement, a desire for his caresses to continue, to take her further along that road which led to womanhood.

So I'd best flit when I can manage it, Linnet told herself half sadly. I can get a cheap room when I'm settled at Cobble's – and that won't stop me coming back as often as possible, because there's no family I love more than the Sullivans, and no place I've been happier than Peel Square.

'My life's going back to normal so it is, after months and months of being strange,' Lucy said joyfully to Caitlin as they walked across Barry's Bridge, heading for school. 'We got a letter from Maeve yesterday and she's coming home and bringing that feller, Caleb, with her. She's sad because she's given up; she doesn't think she'll ever find me sister, but I don't mind that because I never knew her. So she's coming back to us, Cait, and aren't I glad? That Clodagh's very nearly driven me mad with her "do this, do that", and never even a thank you from her.'

'She'll be back just in time to see you leave school,' Caitlin said rather gloomily. 'Then you'll be after gettin' a job, unless you stay on the farm, of course. Are you goin' to tell Maeve what you really want to do, Luceen?'

'What? Acting on the stage, you mean? Well, it might upset her,' Lucy said thoughtfully. 'When I mentioned it to Grandad he was so cross I pretended I was only teasing, but Maeve's not like that. Still, I won't say anything yet.'

'When I said how good you were in the school play

my mam said you'd get ideas like your mam, Evie, did, and look what come o' that,' Caitlin said. 'You never said your mam was an actress, Lu.'

'I didn't know she was until Grandad said, when I talked about the play,' Lucy admitted. 'And anyway, from what I've managed to find out she wasn't ever an actress, precisely.'

Caitlin smiled and patted her hair which had recently been cut in a bob. The new hairstyle suited Caitlin very much better than Lucy had imagined it would, and sometimes Lucy looked at Caitlin's shining dark cap of hair which was cut to show the nice shape of her head and which complimented her round, rosy face, and wished that she, too, might have a bob or a shingle. But if she was really going to be an actress she might need her long hair, so she kept the scissors in their place and did not even try to cut herself a fringe, tempting though it was.

'If your mam wasn't an actress, but she was on the stage, what was she?' Caitlin asked now. She stopped to lean over the bridge and Lucy knew she was trying to see her reflection in the smoothly rushing water below. 'Was she a stage manager or something?'

'No, not really. She danced and sang, she didn't act,' Lucy said rather shortly. She did not want Caitlin, or indeed anyone, to know that during Maeve's long absence she had done a very sneaky thing.

If it hadn't rained and rained and kept her indoors, she told herself defensively now, she might never have gone wandering into Maeve's room and pulled open the bottom drawer of the big old chest which stood against the sloping eaves. Once it had been full of sheets and pillowcases, with Maeve's initials embroidered in the corners, jostling for position with six lacy nightgowns, six pairs of silk knickers, petticoats, bust bodices, all the paraphernalia of a girl's bottom drawer, her trousseau, carefully stitched so that she did not go empty-handed to her bridegroom.

But over the years the other girls had married and Maeve had not and Maeve's generous spirit had refused to hoard all the beautiful things she had so lovingly made. So she had given away the bedding, the clothing, everything the drawer had once contained. Now it contained some material, the last pair of embroidered sheets which Lucy knew without having to think about it would be given to her when she married, and, right at the bottom, where the lavender bags and the pot pourri of rose petals were kept, letters.

They were not love letters, she knew that. Maeve didn't receive love letters. Besides, they weren't wrapped in pink ribbon and they didn't have flowers pressed between the pages, two things which, Lucy knew, were obligatory in love letters. They were just kept in big brown paper bags, and when she looked at the signature on the first one and saw it was her own mother . . . well, surely it was her right to read on?

Reading them, starting with little Evie's very first letter home, had been a pleasurable business at first. Her mother had been interested in baby Lucy, had talked about her Career – always with a capital initial letter – and her other child, the oddly named Linnet. She had touched on the beautiful rooms over the fine emporium on a street convenient to the theatre, on her social life, which was apparently lively and very much of the champagne-in-slipper variety, and on her admirers, who were many and various and all, it seemed, rich and adoring. But as she read on, even Lucy noticed the change in little Evie's attitude. There was defiance, a repeatedly reiterated conviction that Stardom and Acceptance (more capitals) were just around the corner, were kept from Evie by a malignant fate, by ill-luck, by the sheer vindictiveness of others. There were opportunities missed by a hair's breadth, evil acts by fellow Thespians which had caused her apparent downfall, misunderstandings galore. In short, Evie had not succeeded and did not intend to let those at home believe she was in any way to blame.

And, of course, it also came out, in those rather ingenuous letters, that little Evie posed on stage clad in nothing but feathers, or fans, or a large hat strategically wafted, that she sang songs and danced exotically, but that she had never acted a part.

And, inevitably, Lucy concluded, as just by reading on she began to build up a picture of her mother, the letters got shorter and shorter, the intervals between their arrival at the farm longer and longer. Very soon they were scarcely more than notes, particularly after little Evie had reached New York, though there was one letter where she spoke of her wonderful admirer, Mr Fuego, who was going to see her a 'Star' at any cost.

'He's crazy for me, Maeve me darling,' she had written exultantly. 'Nothing's too good for your little Evie – you should see the apartment he's bought for me, the view over the river alone must be worth thousands of dollars.'

Only after that there was no more mention of Mr Fuego – and neither, Lucy slowly began to realise, of the other child. Well, there were mentions, but they were what you might call off-hand, almost as though – almost as though Linnet wasn't with little Evie after all.

I do believe, Lucy told herself incredulously as she tucked the last letter guiltily back into its big brown envelope, I do believe that the reason why Maeve hasn't found Linnet is because she's not in America at all. I think little Evie left her in Liverpool all those years ago and simply dared not confess it to Maeve!

But it was guesswork, so she didn't tell anyone, not Caitlin, not Granny Mogg, not Finn. Why should I? she thought. I'm not really interested in that other girl, it doesn't matter to me whether she's in New York or – or Timbuktu for that matter. But if Maeve really wants to find Linnet I suppose I'll have to admit I read the letters, and then perhaps I ought to tell her what I think. And if Maeve agrees and thinks it's important then I suppose the two of us could go over to Liverpool together and find the girl with the silly name.

But despite herself the letters had, at last, stirred a degree of interest in this sister that she could not remember. A girl a year or two older than me, but maybe very like me, she thought. A girl who's lived with the theatre all her life, who must have met most of the great actors and actresses, played in their dressing rooms, run about on the stage whilst they rehearsed! Knowing her might be quite useful if I do decide I want to be an actress, she decided; she could give me all sorts of tips and advice. Probably she would know just how one would go about getting a job on the stage. Think of that, Lucy Murphy, think of that!

Linnet guessed that Mrs Sullivan had had words with Roddy because the next day she received an incoherent and mumbled apology from a young gentleman very red about the gills.

'Mam said it weren't fair, I put you in an awkward position,' he muttered, staring fixedly at the table, for he had chosen to make his apology in his dinner break whilst Linnet, naturally, was at her busiest, flying round the small room sliding platefuls of scouse and dumplings, apple pie and steak pudding, before the customers. 'I din't think, Linnie, I din't mean no 'arm. Only you're me pal, an . . .'

'It's all right, Roddy, honest to God it is,' Linnet said distractedly, trying to move on to the next table without seeming rude, but Roddy had drawn her attention by grabbing her apron and he still held a corner of it, crumpled up in one large fist. 'Look, what do you want to eat?'

'Oh . . .' Roddy looked round vaguely as though he would find a plateful of something nice on the floor or the walls. 'Oh . . . anything, you choose.'

'Right, scouse and dumplings,' Linnet said briskly. 'Let go me pinny, there's a good feller.'

'Oh . . . sorry, I didn't know I were still 'angin' on,' Roddy said. 'Linnie, can I meet you after work?'

'Course you can; we're still pals, our Roddy,' Linnet said, moving to the next table. 'Why, you're like a brother to me and I wouldn't stop meeting me brother because of a bit of a tiff, like, would I?'

Roddy scowled but made no comment and Linnet continued with her work but the whole episode had made her think. She loved living in the square with the Sullivans but she knew she would have to move out and it looked as though sooner might be better than later. The trouble was she couldn't possibly afford a room, or even a bit of a room, on ten bob a week.

And later that evening, when Roddy, after a significant glare from his mother, had gone off up to bed muttering about gettin' an early night, she and Mrs Sullivan sat down and talked it through.

'We loves 'avin' you, queen, not only for yourself but because I ain't never 'ad a daughter an' I've always wanted one,' Mrs Sullivan said frankly. 'But Roddy's mortal fond o' you, an' he's growin' up, same's you are for that matter. An' we're bleedin' short o' space so you don't get no privacy. An' you're a sight too young for marryin', an' besides that would only solve one o' the problems.'

Linnet, who had no intention of marrying anyway, let alone at the tender age of sixteen, did not understand at all what problem marrying would solve but she did not like to say so. 'If I could earn a bit extra in the evenings ...' she said hopefully. 'I'm free by eight most nights. Isn't there someone round here with daughters who might let me have a mattress on the floor?'

Mrs Sullivan threw both hands in the air. 'Well, you've an 'ead on your shoulders, Linnet Murphy, why din't I think o' that?' she declared. 'Me cousin Myrtle's gorra daughter an' they're always short of the readies. They live a ways from 'ere, but you'd manage. It's a back to back up on Lawrence Street. Want me to 'ave a word?'

'I suppose you'd better,' Linnet said sadly. 'Oh Auntie Sullivan, I'll miss you, and the others, something cruel, but I know you're right and it's only fair. What's your cousin Myrtle's daughter called?'

'Bessie. Bessie Brinton. She's a year or so older'n you but you'll gerron together. A nice gel, Bessie.'

They got on and Linnet, handing over eight bob a week to the Brinton family, was grateful for a roof over her head and cheerful company, but wished, wistfully, that Mrs Sullivan had managed to pass on to her feckless cousin Myrtle some tips about housekeeping in general and cleanliness in particular.

The Brintons had bed bugs and accepted them as a fact of life, whereas the Sullivans, who also had bed bugs, fought them with fire and brimstone, soap and water, much boiling of sheets and hanging out of mattresses. And fleas marched off Tammy Brinton's four large, half-witted mongrel dogs when they grew tired of eating nothing but dog and had many a good meal on poor Linnet's white skin.

'I don't mind for meself so much,' Linnet told Roddy, scratching furtively as they sat in the cinema watching Agnes Ayres rolling her eyes and pouting at her leading man. 'It's passing them on I hate – and if Ma Cobble were to see a fleabite on me neck, what d'you suppose she'd think?'

'Norra lot,' Roddy said rather gloomily. In a moment of cinematic passion he had tried, personally, to mark Linnet's neck and had received an eyewatering clout on the nose for his pains. She did not know what he was up to she had informed him crossly, but she didn't fancy trying to explain to Mrs Cobble that she had been attacked by a leech. 'Everyone 'as fleas, chuck. We does our best, but in summer they're everywhere.'

'The Brintons' fleas are as big as their bed bugs,' Linnet said. 'You know I'm doing shorthand and typewriting in me evening classes, Roddy? Well, one day I'm going to get an office job and I tell you, people in offices don't like fleas one little bit.'

'Well, the answer's there awright – move back in wi' us,' Roddy said joyfully. Linnet giggled and dug him in the ribs.

'So you can sneak down in the night and bite me neck and make 'em think I'm living with Dracula?' she said derisively. 'I should just say so, Roddy Sullivan!'

Linnet's job with Mrs Cobble lasted a year, until the delinquent Millie's child was old enough to be left with Millie's mam.

'I'm that sorry to lose ye, chuck,' Mrs Cobble told Linnet when she explained that Millie was returning. 'But you'll do well, I'll give ye a good reference, tell anyone what asks that they couldn't tek on a better gel. Honest, 'ard-working, clean . . .'

'I do understand, really I do, Mrs Cobble,' Linnet

assured her fat and friendly little employer. 'And I'll never forget you because you've been so good to me. But you know I've been doing night-classes? Well, I'm a fast typist now, and me shorthand's not bad either. I think I'll go for an office job, if I can get one – and there's one advertised in the *Echo* this very week.'

And within a few days, before she had really digested the information that she would be out of work the following week, Roddy had called for her after work, taken her arm, and suggested a trip to the cinema to see her all-time favourite, Gary Cooper, who was starring in a film called *Lilac Time*.

'Because I miss you, now you don't live at our 'ouse no more,' he told her, only half teasingly. 'We can sit an' 'old 'ands an' 'ave a bit of a cuddle, eh?'

'Can't, it's night-school,' Linnet told him, tucking her hand into his arm nevertheless and walking along beside him. 'But I'm out of Cobble's as from Monday. Millie's coming back.'

Roddy stared down at her, lively dismay changing, abruptly, to hope. 'You'll move back in wi' us, of course?' he said ingenuously. 'I won't muck about like when I kissed you in the kitchen an' me mam walked in, but it 'ud be nice to 'ave you near, again.'

But Linnet, who was happy enough with the Brintons, apart from the bugs, made noncommittal noises. Though she had missed the Sullivans and Peel Square horribly at first, she knew that when the time came for her to move on it would not be to return to the Sullivans, much though she loved them. She was beginning to realise that independence, once gained, is important and not to be willingly given up. And though there were drawbacks in Lawrence Street, at least the Brintons never asked her where she was going or who with. Linnet, who had accepted an invitation from an Irish fish porter to go to the Rotunda with him, knew that she would never have got away with the outing had she been living in Peely. It hadn't been a particularly good evening – the smell of fish had seen to that – but at least she had gone, discovered that the fish porter wasn't her Mr Right, and returned to Lawrence Street with no one the wiser. The fact that Mrs Sullivan would have worried in case she was taken advantage of she dismissed with the insouciance of youth. Linnet Murphy could take care of herself!

'Well, if you've got no gelt, queen, I don't see as you've much choice,' Roddy said presently. 'Wish you an' me could 'ave a place between us . . . but full-time butcherin' ain't all that well-paid and me mam needs wharrever I can spare.' He sighed deeply. 'If you ever feel like makin' an honest feller of me, our Linnie, you've only gorra say the word.'

Linnet laughed. 'It 'ud take more than me to make an honest feller out of you, Roddy Sullivan! But what I meant to tell you was that I've got an interview for a job – an office job! It's in one of the big insurance offices on Exchange Flags and it's for an office girl with good prospects for advancement the advertisement says. What about that?'

'You won't want to go around wi' a butcher's boy when you're in an office,' Roddy muttered after a moment. 'I 'ates butcherin', but what else is there? You get a couple o' hundred fellers after every bleedin' job what comes up, what chance 'ave I got? At one time I used to think I'd leave the Pool, go down south, but it's as bad there as 'ere, so they say. I dunno, queen, I'm sure.'

'You're me best friend, our Roddy, and I wouldn't want to go out with anyone else. Well, not unless you count Gary Cooper or Mr Miles Guest, that lovely man who stars at the Playhouse when they do dramas.'

Roddy snorted. 'Bleedin' fillum stars! Well, if they're

the only fellers you've got an eye to I guess I'm awright for a bit. But if you get that job, an' I'm sure I 'ope you will, then you'll be off wi' some bleedin' insurance clerk or other an' not a glance for a butcher's boy, I tell you.'

'Then don't stay a butcher's boy,' Linnet shouted, losing patience and jerking her arm out of his. 'You do talk so big, Roddy Sullivan, but you've not applied for a job for ages, so how d'you know you can't get one? Look, you'd best push off now, 'cos I'm going to me class and it's all I can do not to fall asleep at me desk without you upsetting me. See you tomorrow.'

'I'll walk to the school with you,' Roddy began, but Linnet shook her head impatiently.

'No point, we're nearly there and you've not had your tea yet. Get off home there's a good feller – I'll see you tomorrow, all right?'

Roddy sighed. 'All right,' he agreed resignedly. 'See you tomorrer, then. Same time, same place?'

'That's it. And by then I'll know whether I've got the job, because the interview's in the morning.' Linnet paused in her onward flight and turned her face towards him. 'Wish me luck, our Roddy!'

'Oh, dammit, good luck, our Linnie,' Roddy called back. 'Good luck for the mornin'.'

Roddy watched her out of sight and then turned back towards Peel Square. She was the loveliest thing, his Linnet, but he was so scared of losing her! The trouble was, they'd known each other for too long so she took him for granted, never thought of him as a man but only as the boy who had teased her and taken care of her, alternately bullied and spoilt her. But he didn't know how to change things, that was the rub. His mam, bless her, was always giving him advice, mostly on the lines that Linnet would take him seriously one day, when there was a bit of distance between them.

So what to do? Linnet made no secret of the fact that she hated his butchering, the smell which hung round him, his whole job, in fact. She had as good as told him to do something different today and of course she was absolutely right, he'd not tried for a job for a year or more. Never, in fact, since Sampson the butcher had taken him on, agreed to train him as a proper, time-served butcher, and begun to pay him a halfway decent wage.

And there were jobs. His father had been a seaman and his reputation had been good. More than once Da had said, almost wistfully, that his lads could do worse than follow in his footsteps. And they always wanted seamen – stokers, deckhands, all sorts but he'd not looked in that direction because he was afraid of leaving Linnet even for a few weeks, afraid of what he might find when he came back.

Oh, well. Butchering wasn't that bad, and he was able to meet Linnet out of work two or three times a week, he took her home, dancing on a Saturday night, to the flicks, even to New Brighton to hang around the amusement arcades and paddle in the water.

And an office girl wasn't such a marvellous job, after all. It was a bit better than being Mrs Cobble's gofer, perhaps, but it wasn't as though she was a proper secretary. Roddy turned in under the brick arch, crossed the paving in a couple of strides, and pushed open the front door.

'I'm home, Mam,' he called. 'Gorrany tea on the go?'

Linnet got the job as office girl and found, to her delight, that it paid better than the job at Mrs Cobble's and finished earlier, too.

'And I'm also teaching a beginners' evening class in typewriting and they pay me a bob a session, and I can manage four sessions a week,' she told Roddy triumphantly as he walked her back to Lawrence Street when she finished at Mrs Cobble's for the last time. 'And I may be getting a room of me own! I like Mrs Brinton, she's awful nice, but . . . oh, Roddy, a room of me own! D'you want to come and see it with me? It's on the Boulevard – you know, that big, wide street with the trees and the grass. Do come, then you can tell your mam what it's like.'

Roddy, secretly thrilled to be asked, pretended reluctance but allowed himself to be persuaded, so next evening found the two of them mounting the stairs at number 8, The Boulevard, Roddy cautiously, Linnet eagerly, whilst ahead of them a young woman with a couple of kids clinging to her skirt led the way, calling remarks back over her shoulder as she climbed the stairs.

'It's ri' at the perishin' top, Miss Murphy,' she said cheerfully. 'Still, your legs is younger than mine . . . an' you ain't carryin', either.'

'Carryin' what?' Linnet hissed and Roddy, grinning, tapped his own stomach significantly.

'She's 'avin' another kid,' he whispered hoarsely. 'I tell you what, our Linnet, a week of livin' 'ere an' you'll think Havelock Street's flat as St George's Plain!'

'It's a long way up,' Linnet agreed, 'but think of the view, our Roddy! Ah, we're there.'

The young woman pushed open a lopsided, creaking door and gestured them to go ahead of her. The reason was soon clear; the room was so tiny that a narrow bed, Linnet and Roddy filled it completely. An expectant mother would have had great difficulty in simply getting through the doorway.

'It ain't a room, it's a bleedin' cupboard,' Roddy announced, looking round him. 'You'll 'ave to undress on the landing, queen, or you'll skin your elbows on the walls.'

'It's very nice, really,' Linnet murmured. 'It is a bit small, but I'm not very big myself.'

A bell sounded below them and the young woman's large and untidy head appeared in the doorway. 'Gorra go,' she said cheerfully. 'That's the doorbell. Look all you want, then come down an' tell me if you're takin' it.'

She lumbered down the stairs and Linnet turned to Roddy. 'Don't say it, I know it's tiny, but there's a bed and a window . . . and she said I could use the kitchen to cook me meals. She said all the rooms are small, Roddy, and it is cheap, honest.'

'And you like this better than me Aunt Brinton's? Well, I can see you might,' Roddy said handsomely. 'It looks clean an' at least you won't 'ave to share a bed wi' Bessie. Wharrabout visitors?' he leered at her. 'You've gorra be really pally to 'ave a visitor in 'ere. I mean you go to scratch your – your elbow and you'll find yourself scratchin' someone else's kneecap.'

'Oh, ha ha,' Linnet said crossly. 'She's only asking eight bob, Roddy, and that's about what I can afford, so I'm going to take it.'

'Who's next door?' Roddy asked suddenly. He tapped on the wall; the sound echoed hollowly back at them. 'This ain't a wall, Linnet, it's a partition, just a piece o' wood. Dear Gawd, you could get through it wi' a tooth-pick . . . you could wake up one mornin' an' find an eye glarin' down at you through an 'ole in the wall!'

Linnet giggled. 'It's all girls so what would it matter? There's a married couple with two little boys but all the rest of us are girls. That's another reason why I like it,' she added honestly, 'because we're all about the same age and none of us will have much money. I'm going to take it, so I just hope you'll give Auntie Sullivan a good report about it.'

'She'll be up 'ere inspectin' the day you move in,'

Roddy assured her. 'You know me mam – she worries about you, queen.'

'Yes, I know. But – but Roddy . . . it's me own place!'

'Yeah, I know. An' it's a decent little room,' Roddy said, suddenly magnanimous. It was the thought of a houseful of girls, Linnet imagined. 'You'll be awright 'ere, our Linnie, though you've a powerful trek to work.'

'I'll catch a tram; or leave early,' Linnet assured him. 'Let's go down and tell the lady "yes" then, shall we? Oh, Roddy, a place of me own!'

Chapter Seven

Mrs Sullivan was at the low stone sink, up to her elbows in suds, when Roddy came into the kitchen with a bounce in his step and a sparkle in his eye. He had taken pains over his appearance that morning and felt very much the young man about town, with his hair Brylcreemed and a clean white shirt on under his best suit. And at this precise moment he was so happy it was all he could do not to burst into song. He was carrying a big, newspaper-wrapped parcel which he put down on the kitchen table with a thump.

'Present for you, Mam,' he said laconically and then, unable to contain himself a moment longer: 'I got the job, they told me straight off I'd gorrit.'

'The job? You got the job? Well, son, I won't pretend I'm not glad because we could do wi' the money, but we'll miss you, me an' your dad.' Mrs Sullivan turned impulsively from the sink and gave her son a kiss on the cheek, her pink, water-wrinkled hands held carefully clear of the suit. 'When d'you start?'

'It's sail, Mam, you should say, when do you sail? And it's Tuesday morning, wi' the tide.' He heaved a sigh and a grin spread slowly across his face. 'Eh, it's good to be doing a proper job again and it'll be good to 'ave money in me pocket, an' all. First t'ing I did once I knew was go round to the market an' give in me notice to old Sampson an' he let me 'ave a leg o' pork, cheap.' He unwrapped the newspaper and displayed the meat. 'See? That'll mek a meal or two, eh?'

'It's a grand piece o' meat,' Mrs Sullivan said, turning back to the sink and plunging her arms into the suds once more. 'It'll do us for the best part of a week, hot an' cold. I tell you someone who won't be too pleased that you're goin' to sea, though, an' that's young Linnet. She's rare fond o' you, lad, for all she pretends otherwise. She'll miss you turble bad.'

'I wish I believed that,' Roddy said gloomily. 'She's that keen on 'er bloomin' job, she talks about nothin' else when we go out. I met 'er out of work the other day an' she were talkin' to a feller.' He snorted disdainfully. 'A bleedin' insurance clerk, whatever that may be – not quite like a seaman on the SS *Mary Rose*.'

'Well, I hope you haven't signed on because of the things Linnie said about butchering,' Mrs Sullivan said absently, pulling a sheet out of the water and beginning to wring it viciously. She had lost her job at the bakery on Derby Road when they started to cut down on staff and now she took in washing, a miserable, badly-paid business much hated by her family. 'She only said butcherin' were a low business to get a rise out of you, son. She knew it were a decent trade, really. Only the money weren't so good, I'm bound to admit that.'

'The money went down as soon as jobs began to get scarce,' her son pointed out. He crossed the kitchen and opened the back door into the noisome little yard in which the mangle stood. 'Old Sampson weren't a bad boss, but when folk start askin' for smaller and smaller parcels of meat something's gorra go. And I'd been there a good while. Lemme give you an 'and with them sheets, Mam, they're too 'eavy for you.'

'Oh go on wi' you – not that I'm not grateful for your young arms,' Mrs Sullivan said breathlessly, heaving the sheet out of the cooling water. 'Grab a hold o' this, then!'

'You go on wi' the washing, whilst I mangle,' Roddy

advised her. He went into the yard, dunked the sheet in the big rainwater barrel which his mother used as a rinse and then fed it through the mangle twice to get the last drop of water out. Then he shook it, pegged it on a section of the washing line and returned to the kitchen. 'I wonder what Linnie's doin' tonight? I might pop round, later.'

'Go sooner,' Mrs Sullivan advised, wringing a second sheet over the suds and then handing it to her son. 'No point in not tellin' her as soon as you can. Get yourself some bread an' scrape an' a cuppa – you can make me one, as well – then go round to Exchange Flags. They don't finish till six, you've plenty of time.'

'Right, I will.' Roddy rinsed the next sheet, mangled it, pegged it on the line, then rubbed a hand thoughtfully across his chin and heard the resultant rasp with mixed feelings. Seamen could have beards, and it would be grand not to have to shave each day, but Linnet liked a feller to be tidy. Perhaps he'd have a shave before he left, dazzle her with a smooth chin as well as with the news that he had joined the merchant service as a deckhand and would be off the following week.

'All done?' Mrs Sullivan appeared in the doorway with an armful of pillowcases. 'My, I'll be glad when these are done, that Mrs Pedham from the Angel on Dale Street believes in gettin' value for money – still, once they're ironed young Jack delivers 'em and she pays up prompt, I'll give 'er that.'

'I wish you didn't have to do it, though,' Roddy said. 'When I send my allotment home, perhaps you'll be able to ease off a bit. Or you might get another cleaning job.'

'Aye, an' pigs might fly,' Mrs Sullivan said. She wiped sweat off her forehead with the back of her arm and decorated herself with soapsuds. 'Never mind, eh? You don't hear me complainin'.'

'Oh you, you never moan,' Roddy said affectionately.

He went over to the fire and pulled the kettle over the flame, then went to the cupboard and got out a screw of tea, a tin of condensed milk, a half loaf of bread and a packet of margarine. 'What d'you want on your bread and scrape? Can we spare some conny onny?'

'There's nothin' I like better on a buttie than conny onny,' Mrs Sullivan admitted. 'But will there be enough to wet the tea? I don't fancy me tea black an' I've no fresh milk.'

Her son peered into the opened tin of condensed milk.

'Aye, plenty for both,' he decided, standing the tin to one side and beginning to saw at the loaf with the ancient bread-knife. 'Soon have a feast ready, our Mam. Then I'll be off to see Linnet.'

Linnet was finishing off a letter for Mr Cowan, typing away as fast as she could, when he came into the pool and looked around in the rather helpless way men often did when they found themselves amongst so many women – and all working away like mad things, of course, since there were many more shorthand typists in the city than there were jobs. She smiled at him, then waved a hand.

'If it's the letter to General Accident you're after, Mr Cowan, it's over here,' she called. 'I've all but finished it . . . just got the last para to go.'

Mr Cowan looked relieved. He was a bespectacled, dark-haired man in his forties who prided himself, Linnet imagined, on always being spotlessly turned out. He had patent-leather hair – well, it shone like patent-leather – an impeccable dark suit, a severe navy-blue tie with tiny red dots on it and a pencil-line moustache. He was also one of the shy ones.

Linnet had realised soon after starting her first job that the men in the office could be divided into two types: those who were shy with girls and those who felt it obligatory on all occasions to flirt with everything female, even the likes of stout Miss Harper and stringy Miss Elphinstone, who ran the typing pool between them. On the whole, she preferred the shy ones. Rude jokes whispered in one's ear were bad enough, but a squeeze in the confines of the jerky old lift or a hand lingering too long on shoulder or hip could lead to all sorts of trouble. Or so she believed, for she had not been with the Eagle and General Life Insurance Company long enough to be sure how her superiors would behave towards a girl who forgot herself sufficiently to allow a young man to take liberties.

But Mr Cowan was definitely diffident, which was strange because he was married, with a child, and married men, in Linnet's experience, were not generally shy with girls.

But now Mr Cowan was making his way through the desks to Linnet's side and Linnet, with great panache, was finishing off the letter, checking it with a swift glance, and ripping all four copies out of the machine. The top copy was to be sent to the customer, in this case to another insurance company, the second would be added to the fat file, the third would go back with Mr Cowan for his personal file and the fourth, the pink one, would go in Linnet's desk drawer so that any errors, discovered later, could be traced back to her.

'Nearly ready, sir,' Linnet said cheerfully as Mr Cowan bent over her desk and began to read the letter across the top of her head. 'I'll just do you an envelope.'

She took a suitably sized envelope out of her desk drawer, typed the name and address swiftly onto the front of it, and slid the envelope into place. She dealt quickly with the flimsies, then turned to Mr Cowan, who seemed to have finished reading and was fiddling in his pocket, no doubt for the fountain pen with which to add his impressively curly signature at the end of the page.

'Is it all right, sir? Only if so, it can be sent straight down with the rest of our post rather than going back to your office for checking and signature and then coming back here.'

'It seems to be correct,' Mr Cowan said rather stiffly. Linnet was just thinking that he was a bit mean with his praise when he added, 'You type very nicely, Miss er . . . er. I've yet to find an erasure on a letter sent up by you.'

He could tell who had typed each letter by the initials at the top of the page, of course. LM for Linnet Murphy and AC for . . . well, for Mr Cowan was the best she could do since she had no idea what his first name was. So now she turned in her chair and smiled up at him, glad to feel that she was a little bit appreciated in this huge firm she had so recently joined.

'Thank you, sir,' she said eagerly. 'I do try not to make mistakes because rubbing out looks so messy.'

It was not precisely what she had meant to say – it sounded rather smug put into words like that – but it pleased Mr Cowan.

'Exactly what I always think,' he said. 'I must have a word with your supervisor.'

When he had taken the letter and gone Miss Everett, who sat next to Linnet and was the nearest thing to a friend she had in the new offices, leaned across the narrow aisle between them. 'Well, you've made a conquest,' she said archly. 'Our Mr Cowan seldom speaks to the typists. Ever so shy he is – he's been worse since his wife died.'

'Died? But she couldn't have been all that old,' Linnet said, beginning to tidy her desk in preparation for going home when Miss Harper or Miss Elphinstone rang the bell. The Eagle and General was very like school if you discounted the number of young men prowling around.

'How old is he, forty-two or three? How did she die?'

'You sound like Cock Robin,' Miss Everett said, giggling. 'Oh no, it's who saw her die, I said the fly with my little eye, I saw her die.'

'Oh don't be silly, Miss Everett,' Linnet said, carrying an armful of files over to the filing tray for the office girls to take back to the basement presently. 'It was a perfectly ordinary question.'

'Yes, of course. Sorry. She died of a fever . . .'

'And no one could save her, and that was the end of sweet Mollie Malone,' sang Linnet under her breath, returning to her desk. 'There you are, I can be silly as well. And it did rather fit in with the song, wouldn't you say?'

'You're a card, Miss Murphy,' Miss Everett said, rather as though she meant something much ruder, though. 'She died of milk fever, I should have said. It was awfully sad. She'd just had a little baby girl, you see, so Mr Cowan was left with the kid, to manage as best he could.'

'Heavens. And how does he manage?'

'Oh, I don't know; I believe he has a mother,' Miss Everett said vaguely. 'I say, did he say he wanted a word with our supervisor?'

'I believe he did,' Linnet said. She put her shorthand notebook into her top drawer and arranged her pencils alongside it, then she straightened her typewriter, which would move sideways, crablike, across her desk as the day wore on, and unfolded her leatherette typewriter cover. 'I expect he was going to tell her she'd done a good job getting me to work here.'

'Oh, the conceit! No, but you see, Mr Cowan's just been upgraded. Mr Smith retired ten days or so ago and Mr Cowan will be doing his job. And that means he'll need a secretary and won't be using the pool any more.'

'Oh, that's a pity,' Linnet said, just as the bell tinkled for the end of the day. All over the long room with its lines of desks and its myriad young ladies, typewriter covers were slammed down over the machines in almost perfect unison, as though the girls had been practising for weeks. 'Just when he's noticed my work . . .'

'You *are* slow,' Miss Everett said in a superior tone. She picked up her handbag and headed for the door, speaking over her shoulder as she went. 'He's looking for a secretary, Miss Murphy, and at least half the typing pool are hoping he's looking at them!'

All the way along the corridor and down the stairs, Linnet mulled over the remark. She could see why Miss Everett had said it but she was sensible enough to attach very little importance to it. Had she not worked like anything at her first job, at the Majestic Assurance Company, staying late, arriving early? First as an office girl, then a junior typist, finally as a trainee shorthand typist? And despite two years' service, had she not been told to pick up her cards when the bosses decided to cut down on staff? There's a depression on, the remaining girls had said wearily as they waved goodbye to half the staff and prepared to do twice the amount of work for rather less wages. You can't even complain when there's a hundred people fighting for every job – you dare not complain. She knew she had been lucky to get this new job.

Still, unlikely though it was that she would be given preferment, she could dream, couldn't she? She stood at her tram stop and stood, also, on the tram when it finally came clattering along, because it was crowded with homegoing workers, all as eager to get away from the city centre as she. She was pressed and pushed and pulled, but at last they reached The Boulevard and she dismounted, sighed and began to walk towards her home.

The sound of someone running along the pavement and shouting breathlessly wasn't all that unusual, but she glanced back anyway, just in case she had left her handbag on the bus or missed a friend – and she had. It was Roddy.

'Hello, our Roddy,' Linnet said as he panted up beside her. She remembered that he had been for an interview for a job on board a ship and guessed from his whole manner that he had been successful, but knew he would want to tell her himself. 'What happened? Any luck?'

There had been other jobs, other interviews; she could still remember the droop of his shoulders when someone had turned him down. But that had been when he had been kicked out of his previous job, before Sampsons on St John's market had taken him on. Then he had been unemployed and beginning to believe himself unemployable. This time he had a job, a steady one, and simply wanted to change from one wage packet to another, or that was how she saw it. And going to sea could be dangerous – she did not know if she approved.

'I gorr . . . I mean I got it.' She had nagged him to improve his speech and now she patted his cheek affectionately, grateful that he realised she was doing it for his own good and did not laugh at her or ignore her advice. 'We sail on Tuesday, at high tide, queen – I'm a deckhand on the SS *Mary Rose*.'

'That's wonderful, Roddy . . . but I'll miss you very much, you know. How long will your voyages be? Is she a liner, or a cargo ship? I bet you're excited . . . how do you know you won't be seasick?'

'She's a cargo ship, a sizeable coaster, in fact. She's out of Liverpool and carries timber, bricks, all sorts, up and down the coast and across to the Scottish islands, sometimes over to Sweden, and to Ireland, as well. Which means we could be away a week, or six, depending. But I don't mind, me Dad was on cargo ships, he says they're all right provided you keep out of the holds. How about comin' out wi' me tonight, to celebrate, like? I shaved on purpose an' I'm still wearin' me best kecks!'

'We-ell . . . were you thinking of going to the flicks?' Linnet asked hopefully. She did love the cinema, particularly the talkies, which had put the old silent films completely in the shade. 'I've not been to the Rotunda for absolutely ages.'

'I thought a dance; then we could cuddle,' Roddy said with all his usual forthrightness. 'I like to get me arms round you, Linnet Murphy, an' hold you to me manly bosom!'

It made Linnet laugh but she took hold of his arm and gave it a pinch, then stood on tiptoe to kiss his cheek.

'Roddy Sullivan, you are a darlin',' she said vigorously. 'Tell you what, though I know it's not at all the thing, come back to my room and I'll make us a little supper, then we can decide where to go later. What do you say?'

'Gee whizz,' Roddy said in true cinema fashion. 'You say the cutest things, Miss Murphy – sure I'll come to your place!'

'Well, I know people might talk, but you're like a brother to me, always have been,' Linnet pointed out righteously. 'And whilst I do the cooking you can tell me all about your new job. Now, why are you pulling that long face, our Roddy?'

'I am not your bleedin' brother,' Roddy shouted, causing several heads to turn accusingly in their direction. 'Nor I don't want to be. I want . . . I want . . .'

'I want never got; do you remember how your mam used to say that to us when we were kids?' Linnet said diplomatically. She caught his hand and squeezed his fingers hard, then smiled up into his face. 'She says it to Freddy and Jack still, I expect. Oh Roddy, don't scowl, it spoils your nice, friendly face. Come on, I'll race you to No 8!'

In all the excitement of going round to the Sullivans' and helping Roddy decide what he should pack for his first voyage, Linnet completely forgot the brief visit of Mr Cowan to the typing pool and Miss Everett's remarks. In fact, when she went up to Canning dock to wave Roddy off very early on Tuesday morning, with a light mist hovering over the face of the Mersey and the streets strangely hushed, she found herself crying so hard that work scarcely seemed important at all. Roddy was her childhood companion, her dearest friend, and he was going away, into danger, where she could not follow!

'The lad'll only be away five or six weeks, aren't we daft?' Mrs Sullivan said through her tears, clutching Linnet's arm. 'Why, when 'e comes 'ome it'll be like me 'olidays, that's all!'

'I know, but I like seeing him on a Sunday, I like talkin' to him,' Linnet said, rubbing her eyes with the backs of her hands. 'He's grand to talk to, is your Roddy.'

The two women stared out across the shining flag-stones of the dock as the SS *Mary Rose*, siren sounding forlornly across the oily water, disappeared into the mist. Then they dried their eyes, blew their noses, said six weeks would soon go and wasn't it a great chance for him, and went to a canny house nearby to eat bacon and eggs and drink strong tea before departing, Roddy's mother back to her home and Linnet to the insurance office on Exchange Flags.

'Miss Murphy? Miss Harper wants a word with you. Go to her room at once, please.'

'Of course, Miss Elphinstone. I'll go right away.'

Linnet felt her cheeks grow hot with apprehension but

she typed to the end of the line anyway, then stood up. Summonses to the office usually meant that you had done something wrong but though she racked her brains as she walked sedately across the typing pool she could think of nothing. She had been in early this morning because of seeing Roddy off, she had started work immediately, however, and had not waited until her normal arrival time. What could it be? And did she look neat and tidy, because Miss Harper was always nagging them about personal appearance? She would have liked to rush along to the ladies' cloaks to check her hair, make sure that her nose wasn't shiny and that she hadn't managed to transfer the ink from her typewriter ribbon to her cheeks or chin, but she would have to take a chance. Miss Harper disliked being kept waiting even more than she disliked a slapdash appearance.

Miss Elphinstone, being the junior of the two supervisors, usually worked at her machine at the long desk in the typing pool, opposite the door, whilst Miss Harper, as senior supervisor, could mostly be found in a tiny cell of an office just up the corridor. Here she checked the work going in and coming out, took calls from members of staff who wanted a shorthand writer to take dictation, chose who should go where and generally made sure that the pool ran smoothly. Linnet had only worked here for five weeks but already she knew that Miss Harper also brewed coffee in the office, sent out for sandwiches which she munched whilst hiding behind a large sheet of legal paper, and took personal calls on the telephone which stood on the right-hand side of her desk. Miss Elphinstone, who helped out when the typing pool was frantically busy and never let 'her girls' down if she could avoid it, was popular amongst them, to an extent at least, but Miss Harper was much disliked.

'She can be vindictive,' Linnet had been warned. 'If she takes agin you she can make trouble. It's best to be very, very polite to Miss Harper and don't you ever call her just "Miss", 'cos that's asking for trouble; she likes us to use her full name.'

So Linnet tapped on the door, waited a moment, and then walked in.

Miss Harper was sitting behind her desk, apparently writing in a large ledger. There was a strong smell of coffee in the air and an empty cup stood beside the streamlined white typewriter which was a sign of Miss Harper's power and influence – everyone else, including Miss Elphinstone, had a black machine. There was talk, of course, about how she got the machine; but I don't believe a word of it, Linnet told herself, she's too fat and spiteful and although Mr Cripps, the manager, is old and has bad breath, he surely wouldn't . . .

'Good morning, Miss Harper. Miss Elphinstone said you wanted to see me.'

Linnet stood as the nuns had taught her; feet demurely side by side, hands clasped before her, eyes on the ground. Then she looked up, because she knew people thought you were sly if you didn't look them in the face and saw Miss Harper was staring at her. She was looking at Linnet as though she couldn't understand something; her eyes were going up and down, up and down . . .

'Ah, yes. So you're Murphy, I couldn't quite recall. You've not been with us long I believe, Miss Murphy.'

'Just five weeks, Miss Harper,' Linnet murmured. What was this all about? And why was the wretched woman staring at her like that, as though she was searching for a pair of horns growing out of Linnet's newly shingled head?

'So short a time? And already you've managed to catch a gentleman's eye. Tell me, just how did you do it? I can't say your looks are in any way exceptional – I'm not saying you're plain, precisely, but you certainly aren't as eye-catching as, say, Miss Franchini, yet no one's approached me about her, yet.'

Miss Franchini was a flashing-eyed brunette, the result of a liaison between an Italian seaman and an Irish barmaid from a waterside pub. She was very beautiful but liable to throw tantrums – and typewriter rubbers – when things annoyed her. Perplexed, Linnet tried to remember whether she herself had ever lost her temper whilst working for the company, and decided she had not. So what on earth was Miss Harper going on about?

'I'm sorry, I don't quite . . .'

'You don't quite what, Miss Murphy? What have I said that has puzzled you so? Surely you must realise why I've called you into my office?'

Linnet shook her head. There seemed little point in pretending; she was completely in the dark. 'No, I'm afraid . . .'

'Oh, come now! Mr Cowan came to me a fortnight ago and said he would like you to do his work for a while. Since then, he's been over to your desk on at least two occasions – at least! Surely you did not imagine that he was so enamoured of your work that he had to see you personally on two occasions, when he could just as easily have telephoned through to me that the work was urgent? I don't know what you said to him, Miss Murphy, or what you offered . . .'

'I said nothing, except that his letters were in my "out" tray,' Linnet said firmly. 'As for offering . . .'

Miss Harper cut in at once, and Linnet saw that her cheeks were faintly flushed. 'No, that was badly put. Anyway, you'd best pack your personal belongings; you're leaving us.'

'Today? Without working out any notice? But I don't

understand, I've done nothing wrong, there have been no complaints . . .'

'Yes, you're leaving us. But only, you little simpleton, to move up to the second floor as Mr Cowan's secretary. As if you didn't know!' Miss Harper hissed, her eyes narrowing. 'Why, you must think I was born yesterday!'

A dozen retorts, all of them unkind, danced into Linnet's head, but she banished them firmly. This was a good job, and a secretarial job was beyond her wildest dreams. She would not put it past Miss Harper to be saying all this as some form of nasty practical joke, but just in case . . .

'Thank you, Miss Harper,' she said, instead 'I'll go and get my things together.' And before the older woman could say another word she had turned and left the room.

Back in the typing pool, it was a nine days' wonder, of course. Only Miss Everett said that she had known all along and that wasn't Miss Murphy a dark horse?

'Come back and see us,' the girls begged as she emptied her desk drawers and filled the large paper sack which Miss Elphinstone had given her. 'Don't go all snobby on us, come back and have your sandwiches with us now and then.'

'Of course I will,' Linnet said stoutly. 'Besides, I probably won't be a secretary for long, not once they realise I've never been one before and don't know the ropes. Oh, I'll be back in the pool before you can say knife, see if I'm not.'

And she might have been, but for two people.

Mr Cowan was the first, and he was on her side from the start. He made it plain that he had chosen her out of the typing pool because he thought she would suit him, and suit him she did. He explained, slowly and carefully, what he wanted her to do and was always quick to congratulate her when she got things right – a very different attitude from that of Miss Harper, who took rightness for granted and grew furiously angry over the tiniest mistake.

The other was Miss Beasley, whose room she shared, for even someone as important as Mr Cowan did not have a private room for his secretary. Miss Beasley was twenty-four, engaged to be married to a successful plumber called Joseph Cartwright, and very elegant. She was tall and slim, with white-blonde hair and large light-blue eyes. She dressed in impeccable dark suits and crisp light-coloured blouses and had a pleasant manner though rather a strident voice. She talked in a very posh way when her boss, Mr Griseworth, was about, and with a local accent when she and Linnet were by themselves. And she was the epitome of secretarial efficiency. She told Linnet she was, using those very words, and when Linnet said, half-laughing, that she didn't know what an epitome was, she threw over a worn copy of Nuttalls's Dictionary and told her new colleague to look it up.

'You've gorra be good at your work, queen,' she said on Linnet's first day, "cos if you get sent back to the pool old Harps'll make your life a misery. Still, I reckon you must be good or old Cowie wouldn't have got you to work for him, but there's good an' good, if you understand me. This job ain't just shorthand an' typing, not once they make you a secretary it ain't. It's book his ticket on the train, get seats at the theatre, take his best suit in for cleaning, buy flowers for his wife on her birthday – remember her birthday come to that, when sure as eggs he's clean forgot. Oh aye, you'll be mam and dad to the feller, you'll all but wipe his bum for him, and if he thanks you a couple of times a year you'll be walking on air, ready to lay down your life for the bugger.'

The bad language, coming from such an unlikely source, made Linnet giggle. 'Is that all true, or are you kidding me?' she asked incredulously. 'I wouldn't know where to start – I've never even used a telephone, you know, and the thought of doing that scares me, let alone booking tickets.'

'Stick with me, honey,' Miss Beasley said, imitating the latest American star to hit the silver screen. 'And you won't go far wrong. By the way, I'm Rose. You?'

'Oh . . . I'm Linnet. Hello, Rose.'

'Hello, Linnet. First names are friendlier, I always say, but we'll only use them when we're by ourselves or out o' the office, because it sounds unbusinesslike. Now come over here and I'll show you how to make a telephone call.'

Linnet was perched on the windowsill in the communal kitchen of No 8, eating toast and looking out at the backyard criss-crossed with laden washing lines, when the door burst open and one of the other residents came in, backwards, having opened the door by butting it with her bottom. She was carrying a heavily laden tray.

'Morning, Margaret; what've you got there?' Linnet asked, eyeing her fellow resident as Margaret thumped the tray down on the wooden draining board. 'It looks like a year's washing up to me.'

'Cheeky mare – it's only a week's,' Margaret said. She was a square, muscular girl of Linnet's own age, clad, today, in a black skirt with stains down the front and a faded gingham blouse. Her substantial legs were bare and she wore down-at-heel pumps on her feet. 'I don't see the point of washin' up while there's a clean cup in the 'ouse. Ain't it a grand day, though? You're workin' this morning, I suppose, but I'm catchin' the tram an' goin' up to the market. Anything I can get you whiles I'm there?'

'Oh, Margaret, you're a pal – Rose and I thought we

might go out this afternoon as it's so sunny so I shan't get a chance to do me shopping. I could do wi' some veggies – spuds and a cabbage would be grand, though if they're selling something nicer, like peas, I wouldn't mind a pound of 'em. And a bit of meat, enough for two, in case I have a visitor.'

'Oh, aye? Roddy in port, then?' Margaret tried to look arch but only succeeded in looking nosy, her black eyes glittering with curiosity and a hopeful smile curving her mouth. She did like to be first with the news did Margaret!

'No. Not for another week.'

'Oh? Then who might you be cookin' for, come Sunday?'

'Honestly Margaret, it could be anyone, I know enough people! There's Roddy's mum, she pops round from time to time, and then there's me friend Rose from work, and Anita, me old school pal . . .'

'Which? Which one will you be entertainin', come Sunday?'

'None of 'em, so far as I know. It's just that a bit of meat for two can be eaten cold on Monday, or, if I *do* have an unexpected visitor . . . see what I'm getting at?'

'You're tellin' me loud ones, that's what,' Margaret said with unimpaired cheerfulness. 'Makin' me think you was entertainin' someone! I thought it might be the feller you work for – I'd be made up if I could just set eyes on him – but no, you was havin' me on. So it's peas if they've gorrem, cabbage if they ain't, an' a bit o' meat for two. Want some wet nellies for your afters?'

'I don't think they'd keep all that well,' Linnet said, wrinkling her nose. 'Get me some fruit for a pie, would you, chuck? Anything they're selling.'

'Right. Where's your chink?'

'Oh, hang on.' Linnet slid off the windowsill and went

194

over to her handbag hanging on the back of the door with her jacket; there was no point in climbing the stairs more than you had to each day, so she usually left for work as soon as she'd eaten her breakfast. She fished around in the bag and produced a shilling. 'Will this do?'

'That'll do,' Margaret allowed. She took the money and slid it into her apron pocket. 'If you're out when I get back I'll hang onto the stuff, awright?'

'Grand. Thanks, love,' Linnet said as Margaret disappeared, slamming the door behind her. She liked most of the other residents in the big, once-grand old house, and Margaret was no exception, though some of the other girls said she was no better than she ought to be and that the young men she brought home were not, as she claimed, cousins but customers. It could have been true; Margaret was sloppy to the point of sluttishness in the house but dressed up to the nines just to walk down to the corner shop. But whatever her occupation, Margaret was kind, generous when able to be so and good company, and who could ask for more?

Not me, certainly, Linnet thought now, washing up her cup and plate and standing them on the stained dresser beside the rest of her kitchen utensils. Again, with a kitchen on the ground floor and a flat under the eaves there was little point in lugging pots, pans and cutlery up and down and everyone in the house did the same so things rarely went missing.

I don't mind Auntie Sullivan and Roddy coming round, Linnet told herself now, automatically tidying the kitchen and rinsing out the tea-towel before hanging it on the piece of string which the girls had looped across the sink for just that purpose. But I wouldn't like Rose to come. She is so nice, but she wouldn't think much of it, though she would have liked Mammy's rooms.

The thought of little Evie brought a lump to her

daughter's throat, for the previous year she had at long last had definite proof of her mother's death. A friend of Mr Sullivan's, a seaman on the Atlantic run, had volunteered to make some enquiries next time he docked at Staten Island and had come home with an old newspaper cutting telling of the death of Evie Murphy, whom theatre-goers might remember as the little Evie of a few years back.

He had even bought flowers and put them on the grave, and had refused Linnet's offer of payment.

'I remember little Evie when she played at the Royal Court,' he said gruffly. 'Mebbe you'll go over yourself, one day. Put the money towards that.'

Linnet thanked him, but she knew she would never go to New York herself. She had been left, more or less forgotten, and though she bore little Evie no grudge, neither was she foolishly sentimental. She had loved her mammy and her mammy, she believed, had loved her, but with little Evie's death Linnet had been cast even more on her own resources and now it took her all her time and energy just to keep herself respectable and fed with a roof over her head. And no one would blame me for not missing someone who I'd not seen for so long, Linnet told herself a trifle defensively. Our lives were running on different tracks long before Mammy died.

She picked up the mop and went swiftly over the floor, then glanced up at the clock which had been Roddy's gift when he came ashore for his first leave. She had put it in the kitchen because they all needed a reminder of the time down here and there was simply no space in her tiny room. But there was no hurry, it was still only half past seven in the morning. She and the other girls got up very early in the summer because the attic rooms in particular grew both warm and airless as the day went on. So they did their housework whilst it was still quite cool and then, when they returned from work, they could sit outside on the strip of grass between them and the road, play games, call out, and relax until darkness fell and their rooms were losing their heat once more.

Time for one more quick cup of tea, then I really must get going, Linnet told herself, bustling across to her teapot and testing the side of it with the backs of her fingers. It was still hot enough for one more cup. She poured the tea and then sat on the windowsill once more, dreaming away to herself and sipping lukewarm tea carefully; it would not do to have a teastain on her cream-coloured blouse nor on the green cotton skirt which was so elegantly long that it brushed her ankles as she walked.

She had to be smart for work. Rose said it was important and anyway, what was the point in having some decent clothes if they were only worn once in a blue moon? Roddy took her out when he was home but the SS *Mary Rose* had a quick turn-round and he sometimes said jokingly that their lips barely met in their first kiss before they were wrenched apart again and he was off once more.

And Linnet was beginning to suspect that Roddy really enjoyed the life, that he would be a seaman, from choice, for ever if he could. Oh he kept declaring that he wanted to marry her and settle down, but settling down meant, presumably, getting a shore-job, and there was so much unemployment in Liverpool that no one with any sense would advise him to do anything so risky. Especially when he was good at what he did now and enjoyed it and had thoroughly disliked butchery.

But she must stop dreaming and get ready for work. Linnet rinsed her cup, emptied her teapot, then stood back and checked her reflection in the window pane. It wasn't ideal but she could at least see if she had a droopy hem or a bad mark on her blouse. But the most careful check did not reveal anything particularly wrong, and since she and Rose intended to go on the overhead railway right along to Seaforth Sands, she would do her best to look neat and pretty – Rose certainly would. In the summer months Rose favoured cotton skirts and tops or well cut summer dresses with white piping at neck and hem. She had a real flair for clothes and Linnet was happy to take her advice when buying a new garment of any description. Rose had been with her when she chose her green cotton skirt and she had great faith in its ability to make her look nice.

Having checked her appearance Linnet reached for her long cream linen jacket and handbag, slid her feet into her sensible walking shoes, cast a last glance around the room and set off. Her step was light and she felt like singing as she crossed the rather dingy hallway. She let herself out into the morning and saw Mr Proud, from next door, tapping his way along the pavement. He would be on his way to the tram stop and since he was blind Linnet hurried to give him a hand. Not in an obvious sort of way, of course, since Mr Proud had his pride, ha ha, but unobtrusively, to ensure he wasn't pushed or jostled at the stop and that he got a seat when the tram arrived.

'Morning, Mr Proud,' Linnet said rather breathlessly when she reached him. He walked fast despite his disability. 'You don't work on a Saturday morning, do you?'

Mr Proud was a piano tuner in one of the biggest music shops in the city; Linnet, who had learned to play to a fair standard on her mother's little upright, often talked wistfully to him of how she had enjoyed using the instrument, and he had promised to find her a good, cheap secondhand model when she had saved up. She knew she could not have it whilst she remained in her tiny room at No 8, but Linnet was an optimist. One day, she told herself, she would get a better job and move to a room where, if she wished, she might entertain a guest now and then, or even swing a cat! But now Mr Proud turned towards her, smiling.

'Ah, it's Miss Murphy, I never mistake a voice. You're quite right, I don't go round to people's homes to tune their instruments on a Saturday morning, but I do play in the store. People who can't play a note buy pianos, you know, but they all fancy themselves experts on tone and touch when they hear someone else play. So I sit down and tickle the ivories for them and if they buy I get a small – very small – bonus. Now have we reached the tram stop? My stick says we have.'

'Your stick says right,' Linnet assured him. 'You're magic, Mr Proud, I don't know how you tell where you are, I'm sure.'

'Sounds reflect differently off different objects,' Mr Proud told her. 'A tram makes different sounds on corners, you must have noticed, and then there's the paving-edge. There's quite a big piece of kerb missing just before you reach the stop.'

'I think you must be the most observant person I've ever met,' Linnet said humbly. 'And I won't tell you that the tram's coming, because I'm sure you know, nor that we've about a dozen people in the queue before us.'

'Thirteen,' Mr Proud said gravely, then chuckled as though he could see Linnet's astonished look. 'Just teasing, Miss Murphy!'

Linnet had been in a happy frame of mind when she got on the tram and arriving at the office to find their small room full of sunshine and flower-scents lifted her spirits even further. She was first in and hung her jacket on the peg behind the door, then turned to take the covers off the typewriters – and simply stared.

On her desk, laid carefully across her machine, was the source of the lovely scent. It was a positive sheaf of pink and red roses – there must have been a couple of dozen lying there, their stems wrapped in the pale pink and silver paper used, Linnet knew, by a very superior flower shop indeed.

A passing messenger boy, peering in through the doorway, whistled. 'Cor, 'oo's gerrin' wed, then, eh? If that's Miss Beasley's feller 'e's splashin' out ain't 'e? That little lot cost a bob or three!'

'I don't think it can be Mr Cartwright, since he sent Miss Beasley a bouquet of pinks and cornflowers only yesterday,' Linnet said cautiously. She approached the flowers as though they might bite her, touching the nearest head with one forefinger. 'And they're on *my* typewriter; it must be a mistake.'

'Well, I didn't deliver 'em,' the messenger boy said positively. 'Ain't there a card, Miss M?'

'No, I don't think . . . oh yes, there is,' Linnet said, considerably relieved. The nightmare of having to lug the flowers around three floors, each one of which contained countless rooms, had just occurred to her. 'Let me see . . .'

It wasn't a card, in fact, but a tiny white envelope. It had no name on, which made her hesitate for a moment, but she slit it open and pulled out the card, turning it over to read the carefully scripted note on the other side.

Miss Murphy; would you do me the honour of lunching with me today? she read, though not out loud. *I should be most grateful for your company and also for some advice. Yours sincerely, A. Cowan.*

'Oo's it from, then?' the messenger boy asked. He was still standing in the doorway but so curious was he that his neck had stretched out like a giraffe and his eyes, apparently on stalks, seemed to start from their sockets. 'Come on, gel, are they for you?'

'Yes, they're mine. From a – a gentleman friend,' Linnet said, picking the bouquet up and burying her nose thankfully in the scented blossoms. She had no intention of telling anyone – anyone at all – that the flowers came from Mr Cowan! 'Do go away, Frankie, and shut my door!'

'Some gentleman! Guess 'e's rollin' in the readies,' Frankie said enviously. 'Bet 'e's old as the 'ills an' ugly, too. Fellers wi' that much money always is.'

'Go away,' Linnet said nervously. Suppose Mr Cowan had come out of his office up the corridor and heard that unflattering view! 'I would like to do some work this morning if it's all the same to you, young man.'

Frankie shrugged and began to withdraw. 'Awright, awright, keep your bleedin' 'air on,' he said airily. 'It ain't nine o'clock yet, nowhere near, so if I want to . . . oh! Sorry, miss, I didn't see you standin' there.'

'I imagine you did not,' Rose said frostily, rubbing her elbow where Frankie had backed into her. She waited until Frankie, crestfallen, had taken himself off, then came in, shut the door, and began to take her jacket off. 'What a crowd on the tram – you don't know how much I'm longing for Seaforth sands – good Lord above, where did you get them from?'

'From Mr Cowan,' Linnet said in hollow tones, completely forgetting her resolve of two minutes earlier. 'Just read the note, Rose! He wants to take me out to lunch today . . . oh Miss Beasley, what on earth am I to do?'

'Goodbye, Seaforth Sands,' Rose said regretfully, then came across the office and took the flowers and the note from Linnet's unresisting hands. She read the note, then looked up and smiled encouragingly at her friend. 'You must go, queen. He's a nice feller is Mr Cowan, he won't eat you. But he might feel like doing so if you turn him down.'

'Turn him *down*? You make it sound like a date, a proper date,' Linnet gasped. 'He's married . . . well, he's a widow, then. Widows don't take their secretaries on *dates*!'

'He's a widower, not a widow, and of course widowers take girls on dates,' Rose said bracingly. 'How else would they ever re-marry?'

'*Re-marry*? Oh, but-but-but-'

'Do stop stuttering, Miss Murphy, and listen for a minute. Mr Cowan is a widower but he isn't an old man despite what you seem to think. Do I seem like an old woman to you?'

'Honest to God, I've never thought . . . never said . . .' stammered Linnet, much embarrassed. When she had first met Rose she had indeed thought her somewhat long in the tooth, but that had not lasted. Now, she and Rose were just two girls, neither of whom was yet wed. 'You're only half-a-dozen years older than me, Rose! Oh, I'm sorry, I mean Miss Beasley. But Mr Cowan must be . . . well, I don't know how old he is, precisely, but he seems . . .'

'He's probably only in his early forties, not even twenty years older than me and not so much older than you, either,' Rose said. 'So stop thinking of him as an elderly man, because he isn't. Why, he couldn't even be your father, not unless he started awful young. And start practising saying, "*Thank you, Mr Cowan, I would be delighted to lunch with you today*," because that's what you mean and that's what you are jolly well going to do!'

'I can't! I couldn't possibly! What about Roddy? Oh how I would like to throw these *bloody* roses straight out o' the *bloody* window and forget they ever came!'

Now it was Rose's turn to giggle; she had never heard Linnet swear before. 'Yes, all right, I can see you're embarrassed by the whole business, but you mustn't be foolish, queen. Just you read that note again, careful like. Go on, do it now, whilst I put the roses in water for you.' She buried her own face in the blossoms, inhaling luxuriously. 'Now that's what I call a good scent,' she said, turning to leave the room. 'We'll be swooning wi' it by lunchtime, see if we aren't!'

When she had gone, Linnet got out the little card and read it again. And gradually, her fears began to subside. It was not a lover-like note, it was quite a sensible one. Mr Cowan wanted company; well, that was understandable, he had a little girl and no wife, he must have problems which he thought another woman might be able to solve. *But why didn't he ask a woman, in that case*? a little voice in her head demanded querulously. *Why ask a girl who's only nineteen*?

Perhaps, Linnet told herself, he simply doesn't know many women. But he does know me, I've been working as his secretary for three whole months and we've always got on very well. When I go through to take dictation we quite often have a little chat. The fact that the chat usually consisted of an enquiry as to her state of health, a polite rejoinder and then a request that she might bring him in coffee and biscuits for two people at eleven o'clock since he would have the general manager in his office at around that time was, she told herself, neither here nor there. Her boss was far too conscientious to indulge in light chat in the firm's time. And besides, on a Monday, when he enquired after her weekend, she often told him what she had done at some length, and he did the same. He had gone to New Brighton and sat on the sands, his daughter – her name was Mollie – had tasted her first ice-cream cone, they had come home with pink and peeling noses.

It wasn't much, but it was something. So when Rose came back with the flowers in a rather nice cut glass vase borrowed from the Claims Department, Linnet, pink-faced but determined, was about to set off for Mr Cowan's room.

'What was I to say?' she hissed as Rose sailed into the room with the flowers held out before her. 'Go on, tell me again or I'll make a pig's ear of it.'

'Thank you for the flowers, they're lovely, and I'd be delighted to have lunch with you,' Rose said, giving a mock curtsy and squealing as water tipped from the vase and splashed onto the floor. 'Go on, off with you!'

Linnet hurried down the corridor, repeating the words Rose had just said under her breath. She tapped on Mr Cowan's door and entered, and for a moment sheer terror rooted her to the spot, just inside the door, whilst she stared at her boss like a sparrow mesmerised by a snake.

She might have stood there for ever, until she dropped dead she thought later, but then she looked – really looked – at Mr Cowan, who had risen to his feet and was staring across at her, his eyes eager yet anxious; 'Like a kid waiting for a pat on the head but fearing a slap,' she told Rose later. He didn't look old any longer, either. He looked quite human, really, considering he was a head of department in a large insurance company.

Linnet cleared her throat. 'Thank you very much for the roses; they're really beautiful,' she said, departing from the script but not minding, now. 'And I'd be delighted to have lunch with you today.'

He smiled at her. He had smiled at her before, often, but not like this. Not a frank, broad smile which showed his teeth and made her smile back at him.

'I'm glad you didn't think I was being – well, fresh,' he said. 'We'll go somewhere nice – d'you fancy the Law-rence Hotel, on Mount Pleasant? The food's very good and the service is excellent. Or would you prefer some-where smaller, more . . . well, smaller?'

'I'd like somewhere smaller, really,' Linnet said shyly. 'I don't know much about restaurants though – you choose.'

'Well, why don't we go to the Albany on Oldhall Street?' Mr Cowan suggested. 'The surroundings are pleasant and it's quiet, too. The offices close at 12.30 today so I'll order a taxi for one o'clock – or do you need more time to make arrangements?'

'No, because R . . . Miss Beasley and I had planned to go to Seaforth Sands this afternoon,' Linnet said, and found she did not regret her missed outing now because she could see she would enjoy herself with Mr Cowan, though differently, of course. 'So a friend's doing my shopping. And I live by myself, of course, so there's no one at home I should tell.'

'Of course. Mollie's nanny usually leaves at two o'clock on a Saturday – she has the weekend off – but she's staying on today until teatime.' He glanced down at the desk, then across at her again. 'I thought, perhaps, we might – might go back to my place and take – take Mollie out with us, for some tea?'

'I'd love to meet her,' Linnet said warmly, and truthfully, too. She liked children but had very little to do with them, apart from two boys of eight and ten who lived in the rooms beneath hers and made the weekends hideous with their fights and quarrels when their parents were out.

Mr Cowan smiled again; well, beamed, really. He looked happy and relieved – and all I did was agree to go out to lunch and then to meet his little girl, Linnet thought with amazement.

'Good, good. And now, Miss Murphy, perhaps we had better get down to business. I've got half-a-dozen letters which should really go this morning . . . if you could fetch your pad and pencil?'

*

Lunch was a rare treat for Linnet, who had never been into a restaurant as smart and discreet as the Albany, let alone eaten such food. Mr Cowan had reserved a table and though there were other diners they took no notice of the quiet couple in the corner and very soon Linnet was chattering away to Mr Cowan as though she had known him all her life.

'Let me pour you some wine, Miss Murphy,' Mr Cowan said when the wine arrived, and Linnet felt her face grow hot. Her mother had warned her that gentlemen who pressed ladies to take drink might, occasionally, mean them harm. But how to refuse without giving offence?

'I've never drunk wine, but I d-don't think I shall care for it, Mr Cowan,' Linnet said, and then added, highly daring, 'I wonder whether I might, if – if it wouldn't inconvenience anyone, perhaps have some water, instead? Only I know that strong drink sometimes makes girls tiddly, and since I'm not used to it . . .'

Mr Cowan laughed. 'The last thing I want is a tiddly secretary, Miss Murphy! Of course you can have water but I'll order you a glass of fruit juice, or some lemonade, if you wish. I'm sorry I didn't think of it, because naturally a girl of your age wouldn't fancy – er – strong drink,' Mr Cowan said. 'Now let me help you to some of this excellent sole, and some of the shrimp sauce, too.'

Linnet was much relieved that she was not about to be pressed into drinking wine, though it looked innocent enough as it was poured into Mr Cowan's glass. It was a light golden colour and little bubbles formed on the bottom of the glass and then rose to the top, behaviour very similar to that of ginger beer, a beverage which Linnet much enjoyed. She watched Mr Cowan taking several glasses of the bubbly golden liquid without any ill effect and halfway through the meal, to her own tremendous surprise, Linnet heard her voice saying, 'The fruit juice is very nice, Mr Cowan, but I – I wonder if I might try just a little wine?' She waited for the sky to fall on her – having refused his early offer to now turn round and ask for wine seemed very daring indeed – but he just said, gravely, that it was a vintage of which most ladies he knew approved and poured her half a glass.

Linnet tasted it; it was absolutely delicious and the little bubbles fizzed pleasantly on her tongue. What was more, when she told Mr Cowan that it was really very nice he poured her a proper glass, and when she finished that the waiter, who had been hovering, brought a whole fresh bottle to the table and poured a little into a fresh glass. Mr Cowan tasted it and nodded, then told the waiter to pour his guest another glass.

'I don't think I'd better,' Linnet said regretfully. She had concluded that the beautiful glow and the warm self-confidence which had enveloped her might well be the work of the wine. Heaven knew what she might do if she drank yet more of the exciting beverage. 'Oh, do look at the trolley, Mr Cowan! What wonderful jellies and trifles and cakes!'

He smiled at her indulgently, fondly almost. 'I like to see you enjoying your food with such gusto,' he murmured. 'So many girls just pick at their plates – I hate that.'

'I'm greedy,' Linnet said, regretfully but without shame. 'I do so like nice food!'

'So do I,' Mr Cowan agreed. 'Ah, here comes the trolley – now you may choose whatever pudding you like best. And I'll have a nice cup of coffee and some cheese and biscuits.'

'I'll have . . . that one, please,' Linnet said, pointing to a concoction in which cream, strawberries and meringues seemed to play a large part. 'No thank you, I don't think I'll need any extra cream. And I'd like a coffee, too, please.'

As she dug her spoon into her pudding, Linnet reflected that, if her mother could have seen her now, she would have been most impressed. It had taken Linnet quite a long time, but eventually she had realised that the admirers and impresarios who had thronged little Evie's life had, in fact, been her mother's lovers. They had bought both little Evie and her daughter nice presents and had taken them out for meals very similar to this one – had given them a gay old time, in fact. Yet I, Linnet thought complacently, have got all this not by agreeing to go to bed with Mr Cowan, but by typing his letters nicely! It seemed a far better bargain than Evie's, to Evie's practical daughter.

Chapter Eight

On Monday morning, Rose was all agog to hear how her friend had got on with Mr Cowan. Linnet would have liked to keep her in suspense for a little, but since she was dying to talk about it and Rose was dying to listen, they very soon settled down to a good gossip, though they waited until their lunch-hour, since both spent busy mornings taking dictation and typing up the resultant letters.

'Well?' Rose said at last, as the two of them set off for the Nelson memorial where, on sunny days, they liked to sit to eat their sandwiches. 'Come on, what happened? Where did he take you?'

'We went to the Albany and had a lovely dinner – lunch, I mean; then we caught a taxi and went right to the other side of the city, to Mr Cowan's house. He lives in the most beautiful street, it's called Sunnyside, and the gardens all have trees and grass and that. The house is awfully smart and huge, Rose, bigger than any house I've ever been in before. And I met Mollie, that's his daughter, and Nanny Peters, and then Nanny Peters went off for the weekend and Mr Cowan and I took Mollie to the park and we fed the ducks and Mollie went on the swings. And then we had a delicious tea with buttered toast first and then cream cakes at ever such a nice little café on Smithdown Road, and after that Mr Cowan took me home in his huge car – I bet you didn't know he had a motor, did you, Rose? – and took me right to my front door. I was afraid he might suggest coming in with me, but he didn't, so I waved him off and trotted upstairs . . . it was a lovely day, honest to God it was.'

'And what did he want to talk to you about?' Rose enquired archly as they trotted down Exchange Passage and headed for the memorial. 'You've not mentioned that, I notice!'

'I don't actually know,' Linnet said slowly. 'I've just realised, he never asked my advice about anything, anything at all. We just had a really nice time, honest to God we did.'

'Perhaps it was a ruse to get you to go out with him,' Rose said shrewdly. 'He's got a private income, you know, as well as his salary. He may be afraid a girl is after his money, but he'd like to know you weren't like that. Besides he's really quite shy when he's not talking about insurance, wouldn't you say? Perhaps he just wanted to meet you outside the office and didn't know how else to persuade you.'

'He was nice, and we had a nice time,' Linnet repeated thoughtfully. 'And Mollie is a darling. There was only one thing which seemed odd . . .'

'What? Was it about the kid or about Mr Cowan?' Rose asked at once. 'Let's sit down quickly, though, queen. I spy a group of tatty 'eaded office clerks headin' for our favourite seat.'

They hurried across to the statue and got to the seats before the young men, who pretended they had never wanted to sit down anyway, and started to throw bits of bread at the pigeons whilst covertly eyeing the two girls sitting on the seat with their heads close.

'Any minute now one of 'em will come across and ask if we've got a light, or the time, or some such,' Rose said gloomily. 'Go on then, chuck. What was odd?'

'Well, it was Mollie. I don't know an awful lot about kids, any more than you do, Rose, but I've helped

Roddy's mam with his little brothers, and I don't think any kid should be as good as Mollie was. She's only just two and a half but she stood by her father and threw bread when he handed her a piece, never shouted out or tried to get near the ducks, never went near the water, even. I thought I'd better hold her skirt, but there was no need. She stayed where she was told to stand.'

'Isn't that good?' Rose said doubtfully. 'I'd ha' thought it were.'

'Oh, it's good, all right, it just isn't natural,' Linnet said. 'And it was the same at teatime. Mr Cowan lifted her onto a chair and there she sat. She drank milk out of a mug, no slopping it around, and then she ate a shortbread biscuit. There were lovely cakes but she never asked for one or reached out, even. I took a little round cake with marzipan leaves and a yellow flower on top and offered it to her and she looked scared . . . she put her hand out a little way, then snatched it back, then looked up at her daddy so – so doubtfully. And when I said, go on love, you take it, she didn't attempt to do so until he'd said the same.'

'Hmm. Do you think he's cruel to her? Is that what you're saying?'

'I don't think so. I don't know him very well, except in the office, but he seems proud of her, and I think he'd be affectionate to her if he knew how, but he doesn't seem to. To tell you the truth, Rose, I didn't take to Nanny Peters, good though she may be.'

'Ah ha, I thought there must be a snag somewhere,' Rose said with a smirk. 'How old is she?'

'Oh, young. In her early twenties, I should think. And pretty, too. But . . . there was something about her . . .'

'Do you think Mr Cowan was angling for her and asked you over to show her that he had other female friends?' Rose asked after a moment, when Linnet had done nothing but stare into space. 'Was that what it was?'

'Oh, Rose, all you ever think about is *that*,' Linnet said, not bothering to elaborate further. 'I don't think it was that, though I suppose it's perfectly possible. Nanny Peters didn't like me; I could tell. And I'm not sure she likes Mollie much either, for all she made a great fuss of her and kept tweaking her curls and straightening her skirts.'

'I see. Well, there's nothin' you can do about it, queen, unless he asks you to go round there again, of course.'

'No, but . . .'

'Excuse me, but has either of you young ladies got such a t'ing as a match about you? Me pal an' I are dyin' for a fag but neither of us thought to bring a box o' matches out wi' us.'

The girls had finished their sandwiches. Rose got to her feet and Linnet followed suit. 'No, we've not got matches, nor don't we know the time,' Rose said, bestowing a false and treacly smile upon the hapless youth. 'Come on, Miss Murphy, these fellers is only after our seats.'

This proved an unfortunate remark leading to many guffaws and a number of rude innuendoes, but the girls had to be back in their office dead on the hour so they ignored the young men and hurried back to the enormous Eagle and General building and their desks.

But all the way back to the office, Linnet was wondering just why Mollie was so extremely – unnaturally – quiet and good, and what she ought to do about it.

The warm and summery days passed pleasantly now for Linnet. Roddy came home and they had a couple of days out. They went off on the ferry, caught a bus at Woodside and picnicked in a wood where Linnet paddled in a stream and Roddy lay on his back on the grassy bank and slept – and snored, too. Roddy still insisted that she was his girl, but Linnet could not stop treating him like a brother which, in a way, she felt he was. This led to several hot arguments and once to a fight because Roddy tried to get amorous when they emerged from the cinema, where they had watched Greta Garbo in *Anna Christie*. Linnet, suddenly finding herself in a doorway with her friend Roddy horribly transformed into a hugging, grabbing octopus with eight hands, most of which were in places she preferred to keep to herself, fought back so successfully that Roddy nursed a hacked shin, trampled feet and the beginnings of a black eye for a week.

Roddy said he was sorry for frightening her, but he said it unconvincingly, with a martyred air, and Linnet, who had really been very scared, moved back from him a little. People, she felt, should stick to their roles in life and since she had cast Roddy as her friend and brother, her friend and brother he should remain. If he wanted to behave like the octopus she had called him – and that had been easily the most polite of the many descriptions she had used – then he should choose as a partner someone who liked that sort of behaviour, someone who did not think of him as a friend and a brother, in short.

So there was a certain coolness between Roddy and Linnet which might have made her very unhappy, had it not been for her steadily growing friendship with her boss. At work, Mr Cowan was much easier with Linnet and she with him. He began to take her around quite a lot, without once trying to hold her hand, let alone do anything more intimate. They went all over the place in Mr Cowan's lovely motor, though he did not take it to work but preferred to use a taxi or even the tram. So it was in a car, the very first one she had ridden in, that Linnet saw the Wirral, Lancashire, and even the Welsh countryside. Mr Cowan was a pleasant and undemanding companion – unlike Roddy, Linnet thought crossly – and seemed content just to have her with him so that he could enjoy her enjoyment as much as her company.

And naturally, when they went out in the car, they took Mollie with them. Mollie would sit on the back seat on a pile of cushions, holding onto the strap and watching the passing scene. When they stopped she would slide down from her throne and get into her push-chair, or sometimes she would walk between them, and she would scarcely ever speak and seldom did any expression other than solemn wonder, cross her small, rosy face. And somehow, no matter how she tried to tell herself that Mollie was simply an unusually good child, this worried Linnet more and more.

On one particular occasion, Nanny Peters had gone out for her afternoon off and the planned trip, to see the shops in Chester, came to nothing because the car sprang a puncture as they were going down the drive. So Mollie and Linnet went to the park to feed the ducks and dabble in the lake whilst Mr Cowan dealt with the puncture and the housekeeper, Mrs Eddis, prepared tea at home.

'We'll have it in the garden,' Mr Cowan had instructed her. 'The raspberries are ripe so perhaps we could have some of them, with some cream? I don't suppose Mollie's ever tasted raspberries.'

And since they were alone, Linnet really put herself out to put Mollie at her ease. She persuaded the child to play ring o' roses, and when they came to the end and they both fell down she made a great fuss, saying, 'Oh, Linnet went bump and now look at her skirt! Did Mollie go bump? Up we get, Mollie-Pollie, let's have a race to the big flower-bed. Racing each other means running to see who goes fastest.'

Mollie looked frightened. 'Mustn't,' she murmured. 'Mustn't run. Mollie sit quiet.'

214

'Yes, Mollie is very good, but now isn't the time for being good, now's the time for play,' Linnet said encouragingly. 'More ring o' roses, then, Mollie?'

Mollie glanced back at the house. Her eyes went very big and dark when she looked at the house. Then she looked up at Linnet. 'Play? Mollie play?'

'That's right. Now take my hands and we'll dance in a ring until we get to the tishoo bit, and then what do you do?'

Mollie thought about it, and then smiled. She wasn't a particularly fetching child but when she smiled . . . oh, poor baby, Linnet thought, to smile so rarely when she has so much! 'Mollie falls down,' she said. 'Linnet falls down too – bump!'

And then, just when Mollie was pink-cheeked, breathless, laughing, Nanny Peters came out of the house. She stood for one moment on the terrace, watching them, and then in a voice which cracked like a whiplash she said, 'Mollie! Here!'

'The kid might have been a dog,' Linnet said afterwards, telling Rose about the incident. 'And she didn't hesitate, or glance at me or anything. She put her head down and walked very quickly up to the terrace and stood by Nanny Peters. And when I went up too and said Mollie and I were just playing a game until tea, Miss Peters said, "Mollie doesn't like rough games. Her skirt's got grass stains on, we can't have that," and she took hold of Mollie's shoulder and the two of them disappeared into the house.'

'What did her father say?' Rose asked, clearly fascinated. 'Did he not ask for Mollie when he came back?'

'Yes. And I said Nanny Peters had taken her away and he gave me a very odd, hunted sort of look and said he supposed that was all right then. But neither of us had much appetite for tea.'

'And what'll you do?' Rose asked. 'Surely you ought to do something, Linnie? You're fond of the kid, I can tell.'

It was one thing to be fond of the child, though, and another to interfere, particularly as all she had to go on was Mollie's extraordinary goodness. It was not natural and she knew it, but she also realised that, unless Mr Cowan said something about it, she had no right whatsoever to do anything other than mention it from time to time. She and Rose talked it over constantly, worrying over it like dogs with a bone, but although Nanny Peters continued to treat poor Mollie with a degree of firmness which worried Linnet whenever Mr Cowan was not present, that was scarcely something about which she could complain. The children of the wealthy, Linnet knew, were brought up to be seen and not heard and her worries over the child seemed trivial when you considered that Mollie was prettily behaved, well nourished, had a wonderful home and a loving father. In short, she was living in the lap of luxury and was a very fortunate little girl when compared with many that Linnet saw in the streets each day.

And then, one Friday morning, when Linnet and Mr Cowan had been seeing each other regularly for six weeks or so, he came into her office and shut the door behind him with what Linnet thought was a definitely furtive air. She was alone since Rose was taking dictation from Mr Griseworth and had been gone almost half an hour already.

'Miss Murphy – are you busy this weekend?'

'Not 'specially,' Linnet said. She had been round to the Sullivans' place the previous day and had learned from Roddy's mother that his ship had docked in Southampton for repairs and would be there for a while, perhaps for as long as three weeks. But Roddy, it seemed, had decided he would be too busy to take time off to come home. He was probably still smarting from their quarrel, but even so Linnet thought he should have got in touch with her himself to tell her their usual meeting was off. He had sent a telegram, but had addressed it to the Sullivan family, obviously assuming that his mother would get in touch with Linnet and let her know. However, because Linnet was smouldering under a definite sense of grievance about what she thought of as 'the octopus affair', she took offence at his behaviour. But, truthfully, she was not looking forward to what she suspected would be yet another confrontation with Roddy, so probably he was wise to stay in Southampton. For all I know he may have a girl there, she told herself, and was surprised at the pang of sheer pain which arrowed through her at the thought. So one way and another, she jolly well hoped that Mr Cowan was going to ask her out this weekend. If Roddy chose to stay with his ship in a port hundreds of miles away rather than come home to Liverpool, then she would go out with Mr Cowan and it would serve Roddy blooming well right!

'I wondered if – if we might go over to New Brighton for – for – for Saturday, Miss Murphy, and – and – and –'

'For the afternoon?' Linnet guessed. 'For the whole afternoon, Mr Cowan?'

He was very pink and flustered, quite different from how he had been with her over the past few weeks; she could not help noticing that a fine film of perspiration dewed his forehead and that he kept pushing his glasses up with one finger with a nervous, almost irritable, gesture.

'Well, yes, and – and – and –'

Linnet took a deep breath. 'Is it Mollie, Mr Cowan? Shall you bring her, too? I'd like that.'

He muttered something; it sounded like 'weekend', but that didn't seem to make sense, so Linnet smiled encouragingly once more.

'Was it Nanny Peters, Mr Cowan? Did you want her to come, as well?'

He looked positively hunted. 'No, no, I don't think . . .' he was beginning when the door opened behind him and Rose entered the room. Talking, of course.

'Well, I dunno, there's enough letters in me book to keep me busy . . .' she broke off. 'Oh, sorry, Mr Cowan, I didn't realise you were in here.'

'I'm just going, Miss Beasley,' Mr Cowan said rather stiffly. 'Miss Murphy, I'd be obliged if you'd come along to my office in five minutes. Bring your pad.'

'He sounded cross,' Rose observed, sitting at her desk and throwing her shorthand pad down beside her typewriter. 'Did I come in at a bad moment, chuck? Was he asking you out again? My goodness, if folk knew about you and 'im they'd start puttin' two an' two together and makin' five! Still, you gerron well, I know. Did you say he was asking you out this weekend? 'Cos your feller isn't home after all, is he?'

'Roddy isn't my feller, he's a friend, and yes, I think Mr Cowan was meaning to ask me out, only he kept stuttering and stammering; but he'll probably tell me easier in his own office,' Linnet said calmly, picking up her own pad and selecting a couple of well-sharpened pencils. 'I'll soon know, anyhow.'

She went straight to Mr Cowan's room and sat down at the chair beside his desk. She put her pad on her lap, opened it, poised her pencil above it. Mr Cowan stared down at her pad but said nothing. After a moment's silence Linnet said, 'Dear Sir, in reply to your letter of the 9th instant . . .'

Mr Cowan looked up and tried to smile, but it was a

218

poor attempt. 'Sorry, Miss Murphy, it's just that . . . I find it very difficult . . .'

'Mr Cowan, do you bring butties – sandwiches – for your lunch?' Linnet said, struck by an idea. 'If so, why don't you and I take our sandwiches somewhere quiet and talk then?' It had occurred to her that her boss seemed to find it easier to talk away from the office. 'We can't go to the Nelson memorial but there's other places . . .'

'I don't bring sandwiches,' Mr Cowan said, and this time his smile was a real one. 'But if you would join me in a quick snack, we might indeed discuss the matter which is on my mind whilst we eat.'

'Oh, but I didn't mean . . . I've got butties,' Linnet said, wishing she had not made the suggestion. Now he would think her a gold-digger, a girl out for the main chance! 'It doesn't matter . . .'

'It does matter,' Mr Cowan said firmly. 'We'll save your sandwiches for the seagulls, shall we? That is, if you'll really come to New Brighton with me tomorrow. And we'll have our talk over lunch; nothing elaborate, just a nice chop and a roast potato or two – Sainsbury's Café do a businessmen's special which is quite good.'

'I'm not a businessman,' Linnet said feebly. How she wished she had kept her silly mouth shut, now look what she had got herself into! 'People will think it very odd if I go to Sainsbury's, sir, that's where all the managerial staff go. Us girls don't go out much at lunchtime, but if we did we'd never go to Sainsbury's.'

'True,' Mr Cowan said thoughtfully. 'How about Anderson's Snackerie, on Exchange Street, up by the National Provincial? The men go to Anderson's Luncheon Bar because they can get a beer there, but the Snackerie is more for women, I imagine!'

'I've heard of it because Miss Harper and Miss Elphinstone and some of the other supervisory staff go there, so you might find yourself the only feller,' Linnet said with a twinkle. 'Still, if you don't mind, I don't mind either!'

'Oh . . . yes, I see what you mean.' Mr Cowan's hunted look was back. 'Well, we'll get a taxi, go further afield. Yes, that's the idea, a taxi.'

'I am *not* getting into a taxi with you whilst everyone in the office giggles and gawps,' Linnet said firmly. 'There's no point in causing talk, sir. When you've been kind enough to ask me out before it's always been at weekends, and because we work Saturday mornings and by the time we leave nearly all the staff have gone, no one knows. But if you want us to have lunch together then we'll just have to be careful. You wouldn't want to be gossiped about, Mr Cowan, I know that much! Oh, I know! We'll sneak out separately and catch the same tram, that way no one will suspect anything.'

This time he really did laugh, the laugh which made his face almost attractive Linnet thought appreciatively, smiling herself. 'Miss Murphy, are you ashamed of me? Look, you walk down to the corner of Dale Street and I'll pick you up in a taxi. Will that suit your sense of propriety?'

'That's a *good* idea,' Linnet said, much relieved. 'Where will we go for our lunch, though?'

'There's a place on North John Street – Cottle's, it's called. It's a fair way from here, so we're unlikely to bump into anyone from the Eagle and General. Will that suit you?'

'That sounds just right,' Linnet said thankfully. 'And now, sir, to your letters!'

They had a pleasant lunch in the half-empty restaurant and Mr Cowan at last unburdened himself of the worry which, Linnet realised, had caused him to ask her out for the first time so many weeks ago.

'I don't think Mollie's happy, yet I can't tell why not,' he said. 'She scarcely ever cries now, though she cried a lot as a baby. But she doesn't laugh much, or run about, or do the things I see other small children doing, either. I've mentioned the matter to Nanny Peters and she's much more experienced than I, but she simply dismisses my fears, says the child is a good, quiet child and I should be grateful. To tell the truth, Miss Murphy, it has crossed my mind that a child whose mother dies within days of her birth might be affected mentally by the loss. I was – I was distraught at the time and paid very little attention to the baby, and who can say what such neglect can do to a child's mind? I did have a word with our family practitioner, an elderly man who's known me all my life, but he said I was worrying unduly and that little Mollie, so far as he can tell, is a perfectly normal child. But I noticed, three or four weeks ago, that she winces away if I make a sudden movement, which seems very odd. However, I told Nanny Peters that the habit worried me and soon after that she stopped, but . . .'

'Who stopped? Nanny Peters or the child?'

'Why, Mollie, of course. She stopped wincing when I moved towards her. She scarcely moves when I'm with her, now. I'm sure I'm doing something wrong, but I don't know precisely what and Nanny just says everything's as it should be and not to worry. And I can scarcely ask Mollie herself if I frighten her!'

'The trouble is, Mollie's too young to explain how she feels,' Linnet said thoughtfully. 'I suppose you could ask her, but I don't think she'd be able at her age to explain how she felt. And frankly, Mr Cowan, Mollie worries me, and for exactly the same reason. She's good and quiet, but much too good and quiet, if you understand me. And if you mentioned the wincing to Nanny Peters and Mollie promptly stopped wincing, don't you think that it may be your nanny who is at fault?'

'Because she stopped the child doing something which upset me? Surely, Miss Murphy, that shows she's taking my feelings into account?'

'It could also show she can frighten Mollie into obedience,' Linnet said cautiously. 'I can't think how you stop someone from wincing back, which is an instinctive movement, other than by a threat so terrible that even a child of Mollie's age remembers it. You didn't ask Miss Peters how she worked the miracle?'

'No. To tell you the truth, Miss Murphy, Miss Peters starts talking about psychology and some strange American doctor who's an authority on small children, and she even said, once, that it's right and proper for a child to be in awe of its male parent . . . I feel very helpless, I really do. Upon my word of honour, Miss Murphy, I would never harm a hair of my daughter's head, but from her attitude anyone could be forgiven for believing that I thrash her twice daily.'

'And it hadn't occurred to you that the only person she sees enough of to be genuinely frightened by her is Nanny Peters?' Linnet asked incredulously. 'Mr Cowan, who else could scare Mollie?'

Mr Cowan shrugged helplessly. 'Who am I to say? Dr Davies recommended Miss Peters personally, which makes it difficult, because when I have a worry about Mollie and take it to him he simply says that Nurse Peters will see to it and that I may trust her absolutely. Only just lately, I felt I must get someone else's opinion, preferably a woman's, who could put me right if it was my attitude which was at fault.'

'Well, you aren't very loving towards her, but it isn't possible for you to show her affection when it only frightens her more,' Linnet said gently, pushing her plate away. 'That was a delicious meal, sir, much nicer than sandwiches. But once you've sorted out Mollie's problem you will have to learn to cuddle her, Mr Cowan. Children need to be cuddled. My mam was a great one to cuddle, and she couldn't be called a particularly good mother, I don't think.'

'If I even hold her hand she pulls back,' Mr Cowan said miserably. 'If I pick her up she goes stiff . . . it's quite frightening. She's not speaking as she ought, either, or not when I'm around, though Nanny says she chatters away happily when I'm out at work or when I'm downstairs, having my dinner.'

'Did Mollie never run to you?' Linnet asked, remembering her own childhood and how she would run to her mother the moment little Evie returned to their rooms from a show or a shopping trip. 'Just run to you, with her arms out?'

Mr Cowan shook his head once more. 'No, never. Right from the time she could toddle – and she walked before she was a year old – she was very quiet. Never ran or shouted, never made demands. To tell you the truth, Miss Murphy, of late I've wondered whether her mind was affected at birth because I understand my – my late wife had a difficult time. Yet if Mollie had been damaged, in short if she was simple, she would not, surely, respond to instruction the way she does?'

Linnet, who had wondered the same thing when she had first met Mollie, shook her head decisively. 'She's as bright as any kid I've met,' she said. 'You don't want to worry on that score. But . . . if I may be frank?'

Mr Cowan looked hunted, but nodded his head with the air of one determined, if necessary, to go to the stake in a good cause. 'Yes, Miss Murphy. If it's something I've done I'd rather know.'

'I think it's possible that, all unknowing, you've employed a nanny who is rather too strict, rather too keen to have a perfect charge,' Linnet said, weighing her words as carefully as she could whilst, at the same time, getting her message across. 'I think that if you sent Miss Peters away for a week or two and took charge of the child yourself, you'd see a marked improvement quite quickly.'

Mr Cowan looked shocked. 'Take care of her myself? But I couldn't possibly do that, Miss Murphy. I'm a man!'

'Yes, that is a disadvantage,' Linnet said, quick to see his point of view, for men, naturally, had nothing to do with small children save to beget them, and though she knew very little about that side of things she did realise that begetting was one of man's pleasures whereas up-bringing was very much a woman's job. 'Well, how about bringing in a friend or relative to take care of Mollie for a week or two? You might even employ someone else, just for a couple of weeks,' she added, highly daring, for she longed to say *sack her and watch Mollie improve*, but realised such a suggestion would not, at this stage, be politic. Mr Cowan was still not sure that his 'perfect nanny' was in any way to blame for his daughter's behaviour.

'But I don't have any female relatives or close friends,' Mr Cowan pointed out, having given the matter some thought. 'And suppose I did employ someone else and they proved equally unsatisfactory? No, no, I don't mean that,' he added hastily, clearly seeing the trap into which he was about to fall. 'I mean I might choose wrongly and be forced to ask Miss Peters to return. And that really could be hard on Mollie; I don't think Miss Peters is the type of young lady to forgive such a slight.'

All Linnet's frank and forthright soul begged to be allowed to tell Mr Cowan that it was about time Miss Peters was subjected to the sort of pressure she was clearly putting his child under, but by now, Linnet's sympathy for Mollie was sufficiently strong to make her see that she simply had to remove Nanny Peters by stealth, for a couple of weeks, at least.

'Mr Cowan, you must have female relatives, or friends, anyway,' she urged. 'You mentioned your mother . . .'

'My mother likes a disciplined child; she holds Mollie up as an example to others and thinks the sun shines out of Nanny Peters' . . . out of Nanny Peters,' Mr Cowan said drily. 'No help there, I'm afraid.' He looked long and hard at Linnet. 'Actually, Miss Murphy, I was wondering whether you . . .'

'Me, Mr Cowan? But I'm like you, I'm at work all day. And besides . . .'

'You have a fortnight's holiday due to you at the end of the year which, I am sure, I can bring forward. It's paid leave, Miss Murphy, and naturally, I would pay you Miss Peters' salary for those two weeks as well. Now I want you to believe me when I say that when I first asked you to come out with me I had no intention of taking advantage of you – of expecting you to help me with Mollie on a personal basis, I mean – but simply wanted your advice. Only we did get on rather well, wouldn't you say? And Mollie obviously likes you, and I let things slide and slide. Is it asking too much, Miss Murphy? Only I'm at my wits' end and that's the truth.'

Linnet glanced across to the window of the snackerie; outside, the sun shone from a clear blue sky and there were smiles on the faces of passersby. It would be really nice to have a couple of weeks' break from the office, to sit in the beautiful garden of the house in Sunnyside, backing onto Prince's Park, or to take Mollie on the tram and the overhead railway to Seaforth Sands, to feed the ducks, go rowing on the lake, visit the orangery and the aviary . . . why, it would be like a proper holiday! She watched a girl in a primrose coloured frock and sandals, with a straw hat perched on her dark hair, walking past hand in hand with a handsome young man and envied her her freedom. She herself could never stroll, not on a weekday. It would be fun, and she did like little Mollie. She turned back to Mr Cowan. He was still staring anxiously, pleadingly, across at her.

'If you really can arrange for me to have the time off, I'd like to do it,' she said slowly. 'But what about putting Mollie to bed and so on, Mr Cowan? And getting her up, come to that? If she's an early riser, could I get there in time?'

Mr Cowan's smile spread, slowly, across his face. He looked as though an enormous weight had been taken off his mind, he even sat up straighter, or so it seemed to Linnet.

'My dear Miss Murphy . . . you would stay in the house, of course. Why, Nanny Peters lives in and there's no breath of scandal because my housekeeper lives in as well and two of the maids. Besides, you'd sleep, as Nanny Peters does, in the little room attached to the nursery. If you mean it . . . well, I should be – I should be eternally grateful.'

'I do mean it,' Linnet said. She wanted to help Mollie and besides, to be paid simply to stay for two weeks in a beautiful house, to have your meals made for you and delivered to you, to go out when you wished, to enjoy all the advantages of wealth without any strings . . . it was an opportunity given to few young girls in her position. 'When do I start?'

'I'll tell Miss Peters that I'm going away and taking Mollie with me; I'll say I'm going to visit a cousin with several children and shan't be needing her services for two weeks. I'll tell her she can have a holiday with pay,' Mr Cowan said. Linnet realised that he must have been planning this all along, hoping she would come up with some such suggestion. He might have come straight out with it, she thought, but without resentment. A worried father, who loved his daughter and wanted what was best for her, could be forgiven many things. 'If you could start your holiday at lunchtime a week on Saturday, Miss Murphy?'

'If you can arrange it, Mr Cowan,' Linnet said happily. 'I can't wait to see Mollie's face when we wave Nanny Peters off!'

Roddy was annoyed with himself, almost as annoyed as he had been with Linnet. Brother and sister, indeed! He had never thought of her in that way and doubted whether Linnet, an only child to all intents and purposes, had the faintest idea of the way in which brothers and sisters regarded each other. Roddy, cursed with two older brothers and three younger ones but no sisters at all, was still sure that what he felt for Linnet – and what she undoubtedly felt for him – was a very different emotion to the mixture of exasperation and downright dislike which was how he often regarded his brothers.

But you can't bleedin' tell a woman anything, 'cos they know it all, Roddy told himself, crossing East Street to have a look in Edwin Jones' windows. A look was sufficient, however; the windows were full of mouthwatering things, but the prices! Roddy moved on, glumly, further down the street, still looking in windows as he went.

He would have thoroughly enjoyed Southampton and window-shopping if it hadn't been for the fact that he was missing Linnet, and sorely tempted to simply go down to the station, jump on a train, and storm up the Boulevard to her door. He could imagine the scene; himself at the door, Linnet pulling it open, eyes rounding with surprise and pleasure, himself pressing into her hand the beautiful present for which he was at this moment searching, saying how sorry he was for – well, for pushing his attentions upon her after their visit to the flicks that night . . . her warm smile, her open arms, her kisses . . .

It was a strange thing, Roddy thought broodingly, how a woman could look you in the eye and deny what was in her heart. Linnet loved him, she must do, because he loved her, didn't he? Had loved her from the first moment they'd met, when the little silly had got in the way of his toboggan – how like a girl! – and been knocked for six, and had been rather good about it. He'd liked her then because she was a spunky kid, never moaning about her scraped knees or her bruises but simply telling him off for muckin' up her messages. The Irish accent of her had fascinated him, too, though that had gradually faded and grown less over the years. But her satiny hair, the jut of her chin, the way her eyes smiled at you even when her mouth was serious, the sprinkling of golden freckles on her fair little face . . . God, she was his, she had to be, there could be no doubt of it! Why could she not see what was so patently obvious to him, that they were made for each other, could have no sort of life apart?

Still, it had not been wise to jump her in that doorway. Roddy touched his eye gingerly; she had a left hook which many a feller might have envied, you had to say that for her. A feller expects a female to kick and scratch so he bore no grudge for his bruised shins, but that left hook! She'd meant it, the little vixen, she'd packed all she had into that punch and taken his mind right off – well, off what it had been on. For a moment he had seen stars, and by the time his head had stopped whirling and his eye watering, she was marching off down the street, calling back some pretty unpleasant remarks from what he could recall. The one that stung had been *nasty, grubby little boy*, but she hadn't meant that, he was sure of it. And then, when he'd finally caught up with her and tried to apologise – without actually admitting he had been in the wrong, mind – she had said she looked on him as a brother. A bleedin' brother, when she'd never had even one of them and he'd had five! He had tried to tell her that a brother didn't behave towards a sister as he had always behaved towards her and she had said, frostily, 'I should think not!' and of course then he saw he'd put his foot in it again and had tried to make amends only she wouldn't listen. She had simply gone on walking, and walking fast, too. Roddy, with trampled feet and bruised legs, to say nothing of scratched hands and an incipient black eye, had not felt equal to arguing with her all the way from the Paramount Theatre on London Road to the Boulevard so had lapsed into sulky silence long before they reached the tram stop.

And a tram, even a Green Goddess, with its leather upholstery and wonderfully comfortable seats, is no place to make up a quarrel. Linnet flounced into the vehicle and sat down and Roddy, naturally, sat next to her and she kept shrinking away until she must have been pressed so hard up against the window that it hurt. Then Roddy tried to tell her how he felt about her and the man in the seat in front turned and, raising his voice to combat the noise, for even a Green Goddess wasn't exactly silent, told Linnet to save 'erself for 'er weddin' night an' be damned to the feller, and then laughed with great coarseness and advised Roddy to 'gerrin a cold bath' and do other things which would, he insinuated, resolve Roddy's state both of mind and body.

And Linnet had given Roddy one long, startlingly horrible glare and had turned to the window. For the rest of the ride and all the walk home she had been totally silent, never saying a word in reply to his lengthy and disjointed monologue. And when they got back to her place she had shut the door in his face, very nearly adding a swollen nose to the black eye she had inflicted earlier.

He had been cross – well, bloody annoyed, in fact. He had vowed he would never speak to her or ask her out again. But the annoyance hadn't lasted, not with him, because he was a magnanimous male and not a foolish and misguided female. Linnet, however, had borne a grudge, and borne it so effectively, what was more, that when he had gone round to Exchange Flags and hovered, she had simply pretended not to see him, had walked by him without a word or a look. Painful stuff, no matter how hard he tried to tell himself that she was misguided but would see the error of her ways very soon.

So when the *Mary Rose* had put into Southampton for repairs he had decided not to send her a telegram explaining that he would not be home for some time. Why should he? She had refused to accept his apologies, refused even to speak to him. If I play her game, ignore her, make her suffer, then she'll see reason and be nice to me again, his thoughts ran, incoherently it is true, but hopefully. And then, when she realises what she's lost, I'll return, laden with gifts, and it'll all be good again.

Only . . . only women were so *unreliable*, so confoundedly strange when it came to matters of the heart. Suppose she didn't repent of her nastiness to him? Suppose she kept it up, went on refusing to speak, or go out, or be good friends? Suppose, in short, he had sacrificed that good friendship, which was so valuable to him, for a quick fumble in a doorway after a romantic cinema show? Suppose he had lost her?

Roddy had been mooching along the street, hands in pockets, his mind a million miles away, but when that thought entered his head, so did an icy determination.

He could not lose her, she was the most precious thing in his life. He must make her listen to him, he must, he must!

He would get on the first available train home in the morning and would put his case before her just as soon as he could. Only first, of course, he must buy her a present so magnificent that the ice round her heart would melt and she would fall on his chest in gratitude.

Determinedly, he began to retrace his steps towards Edwin Jones' magnificent emporium.

After considerable thought, Linnet decided she would have to tell Rose where she was going, but most definitely not her landlady. She might have told Mrs Sullivan, who was very interested in the whole affair, but perhaps because of her quarrel with Roddy she had not been visiting the Sullivans as often as usual and suddenly it began to seem a rather odd sort of thing to do, to have a holiday looking after her boss's little girl. Mrs Sullivan was far too practical to assume that Linnet was fishing for a rich widower, but she might wonder what her young friend was playing at. Sometimes, indeed, Linnet wondered herself. She did not think of Mr Cowan as a gentleman friend, though he was both a friend and a gentleman, nor did she consider their friendship in any way romantic, though that was exactly how Rose saw it. Linnet liked the lifestyle Mr Cowan enjoyed and at times played with the idea of being the next Mrs Cowan, but she knew, really, that it was just a foolish daydream and nothing more. Mr Cowan was too old for her no matter what Rose might say, and he was too rich, as well. Men with houses in Sunnyside, with housekeepers, nannies, maids, gardeners, did not marry little secretaries. Besides, Linnet reminded herself, she did not want to marry anyone, not yet. Life was far too full and exciting.

But having a holiday in his house, acting as nanny to his little girl – that was different. And if she was right and Nanny Peters was the cause of Mollie's strange behaviour, then Mr Cowan would be grateful, Mollie would start to act like a normal child, and Linnet could crawl back under the wallpaper, she supposed a little sadly. She might enjoy her excursions into the good life, but she was, at heart, a realist. Once she had served her purpose and sorted Mollie out, then Mr Cowan's secretary would be just that once more.

So on the Saturday that her holiday job started Linnet told her landlady that she was going to the seaside with a friend from work. It said a lot for her dull reputation, she thought afterwards, that her landlady immediately assumed that the friend was a woman and the holiday resort New Brighton.

'Ave a good time, queen,' she called as Linnet, suitcase in hand, set out for the tram stop. 'Send us a card!'

Nodding and smiling, Linnet decided to persuade Mr Cowan to take her and Mollie to Llandudno next day; there she could buy a supply of cards which she could post, judiciously, over the coming fortnight. Few people, she guessed, would bother to look at the postmark and if they did would assume it had been marked twice, in error.

At work everyone apart from Rose – and Mr Cowan, of course – assumed she was going to stay with relatives who lived in North Wales. That was what they did so why should she be any different? What Nanny Peters thought Linnet had no way of knowing, but when she arrived at Sunnyside she learned from Mrs Eddis that Nanny Peters had gone off for her own holiday in no very good frame of mind.

'Said she didn't want no stranger lookin' after 'er little Mollie,' Mrs Eddis remarked, having forcibly removed

Linnet's case from her grasp in order to carry it up the stairs and casting a curious glance at the 'replacement nanny' as she did so. 'Said no one understood the kid like she did, that she'd ha' sooner chose someone to come in 'erself.' She reached the head of the stairs and stood for a moment to catch her breath. 'Made me wonder, that did.'

'What did you wonder, Mrs Eddis?' Linnet asked. 'Here, let me.' She reclaimed her suitcase firmly and this time Mrs Eddis let her do so. 'Did Mr Cowan not say that Mollie knew me?'

'No, Miss, nor he never said it were you,' Mrs Eddis assured her. 'Just kep' sayin' a friend were comin' in. And I wondered, 'cos we don't reckon, Ethel an' me, as 'ow Miss Peters were too good wi' Mollie.'

'You never said anything, Mrs Eddis,' Linnet said with a mildness she was far from feeling. Why on earth hadn't the woman told Mr Cowan of her suspicions? It would have confirmed his own fears and he would, presumably, have acted more speedily.

'Well, no, Miss. The nanny was chose by Dr Davies . . . it didn't seem right to question it,' Mrs Eddis said, going ponderously ahead of Linnet up the corridor and speaking over her shoulder. 'Still, all's well that ends well, they say.' She threw open a white-painted door. 'Your room, miss, wi' the connectin' door to the nursery.'

It was a pleasant room with a wide windowseat and a view over the park. Linnet put her case down on the chest of drawers and studied her surroundings with awe. There was a pink rug on the floor, pink curtains at the windows and a pink shade on the electric light overhead. The bed had a white lace counterpane flung carelessly across it, and there were two chairs, both basketwork, with fat embroidered cushions on the seats. It did not look as she had imagined a nanny's room should look to

Linnet, though she knew herself to be ignorant in such matters.

'Nice, ain't it?' Mrs Eddis said behind her. 'She did 'erself awright, did Nanny Peters. Kept bringin' stuff in ... most o' this stuff were in the spare room but it weren't used, so . . . but I mustn't stand 'ere chattin'. Make yourself at 'ome, miss, and ring if you want anything. Ethel will be up before the cat can scratch.'

'Where's Mollie?'

'Havin' a rest in 'er room. It's just through there, miss.' The housekeeper indicated a door to the right of the bed with a jerk of her chin. 'She'll sleep till she's roused, miss. Ever so good she is.'

But in fact, when Linnet looked into the nursery Mollie was lying in her bed, straight as a die, with her eyes wide open. She closed them as soon as she realised Linnet was there, though, so Linnet said cheerily, 'I've just popped in to see if you're awake yet, dear. It's time for some tea, but before we have it I thought we might have a play. But if you're still tired, of course . . .'

Mollie sat up. She had a small, triangular face, big, grey-green eyes and straight, very dark brown hair. 'Play?' she said looking round her carefully.

'Yes, play. Nanny Peters has gone away, she isn't coming back for a long time so we can play if we like. What would you like to do until teatime?'

Mollie slid carefully off the bed. 'Ring o' roses,' she said in her small, flat voice. 'Ring o' roses, please.'

Linnet went to take her hand and saw Mollie go rigid. Carefully and slowly, she said, therefore, 'I don't know your house very well yet, Mollie. I'm a bit afraid of getting lost. Will you take me down to the garden?'

Mollie looked at her. You could see all sorts of emotions warring on the small face. Then, wordlessly, she took Linnet's hand and led her, not out of the nursery

door and onto the landing, but through the pink bedroom. She looked around carefully, then she peeped into
the suitcase, unpacked but open now on the chest of
drawers, then she looked up at Linnet. Linnet could read
the unasked question.

'I'm sleeping here now, Mollie,' Linnet said reassuringly. 'Nanny Peters has gone away. She'll be sleeping
somewhere else.'

Mollie didn't smile, but it was as though she relaxed
all over. She even gave a tiny sigh. Then she pulled Linnet
over towards the door. 'Ring o' roses now,' she said.
'Mollie *play*!'

The rest of the day passed in a flash. Mr Cowan, who
had deemed it politic to keep out of the way for a bit,
returned to his home to find his daughter and Miss
Murphy playing games in the garden – very discreet,
careful games for the most part – and then the three of
them had tea on the terrace, the tea augmented by delicious cakes and tiny sandwiches. Then Mollie went with
both of them to the park, fed the ducks and even ran on
the grass. Mr Cowan marvelled at the change in his child
and watched whilst Linnet made her a daisy chain and
Mollie wore it proudly, keeping it on for the rest of the
time they were in the park, during the walk home, and
only shedding it, reluctantly, when Linnet promised to
put it in water until the following morning.

'And now it's time for your bath and after that Daddy
is going to read you a bedtime story,' Linnet said and Mr
Cowan, primed, said that indeed he was and it would be
a jolly good story, too. 'Do you want to come and watch
me bath her?' Linnet asked, when she and Mollie were
going upstairs. 'Mollie is going to swim and splash, you
ought to see that!'

But Mr Cowan thought it might be wiser to let Mollie
swim and splash alone for a day or so, and settled down

with his *Evening Echo*. But he had scarcely done more than read the headlines when he heard a bell pealing vigorously and a couple of minutes later Ethel came hurriedly into the room.

'Oh sir, Miss says would you go up to Miss Mollie's bathroom, please. She really thinks you ought, sir.'

Mr Cowan immediately folded his paper and ran up the stairs two at a time. Miss Murphy was very inexperienced, suppose she had unknowingly done the child some harm? He burst into the bathroom to find Mollie sitting serenely in the tub surrounded by bakelite ducks. She jumped and gasped at his sudden entry but Linnet put a soothing hand on her shoulder and thereafter she ignored them both but continued to move the ducks around whilst her lips moved soundlessly and her eyes never left the toys.

'What is it, Miss Murphy?' Mr Cowan said quietly. 'The maid said . . . oh, my God!'

He had seen what Miss Murphy had brought him in to see – the child's upper arms and much of her torso were black with bruises.

'*That* is how Nanny Peters kept order,' Linnet said in a deceptively even voice. 'Nips, pinches, blows from a hairbrush – I daresay we shall never know the half of it. That is the reason Mollie always wore long-sleeved frocks – I did wonder why, but I never dreamed that woman would do anything so wicked. Sir, you'll surely dismiss her after this?'

'I shan't have to,' Mr Cowan said grimly. 'She must know she would be found out – she'll never dare show her face in these parts again. What an evil woman!'

'Yes. But at least Mollie's so young that the harm can be undone,' Linnet said. 'And I intend to spend the next fortnight doing just that!'

*

For the whole of the first week the sun shone every single day, and after a week of constant outdoor play, the company of other children in the park and the loving attention of Linnet and her father, Mollie positively blossomed. She began to chatter freely, she ran, she even shouted. At first she was delighted with any story her father told but she soon had the confidence to choose which story she preferred and very rapidly learned the words so that she could correct her father if he went wrong. As her confidence improved she actually seemed to grow prettier and everyone who came to the house remarked on the change in the child.

Linnet wondered if Mollie would begin to grow quiet again as time went on and once, when they were coming home from a day at the seaside, with Mollie leaning drowsily against her shoulder, Linnet said to the child, 'You'll never see Nanny Peters again, you know.'

'I know,' Mollie said. 'You're my nanny now, Linnet. I do love you.'

'Well, I don't . . .' Linnet began, but Mr Cowan turned towards her and put a finger to his lips.

'Hush,' he said. 'It's too soon. Later, Miss Murphy.'

When they got home and Mollie was safely bathed and bedded, Linnet went down to dinner with her employer and over steak and duchesse potatoes raised the question, once again, of a nanny.

'Because it won't do for her to grow too fond of me so that she resents the change,' she pointed out. 'She's had a bad time, sir, she deserves better than that.'

'She deserves to keep you,' Mr Cowan said calmly. 'And I hope she will. You are a delightful person, Miss Murphy, and I am beginning to think it isn't only Mollie who can't manage without you. You've made us both very happy – wouldn't you like to stay with us, Mollie and me?'

'I'm a secretary, Mr Cowan,' Linnet said uncomfortably. 'I'm not *really* a nanny, I'm not trained or anything. I love it here, and I love Mollie, but . . .'

'Well, you've another five days to go; let's see how you feel at the end of that time,' Mr Cowan said comfortably. 'In the meantime, I'm going to ask you to do another job for me – would you choose me a nice, sensible girl to act as nurserymaid? That woman said it wasn't necessary and to my shame it never occurred to me that it wasn't true, it was just because the fewer people who knew what went on in that nursery the better Miss Peters liked it. I simply accepted her at her own valuation, I'm afraid. But I'll never do so again, which is why I'd like you to find me a nurserymaid, Miss Murphy.'

'Oh . . . but I wouldn't know where to get a nurserymaid from,' Linnet said, worried at the thought of having to find a member of staff for her employer. 'I'd rather you or Mrs Eddis did it, sir.'

'Don't worry, I'll speak to the people at the employment exchange and get them to send half-a-dozen suitable young women up to the house. All you will have to do is talk to them informally and choose someone who will be kind and good to my little girl.'

'Oh, I can do *that*,' Linnet said, much relieved. 'I'd like to do that, sir.'

That conversation took place on a Tuesday. On the Thursday, seven nervous young women arrived at the kitchen door and were shown, one by one, into the small drawing-room where Linnet, at first extremely nervous too, soon settled into her stride and positively enjoyed interviewing.

'I advise you to employ Emma Alcott, Mr Cowan,' she said at dinner that night, having seen all seven of the applicants. 'She's bright and sweet-natured, very clean and intelligent and she really loves children. I don't think you could do better than Emma.'

'Good. Then would you ring the exchange in the morning and tell them your decision? The agency advised me on wages and on terms and conditions so you needn't bother about that. Just confirm that Miss Alcott has the job and ask her to start on Monday next.'

Oddly enough, it was that remark which made Linnet think. She agreed to ring the agency next day and went to bed, but not, alas, to sleep. Her mind was far too active for slumber. Next Monday the new nurserymaid, the sweet, pretty little Emma Alcott, chosen by Linnet, would start work. And on that same day, she, Linnet, would be back at her desk, taking dictation, typing up letters, filing, running errands, coming in early and leaving late. She would have butties for her lunch and not homemade soup, a crusty roll, a beautifully served salad with a lemon cream or a dish of strawberries to follow. She would drink tea and not coffee, would cook her own dinner and after she had eaten it would make do with her own company most of the time. Here, Mr Cowan shared her dinner, then they talked quietly in the twilight, or made plans for the next day. He told her amusing stories about the office and she told him how funny Mollie had been. They enjoyed each other's company until bedtime when Mrs Eddis came through with a tray on which rested two cups of hot chocolate and a tempting display of biscuits. Linnet checked that Mollie was sleeping soundly, undressed, got into her comfortable bed and slept soundly until morning.

Since Mollie's new-found confidence, the child padded into the room each morning and roused Linnet, who enjoyed being woken by a soft little hand on her face, a soft voice telling her that it was 'Morning time now, time to wake up, Linnet!' and always moved over to let Mollie come down the bed with her so that when Ethel came in with a tray of tea it was two faces she saw on the pillow, and two smiles which greeted her.

Back in the Boulevard you'll wake alone, make your own tea, get your own breakfast, come to that, Linnet reminded herself, turning her hot pillow over to get at the cool, uncrushed cotton. But that's freedom, isn't it? That's being a working girl, independent, a career woman in the making. That's what you want – isn't it? You'll be gossiping with Rose, smiling at the clerks and keeping the office boys in order, seeing Mr Cowan across his desk and nowhere else . . .

She turned over again and stuck her feet out of bed because it was a warm night and no doubt the reason she couldn't sleep was the heat and nothing else. But the moment she got comfortable her thoughts returned to her problem. What to do for the best? Having your own little room and being free between six in the evening and nine the next morning was important – wasn't it? Everyone knew that domestic service of any sort was low because you did not have the same amount of freedom and freedom was important – wasn't it? She turned over again and threw one of her pillows on the floor. She would sleep better flat, perhaps.

She had been surprised at the salary which Nanny Peters received, though. If you took into account the rent which Linnet paid for her room and the tram fares to and from work alone, then a children's nanny was laughing all the way to the bank. A nanny had uniform provided, the use of the whole of her employer's home plus, of course, the privacy of her own domain and her keep. A nanny's salary, then, was pocket money. Why, I could save just about all of it and after a few years I'd have enough to buy all sorts, Linnet thought, excited by the prospect of such riches. Rose won't earn money like that ever, probably, and she's really senior compared to me. If I ever *did* decide to get married then I'd have a real little nest-egg towards me own home, whereas even the best of secretaries found saving a tiny sum each week hard work.

She would miss Rose, though, and the companionship of the tall house on the Boulevard: scatty Margaret, prim Ellen, Mr and Mrs Prettywell and their horrid little sons, she would miss them all in different ways. And there was her room, which she had lovingly furnished, and her visits to the Sullivan family, still living in Peel Square. But nannies do get time off, she remembered, just in time to stop herself starting her arguments all over again. I can visit the Boulevard, Rose and the offices on Exchange Flags, and the Sullivans in Peel Square. If Roddy and I are friends again soon I can even take my days off when his ship docks so we can go out together.

Sleep came at last with the problem, Linnet would have said, unresolved. But when she was woken by Mollie climbing into bed with her next morning her mind must have made itself up whilst she slept for the first thing she said was, 'I'm staying here, Mollie, I *am* going to be your nanny!'

Mollie, enthroned upon her friend's stomach, simply leaned forward until their foreheads touched and gazed at Linnet out of eyes which looked, at such close quarters, as big as ponds. 'Buttie kiss!' she demanded. 'Give Mollie buttie kiss!'

'Butterfly, silly Mollie,' Linnet said, giggling. 'Put your cheek near my eye, then.'

Mollie complied and gurgled with delicious amusement as Linnet slowly batted her eyelashes up and down the child's soft cheek. 'More!' she said immediately Linnet stopped. 'More buttie*fly* kissings!'

'Not now, chick. I want to catch your daddy before he.

goes off to work. We won't wait for our tea to arrive, we'll get ourselves dressed and go down to the breakfast room at once.'

'And that is a firm decision, Miss Murphy? You will stay with Mollie and me? I'm delighted, absolutely delighted – it is a great weight off my mind. And since you're sure you'll do the job, do you think it would be best to ring the agency and tell them that we no longer require Miss Alcott? She was, after all, only an insurance policy against a bad nanny or a period during which I might have had to manage without a nanny at all.' Mr Cowan smiled at Linnet. 'With you in charge of the nursery, Miss Murphy, I shall have no qualms,' he finished.

Linnet had sat down opposite her employer at the breakfast table without getting her breakfast, eager to tell him that she had decided to stay before she did anything else, but now she stood up and walked over to the sideboard. She lifted the lid from one of the silver tureens and helped herself to scrambled egg, then kidneys.

'Thank you, sir,' she said quietly. 'I'll ring the agency as soon as they open, and then I'll catch a tram into the city and do all that has to be done. What about giving in my notice at work, though?'

'I'll handle that,' Mr Cowan said at once. 'If you just write a little note I'll see to the rest.' He stood up as Linnet returned to the table and leaned across it, a hand outstretched. 'Welcome to my home, Miss Murphy,' he said, smiling broadly. 'I hope you'll be very happy in your new job and I know that Mollie and I are happy with your decision!'

Chapter Nine

Lucy was in the kitchen getting breakfast when the back door opened with caution and Caitlin came quietly into the room, her face anxious.

'How's Granny, Lu? I went down to the castle early, before the sun was up, but there was no sign of Finn and I just can't think of any more ways to get in touch wi' him. He won't be with the tinkers, he'll be at a farm somewhere, he could be ten miles up the road or a hundred!'

'Oh, well, you've done your best, Cait, which is all anyone can do. But she'd dearly like to speak to Finn one last time and well we both know it. She's goin' down quite fast, now. I wish I could think of something, but haven't I tried and tried until me brain nearly burst with it? As you say, he could be anywhere, curse the feller!'

'I told Arny Aniseed when he came by days and days ago to put the word around for Finn,' Caitlin said discontentedly. 'I made sure Arny, gossip that he is, would do the trick. It makes me wonder if Finn's further off than we think, alanna. I pray to God he's not hurt, lyin' in a hospital bed somewhere not knowin' his own name.'

'Now why on earth should you think that, you foolish girl?' Lucy asked irritably. The fact that the same fear occurred to her nightly did not make Caitlin's voicing of it any more acceptable. 'Will you not go putting daft ideas into me head – I've worries enough without that.'

'I know, and sorry I am that I said it,' Caitlin murmured, not sounding particularly sorry, however. 'But facts must be faced – is she in her right mind, still?'

Caitlin's own grandmother had gone senile towards the end but Granny Mogg, though failing fast, was still bright as a button mentally and, in fact, was quite an awkward patient. She had been living at the farm for six months now, ever since the girls had gone down to the castle with a basket of goodies for her – very like Red Riding Hood, as Lucy had remarked – and found her collapsed at the foot of the stone stairway. She had clearly fallen but how far or how badly she was hurt they could not say. They had hurried home, fetched the farmhands and a gate to carry her on, and brought the old lady back to Ivy Farm, where she had been, at first, put in bed upstairs in the best spare bedroom.

But it had been terribly hard work traipsing up all those stairs whenever Granny shouted – which was often – and besides, once she came to herself she announced that she'd acted like an owl and roosted in an old tower for years, but that she was a tinker and tinkers preferred to die at ground level.

'You aren't goin' to die, Granny Mogg,' Lucy had said comfortingly. 'The doctor says it's just a little concussion, so he does, with a poor old busted leg thrown in for good measure. You'll be right as rain when the bone mends.'

'No I shan't,' Granny Mogg said obstinately. 'I'm a tinker, amn't I? I told fortunes round the fairs and the ceilidhs for years, d'you not t'ink I know me own fate? Anyhow, man born of woman is bound to die, same's pigs an' sheep an' all other earthly critturs. What makes you t'ink I's any different?'

Put like that it was a hard argument to beat so Lucy and her grandfather made up a bed in the small parlour and they carried Granny Mogg down and laid her tenderly between the sheets. And there, for six months, she had remained, frequently grumbling, occasionally escaping, to be found wandering the meadows with the enormous white nightgown they had found for her hiked up indecently high and someone else's gumboots on her skinny little legs.

She always came back willingly, however, having merely wanted, she said, to 'breathe real air an' feel the touch o' rain an' smell the sweetness o' the 'edgerows'. Lucy never pointed out that the window in the small parlour was open all day if the weather was clement enough and that she picked any wild flower she could find for the little green glass vase on Granny's bed-table. She knew that Granny, who had never lived under a roof until Finn ensconced her in the ruined castle, found having four stout walls around her irksome and secretly sympathised with her desire to simply escape from it all for a while.

Because a couple of years ago Maeve had finally come home with her friend Mr Caleb Zowkoughski, only to announce that she and Caleb were now man and wife. Lucy, cheated of a wedding, had probably looked sour, but Maeve had explained that she was not getting any younger, that she and Caleb were very much in love, and that they wanted a family.

'We felt we'd waited long enough,' Maeve had told her father and niece, sitting in the kitchen mending linen, for Lucy had saved her a pile of worn sheets and torn shirts. 'We knew we loved each other so we married. And as you know Caleb is an attorney and a very successful one, bless him, so when our little holiday here is over we're goin' to return to New York because that's where Caleb's business is.' She had looked lovingly at Lucy. 'My dear girl, in a year or two you'll be after meetin' a young man, after fallin' in love, after leavin' home. So I don't feel I'm lettin' you down, d'you see? You'd go from me soon anyway. But if you'd like to come home with us, to New York, and meet some young men . . .'

Home! She had used the word without a second thought and Lucy knew, then, that Maeve was lost to them. And as for leaving Ireland to go chasing across the Atlantic looking for romance, wasn't that just the sort of silly thing her mammy had done, and wasn't her main aim in life to prove that she was not at all like little Evie? Even her fleeting urge to be an actress had died a natural death now that she had to run Ivy Farm. So she kissed Maeve and shook Caleb's hand and wished them well, but refused to go back to the States with them.

'Sure an' aren't I just as happy as a bird here, in me own place?' she demanded. 'I've me friends, me work here on the farm, everything I could want. And I've mebbe met the man I'll wed one day already, so no point in searching further, Maeve. But I hope you'll come back and dance at me wedding and wish me well.'

Maeve hugged her and said she'd miss her, promised to come back for the wedding, hugged her father, hugged Caitlin, wept bitter tears . . . but went, left them to get on with it. Her letters came regularly, but it seemed to Lucy as though they said less and less. She had borne a son, they called him Padraig after her father, she hoped for a girl next so she could name the child Lucy, after her dearest. She had a nice house, she called it a 'brownstone', which seemed a strange thing to call a house, and a big yard, which apparently meant back garden. She held coffee mornings – Lucy and her grandfather exchanged puzzled glances – in aid of various charities and went to sewing bees and fourth-of-July parties. She lived, in short, a life which was so foreign to the Murphys that they simply stopped reading the letters properly and were just glad that their Maeve was so obviously, patently, happy.

Lucy wrote letters back, of course, but because she suspected that her news was not important to the new

Maeve, they were always a little stilted, a little artificial.

But right now, Caitlin had asked a question and Lucy, after a moment's thought, answered it. 'Granny Mogg's completely, totally, sane, if that's what you're meanin' when you say is she in her right mind. But she's livin' in the past today, and she wants Finn mortal bad. If only, if *only* we knew where he was and could get a message to him!'

'Why don't you get her to look in her seeing bowl?' Caitlin said suddenly. 'If she's in her right mind but livin' in the past she might pick him up easier.'

Lucy would have liked to scoff, but it was the first suggestion which, she thought, really might stand a chance. Of course she didn't believe in what Granny Mogg said she saw in the sweetie jar, but she had been right last time. Little Evie had died a violent death, Maeve had confirmed it, and though Maeve had looked and looked for Linnet, even going round to the address in Juvenal Street where her sister and the child had once lived, on her way back to Ireland, she had been unable to trace her niece.

'They did used to live 'ere,' the landlady had said, glowering sullenly at Maeve. 'But they left – went off to Americky. Never heard a word from either of 'em since, nor want to. They left owin' me money,' she added crossly.

So Maeve had admitted defeat, and had told Lucy that although she hoped the two sisters would meet up one day, it clearly wasn't going to be just yet. And Lucy had never mentioned that she was sure Linnet was in Liverpool and not the States because hadn't Maeve tried Liverpool and hadn't that sour old landlady told her the Murphys had gone to America? So she salved her conscience and put her sister right out of her mind once more.

'Well? What d'you think, Luceen?' Lucy broke a couple of eggs into the hissing fat and was about to answer when the back door rattled open and the men trooped in. Caitlin raised her voice. 'If you think the seeing bowl might have a chance we could do it after breakfast.'

'I'll take her through some tea and bread and butter in a minute and see what she says,' Lucy said, skilfully lading sausages, bacon, fried bread and two eggs onto a plate and handing it to her friend. 'It's a good idea, alanna, and it might just work. She's a clever old gal, our Granny Mogg. Give this plateful to your da' whilst I dish up for the rest, would you?'

And as soon as the men were sitting at the table, elbows squared, eating the food, she poured Granny Mogg a cup of tea, buttered a thinly sliced round of bread, and carried the tray through to the small parlour.

Granny Mogg was lying back against her pillows, her eyes closed. Her small, thin little face was pallid and there was an ominous shine on her brow and a blue line round her sunken lips. But she opened her eyes when she heard Lucy take the chair by the bed and gave both girls the ghost of her old, warming smile.

'Ah, tis good to see ye both together,' she said faintly. 'Was ye goin' to bring me me seein' bowl, then?'

In the astonished silence which followed you could have heard a pin drop. Lucy broke it. 'Yes, Gran,' she said baldly. 'How did you know? You couldn't have heard us talkin', surely?'

Granny's shoulders moved in the slightest of shrugs so Lucy held the cup of tea to her lips and jerked her head at Caitlin.

'Go and fetch it through,' she whispered. 'And try not to let me grandad see what you're doin'. Take a sip o' tay,' she urged Granny Mogg in her normal voice. 'Caitlin won't be long, alanna, she'll be back be the time you've drunk up.'

But Granny Mogg couldn't take more than a couple of tiny bird-sips. Then her head fell sideways on the pillow. 'Savin' me strength for the seein' bowl,' she whispered. 'Oh I does want Finn bad, alanna, I wants him wi' such a gnawin' hunger!'

'If you can tell us where he's at you shall have him,' Lucy promised. 'Ah, here comes Caitlin with your – your bowl.'

Caitlin had filled the sweetie jar with water and brought it in on a tray which she placed carefully across Granny Mogg's tiny, bony knees. 'There y'are,' she said bracingly. 'Want the curtains drawed across?'

The old head shook, then the old hands reached out and cupped the sweetie jar and through the almost transparent fingers the pale September sunshine seemed, suddenly, to fill the water with a thousand reflections, a thousand tiny pictures. The room, the girls' faces, the old woman's burning eyes . . . and something else, another scene, another face . . .

'Sure an' he's comin' this way,' Granny Mogg whispered slowly. 'Ye know the lakes? Where the old Quane stood wit' her ladies? He's passin' by there this minute . . .' she leaned forward, her eyes fixed, intent. 'Oh come to me, me lovely lad, me broth of a boyo, come to Granny Mogg for her eyes long to see ye!'

'Lady's View! But that's miles and miles away, up by Killarney,' Lucy said. 'It'll take him a month o' Sundays to get here, unless . . . is he on foot, Granny? Or is he after gettin' a lift?'

'He's on foot,' Granny said. 'You'll bring him to me, alanna? You'll not let me die wit'out seein' me boy?'

Lucy smiled at the old woman and took her hand. Useless to deny that she was dying when her face was like a fine, crumpled lawn handkerchief and her eyes already had that vague, other-worldly look. But Granny Mogg did not fear dying, she just dreaded going away without saying goodbye to her boy, Lucy knew that.

'I'll fetch him back, Granny,' she promised. 'Caitlin will give you your bread and butter, I'll leave right now. And I'll be back before the cat can spit; you know me, I get things done!'

'Aye, you'll be back,' the old woman said. 'He's doin' 'is best but foots is slow. You fetch 'im for old Granny.'

Lucy nodded again, smiled, and left the room, her mind whirling. She could fetch him back now they knew where he was but how? If she rode down to the lakes on either of the carthorses it would be quicker than walking, but not, surely, quick enough? Granny was mortally ill, she knew that, her life was moving rapidly towards it close. She must get Finn back, she must!

She went through into the kitchen and her grandfather raised his head.

'Has she gone?' he asked mildly. 'Poor old 'oman, has she taken her leave of us?'

'No, but it won't be long now. She told me where Finn could be found and she wants to see him,' Lucy said. No point in explanations. 'He's up at Lady's View, on the lakes. Grandad, how can I get there quickly?'

'In Tommy Muldoon's delivery van,' her grandfather said at once. 'It's new, but he'd drive you there as it's an emergency, I daresay. He goes up to Killarney now and then.'

'Oh bless you, Grandad! I'm off; I'll be back as soon as I can,' Lucy said. 'Pray God she lasts!'

Finn was walking at his best pace, arms swinging, legs going like clockwork. He calculated that if he continued at the same pace all through the day and night he might, just might, get to Ivy Farm in time. So when a brand-new delivery van, coming from the direction of his destination and heading for Killarney stopped beside him, his only thought was to wish it had been going the opposite way. He knew he would be hard pressed to arrive in time and a lift right now would have been a gift from the gods. When he looked up at the cab, however, expecting to be asked the way to Killarney or some outlying village, there, smiling down at him, was Lucy: guinea-gold hair gleaming in the sun, so many freckles that you couldn't put a pin between them, long grey-blue eyes narrowed into slits because she was so delighted to see him.

'Finn! Oh, thank God! This is Mr Muldoon, he's very kindly brought me to fetch you. Granny Mogg's . . . she's . . .'

'She's dyin',' Finn said, when Lucy's voice was unaccountably suspended. 'Poor old gal, but sure an' isn't she a good age.' He turned to the van driver, a well-set-up man in his thirties who was smiling down at him. 'Nice to meet ye, Mr Muldoon; you have my thanks for this day's work.'

'A pleasure, Finn Delaney. Hop aboard and we'll be off.'

'How did you know she was dyin'?' Lucy said. Tears stood now in her long blue-grey eyes. 'We couldn't find you, Finn, we were so worried.'

'I knew she'd not last much longer, so I set out as soon as I could. How did ye know where to find me, alanna?'

'I didn't; *she* found you in the . . . the seein' bowl,' Lucy said, leaning well out of the cab and whispering the information. 'Finn, do answer me – how did you know when the time had arrived to come to Ivy Farm?'

He grinned up at her, then set his foot on the step and swung himself into the van beside her. 'Move up, don't be hoggin' the seat,' he said briskly. 'Sure an' Granny

Mogg isn't the only one who can see further than most. And there'll be others comin' from the countryside around, later. Tinkers take care of their own.'

Lucy looked at him, her eyes rounding. 'But they don't know where she is,' she whispered. 'You've kept her safe all these years because they don't know where she is.'

'Some of 'em know,' Finn told her. 'Some of 'em, the old'uns, they know all right. How's she been?'

'Cheerful. But frail . . . very frail.' Lucy reached out a hand and took his fingers in hers. 'Oh, Finn, you've been gone a long time, we've missed you turble, Granny an' me.'

'I had money to earn,' Finn said shortly. 'I'm glad o' the lift, though. I wouldn't want to fail in me obligations. Whose idea was it to bring the van for me?'

The engine was noisy so speaking softly, almost into each other's ears, they could be sure of a private conversation, particularly as Mr Muldoon seemed to enjoy a tune and accompanied every mile of the way with loud and continual song.

'A bit of Caitlin and a bit of me grandad,' Lucy said at once. 'What were you doin' this summer, Finn, to stay away so long? Did you find a good-payin' job at once?'

'I've been drivin' a jauntin' car in Killarney and makin' the visitors laugh,' Finn said proudly. 'Me and Derry Crewe bought the jauntin' car between us, but I drive it mostly. A lot of Americans I do drive and they're generous to a poor Irish tinker so they are. I tell 'em stories, I sing 'em songs, I advise 'em where best to fish for trout an' salmon. Finn Delaney's a name to conjure wit' in Killarney, an' long may it stay so!'

'You're a divil of a feller, Finn Delaney,' Lucy said rather sourly. 'And were many of the Americans young and pretty – and female?'

'Divil a bit of it – ugly old maids every one,' Finn said,

untruthfully but with considerable tact. 'Not a sweet little colleen amongst 'em to rival the rose of Cahersiveen.'

As they drove along the pretty winding roads, the hedges heavy with wild roses and honeysuckle, Finn thought about the girl who sat beside him, with her burden of golden hair, the dusting of freckles across her little nose, the sweet, mischievous smile. And when he told her that there wasn't a girl to rival herself he saw that smile break out, saw how she cast her eyes down so that the expression in them was shielded from him by her long, curling lashes. And it made him smile, in his turn.

Women! They were all the same, and most of 'em were after Finn Delaney, with his strong, supple body and needle-quick mind! He was always willin' to oblige 'em, of course, particularly the lovely, wayward tinker girls with their long black hair and generous ways. But Lucy Murphy was safe from him; she was a young lady, a rich farmer's granddaughter and the apple of her grandad's eye. Finn Delaney had more sense than to meddle there, no matter how tempted. So he smiled at Lucy and squeezed her hand and then leaned across her and started to tell Mr Muldoon all about the summer he'd spent driving his jaunting car round the streets of Killarney, out under the strawberry trees to Lady's View, and further afield still. And Lucy listened and smiled peacefully now and then and it occurred to him that she was a very restful female, that she made no demands on anyone, that he could not have chosen a better person to care for Granny Mogg.

One day, he found himself thinking, one day, when I'm old and want to settle down . . . but he killed the thought, because he knew he would never be old, never want to settle down. He was a rover, an adventurer, and once Granny Mogg was gone he would go, too, and probably never come back to the flat watermeadows and the good fishing, to the old, ivy-clad farm in the hollow of the hills. Never again would he see the colleen with the long, blue-grey eyes and the sweet smile, because he could not take her from her rich farmlands and her loving family and give her nothing in return but a campfire, a ragged sacking tent, a jaunting car and the love of a feckless, faithless tinker.

They arrived in time. They entered the room, Lucy clutching Finn's sleeve, and Granny Mogg was sleeping, smiling in her sleep. But she woke at once when Finn spoke her name and began to talk to him, though in Gamon which was the tinkers' own tongue and not a language which Lucy understood. She spoke fiercely at first, then more mildly, and Finn knelt by the bed with her little, bent claw in his big, tanned hand and nodded, shook his head, answered in the same tongue.

'What does she say?' Lucy asked at one point, and saw that Finn's eyes, which were darker than the darkest peat-pool on the marsh, had filled with tears. But he answered her patiently and seemed to feel no shame to let the tears run down his lean cheeks since he did not bother to wipe them off.

'She's arrangin' her will,' he said quietly. 'She has property – oh, not the sort of property which you mean, but property, nonetheless. She has told me who is to have what and now she is content. Very soon she'll start on her long journey.'

Granny Mogg died that night, though Lucy was not present when the old woman breathed her last. Finn told her to go to bed, said he would watch with Granny Mogg all through the night, and next morning, very early, when Lucy peeped into the small parlour, Finn turned and smiled at her and came over to the doorway in which she hovered.

'She's gone, and gone whilst she slept with no pain or fuss,' he said simply. 'Just before midnight, it was. Don't fear that she died within doors, either, for that she would not have wanted. I carried her outside, for she weighed no more than a tiny child, down as far as the gate which leads to the watermeadows. And there she breathed two harsh, hard breaths and then no more. Peaceful, she went, which was as she would have wanted it.'

Lucy looked at the bed; very tiny and wizened did Granny Mogg look as she lay there, on top of the covers now with her limbs straight, her arms crossed on her breast, her eyes closed, her mouth, which had laughed so much, severe in death.

'She looks peaceful,' she breathed. 'Shall I fetch the midwife, to lay her out?'

Finn laughed. 'A midwife, for a tinker? No, there's no need. The others will be here by now, I'll go out and fetch a couple o' wise women in to her. They'll do what's necessary whilst you an' I make tea and take it out to the rest. The pyre will be the sod hut, of course, and as many branches as they've brought with them.'

'There's no one outside . . .' Lucy began, and stopped. She could hear small sounds now, which had not been there two minutes earlier. A mule shifted its feet and whickered and a donkey answered. A shod animal, a horse probably, clinked its hoof against the paving stones and a child called out in a shrill, carefree tone.

'That's the Tuam tribe; the others will follow before noon,' Finn said. 'They'll collect wood for the pyre, though the hut will catch easily; we've had no rain for ten days, a fortnight. And they'll have to set up camp, of course.'

'Right,' Lucy said. She bent over the bed and kissed

the still, small face. 'Goodbye, dear Granny Mogg; you'll be sadly missed.' She turned and went before Finn out of the room, along the passage and into the kitchen. To her surprise the fire was already blazing and as she and Finn entered Padraig Murphy turned to face them. He smiled.

'Sure an' isn't it a grand sight, all those people an' animals assemblin' in me haggard wit' the sun comin' over the top of the hills an' the mist risin' from the water?' he said, gesturing through the low kitchen window. 'And won't Granny Mogg have a send-off to be proud of indeed indeed, and her only a bit of a woman?'

'Thanks for putting the kettle on, Grandad,' Lucy said. 'Finn thinks we ought to make tea for them because he says they'll be busy now, finding wood for the pyre and setting up camp. And he's gone to fetch two of the women to – to lay Granny Mogg out.'

'Aye, aye. No confinin' coffin for a tinker, just a winding cloth,' her grandfather said absently. 'An' the warmth of the fire on your old bones to speed you on your journey. It's not such a bad way to go, alanna.'

'I know, but I'm going to miss her,' Lucy muttered. She was not ashamed of her tears, but she was afraid Finn would think less of her for them. Granny Mogg was out of pain and had passed over; there should be no need to cry for her now. 'I'll go and fetch more water.'

And for half an hour she and Finn carted water, made tea in the buckets which the tinkers brought to the back door, and kept themselves busy.

'I don't know that I want to see . . . the other business,' Lucy said, when Caitlin came over to help her to prepare breakfast for the farmhands. 'I think it will upset me . . . and they don't show much emotion, do they? Tinkers, I mean.'

'I'm going,' Caitlin said, surprising Lucy, for of the two of them Caitlin was usually the one to shrink back from unpleasantness of any sort. 'I want to say goodbye to her. It's – it's the last thing we can do, to give the old girl a send-off.'

'I wonder, will they have a ceilidh afterwards?' Lucy said. 'Folk do, though it's called a wake. And you're right, Caitlin; I'll come with you.'

So the two girls were present when the sod hut was pulled down, the fire lit, the delicate body consumed by the flames. And Lucy voiced what they both thought when they returned to Ivy Farm.

'It was beautiful,' she said wonderingly. 'I never thought it would be, but it was. I'm glad I went, and one day, when I'm really old, I shall ask if what's left of me can be turned to ash and spread on the waters of the lough whilst all around people mourn and tear their clothes and let their tears flow without shame.'

It was over and Finn knew that he should go. But before he could leave there was the bequest to Lucy, for she was to have Granny Mogg's ancient gold necklace, and that necklace could not be handed to a buffer woman, a woman who was not of the tribe whilst the women of the tribe could see or there would be trouble. The necklace had been passed down, from mother to daughter, for centuries, probably. But Granny Mogg had no daughter and her granddaughter-in-law had let her husband cast Granny out to die alone in a ditch, so she deserved – and would get – nothing.

The tribes did not have many laws, but the wildest and least law-abiding tribe would do its best to see that the wishes of the dead were honoured. Granny Mogg could leave her possessions to whom she pleased, there was nothing to say she could not leave her necklace to a buffer woman, but Finn was realist enough to know that there were women in the Tuam tribe, good enough women, who would do almost anything to get hold of that necklace. It was thought to have magical properties, it was revered and valued . . . but if Lucy kept it for special occasions and took care of it there was no reason why anyone should ever know she had it. They would think Granny Mogg had hidden it, or that it had been burned with her, on the funeral pyre. So Finn told himself that he could not leave until he had shown Lucy the necklace, handed it over and made her promise to keep it hidden whilst the tinkers were in the neighbourhood. Which meant remaining in the area for a few days, at least.

It was harvest time, so he had work in plenty. He worked for Padraig and Padraig said he had never had a better worker.

'Come back next year, boy, and you can sleep in the attic room and feed wit' the family,' he said heartily. 'Never did I know such a feller for work – ye can beat even Kellach who is at the height of his strength. Stay, if you will, for there's always work to be done on a thriving farm like this.'

Finn smiled and said he would think about it and wasn't Mr Murphy the best of men to make an offer so generous to a poor tinker? But he knew he must go, and soon.

'He won't stay; he's never stayed,' Lucy said in private to Caitlin. 'He's got to move on, it's in his blood. I pity the woman that falls in love with Finn Delaney, for he'll never stay in one place long enough to be caught.'

'He's grown awfu' handsome,' Caitlin murmured, with her rich, dark hair falling softly over her dark eyes and hiding the expression in them. Does she know I'm sweet on him Lucy wondered? Does she feel the same about him? Sad it is that we, who once shared everything, can grow secretive and solitary and keep the secrets of our souls from each other, just because a man has entered our lives.

'Yes, he's handsome,' Lucy agreed. 'But sure it's not looks that are important when you're after marryin' a feller.' Caitlin's eyebrows rose and no wonder; how my mouth gabs out the things I most want to keep to meself, Lucy mourned, and once more her mouth opened and words came out. 'Not that I'm thinkin' of marriage, me. Not for many a long day.'

She shot a quick look at Caitlin. Caitlin's cheeks were rosy and her eyes were very bright. 'Nor me,' she said quickly. 'Why, we're neither of us in our dotage yet; plenty of time for that kind o' thing.'

She is in love with him, Lucy thought, with a mixture of dismay and elation, because at least as things stood they'd both made fools of themselves. And fools was what they were since wasn't it as plain as it could be that Finn wasn't for the likes of them? Handsome, yes, charming, yes, but – but fickle as the west wind, and about as easy to grasp, Lucy reminded herself, and tried to work up a proper scorn for a man like that.

And then he came to her on a fine summer evening and said would she like to walk with him down to the lough now, and take a look at the castle and watch the sun setting over the mountains? And Lucy's mouth opened to say no she would not, she was far too busy and besides, what was the point? Only her heart got in before her head and her heart made her mouth say, 'That would be nice,' and then it made her body get up and walk beside him, out of the farmhouse, across the haggard, down the lane and into the sloping meadows, just as the sun was casting its last long, golden rays across the water.

'I've enjoyed bein' a part of your family so I have Lucy Murphy,' Finn said, as they walked.

He's going and he's going to tell me so, he's going to

say he'll never return, that we must say goodbye, Lucy's acute imagination observed dispassionately whilst her voice murmured politely that they had enjoyed his company and that Grandad thought him a marvellous hard worker.

'Ah, well, we can work, us tinkers,' Finn said. 'I didn't tell you before, alanna, but Granny Mogg wanted you to have something of hers to remember her by. It's in here.'

They had reached the castle and he gestured to the archway into the keep.

'I don't need anything to remember her by, I'll remember her all my life,' Lucy said with a rush of affection for the old woman. Whilst Granny Mogg lived, you came here twice, sometimes three times a year, her heart said soundlessly. I'll never forget her for that reason alone, though there are a thousand others.

'Well, maybe. But she wanted you to have it. It's in her old room. Will ye come up?'

'Of course I will,' Lucy said, momentarily affronted. 'It wasn't me that didn't like the stairs, Finn, it was Caitlin. I'll go first.' And she shot up the stairs so fast that Finn was left far behind laughing up at her as she pushed against the door and burst into the small, round room.

She had not been up here once since Granny Mogg had moved into the farm and she looked round, momentarily distracted. It had not changed at all, not one iota. The bracken bed was still piled up against the wall, the table was in the middle of the room, the chair pushed beneath it. Only the smell was different; now the little room smelt of mice and loneliness.

Finn came into the room and closed the door behind him. He went over to the bracken bed and shifted it from the wall and showed Lucy a small loose stone there. He pulled it out and pushed his hand into the hole, drawing it back with something wrapped in a piece of what looked like black velvet. He unwrapped the velvet and gold shone dully.

'Here,' he handed her the necklace and Lucy gasped, unable to believe that she was being offered something so heavily, richly glowing, but she took it and stood quite still, looking down at it.

It was very, very old, and every link was wrought in the shape of a bee, and each bee clung with its front or back legs to the bee before and behind it. It was the most beautiful thing she had ever seen, ever touched, and the gold was soft and richly coloured, but the necklace was heavy and cold in her hands and suddenly she was afraid. She shook her head and handed the heavy gold chain back to him.

'I don't want it; truly Finn, it frightens me. You must have it – I give it to you freely because . . . because I loved you, when I was a little girl. Take it and give it to – to your wife, when you marry. Please, Finn! I would rather you had it than anyone else in the world.'

He stood there, holding the necklace, his expression suddenly diffident. 'No, I can't take it, Luceen. It's the only truly valuable thing Granny Mogg possessed, it was her grandmother's, and her grandmother's grandmother's before that. It has come down in her family for generations but tinkers don't regard that, no one would blame Granny for not wanting her daughter-in-law to have it, not after what happened. She had no daughters of her own and she knew you loved her – she loved you. Please take it.'

Lucy put her hands behind her and shook her head. 'I can't. Besides, I've given it to you, as a present for your future wife. You can't refuse me that, Finn. Now can we go home?'

He looked at her for a long moment; his eyes seemed to burn into her very soul and she was sure he knew how she felt about him and despised her for it. But presently he reached out and took her hand and his fingers were warm and light, their grasp friendly.

'Thank you, alanna, for your gift. I'll wear the necklace round my own neck, for safe keeping, until the time comes to pass it on to another. And now I suspect you know what I'm going to say.'

'You're leaving,' Lucy said calmly.

'Yes. And I shan't...'

'You won't be coming back. It's all right, Finn, I understand. But – but you won't go for ever, will you?' Her composure slipped suddenly and she looked down, afraid he would read the naked love in her eyes. 'You'll come back one day, will you not, if only to dance at my wedding?'

He grinned then, a broad, natural grin, and transferred his hands to her shoulders, shaking her slightly.

'Little goose! I cannot for the life of me imagine you a sober wedded wife but no doubt it'll come to that one of these fine days. So if you want me at your wedding, you must send for me.' He stopped smiling suddenly and was serious. 'Alanna, I shan't come back because I turn my face forwards, always. Only Granny had the power to bring me back season after season, year after year. But now she's gone and I must go onward, I must see more of this land. If you ever need me come to Killarney and talk to the man who drives the yellow and green jaunting car; if it isn't meself then it'll be me good friend, Devvy. He'll tell you where I'm to be found, if I'm still on this earth.'

'Oh, Finn, don't say that,' Lucy quavered. 'You aren't going to die, are you?'

'Man born of woman is bound to die, Granny Mogg used to say. And remember, we're talkin' of the distant future, when you're going to invite me to your weddin'!

By then I'll be an old feller, if not a dead'un. Now come on, let's see you smile.'

She smiled though tears trembled in her eyes and Finn smiled too and then, very gently, he took her in his arms. He kissed her with tenderness, then with passion – and then he simply let her go and moved away from her.

'Enough of that, Luceen. Let me walk you home.'

Without another word they walked home; he saw her into the farmhouse, called out to her grandfather, said he needed to have a word with Kellach before he went to the barn to sleep. He walked away jauntily, without looking back, and Lucy went up to her room, undressed, washed, put on her nightgown, got into bed.

And once in bed she thumped her pillow and then turned over and sobbed into it, for she knew she would not see Finn when she awoke next morning. That kiss – those kisses – had been their farewell.

But he did the right thing, leaving, her mind said comfortingly just before she fell asleep. It isn't everyone who could live a tinker's life, and I don't even want to try. I love the farm, and Grandad, staying in one really beautiful place surrounded by people I love and respect. And some day soon I'll meet a man who matters to me more than anyone else on earth, and we'll marry and make beautiful love and settle down to raise a family.

But learning to live without even the hope of Finn was going to be awfully hard.

Maeve, in her neat brownstone house in New York, entertained Caleb's friends and made friends of her own. She soon had a thriving social life and worked for any charity which needed her, because Caleb was an increasingly popular and successful attorney and insisted that she employ staff to help in the house. Caleb wanted her to have a nanny for little Padraig, too, but Maeve drew the line at that. Could she not look after her own child as, once, she had looked after little Evie's? She pushed Padraig's pram in the park and although she did have a maid, a nice little girl who came from the old country, as Maeve did, as well as a cleaning woman who did the rough work, a gardener and a boot boy, she did most of the cooking and all of the food buying, trekking all over New York to get the proper ingredients for her soon famous dishes.

'Maeve's soda bread is out of this world, and her fruit puddings are better than mother made,' Caleb's business associates said. 'She's a fine woman, she worships Caleb and that li'l feller of theirs.' And they looked accusingly at their smart wives who never touched a mixing bowl and scarcely knew their own nanny-reared children.

So Maeve was happy and busy and though she often thought of home, of big Padraig and of Lucy, it was comfortably, fleetingly. They lived their own lives far away and their lives impinged upon Maeve's not at all.

But the little daughter she longed for did not put in an appearance, and for fear that little Padraig would grow up spoiled and selfish Maeve pushed him across to Central Park every afternoon, even when it rained or when snow piled up at the pavements edge, so that he might play with other kiddies on the grass, the swings, by the lake.

On a particularly pleasant October afternoon, when she was pushing the pram with Padraig just awoken and inclined to be grumpy, in it, she slowed by the lake to let him see the ducks, and what must the naughty boy do but heave off his brand new tweed hat with the velvet bow on top and throw it in the lake, where it bobbed amongst the interested and investigative ducks like a tiny curragh. And not only was the hat new, it went with his little tweed and velvet coat and had cost a great many dollars, so Maeve gave a cry of distress and looked round for a stick to prod it out before the ducks decided it was good to eat after all.

The only stick available, however, fell short by a good two feet of the object she was fishing for. With a sigh, Maeve began to unlace her sensible shoes; there was nothing else for it, she would have to wade in, and oh, though the sunshine was warm, she just knew the water would be cold! She gave her son, sitting up in the pram and beaming at the ducks, a black look, then rumpled his soft hair. He was only being a boy, bless him!

But as luck would have it, Maeve did not have to paddle. A young fellow in a seaman's jersey and rough navy trousers had seen her plight. He didn't even bother to remove his boots but simply walked a foot or so into the water, fished for the hat with the very stick Maeve had so unsuccessfully used, and returned the hat to her with a grin.

'Oh, that was so kind; thank you very much; I'm afraid me son's getting full of mischief and would rather walk than ride,' she explained, smiling at the young man. 'But he'll outgrow that, I hope.'

'Oh, all kids gerrin 'ot water when they're fed up of ridin' and would rather walk,' the young man said easily. He leaned over the pram. 'Oo's a bad feller, eh? But your mam's goin' to get you out o' there any minute, 'cos it ain't far to the playground.'

'You're right, I am. And what are you doing so far from home, may I ask?' Maeve said, as she began to push the pram towards the playground and the young man fell into step beside her. 'You're from Liverpool, England, or I'm much mistaken. I'm Irish, but I spent some time in your city a couple of years back and I could recognise that accent anywhere. What are you doing in New York?'

'I've got five days ashore so I come wi' me bezzie up

the river to tek a look around,' the young man said. 'How come you're here, missus?'

'It's a long story,' Maeve said, with no intention of telling it. 'What's a "bezzie"? That's a new one on me!'

'Best pal,' the seaman said. They reached the play area and Maeve unfastened her son from his prison and lifted him onto the ground, then sank down on the nearest seat. The seaman sat down too and held out a square, capable hand. 'Me name's Roddy Sullivan; nice to meet you . . . ?'

'I'm married to an American, I'm Mrs Caleb Zowkoughski,' Maeve said, shaking the hand vigorously.

'Nice to meet you, Mrs Zowkoughski,' the young man said. 'And what's the young feller-me-lad called?'

'Padraig, after me father back home in County Kerry, but we call him Paddy, usually. And when will you be back in Liverpool, Mr Sullivan?'

'In two weeks, if we're lucky,' the seaman said rather gloomily. 'We're runnin' timber from Canada to Liverpool this trip, wi' a two-day turnaround, but next time we'll be away very much longer – weeks an' weeks, because we'll be coastin' up and down America an' the West Indies, movin' timber. On our nex' trip we shan't make our 'ome port for a while, worst luck.'

'Why's that?' Maeve asked. 'I thought all young men wanted to see the world.'

'Oh aye, but I've 'ad a row wi' me young lady. It were all a mistake, she took wharr I said wrong, I never meant . . .' Mr Sullivan said, going a little red around the gills, Maeve noticed. 'You know 'ow women can be, Mrs Zowkoughski – bleedin' unreasonable, if you ask . . . oh, sorry, I meaned very unreasonable, o' course.'

'Tell me about it,' Maeve said tactfully, since it was all too clear that he had every intention of doing just that. 'Perhaps just telling someone will help.'

Roddy liked his companion; she seemed sensible and practical. Perhaps, he thought, hope rising, she really could advise him. She was a woman, after all, and would surely understand another woman's strange behaviour. So he outlined what had happened to cause the quarrel.

'She 'ad a good job in an insurance office, she were 'appy there. And when me back's turned for three lousy weeks, what does she do? She moves in wi' a rich old bloke from work, that's what.'

'Married him, do you mean?' Mrs Zowkoughski asked. 'In three weeks? That seems rather . . .'

'No, she din't marry 'im 'cos 'e's married already,' Roddy said unhappily. 'She just moved in, or that's wharr I were told.'

'Just moved . . . and he's already *married*? Oh, I suppose he's a widower, is he? But even so . . .'

'The old b . . . gent's very rich,' Roddy explained. 'He's gorra ruck o' servants, a motor, a big 'ouse . . .'

'Is she a gold-digger?' Mrs Zowkoughski asked. 'Well, I suppose she must be, if she was prepared to – to do that just because he was rich.'

Irrationally, Roddy immediately thought Mrs Zowkoughski prejudiced; it was not Linnet's fault, it was all down to the bleedin' millionaire she'd met up with, he'd taken advantage of her, that was clear once you'd thought about it.

He said so and Mrs Zowkoughski said judiciously that though it was wrong of the man to have offered a young girl everything but marriage at least she then had a straight choice, to behave well or badly. His young lady had chosen to behave badly in Mrs Zowkoughski's opinion, and Mr Sullivan had every right to be seriously annoyed with her.

'I advise you never to speak to her again, but to find yourself another young lady. After all, there are plenty about,' she said, smiling at him. 'I'm sure you can do better for yourself than yearning after a rich man's leavings, for that is what she'll become, unless he decides to offer her marriage after all, that is.'

'But she's only a kid, she's not seen much o' the world,' Roddy said rather wildly. He had thought he wanted the very advice he was being given but now he realised that what he truly wanted was someone to tell him to try again. 'She's got no mam to advise 'er, nor nothin'. She must ha' thought she were doin' the best for 'erself. It ain't as if I've ever asked 'er to marry me . . .'

Mrs Zowkoughski leaned across the bit of bench which separated them and took his hand. 'Go back home and tell her you love her,' she said warmly. 'Because it's plain that you do. Give her a chance to be sensible and she'll probably be happy to abandon her old man and his money for the chance of true love.'

'I will, then,' Roddy said, getting to his feet and giving Mrs Zowkoughski his most charming smile. 'I'll do just as you say, missus, an' thanks for listenin'. I'd best be on me way now, I'm meetin' some pals in a fish restaurant on 52nd Street an' that's a good walk from 'ere.' He waved to the little boy playing on the grass and strode away, his step lighter than it had been for a while. She was right! He would definitely give Linnet another chance, after all she didn't deserve to lose him because of one little mistake!

As he walked, though, he remembered that he had not told Mrs Zowkoughski Linnet's name – nor, indeed, nearly all the story; would her advice have been the same had she heard that the quarrel had not just been a quarrel but a fight as well? Because when he'd gone happily along to Exchange Flags to meet Linnet out of work and been told that she was living with some rich feller on a posh little street backing onto Prince's Park he'd seen red at once, and was still seeing it when he arrived outside the house and met Linnet, humming a tune beneath her breath, heading for the post box at the end of the drive to post a letter.

'Hello, Roddy!' she said, giving him a great big smile as though she expected to be greeted with equal enthusiasm. 'I didn't know you were ashore, how . . .'

She got no further. 'Don't flannel me, an' you'd best go back in there an' pack your bleedin' bags, queen,' he had hissed at her, grabbing her arm. 'Why, what a way to be'ave, an' you supposed to be such a little lady!'

She had got cross – how she dared, when you thought what she'd done! But she had, nevertheless.

'Let go my arm, Roddy,' she said, pulling against him. 'I'm not packing any bags, what on earth's got into you? I'm not just staying over, you know. I live here now, permanent.'

'With a feller old enough to be your father; I know,' he jeered. He had seen a middle-aged man edge a long-bonneted motor car cautiously out of the drive moments before Linnet had come singing into view. 'Well, I'm back now, and I won't stand for it, d'you hear? I won't let you lower yourself . . . many a man wouldn't want to 'ave nothin' to do wi' a girl what be'aved like you 'ave, but anyone can make a mistake and . . .'

'Roddy Sullivan, how dare you? I've not made a mistake, it's the best move I ever made! I get more money, I'll be able to save easier, and Mr Cowan's kind and generous. He'll take good care of me, he's already promised that as soon as I've settled in . . .'

'Not marriage? Don't say the old lecher's promised marriage, flower?' Roddy had gasped, suddenly truly afraid. It was hateful that his little Linnet – his, his! – had been tricked into moving in with an ugly old man, but suddenly he realised that her living with the feller, though it hurt like a knife through the heart, wasn't the end. But marriage! If she married him then that was it, he might as well leave right away. 'You wouldn't marry 'im, chuck? Marrying's for life, you know. You've made one bad mistake so don't make another what you can't alter.'

Linnet wrenched herself free of him and walked past him, nose in the air, cheeks scarlet with what he hoped was shame but suspected was rage.

'Bugger off, Roddy,' she hissed over her shoulder. 'I hate you! I thought you'd be pleased that I'd done well for meself. You call yourself me friend but instead you're just nasty, as usual. Well, if you think I've done the wrong thing then just bugger off, d'you hear me?'

He heard and was stunned. Linnet never swore, he didn't know where she had learned such language! Probably from her precious Mr Cowan, he thought bitterly, totally forgetting the many times he had sworn far more colourfully in front of her when they were kids. He tried to catch her arm again but she turned on him with such fury that he desisted, trailing behind her to the post box and back to the drive, telling her that she was going to regret what she'd done, but that he, Roddy, was prepared to be magnanimous about it. If she left right now he would see there was no talk, they could be married in a jiffy just in case . . . he paused delicately . . . in case her loaf had already been cut and there was a bun in the oven.

Afterwards, he was inclined to think that even such tortuous frankness had been a mistake. She turned and stared, a frownline appearing between her soft brows.

'Wha-at?' she said slowly. 'Why can't you say what you mean instead of talking in ri . . . oh! Oh, how *dare* you, Roddy Sullivan, how dare you even *think* such a . . . go on, I told you to bugger off, now bloody do it!'

And when poor Roddy tried to lay a hand on her arm and explain again that she had been taken in by an older man, that he, for one, did not blame her, she hacked him in the shins with a small but sturdy boot, at the same time swinging that wicked left hook – which, as a member of the weaker sex, she should never have possessed – and catching him right on the bridge of the nose. He staggered back – anyone would have – and cracked his head on the gatepost. And then, believe it or not, the wretched, unfeeling girl laughed. Laughed, as he clutched first his bleeding nose and then the great lump on his scalp and tried to see if his leg was broken!

'That's right, have a good cry,' she said tauntingly. 'And then go home to your mam and I hope I never see you again as long as I live.'

A good cry! His bleedin' eyes were waterin' from the unladylike punch and she accused him, Roddy Sullivan, of crying! All his love and concern for her vanished on the words.

'Bugger off yourself, you nasty little bitch,' he shouted. 'And you never will see me again, don't you fret – not as long as either of us shall live!'

And with that he had turned and left her, limping back to the tram stop and wishing Mr Cowan joy of her. Just let him cross her once, he told himself, and he'll feel that boot somewhere soft and see a fist atravellin' towards him, and serve him soddin' well right. A tram stopped alongside him and Roddy swung himself aboard. Oh, aye, Linnet's boot in his essentials would put a stop to his 'orrible ways, the dirty old man. But later, lying in his bed at home having refused to tell anyone why he had a swollen nose and a great lump on his head, to say nothing of a limp which Long John Silver might have envied, he did just what Linnet had accused him of.

He cried.

After the interlude in New York Roddy was desperate to

271

get back and the moment his ship tied up in Canning Dock he set out for home. He wanted his mother's advice.

'It's Linnet,' he told Mrs Sullivan once the preliminaries of greeting were over. 'She's not workin' in Exchange Flags any more, she's – oh, she's – she's –'

'She's nannyin',' Mrs Sullivan said placidly. 'She's gerrin' good money, our Roddy. An' Mollie, that's the feller's little girl, she's a good, pretty little kid. I reckon our Linnet's falled on 'er feet this time.'

Afterwards, Mrs Sullivan told her son that his jaw had dropped so low she feared he'd broke his foot but at the time she just went on ironing as though she had not shocked him into total, dazed silence. She finished a shirt and reached for another, got halfway through it and changed irons, since hers was cooling, for the one which was heating up beside the fire.

'Well, our Roddy? Goin' to see her, are you? She didn't say much when she come round – well, not about you, anyroad – but I suppose you 'ad another bleedin' quarrel?'

'I th-thought . . . I thought . . . I told 'er . . . oh, my Gawd!' Roddy slumped down onto the hard kitchen chair and buried his head in his hands. 'She'll kill me, she'll kill me stone dead our Linnet will! Oh, Mam, the things I said, the things I *thought*! She'll never look at me again, she'll . . .'

'I dunno why it didn't cross what passes for your mind that gels don't usually wear a uniform to live a life of sin,' his irrepressible mother said, ironing steadily. 'Or are you used to seein' our Linnie in a navy skirt an' jacket an' a white blouse wi' navy pipin'?'

'Oh, Holy Mother of God, I just thought she were lookin' even lovelier than usual,' the hapless Roddy groaned between his fingers. 'What'll I do, Mam? Will she see me, d'you think?'

'I dunno. You could try apologisin', I suppose, if you can bring yourself to admit you were wrong,' his mother said rather tartly. 'How you could ha' thought, for one minute, that our Linnie 'ud sell 'erself for a big 'ouse an' a motor . . .'

'But what was I to think?' Roddy groaned. He emerged from his hands and stared hopefully at his mother. 'They telled me she were livin' wi' a rich man on Sunnyside, no one said nothin' about bein' a nanny . . .'

'Take 'er a few flowers, a present,' his mother suggested, when he ran out of words and slumped back in his chair once more. 'Tell you what, son, drop 'er a line. Only this time *say sorry*, don't jig all round the point tryin' to justify what you've done.'

'I will,' Roddy said eagerly. 'I'll do it now.' He got up and was dragging his ditty bag across the floor when he turned back. 'You don't think 'e'll try it on wi' our Linnie, then? Or ask 'er to marry 'im?'

Mrs Sullivan shook her head sadly at him and carried a neatly ironed shirt over to the table to fold it. 'Don't you ever learn, son? Wharrever our Linnie does next depends on *you*. On *you*, you great lummock, understand? Now git an' write that note.'

In the room he shared with his brothers, Roddy got out pen and ink and the last sheet of his paper. He wrote the most abject of letters, apologising unreservedly for everything he had said and thought, assuring Linnet that he would always be her devoted friend, would do anything in his power to help her should she ever need it, would go to the ends of the earth and back to please her. Then he got out his savings and set off for Church Street. Once, when he and Linnet had been walking up Church Street, they had seen, in the window of one of the jewellers there, a slender gold bracelet with semi-precious jewels set between the links. Linnet had spent a long time with her nose pressed against the glass, admiring the bracelet. Well, now she should have it for her own and he prayed that it would melt the ice around her heart so that she would forgive him.

He longed to go to the house in Sunnyside himself and confront her, beg her forgiveness, but Roddy was learning at last. He was only here for one more day and if she didn't receive the letter first who knew what she might say – or do – to him? So he bought the bracelet, wrapped it in softest tissue paper, made it into a neat parcel, sealed it with red sealing wax and posted it and the letter to Linnet, at the Sunnyside house.

He hadn't said a word in either the letter or the note he sent with the parcel about not giving in if Mr Cowan tried anything on, because he knew she wouldn't, not really. He didn't even tell her that marriage to such an old man would be a miserable affair compared to marriage to him because that, too, would undoubtedly be seen as more nastiness. He just posted his parcel and his letter and walked back to the house in Peel Square with his fingers crossed.

And then, because he had no choice if he was to keep his job, he rejoined his ship and sailed away, without knowing whether his hot-tempered little love had accepted his apology or was even now burning his letter on a slow flame and stomping his bracelet underfoot.

He didn't really think she would do anything like that, though. Linnet had always been quick-tempered but she didn't have a mean bone in her body. She would read his letter, accept his grovelling apology, and wear the bracelet to show him, if he happened to pass by, that all was forgiven and they were friends again.

Or he hoped she would. But as his ship laboured through the heavy Atlantic swell there were times when he had his doubts; times when his eyes watered and he recollected the left hook and prayed fervently to God and the Mother of Jesus that he hadn't put his foot in it with Linnet for the last time.

'Holy Mother, keep her safe, make her love me,' he prayed. 'I'm a bit hot-tempered meself but I don't mean a word of it. I'm gentle as a lamb really, I swear to God I am. And may that old lecher Cowan burn in hell if he hurts one hair of her head!'

Chapter Ten

Linnet had got over most of her feelings of outrage that Roddy could have believed she was the sort of girl to take a lover – especially one as old as Mr Cowan – in the weeks which followed their quarrel. But she still felt quite cross with him, so when his letter arrived one Monday morning she didn't open the envelope at once. She put it in the little drawer of the bedside table in her room and left it, she told herself, to simmer.

And next morning, the package arrived. It was a pretty little parcel, with the scarlet sealing wax and the white outer paper, painstakingly addressed in Roddy's best hand – and he could write beautifully when he chose. But she didn't open it, she let it lie beside her breakfast plate where she could eye it broodingly from time to time.

What was in it? What could it possibly contain? In the end she carried it upstairs and dropped it into her bedside drawer and went down again to take Mollie out to the park since she knew her charge needed fresh air even on a rather chilly October day, when the wind was in the east and the sky threatened rain. So she and Mollie would go to the park where Mollie would play with any other children also there, and then they would come home again and Linnet would help Mollie with her big jigsaw puzzle, the one with pictures of animals, all with their names written on them. The jigsaw was an instructional one and was, Linnet hoped, helping Mollie to learn her letters.

Then they would go into the breakfast room where the

maid would serve them a light luncheon. After that they would go to the nursery and Annabel Withers, who lived up the road, would come to tea with Mollie and they would play together, sometimes pleasantly, sometimes not, depending on their mood.

Annabel's nanny, Edie Ryan, was only a year or two older than Linnet. She was a jolly, pink-cheeked girl who truly loved her charges – she had three, but two of them were in school, only Annabel being below school age. Linnet and Edie had speedily become friends and now they took it in turns to entertain each other's child to tea so that the one not on duty could have a bit of time to herself. Linnet, putting her charge's leggings on with minimal help from Mollie, found herself wishing that it had been Mollie's turn to visit this afternoon and not the other way round; then she could have opened her letter and her parcel at her leisure.

But the day passed. Mollie was fed, bathed, put to bed. Linnet went down to the dining room and had dinner with Mr Cowan, quieter than usual because of the letter and the parcel. In fact, as soon as the pudding was cleared away she excused herself; she would go to her room if Mr Cowan did not mind, she had some work to do.

'But I do mind,' Mr Cowan said, smiling sweetly at her. 'I enjoy our quiet evenings together, Miss Murphy. I like to hear what you and Mollie have been up to whilst I've been toiling away at Exchange Flags.'

It would have been rude to say that the enjoyment was all on his side as well as untrue – usually Linnet enjoyed their evenings, too. So she went with him into the white drawing-room and they talked for a little and Linnet kept forgetting what she was saying and staring into the fire until Mr Cowan gave her a searching look and asked, in a rather stiff voice, if she had a headache.

'Yes, I have,' Linnet said, trying to look pathetic. She

knew she could scarcely look pale, what with the warmth from the fire and the meal she had just eaten. 'If you don't mind, Mr Cowan, I think I'll go up early.'

He must have guessed she wanted to leave him but he just smiled and bade her goodnight. He is a nice man, Linnet thought, conscience-stricken. I really shouldn't lie to him – but what am I to do? If this was an ordinary job I'd walk away from it at six, but as it is I'm on duty twenty-four hours a day, or it feels like that. Nannies really do earn their salaries!

Up in her room, she closed the door firmly and went over to give the fire a poke. It was a tremendous luxury having a fire in her bedroom, a luxury which was all the sweeter because it was always lit, as if by magic, when she came up to bed. All she had to do was put a bit of coal on occasionally, or liven it up with the poker. Having dealt with the fire she went over to her bedside drawer and got out the letter and the packet. Then she drew her chair up close to the hearth, sat herself down, and decided to open the letter first.

It was a nice letter. He was truly sorry, he said, for everything he had said and thought about her living with Mr Cowan. He explained painstakingly that he had jumped to a wrong conclusion, told her how he had heard the news originally, explained that he was now bitterly ashamed of himself. He begged her forgiveness and said he would always be her friend. You could almost say he grovelled, Linnet mused, putting the closely written sheets back into the envelope and reaching for the packet. But Roddy need not worry because she had always known he was her friend and she would always forgive him as he, she knew, would always forgive her. That punch on the nose had been quite well received, all things considered. Linnet knew young men who would have punched her right back.

She undid the packet and the bracelet slithered out and fell into her lap, making her gasp. It was beautiful, really beautiful, easily the nicest thing anyone had ever given her – and it must have cost poor Roddy an awful lot of money, he must have spent every penny he'd saved, one way and another.

She slipped the bracelet round her wrist and fastened it and a tiny little note fell out and fluttered to the floor. Linnet bent and picked it up.

Hope you love it like I love you, it said simply. *Your Roddy.*

Over the weeks which followed, Linnet learned a thing or two about being a nanny which she had not even considered when she took the job.

The first surprise came when Mr Cowan asked her, quite mildly, if she would mind not wearing her new bracelet whilst she was on duty.

'It's very pretty, Miss Murphy, and I'm sure you enjoy possessing it,' he said. 'But it will give rise to talk – I'm sure I need not say more.'

Linnet murmured that she would take it off straight after breakfast and did so, but she could not imagine what sort of talk a bracelet could give rise to, and that night, at dinner, she taxed Mr Cowan with it.

'As you see, sir, I'm not wearing my bracelet since you desired me to take it off, but I have to admit I'm curious. How could it possibly give rise to talk? Surely no one thinks I would steal such an object?'

Mr Cowan shook his head chidingly at her. 'Come, Miss Murphy, I know you are very young, but what do you suppose my housekeeper thinks when she sees you for a month bare-wristed and then you turn up at breakfast one morning with a gold bracelet to which you seem so attached that you keep it on three days running?'

'It was sent to me, through the post,' Linnet said, her

cheeks hot. 'I expect Mrs Eddis wondered what was in my packet – well, now she knows. I don't see how anyone could think different, sir.'

'People sometimes believe what they want to believe,' Mr Cowan said. 'You are a young and lovely girl, living in a widower's house. Some people will say that I gave you the bracelet. Others will conjecture why I gave you the bracelet. Few indeed are those who will suppose it was sent you as a present through the post.'

If Mr Cowan had known about Roddy's black eye, Roddy's swollen nose, he might have been glad that a great stretch of highly polished walnut dining table sep-arated him from his daughter's nanny. And Linnet man-aged to control an urge to fly across that same stretch of dining table and box his ears for him, because she realised he was only saying what he thought to be the truth. Poor man, as if she would have accepted a valuable present like a gold bracelet from an old widower and one, more-over, who was her employer!

'Well, if anyone has such evil thoughts, sir, I hope for their sake that they don't speak them aloud,' she said. Her voice was icy but her cheeks, she knew, flamed. 'The bracelet comes from a very old friend.'

Mr Cowan grinned then, and he looked younger and a good deal less censorious. 'A very old friend, Miss Murphy? As old as me?'

She had to smile, but did not answer him directly. 'I hope, if anyone ever says anything like that in front of you, sir, that you'll tell them roundly that I am not that sort of person, and that you are not either, Mr Cowan.'

'I'm very sure, Miss Murphy, that no one would dare to say anything of that nature to my face,' Mr Cowan said smoothly. 'However, I'll bear what you say in mind.' And then, whilst she was still thinking it a poor sort of reply, he changed the subject.

Another thing which Linnet learned about being a nanny was how very boring it could be. She loved Mollie and enjoyed her company, but she still got bored because there was simply not enough for her to do. Nanny Peters had prepared and cooked all Mollie's meals, but because Linnet had had no formal training Mr Cowan decreed that she and Mollie should be fed from the kitchen. The kitchen staff did not much like having to make a luncheon each day as well as doing a high tea for Mollie, but they had no choice but to obey and Linnet, too, could scarcely insist that she would enjoy cooking Mollie's luncheon, particularly when cook brought them such very delicious meals.

So Linnet, finding herself with leisure for the first time in her life, began to long for the office life she had so gladly shed, for a friend like Rose to giggle with, for the other lodgers back at the Boulevard – even the noisy little boys would have been a relief during the long, silent afternoons when Mollie was out to tea, or playing quietly with her toys.

It might have been better had the month been June instead of November, because it rained and rained, turning a visit to the park or the aviary to a purgatory of cold hands and wet feet, and although she could, in theory, have left Mr Cowan in charge of Mollie in the evening whilst she went to the cinema or even the theatre, she didn't much fancy trudging through the rain at either end of the journey.

The outings with her employer stopped because of the weather, too, though he told her he would take her and Mollie Christmas shopping in Chester as soon as the weather improved. Linnet thought Chester a delightful city – the rows intrigued her, and the old, Elizabethan shop-fronts – but would rather have spent a day going round Blacklers, Lewises and the Bon Marché on Church

Street. Christmas shopping would be fun, but it was too early yet, so she wrote letters to Roddy which she could not post, lacking an address, read books from Mr Cowan's library and moped.

And her days off, which had been promised, always seemed to disappear into thin air, because they were so difficult to arrange. She had not once visited Margaret or her other friends from the Boulevard, and had only managed to spend half a day with the Sullivans on one occasion. She was supposed to have a whole day off each week but who would look after Mollie whilst she went gadding? She asked Mr Cowan, timidly at first, and he said she had best speak to Mrs Eddis and Linnet wished very heartily that she had not agreed with her employer that she had no need of a nurserymaid once she took up the job. Nice, efficient little Emma Alcott was gracing someone else's nursery by now, allowing some other nanny to get away from her charge from time to time. But Mrs Eddis, though pleasant to Linnet, made it very clear that neither she nor the maids could take on the extra responsibility of Mollie.

'You could go out for an hour if you let one o' them other nannies take care of the kid, or you could go round to your friend's place and take the kid wi' you,' she suggested after Linnet had been living at the house for several weeks without a single afternoon off, let alone a whole day. 'The boss won't know – 'e probably wouldn't care if 'e did know, come to that.'

It sounded fair enough so after luncheon one day Linnet dressed Mollie in her scarlet coat and leggings and the little round scarlet hat like a pudding basin, put on her own navy overcoat and round velour hat and set off for the tram stop.

It was a very cold day; last night's rain had frozen to ice in the puddles and Mollie's little nose was as red as her coat and hat, but they hurried along, hand in hand, and hopped on the tram as soon as it arrived, both in the best of spirits at the thought of a break in their routine.

The nearest tram stop to Peel Square was Arden Street on Scotland Road but Linnet didn't get off there because she wanted to get some cakes at Ernest Beasley's. She and Mollie had fun choosing what Beasley's called 'pastries', and watched with watering mouths as the cakes were tenderly placed in a white card box with *Beasley's Bakery* on it.

'It's a nice present, isn't it, Linnet?' Mollie said, dancing along beside her nanny. 'Your friend will like the dear little cakes – and so will we, won't us?'

Linnet laughed and assured her charge that the cakes would give everyone pleasure and presently they turned in under the arch and entered Peel Square. It was, as usual, full of children playing a variety of games – hopscotch, jacks and ollies being the ones Linnet recognised – and Mollie hung back wistfully as they reached the front door. It was clear that to a child, Peel Square was a playground paradise and Mollie wished very much to stay out there whilst the adults talked.

Mrs Sullivan was delighted to see them, received the box of cakes with genuine pleasure, and made a great fuss of Mollie.

'Aren't you a big girl, young Mollie?' she said. 'Never did I see anything like it – you'll be as big as our Teddy at this rate!'

'I will,' Mollie squeaked. 'I do grow, don't I, Nanny Linnet?'

'She only calls me nanny when we're in company, it's plain Linnet most of the time,' Linnet said, giggling. 'Well, Auntie Sullivan, how are you – and the rest of the family, of course?'

'We're all well, even that stupid Roddy,' Mrs Sullivan said. 'Writ to you, did 'e?'

'Yes. We'd had a quarrel so he wrote to say sorry. He sent me the loveliest present . . .' Linnet shot out her wrist and the bracelet, donned for this special occasion, fell in a charming loop across her slim white hand. 'What d'you think, Mrs Sullivan? Isn't it the prettiest thing?'

'I think our Roddy's got good taste; and 'e's learnin' some sense an' all,' Mrs Sullivan said approvingly. 'You're fond of 'im in spite of everything, ain't you, queen?'

'Yes, he'll always be my good friend,' Linnet assured her. 'But he does lose his temper, and then I lose mine . . .'

'And my boy ends up wi' a black eye,' Mrs Sullivan murmured. Linnet shot her a conscience stricken look.

'Oh . . . oh, that! He – he walked into me . . . but it was a mistake, we made it up.'

'Glad to 'ear it,' Mrs Sullivan said. 'Now, young Mollie, why don't you run outside an' play wi' the other kids?' Mollie complied eagerly and Mrs Sullivan settled down in a shabby kitchen chair and smiled at her guest. 'Put the kettle on, chuck, an' you an' I will 'ave a cosy chat an' a nice cuppa,' she said comfortably. 'The littl'un can't come to no 'arm out there, the other kids'll see to that. Nor there ain't no traffic to worry about, norrin the square.'

At first Linnet kept popping out to make sure that Mollie was all right, but the child was obviously enjoying herself and soon she ceased to worry. Instead, she and Mrs Sullivan caught up on each other's news and presently, when Mr Sullivan came in, she was told all about his job as a nightwatchman and the dog which accompanied him on his rounds – it was a large alsatian called Grab and aptly named, apparently – as well as learning that Roddy was now on a bigger ship than the *Mary Rose*, carrying timber across the Atlantic. He could be away for as much as nine weeks at a time, but the money was good and he enjoyed the work.

'I b'lieve he popped to see you when 'e was last ashore,' Mrs Sullivan said tactfully, as they sipped their hot tea. 'We don't 'ave no address for 'im when 'e's on the timber run so we can't write back, an' 'e ain't ashore for long so 'e doesn't write to us much, either. Still, nine weeks will soon go.'

'In nine weeks' time Christmas will be over and there will be snowdrops in the churchyards,' Linnet said. 'What's the turn-round, Mr Sullivan?'

'After nine weeks 'e'll probably 'ave a week ashore,' Mr Sullivan said after some thought. 'You'll be able to see a bit of each other.'

'Yes. Only I think Roddy will have to come to me, because I'm having an awful job to get any time off.' And in a few swift sentences Linnet explained her position.

'Tell your boss 'e must gerra nurserymaid or you'll leave,' Mrs Sullivan said when Linnet finished speaking. 'Fair's fair, chuck. Everyone's entitled to some time off. I don't deny the child's a nice kid, but you need to gerraway from 'er for a few hours each week.'

'I know I do,' Linnet agreed gloomily. 'But it's not so easy. Mr Cowan's awful kind, but it's much harder to speak to him, somehow, when you're his nanny and not his secretary.'

'Hmm,' Mrs Sullivan said thoughtfully. 'Hmm.'

And then there was a shriek from outside which rivalled description. It had all the hair standing up straight on the back of Linnet's neck even as she scooted for the door. She wrenched it open and almost fell out into the square – and there was Mollie, engaged in a fierce battle with a small redhead over the piece of wood the kids used as a cricket bat. The redhead was the one emitting the terrible screams.

'Matty Stevens, shut your bleedin' gob or I'll shut it for you,' a slatternly looking woman screeched from her blotched and filthy doorstep. 'Come on you two, leggo that bat or I'll crucify the pair of ye!'

Mrs Sullivan peered out past Linnet, who was urging her charge to let go of the bat and come in this instant, not that Mollie was taking any more notice than the red-haired Matty. Both small girls continued to battle grimly whilst the other kids looked on, grinning.

'Break it up, you two,' Mrs Sullivan called. 'Mrs Stevens, we'll gerrours off if you'll do likewise wi' Matty.'

Mrs Stevens sighed and descended onto the battlefield, as did Linnet. Silently, both laid hands on her own child and tugged. Matty screamed once more and then turned and bit her mother's wrist. Mollie, meeker by nature, let go of the bat and said loudly, 'Bad girl, Matty, I'll crucify ye!'

Linnet gasped and shook Mollie's shoulder, whereupon Mollie looked up at her and grinned quite unrepentantly. Mrs Stevens laughed and dragged her small child towards her door. 'They ain't done no 'arm,' she said over her shoulder. 'Turble temper this 'un 'as – I guess it's the red 'air. Sorry, one an' all.'

'She's no worse than mine,' Linnet said grimly. She picked Mollie up and carried her into the Sullivans' kitchen. 'You're a bad girl, Mollie, what were you fighting over, anyway?'

'The bleedin' bat,' Mollie said primly. 'Freddy said I might have a go next.'

'It's norra bleedin' bat, chuck, it's a cricket bat,' Mrs Sullivan said, her voice shaking with laughter. 'Wharrever made you think it were a bleedin' bat?'

'Everyone else called it that,' Mollie said. 'Freddy said

it was my turn next wi' the bleedin' bat.' She allowed herself to be picked up and sat on a kitchen stool, then reached eagerly for the mug of milk Linnet was holding out. 'I'm thirsty, I am!'

'I just hope she forgets it by the time we get home,' Linnet said in a desperate under-whisper as she and Mrs Sullivan began to slice and butter bread and set out the cakes Linnet had brought. 'I don't think her father would be too pleased if she started cussing before her fourth birthday.'

'It ain't cussing, just sayin' bleedin',' Mrs Sullivan objected, cutting bread like a machine in thin, equally sized slices. 'It's just just a way of describin' something, I guess.'

But Linnet, smiling noncommittally, knew that her employer was unlikely to agree with this cheerful sentiment.

When Linnet and Mollie got home, rather late, from Peel Square, they found that Mr Cowan was entertaining visitors. Fortunately, perhaps, it did not occur to him to ask Linnet where they had been, he merely came into the hall as they entered it and said in an undertone: 'Miss Murphy, my elder brother and his wife, Mr and Mrs Edgar Cowan, have arrived for a short stay. I'd be obliged if you would tidy Mollie up and bring her down to the white drawing-room before dinner. They've not seen her since she was a small baby and my sister-in-law is particularly keen to renew the acquaintance. Could you be ready in, say, twenty minutes?'

'I think so, sir,' Linnet said, remembering that Mollie would be showing traces of the jam she had eaten for tea to say nothing of chocolate cake. 'She's been playing out – should I, perhaps, bath her first?'

But Mr Cowan shook his head. 'No, no, that won't be

necessary, Mrs Edgar is very fond of children, she'll not be put off by a touch of dirt. Well, off with you both, I'll see you presently.'

Linnet and Mollie hurried up the stairs and along to Mollie's bedroom where Linnet stripped the child down to her liberty bodice and woolly knickers and then regarded her critically. Battling with Matty had scratched Mollie's left cheek and both her wrists, but other than that . . .

'Bathroom, for a quick wash, darling,' Linnet decided. 'Aren't you a lucky girl, you very own aunt and uncle are here to see you! You won't remember them, but they love you very much. They haven't been to see you since you were a tiny baby.'

She felt it politic to tell Mollie frequently that she was much loved, for Mr Cowan still found it difficult to show open affection towards his little girl.

'Don't 'member,' Mollie said now, as she was washed, brushed and dressed in a clean red woollen dress with patent leather strap shoes and long white socks. 'I'm hungry, Linnet.'

'Well, you had bread and jam and cake, but you didn't eat much at luncheon because you were so excited,' Linnet remembered. 'No time for a snack now, love, but we'll get you a buttie and a drink of milk before you go to bed. Am I tidy? You look very smart indeed.'

'So's you,' Mollie said, eyeing Linnet's navy suit and crisp white blouse. 'Can we go down, now? I'm very so hungry!'

'Ever so, not very so,' Linnet corrected automatically as they made for the stairs. 'Never mind, sweetheart, you'll soon be fed I promise you.'

They entered the white drawing-room rather tentatively, for Linnet had got it into her head than the older Cowans would be difficult and severe, but this proved anything but the case. Mrs Edgar was a plump, pretty woman in her early forties with her richly curling golden hair cut into a fashionable bob and a good deal of make-up on. She was wearing a tea-gown in tangerine silk with coffee-coloured fringes and shoes which exactly matched and when she saw Mollie she gave a crow of delight and held out her plump white arms.

'What a little treasure! Come to Auntie Bertha, Mollie darling, and tell me all about your day.'

Mollie was nothing loath. She settled herself on her aunt's lap and began to prattle happily, and presently she jumped down and ran out of the room to return with a new game which she very much wished to master. Auntie Bertha began to show the child how to flip one tiddlywink counter with another and Mollie was soon absorbed.

This left Linnet time in which to meet Mr Edgar and to tell him how bright Mollie was for her age, how intelligent. Mr Edgar proved to be a taller edition of his brother but, she thought, with more self-confidence yet a softer, less harsh attitude. It was hard to remember how gentle and shy Mr Cowan had been at work because in his own home he was rather dictatorial, but his brother, beaming at Mollie, demanding to be introduced to the new nanny, was clearly immediately at ease.

'So you're Nanny Murphy,' he said jovially, taking her hand and smiling into her eyes. 'You aren't very old and I always think young things get on best together, so you and Mollie should deal famously. I gather from my brother here that Mollie had a bad time with her previous nanny.'

'Yes, she did,' Linnet admitted. 'But that's all behind her now, sir. In a few months she's changed completely, and definitely for the better. Why, she's only just three but already she knows her letters and can count up to ten.'

'That's excellent; we'll have her addressing the House of Lords before she starts school at this rate,' Mr Edgar said jovially. 'Does she eat well? Sleep well?'

Linnet assured him that Mollie was a model child, enjoying her food and sleeping the clock round at nights, but after a few such remarks she heard the scuttle of Edith's feet in the hall and then a tentative *boiiing* as the gong was struck very gently. In the normal course of things Edith would have poked her head round the door and announced, 'Dinner's ready, sir,' for Mr Cowan did not allow the gong to sound for fear of waking Mollie. But since the child was still up and they had visitors to dine Edith clearly thought that a more formal approach was called for.

But it seemed as though Linnet was the only person who had heard the gong, or grasped its message, for the brothers continued to talk and Mrs Edgar went on playing with her little niece. I'd better say something or dinner will be spoiled, Linnet thought, so she went over to Mollie and took her hand.

'Come along, love; that was the gong for dinner, it's time you were in bed,' she remarked. 'You've not had your bath yet, either.'

Mollie slid reluctantly off her aunt's lap, tried to pick up the game board, and everything crashed to the floor, tiddlywinks bounding everywhere whilst the pot into which one was supposed to aim them fairly flew across the drawing-room parquet and disappeared under the chaise longue.

'Oh drat!' Mrs Edgar exclaimed. 'All my fault, I should have held onto it. We'll clear it up in a trice, but I'm afraid we may be a little late for dinner.'

Mollie, scrabbling on the floor with both fists full of tiddlywinks, looked up.

'Late for dinner? Mrs Eddis will crucify you,' she

remarked conversationally. 'I'm going to have a buttie though, aren't I, Nanny Linnet? Because I only had bleedin' bread and jam for my tea.'

Linnet knew there would be trouble, though at the time Mr Edgar had turned away to hide a twitching lip and Mrs Edgar had laughed without attempting to cover up her amusement. But Mr Cowan had looked mortified – and no wonder, Linnet thought crossly. Why on earth did Mollie have to repeat that particular phrase? But that was kids for you.

She didn't have dinner with Mr Cowan, of course, not when he had guests, so she and Mollie had a delicious high tea in the kitchen with the staff. Egg and cress butties were accompanied by tiny chicken pies, a speciality of which Cook was justly proud, and then they had a large helping of trifle, finishing off their meal with milk for Mollie and a large cup of tea for Linnet.

'Bedtime now, you little monkey,' Linnet said, carrying her sleepy charge up the stairs. 'Night night, sleep tight, please make sure the bugs don't bite.'

'What's bugs?' Mollie asked through a mouthful of thumb. Linnet sighed with exasperation at her own foolishness. Fancy using that particular little rhyme on such a delicate day for language!

'Nothing. It doesn't matter. Sleep well, Mollie, and don't wake me too early,' Linnet said, as she did every night. 'Do you want Mr Woggins?'

Mr Woggins was a pink plush rabbit with one eye and huge feet. Mollie nodded, her eyes already mere slits.

'Please, Linnet. On my tummy.'

Linnet placed the plush rabbit on Mollie's tummy and Mollie gave a deep sigh, curled her spare hand protectively round him, and slept.

I might as well go to bed, too, Linnet told herself. No point in going downstairs, Mr Cowan won't need my company tonight and it's awful snug in my room with the fire on and the lamp glowing. I'll read Roddy's last letter and write my diary and then I'll get into bed myself. I'm tired enough, heaven knows, what with one thing and another.

But life was not destined to be so simple. She had no sooner made up her fire and got out her diary than there was a knock on her door. Guessing that it was Edith with her hot drink, Linnet called out 'Come in!' and was astonished when the door opened and Mr Cowan slipped into the room.

'Miss Murphy, I have to speak to you! I couldn't very well send for you downstairs since my brother and his wife are there . . . please explain how Mollie came to use that – that very coarse expression.'

'She must have heard it,' poor Linnet said feebly. 'Other children in the park, or even an adult, shouting out when we're passing along the street. I'm afraid folk do occasionally use bad language, sir, even before children.'

'But she's never done such a thing before! Miss Murphy, where did you spend the afternoon?'

Trapped, Linnet decided she must answer honestly. 'I went to Peel Square, sir. Where I used to live before I got my room on the Boulevard. I – I visited my old nanny, the person who took care of me when my mother was busy.'

She had never told Mr Cowan that her mother had been on the stage, nor that her own upbringing had not been, perhaps, all that it might have been. She felt mean calling Mrs Sullivan her nanny, but it was the only sort of explanation, she felt, that Mr Cowan would understand. In the echelons of society in which he moved, a woman with six or so kids of her own would scarcely take on another one, though this was precisely what Mrs Sullivan – dear, generous Mrs Sullivan – had done.

'Peel Square; I don't think I know it. Is it a good area of the city?'

'It's between Cazneau Street and Grosvenor Street,' Linnet said evasively. 'It's just somewhere people live, that's all.'

'I see. And did you let Mollie out of your sight whilst you were there?'

'Yes, I did. She went out to play with the other kids whilst Mrs Sullivan and I had a cuppa and got the tea ready.'

'And did she, Miss Murphy, hear someone using foul language?'

Linnet sighed. 'She heard a boy call a cricket bat the bleedin' bat, if that's what you mean. Look, sir, if you're cross that I took Mollie with me to Peel Square, I'm sorry, but what choice did I have? I've not had a day off for weeks and weeks because Mrs Eddis won't take care of the child whilst I'm gone, and . . .'

'That, Miss Murphy, is just an excuse. And that reminds me; my sister-in-law remarked on your pretty gold bracelet – now did I, or did I not, tell you not to wear it whilst you were on duty?'

'You told me not to do so, but if you remember, sir, the moment I stepped through the door . . .'

'That's enough, Miss Murphy. I cannot allow you to take Mollie into a poor area of the city where she could easily pick up more than bad language. And I won't have my wishes flouted. If you can't oblige me on these scores then I think, perhaps, that we've come to a parting of the ways.'

'I see,' Linnet said quietly. 'Very well, sir. I'll pack my things and leave after breakfast tomorrow. I trust you'll pay me for the last three weeks?'

They were facing each other and Linnet saw the shock and uncertainty which flashed across his face, but she did not see what else she could have said. There was absolutely no way in which she could promise never to wear her bracelet again in his presence and neither could she guarantee that she would not take Mollie into a part of the city of which he disapproved. Not unless he employed a nurserymaid with whom Mollie could be left, and he had shown no inclination to do that.

'Now wait a minute! Do you mean to tell me you intend to deliberately flout my wishes? That you are going to insist on taking Mollie with you when you visit places like Peel Square?'

Linnet jumped to her feet, her cheeks hot. He was behaving with total inconsistency – ordering her to do something which she could not possibly help!

'Mr Cowan, I didn't intend to *flout your wishes* as you put it by wearing my bracelet! I was in a hurry to get Mollie ready to meet her relatives and I simply forgot I had it on! Is that clear?' She had shouted the words into his face and saw him blink and draw back without any sympathy. He had tried to take advantage of her dependency upon him and it hadn't worked – hard luck!

'Oh! Well, yes, I suppose . . . but Peel Square! You cannot pretend that was a suitable place to take a child, I suppose?'

'I was brought up there, which means it can't be all bad,' Linnet said hotly. 'And since you've refused to employ any help for me and your housekeeper resolutely insists that keeping an eye on Mollie isn't her job, again you leave me no alternative. It is take Mollie with me or don't go out, and if you expect me to work twenty-four hours a day, seven days a week, and never see my own dear nanny or my friends again . . . well, I'm not a black slave-girl sir and I don't intend to be treated like one. And now would you kindly get out of my room?'

She had told Roddy to bugger off, but Roddy was used

to being shouted at and Mr Cowan was not. He looked shocked; he went quite pale.

'Miss Murphy . . .'

'Out! This may be your house, but whilst I'm employed by you this is my room and I won't have you blustering and bullying me in here.' She marched past him, head held high, cheeks aflame, and opened the door. He hesitated, then walked towards it, hesitated again . . . left the room. He turned in the hallway, obviously about to utter some dignified last words, but Linnet, feeling joyfully free and wicked, didn't give him the chance. She slammed the door crisply and shot the bolt across. Then she sat down in her chair before the fire and let out her breath in a long, silent whistle.

Phew! Well, she had burned her boats and right now she didn't give a damn. She would not be treated like a slave, not for all the money in the world, not for the nice food, or the rides in the motor car . . . not even for Mollie, and she did love the kid.

It was a shame about Mollie, because God knew what the child would do when she left. But that was no longer her concern. She could not let herself be bullied and shouted at and never given a day off just for the child's sake. And anyway, Mrs Edgar – Aunt Bertha – seemed a very nice sort of person. She would probably stay for a bit and choose a good nanny for the little girl before she left.

Comforted, Linnet sat in front of the fire for a while, planning her next move. She would not get her old job at the insurance company back, that was too much to expect, nor would her landlady in the Boulevard let her have her old room again, and in any case she could not afford the rent, not until she found herself a decent job. But she would be free to walk the streets, to pop into a canny house for a cheap snack, to go to the flicks when she saw a film she wanted to see, to walk by the river, to sit on Mrs Sullivan's doorstep and chaff with the lads . . . free, free, *free!*

She sat dreaming in front of the fire for a long time. She thought about the companionship she had so missed and the warmth of the other girls at work and in her lodgings. She thought about Mrs Sullivan's untidy, crammed little house, the smell of ironing and cheap meat stewing over the fire, the row of patched boots by the back door. Mr Cowan had a beautiful home, a lovely way of life, a dear little daughter. But she, Linnet, knew now that the Sullivan kitchen with its smell of poverty and love was worth more to her than all the Cowan comforts.

I wouldn't swop a week in this house for an hour wandering the streets of Liverpool, free as a bird and with nothing in my pocket but a big hole, she thought wonderingly. I can't wait to shake the dust of Sunnyside off my feet, I honestly can't wait!

Next morning she was woken by Mollie as usual, then her tea-tray arrived. Linnet dressed herself and the child and went downstairs with a light and springing step. The quarrel was over and she felt peaceful and glad; she would go straight round to the Sullivans' house, dump her small suitcase (it wouldn't have much in it since during the months she had worked for Mr Cowan she had worn her uniform) and then start job-hunting. I'm an experienced office worker, and I'm well-fed and neat, I'll get a job, no problem, she told herself as she and Mollie walked into the breakfast room. She put Mollie into her chair, provided her with a lightly boiled egg, some bread and butter fingers and a mug of milk and helped herself to bacon and kidneys, then carried her plate to the table and sat down. Through the window she could see frost sparkling on the grass and the sun shining brightly; after days and days of rain, Linnet saw this as a good omen. Even the weather approved of her leaving this place!

But she had scarcely started her meal when the door opened and Mrs Edgar appeared. She smiled at Linnet, took a plate out of the hot trolley and began to fill it from the big silver salvers which stood on the sideboard. Then she brought her food over to the table and sat down opposite Linnet.

'Good morning, my dear. Good morning, Mollie. Mollie, darling, have you finished your nice egg? Then if I may I'll get you down and you can go and find your Uncle Edgar who will take you in the garden for half an hour whilst Miss Murphy and I have a chat.'

Mollie was happy enough to run off in search of her uncle, though Linnet thought rather apprehensively that the last thing she wanted was to be left alone with any member of the Cowan family right now. But there was little she could do about it so she continued to eat her breakfast, eyes on her plate, and only looked up when Mrs Edgar spoke directly to her.

'Now, Miss Murphy, what's this I hear? My brother-in-law is in great distress. He tells me you've given him notice and intend to leave today and he is upset that you should want to take such a step. Can you make things a little clearer for me?'

'Yes, indeed. Mr Cowan did not approve of my taking Mollie to Peel Square, in the city, where she played with other kids whilst I visited the woman who brought me up. He wanted my word that I would never do such a thing again. I told him that since he did not employ anyone but myself to look after Mollie, it was take her with me or remain a virtual prisoner in this house and that I could not agree to. So he suggested we should part company and I agreed. Far from handing in my notice, Mrs Edgar, I believe I was dismissed.'

'And you don't really want to leave? My dear, I'm so pleased, because you've done wonders not only with Mollie but with my brother-in-law, as well. He seems much more relaxed and in control and is certainly far happier with his daughter. So if I tell him it was just a misunderstanding . . . ?'

'It wasn't. I understood him perfectly and I believe he understood me. Furthermore, Mrs Edgar, last night I realised what a dreadfully boring life I was leading here. Oh, I don't deny my salary is good, my meals delicious, my work not over-demanding, but I'm never free for one moment to please myself. I never have an afternoon off, not an hour off, even. And that means I'm losing all my old friends and not making new ones. No, upon reflection I believe Mr Cowan was right. We should part company and go our separate ways. Mr Cowan will soon find a replacement for me, I'm sure.'

'But he's so pleased with the way you and Mollie get on, so delighted to find in you a bright, intelligent companion with whom he can discuss his problems. I assure you, Miss Murphy, that he will be deeply hurt and distressed if you insist on leaving.'

'It isn't up to me,' Linnet said, her voice rising a little. 'I was dismissed, Mrs Edgar, and so I'm going to leave. That's all there is to it. And anyway, kind though it is of you to intercede, I do think this is between Mr Cowan and myself.'

Mrs Edgar looked nearly as surprised as her brother-in-law had done when Linnet had shouted at him the previous evening. 'Well, you do speak your mind, Miss Murphy,' she said. 'I'll send Mr Cowan to you; he'll tell you you're mistaken.'

Linnet said nothing and Mrs Edgar got up and left the room. Linnet poured herself another cup of coffee and glanced once more through the window. The sun was fairly beaming in through the glass and she could see Mollie's small figure in the distance with her tall uncle beside her. There was such promise in the sparkling morning that she felt like leaving this moment.

The breakfast room door opened softly and someone cleared his throat uneasily. Linnet did not have to glance across the room to know who it was.

'Miss Murphy? May I . . . ?'

'It's your house, Mr Cowan,' Linnet said evenly. 'I'm just finishing my breakfast. Mollie had hers earlier and is walking in the garden with your brother.'

Mr Cowan came and stood opposite Linnet. He looked as though he had not slept well, if at all. Serve him right, Linnet thought cruelly. I might not have slept either if I'd not decided it was all for the best. Well, I'm leaving and he's going to have to learn to manage without me – let's see how he likes *that*!

'Yes, m-my sister-in-law told me. Miss Murphy, I spoke in the heat of the moment last night – won't you forgive me?'

For the life of her Linnet could not help smiling at him; he looked so stricken, so full of remorse! 'It doesn't matter,' she said. 'I'm sorry, too, probably Peel Square isn't what you want for Mollie – well, I don't suppose Mrs Sullivan wanted if for her boys, either, but it was all that was on offer. But I'll be out of your home soon, and you won't have to bother about me again.'

'But I want to bother about you! And I don't want you out of my home, I want you in it,' Mr Cowan almost shouted. 'I said stupid, selfish things . . . don't make Mollie suffer for my fault, Miss Murphy! Stay with us, please. You can have weekends off . . . I'll hire a nursery-maid, a companion for you . . . anything, if only you'll not go.'

It was awful, it cut the ground completely out from

under Linnet's feet. She stared at Mr Cowan, gaped at him almost, and prayed for the right words so that she might still escape.

'Miss Murphy? I'll ring the agency and get the girl, Emma, the one you recommended. I'll take time off from the office and keep an eye on Mollie myself until the nurserymaid starts. I'll increase your salary – you shall have a dress allowance, like my wife did – if only you'll stay with Mollie and me.'

Linnet wanted to say no, she couldn't stay, not now. She wanted to jump up from her chair and leave the room and pack her case and – and simply run and go on running until she got to Peel Square and the sensible, capable Mrs Sullivan. But she could not do it, could not hurt Mr Cowan so badly. So instead, she nodded reluctantly.

'All right, I'll stay for a while, at least. Until Mollie's at school perhaps. But I'm going to wear my bracelet every day, Mr Cowan, because it's – it's a pledge from my young man. We're going to marry one day, Roddy and me, and I won't hide his bracelet away as if it was some sort of guilty secret. Is that all right?'

She was looking into his eyes as she spoke and she saw the hurt, the deep, painful shrinking. And knew, as she had suspected when he came into the room and gazed so unhappily into her eyes, that Mr Cowan fancied himself in love with her. He hadn't realised it, not until she said she would go, and then he had thought of the long, lonely evenings, the solitary dinners, the responsibility of bringing Mollie up alone, and he just couldn't face it. He had told himself he was in love and had been willing to do almost anything to keep her here, in the house on Sunnyside. She had a horrid suspicion that, if she had not capitulated, he would have offered marriage next. And if he had, and she had turned him down, whatever would he have done then? But even now he had his pride. He would not willingly let her see that she had hurt him.

'Yes, that's fair enough, Miss Murphy, you wear your bracelet whenever you please.' He grinned then, the boyish grin which she liked because it made him look younger and more carefree. She had noticed that when he relaxed and forgot his responsibilities, he could be a pleasant companion who could talk and even joke without having to continually stress his seriousness and superiority. She much preferred that Mr Cowan to the reserved, uncompromising man who thought himself too important to mix with ordinary people and who tried to tell everyone, including Linnet, what they should and should not do. 'Now, Miss Murphy, can we forget our – our disagreement? It shan't occur again, for my sister-in-law has pointed out that you and I should work together to make this a happy home for Mollie, and I intend to do just that.'

'Certainly, Mr Cowan; I've forgotten it already,' Linnet said, pushing her plate away and standing up. 'And now I'd better go and fetch Mollie in. I'm going to take her on the tram down to the Pier Head so she can see the Mersey – she's Liverpool born and bred, sir, but she's never even seen our river. I was shocked, that I was!'

She said it to lighten the atmosphere, and it worked. He laughed. 'There, now you've proved I'm a bad father for I'd not thought to introduce her to the river. Incidentally, Mollie has a great-aunt in Birkenhead; you must take the child over on the ferry and visit her one day. She's a nice old girl, you and she would get on. Or perhaps I could take some time off and come over there with you. And next summer I thought we might go to a hotel in Llandudno for a couple of weeks; you would enjoy it as much as Mollie, I'm sure.'

'That would be nice,' Linnet said politely. She moved past him, opened the door, slid out into the hall. By next summer, she told herself, she would have seen Mollie settled with the new nurserymaid and would have no scruples about leaving. But Mr Cowan had followed her from the room, and as he closed the breakfast room door behind him she turned, smiled at him and spoke as easily and naturally as she could. 'I'll see you this evening then, sir.'

'Indeed. You'll dine with us tonight please, Miss Murphy. A foursome is easier and more comfortable than a threesome and I feel – I feel you are one of the family already. Mrs Edgar would like to know you better and so would my brother.'

'Very well,' Linnet said. She inclined her head and then opened the side door and ran down the garden to find Mollie, glad to end the conversation, which was bound to be rather stilted and awkward considering what had gone before.

Walking back down the garden with Mollie's small hand in hers and the child chattering away beside her, Linnet thought rather sadly that her courage had not been equal to escape when it came to the point. But she knew, really, that it had not been lack of courage which had stayed her hand. It had been a wry fondness for Mr Cowan, and a real love for Mollie. She could not leave them in the lurch, not once Mr Cowan had apologised. But because she had given in it did not mean she was happy with the situation. I can almost feel the prison bars closing round me, she told herself sadly. But it won't be for long, it can't be. Roddy will be home in a few weeks, he'll tell me what to do. He's sensible, is Roddy.

And for the first time it occurred to Linnet that to spend the rest of her life with Roddy, even if they did quarrel a great deal, wouldn't be a bad thing; not a bad thing at all.

Chapter Eleven

Spring had come suddenly, in the middle of April, bringing with it sunshine, wild, warm winds, sudden sparkling showers. And because everything always happens at the same time, Caitlin and Declan Franklin decided to get engaged the same month that the Stations came to Ivy Farm. And that meant, Lucy thought bitterly, that Caitlin, who was such a help, would be too busy with her own affairs to help with the Murphys' Stations. And with Grandad abed and her aunts busy with their own affairs, that left a great deal for Lucy to do. Because it was a big thing for a family, indeed for the whole neighbourhood, when the Stations came. The priest heard confessions and took communion in your home and all your friends and relatives came, so it was a great time for spring cleaning, and for sending letters to distant relations reminding them that the farmhouse had been singled out and that their presence was required.

In this particular part of Kerry the Stations, it was calculated, came round to each house no more than once in ten years, which gave you plenty of time to prepare, or so you would think. Only somehow things which should be done don't get done and the world doesn't come to an end just because you've not put a lick of paint on your doors for nine years. And then the tenth year comes along and you've got it all to do – every wall must be whitewashed, even walls which the priests and the congregation were highly unlikely to inspect, every floor stripped of old polish and then polished anew, every cushion cover, tablecloth and curtain must be taken down, tubbed, hung on the line, ironed, starched, put back in its place. In short, when a farm had the Stations everyone suffered.

It would, of course, be Lucy's first time, because ten years before Maeve had still been living at home, masterminding their every move, mothering them. And what was worse, Grandad was poorly. 'He'll be here for the Stations,' the doctor had said the previous week and Lucy, frightened, said, 'but surely it's not that serious, doctor? Surely Grandad will be here for years yet?'

Dr Leary had patted Lucy's shoulder, tried to smile. But it hadn't been much of a smile because he and Padraig Murphy had known each other all their lives, had drunk together, played tricks on each other . . . had attended each other's weddings and scoffed at each other's foolishness over this and that.

'He'll not last the summer, unless a miracle happens,' the doctor told her sadly. 'But he'll see the Stations out. Will you be wantin' to send for Maeve? I'll add a line to your letter if you like.'

But Maeve had just discovered that she was expecting again and was busy and happy. 'How can I write with bad news and get her tearin' back here, perhaps too late?' Lucy asked the doctor. 'It takes a long time to arrange a trip across half the world – is it fair, doctor?'

'No, it's not,' Dr Leary said, having given it some thought. 'Best say nothing, then. Maeve's not a young woman, to bear a child at her age is no light thing, best not add to her worries until we have to.'

'And Grandad's so happy,' Lucy said. 'He dearly loves the Stations.'

So she and Caitlin worked as hard as they could – despite her new preoccupation Caitlin did not let the Murphy family down – and the farmhands performed miracles on the outside of the house and in the farm buildings. The haggard was cleaner than it had ever been – save when Maeve had ruled when the Stations last came – and everything was planned down to the last detail. Friends and relatives, forewarned, would be arriving the day before if they came far and very early on the day itself if they were near. The old priest and his young curate would arrive early, too, the curate to hear confessions and the priest, of course, to say Mass. When the service was over breakfast would be served, if the day was fine in the yard, and when a long and leisurely meal had been eaten the priests, having done their duty by everyone, would leave, sped on their way by thanks and good wishes, carrying with them the dues they had collected before the service began. And then the real party would start. Huge meals would be set out on the white-clothed trestle tables and every scrap of food would be eaten, there would be singing, talking, dancing and story-telling, and guests who could do so would stay late into the night.

'If it rains it's the barn,' Lucy decided the day before, though the sky overhead had been clear for a couple of days. 'There's too many for the house, they'd be crammed in shoulder to shoulder. No, the barn's definitely best. What do you think, Caitlin? Shall we set up the trestles in the barn just in case the weather turns?'

Caitlin said leave it until the day, because surely the Holy Mother would look on an event like the Stations with approval, and see that the weather stayed good? And since Lucy agreed with her they put off making a decision, so when the day itself dawned bright and fair, without a cloud in the sky, the girls felt their faith had been justified and set about preparing breakfast with light hearts.

'They will all come and talk to me, alanna, so make sure I'm in me best,' old Padraig told Lucy as she brought hot water through so that he could shave. 'I'm wantin' to talk to me man of business when the priests leave, as well as me friends. He's comin', o' course?'

'Would Mr Eamonn miss the Stations at Ivy Farm? He'd sooner lose his right hand,' Lucy assured the old man. 'But if you're tired, Grandad, let business wait. Mr Eamonn can come to see you any time.'

Padraig grinned at her. He had all his teeth still and his grin was a pleasing sight. 'And I've got all the time in the world, so I have? Is that what you were goin' to say, alanna? Well, well, I've had a good life, better than most, and I'm an ole feller now. I don't grudge the leavin', but I want to settle things.'

'But you've made your will, Grandad,' Lucy said gently. 'That's all the settlin' that's needed, isn't it?'

He shook his head at her, smiling still. 'I do as I please, miss! Your aunts are comfortable, you've a good home here, but of late I've thought of your sister often and often. Who knows where she lays her head o' nights? Who knows if she's in desperate need? None of us, none of us. So I'm makin' provision for her, see? Poor child, poor little Linnet. Makin' sure she doesn't go short.'

'That's just like you, Grandad, but we still don't know where she is or how to get in touch with her,' Lucy pointed out. 'Maeve tried, years ago, without success. Why should you have better luck?'

He grinned again, a grin with a good deal of mischief in it. 'Oh, you'll try harder this time, alanna, and this time you'll succeed, mark my words. Because if you don't . . . but no matter, no matter. Hand me me razor and I'll get rid o' that white stubble – it makes me look like an old man so it does!'

By the time she climbed into bed that night Lucy was absolutely exhausted, but she was delighted with her first attempt at hosting the Stations. Everything had gone like a dream, exactly as she had planned it. Everyone had paid their dues, confessions had been cheerful and mercifully brief, relatives and friends had congratulated her and her workers on the state of the farm, the tidy house and the wonderful food.

Grandad had enjoyed himself, too. He had held court, seeming not to find so many visitors tiring, and had actually taken a little of the beautiful broth of beef bones and every vegetable she could lay her hands on, which Lucy had made for him.

'You've done well, Lucy,' her Aunt Clodagh had said as they met, briefly, in the dance. 'Maeve would be so proud if she could see you now! I used to think you were spoiled rotten, so I did, but you've turned out better than I ever thought. You've given us a wonderful day, my dear.'

It was high praise coming from the normally critical Clodagh, and Lucy swelled with pride. I'll remember today for ever, she thought, whirling up the line of dancers on Peder O'Rorke's arm. Peder was keen on her, he told her so often and she knew it was true. Caitlin and Declan, who worked in the grocery in Caher, couldn't wed until Declan had saved enough money to get them somewhere to live. Declan was an orphan so he had no family to help him and the Kellys lived in a small tied cottage, they didn't have room for another soul – and Declan was a good Catholic; the babies would come whether the young Franklins could afford them or no, so you didn't marry until you had at least a roof over your heads.

It was different for Peder and he often reminded her that she had only to say the word . . . he was a farmer's son from further up the valley, there would be no shortage of money to build a nice little house for two newlyweds and no need for anyone to scrimp and save.

'You'd be marryin' land,' Grandad said wistfully, whenever Peder's name was mentioned. 'A farmer's girl should always marry land.'

Sometimes Lucy was tempted, there was no doubt about that. She enjoyed the work on the farm and in the house well enough, but she often felt lonely and realised that, when Caitlin went, she would feel lonelier still. Besides, as Peder's wife she would have a position, a status, which she didn't have as Padraig's granddaughter, no matter how hard she worked. And with Padraig no longer able to tell them when to reap, sow, plant, plough, she had to ask the men or use her initiative.

I'm no good at the planning side of it, Lucy told herself, sitting by Grandad's bed and trying to learn all the things she had spent her childhood trying to avoid and ignore. Why didn't I listen when Grandad talked about sheep, cattle and crops?

But she hadn't and now she was having to ask questions, guess, take a chance. Mr Kelly had always worked hard but had no ideas other than to do as he was told and Tom Flanagan was ill and old. Kellach was a good worker but he had never taken a decision in his life and had no faith in his own judgement.

'Ask the ole feller,' he would say, looking worried. 'Mr Murphy will know, he knows all about it.'

So Lucy found herself alone, relying heavily on her workers to do the work whilst she tried to take decisions on matters of which she knew nothing. Padraig was a tower of strength, but she knew that he would not be here for her much longer and then what would she do? Marry Peder? Sell the farm and move away, to a town somewhere? There was no question of employing a manager, the farm could not, now, afford such a thing.

It'll be Peder, she told herself heavily the day after the Stations, as she made Grandad's early morning cup of tea. He loved the first cup of tea of the day and enjoyed it more than all the others, he said, because it had a special, first tea taste. So she made it carefully, carried it through, set the tray on the bedside table in the small parlour, went over to the window, drew back the curtains to let in the sunshine, the birdsong . . . stopped short . . .

He had not stirred. Very still he lay, propped up by the pillows, his expression serene, his hands with their knotted veins lightly clasped and lying outside the sheets. Lucy knew at once he was dead and pulled the sheet up over him. He died happy, Lucy told herself and she drew the curtains back across the window, shutting out the sunshine, the May blossom and the lilac and laburnum which he had loved to see. But she could not shut out the birdsong. As she went around seeing to all the things which a death makes necessary, she heard the birds singing their hearts out, as though they wanted to remind her that Padraig had loved them, would want the last sound he heard on this earth to be their songs.

And it comforted her.

Lucy and Mr Eamonn were in the solicitor's office, on opposite sides of the big desk, trying to solve the mystery of Linnet Murphy. It was more than a month since Padraig had died and there had been no answers to the many advertisements which Maeve had placed in the New York newspapers, nor had her other enquiries borne fruit. And now Mr Eamonn was explaining the importance of all this to Lucy herself.

'He's left the farm to the two of ye, jointly. You and your twin sister, Linnet Murphy.'

'Twin sister? Did you say *twin*, Mr Eamonn?' Lucy's voice came out high with astonishment.

'Did ye not know?' the solicitor looked at Lucy over the top of his glasses, then he nodded slowly to himself.

'No, I see ye did not; Maeve didn't like to mention it with the other one gone, I'd guess. But Linnet's your twin, so she is, and until we find her nothing can be done. Oh, you can work the farm, but there's money banked by your grandad which can't be released until the two of you can sign papers. You can neither buy nor sell, you must pay the wages from whatever you earn, but you can't pay into the bank or they'll hold the money for probate. And despite my begging Paddy not to tie your hands in this way, he went right ahead. The old divil had done it and died before it could be undone. So try to think where your sister could be, alanna!'

'I'm trying,' Lucy said slowly. She wondered why Maeve had never told her she had a twin, but then remembered her own attitude. She hadn't wanted to hear about Linnet, hadn't encouraged anyone, even Grandad, to talk about her. And Maeve, who loved little Evie, would have hated explaining to Lucy that her mother had taken one twin and left the other. To part sisters was bad, but to part twins . . . well, it would not be easy to explain away. Then she saw that Mr Eamonn was still staring at her, waiting for her to answer, so she rushed into speech. 'There must be something which would help, some clue Maeve hasn't thought of . . .'

And suddenly, she remembered the letters, her mother's letters to Maeve which she had found and read. She remembered, too, her own feeling that perhaps Linnet had never gone to New York in the first place. That she had stayed in Liverpool, left behind as once Lucy herself had been left.

If it was true, if her twin sister had never gone to New York, then there was little point in trying any harder to find her there. If she's in Liverpool I could catch a ship and search for her myself, Lucy thought, and suddenly she knew just what she was going to do.

There was nothing she could do on the farm that the men couldn't do every bit as well, and Caitlin could move in, for a wage, and look after the kitchen side of things whilst she was gone. And I can search for me sister me own self, and see a bit of the world at the same time, Lucy thought exultantly. But she was still in Mr Eamonnn's office and he was still regarding her curiously over the top of his spectacles. Lucy cleared her throat.

'Umm . . . you've made me think, Mr Eamonnn. I do believe I may have an idea where my sister could be. Is it possible to get sufficient money from the estate for me to go away for a week or two? Only I'd like to go myself, this time.'

'But Maeve's in New York, Lucy, she must know the place pretty well by now, and she's had no luck,' the solicitor objected. 'Surely to go all that way . . .'

'Oh, I'm sorry, I should have explained. Years ago, I read some letters my mammy had sent Maeve, and it occurred to me then that little Evie wrote as though she was alone in America. And I thought that probably Linnet had never gone to New York when my mother did, but had stayed behind, in Liverpool. But I said nothing to Maeve, because it didn't seem important. Only now . . . well, if I'm right she could be a lot easier to find!'

It proved easier to arrange than Lucy and Mr Eamonnn had anticipated, chiefly because when Maeve heard what her niece wanted to do she immediately sent a money order through the post which was sufficient to pay all Lucy's travel and would also cover her living costs for around two weeks.

'If you need more, telegraph,' the accompanying letter said. 'I'm so grateful to you, Luceen, for trying to find your sister. Losing her has been an ache in my conscience for many a long year.'

So Caitlin moved into the farmhouse and Lucy wrote

long lists of instructions, got Peder to advise her on what she should tell Kellach to do on the farm in her absence, packed a bag no less than three times – once with her best clothes, then with her oldest, then with her best again – and finally booked her tickets.

'I'm leaving on the first train tomorrow,' she told Caitlin importantly the night before she left when the two of them were in the kitchen making last minute arrangements for the weeks to come. 'I'm going to Dun Laoghaire to catch the ferry to Holyhead, then I'll get on another train for Liverpool. And when I get to Liverpool Mr Eamonnn says I should stay for the first night or so at the big hotel just outside the station. Until I get me bearings. Oh, Caitlin, I'm so excited!'

'Why, Luceen? Let's face facts, I've never t'ought you had much time for that sister of yours. You were always quite rude about her – "silly name" you used to say whenever she was mentioned.'

'Ye-es. I was a bit jealous, because Mammy took her and not me. It seemed like a slight, though I knew I was better off here with Maeve. And then when Maeve kept worrying about her – what she was doing, how she was managing – I felt jealous that she worried more about a girl she'd not seen since she was a tiny kid than she worried about me. I was just being selfish, really, but that's how it was. But once I knew that me and Linnet were twins, I felt as if I'd been cheated, as if I was only half a person and hadn't realised it till that minute.'

'I'd have loved a sister of me own . . . but I t'ink I know what you mean,' Caitlin said. She shot a sideways look at her friend. 'When I first brought Declan to meet everyone . . . well, I kept hopin' he didn't have a fancy for blondes, that he liked dark girls best. If I'd had a twin I'd ha' scratched her eyes out if she'd so much as glanced at him.'

'There you are, then, you do understand,' Lucy said triumphantly. 'But now I've got to find Linnet because without her I can't even begin to run Ivy Farm properly. Yet if I do find her, and bring her back . . . oh, I don't know. Sharing isn't – isn't something I've done much of and I don't know how I'll take to it and that's the truth. Why, the other day I found meself thinking I was glad Grandad wouldn't be here just in case he doted on her more than he used to dote on me! Would you believe a person could be so small-minded?'

'Marry Peder,' Caitlin advised. 'Then you can divide the farm. You can move in wit' him and this twin of yours can try her hand at farming here.'

'She won't know anything about farming,' Lucy objected. She went over to the pantry and took out a large tin with a picture of the English Houses of Parliament on the lid. Opening it to show the fine fruit cake within she added, 'Give this to the fellers for their elevenses tomorrow, would you? It should last a day or so, and then you could bake another. There's a tin of shortbread in there, though, so if you don't get time to bake . . .'

'Listen to the woman – as if I'd not spent the last few years in this kitchen alongside you, bakin' and roastin' and cleanin' wit' the best of 'em. Go and put the kettle on and we'll relax over a nice cup of tea. And, Lucy . . .'

'Yes?' Lucy said, as the silence stretched. 'Don't be embarrassed; say what you want to say.'

'We-ell, be nice to this girl Linnet, won't you? You've been awful lucky compared with her, you know. You've had Maeve, the farm, your grandad, and now you've got Peder if you want him. 'Tweren't her fault that your mammy took her away when she left and she didn't do all that well by her, seemingly. This sister of yours, she didn't even have her mammy for very long; from what you've told me, she's only had herself.'

'It's all right, I know,' Lucy said gruffly. 'I spent most of last night putting meself in her shoes and I'm going to be sweet as honey when we meet. But you can't make yourself like someone, you know, and I don't suppose I'm liable to like her after all these years. But I promise you, Cait, that she'll never know it. And now let's have that cup of tea, and we'll take a slice of me beautiful fruit cake, too!'

When Lucy got off the train at Lime Street Station in Liverpool she was tired, travel-stained and aching in every limb. The first train journey had been quite enjoyable – she had seen new sights, had admired, or deplored, the meadows and fields through which she travelled with a farmerly eye, had chatted to folk in the train and exchanged titbits of information about Cahersiveen and the people who lived there.

The ferry might have been fun, an adventure, had there been two of them, but when you were on your own new experiences, Lucy discovered, tended to be nerve-racking rather than amusing. She had never been on a ship before either nor gone further, at home, than the mouth of the lough in a neighbour's fishing boat. Now she was seeing waves of terrifying height and contrariness – she had imagined that out to sea waves behaved as they did nearer shore, but this proved to be anything but the case. The wind got up, the ship ploughed on, and the waves, instead of lining up neatly, seemed to attack the ship from every angle and to rear to impossible heights above the suddenly dangerous deck.

It was not long before Lucy, green of face and unsteady of foot, made her way below to cower in a corner, occasionally, alas, throwing up into a sturdy brown paper bag given to her by a sympathetic stewardess.

'Happens to us all it does, love,' the stewardess said in

a strange, sing-song accent. 'Better you will feel as soon as we dock. Now sit there and I'll bring you some seltzer. That sometimes helps.'

Lucy drank the seltzer, which was just very fizzy water, but it didn't help; well, it wasn't down there long enough, Lucy thought ruefully, reaching for a replacement bag. The only comfort was that all around her horrid noises proved she was not alone. Most of her fellow voyagers were casting up accounts simultaneously, it seemed.

The journey took about four hours and by the end of that time Lucy felt like a rag doll whose stuffing had been removed. When they docked she couldn't get off the wretched ship fast enough and onto dry land, but she felt too weak to make a break for the shore so simply allowed herself to be carried along by the crowds, and was soon standing apathetically in a line to climb aboard the train.

'Come along there, we're late,' the ticket collector said as he directed people to empty compartments. 'Ah, you gerrof at Crewe, queen. Tell someone in your carriage you want Crewe, you're awful green still.'

'Crewe? But I want to go to Liverpool,' Lucy said thinly. All her excitement, her spirit of happy independence, was at the bottom of the Irish sea in a brown paper bag. Never had she so longed for home and a bed which didn't move around! And her stomach ached with emptiness, yet she knew she would not be able to eat anything, probably for weeks. This is your fault, Linnet Murphy, she told her absent twin fiercely. If you'd not hidden away from us and then somehow got into Gramp's head when he was dying, none of this would have happened. I'd have inherited the farm and married Peder and never, never crossed the sea to get to this horrible old land – I wish I were back at Ivy Farm so I do!

'That's right, you want Liverpool so change at Crewe,'

the ticket collector said patiently. She was just thinking him rather a nice man when he turned to the man behind her and said bitterly: 'Bleedin' ignorant bogtrotter! These micks are all de same – never 'eard of Crewe station, an' it's only de biggest in de world, just about.'

Horrible ole divil, he's no right to be rude about the Irish, Lucy thought with unusual venom, sinking into a seat and leaning her weary head back against the plush upholstery. Bog-trotter indeed, just who did he think he was? I wish he might say that to a man – a man would have t'umped him for that!

But wishing wasn't much good; if wishes were horses then tinkers would ride, Lucy told herself, and got a stab of pain at the words. Oh, Finn, Finn! But you've forgotten him, she reminded herself fiercely, you've not so much as wasted a thought on him since Granny Mogg's death, and that was three years and more ago. Don't, for the love of God, start all that up again, don't start thinking of him now!

And for once, she obeyed her own injunction. She felt the train jolt and lurch, heard the whistle blow and various people call out, laugh, begin to push into the compartment. And then she was asleep and dreaming of green Cahersiveen meadows and the sea lough, blue beneath the sun.

'Wake up, luv! You're t'lass who wanted Crewe, aren't you? Well, we've arrived . . . come on, luv, do wake up!'

The voice was strange, the accent stranger, but the word 'Crewe' brought Lucy surging up from the depths of sleep. Groggily, she sat up; where was she? A bleary glance round confirmed that she was not at home but then she was pulled to her feet and her bag thrust into her arms.

'Move thysen', luv, or you'll be carried out of t'station!

316

You want to change 'ere for Liverpool. Hey don't forget thy coat!'

Half asleep still but rapidly coming round, Lucy scrabbled for her coat, her bag, her various possessions, and then stumbled out onto the platform. The train had been stuffily warm but the air on the platform was bracing, not to say cold, Lucy thought, trying to retract her head into the collar of her coat as a tortoise might when the chilly wind nipped at her sleep-crumpled cheeks.

'The train now standing at platform four is the twenty-one forty for . . .' a list of stations followed and just as Lucy was about to go in search of a porter the voice concluded, 'and Liverpool Lime Street.'

That was her train! But where was platform four? Lucy took a look around her and realised, for the first time, that this station was *huge*, absolutely massive. There were signs at various points, people scurrying about, a flight of stairs leading to an upper area, but she could not see a sign saying platform four nor another sign pointing to the Liverpool train. She was trailing miserably along the platform when an official-looking figure passed her. Quick as a flash, she grabbed the uniform-clad arm.

'Oh, excuse me, can you tell me where platform four is?'

The man looked down at her.

'Up the stairs, turn left, down the stairs, at the bottom of the second flight of stairs, turn left,' he said in a flat, uninterested tone. 'Better run, miss, if it's the twenty-one forty you're after. It's almost time 'e left.'

Lucy ran. She missed it.

Emerging onto Lime Street at eleven o'clock at night was quite an experience for a country-bred girl. Instead of being in darkness, as Lucy had assumed it would be, the street was brightly lit, and the gas lamps' flaring white light illuminated a number of smart and beautifully dressed ladies strolling idly along the pavements.

The theatre is near, I remember someone telling me so, it must have just opened its doors for the audience to leave, Lucy thought, staring with considerable admiration at the lovely ladies. It then occurred to her that it was not usual for a great many women to go to the theatre unaccompanied, yet there did not seem to be any gentlemen accompanying the ladies.

Then a gentleman came along. He was walking swiftly, not paying very much attention to his surroundings or not appearing to do so, anyway. And the ladies converged on him. They knew him, obviously. One asked him if he had found himself a bed for the night, another suggested that she was always willing to give any assistance she could to a kind gentleman like him, a third advised him not to consider Mimsie or Sal but to choose a decent girl like herself. Or that was what Lucy thought they said; their accents were by no means genteel and she had to listen carefully or she would have assumed they were speaking a foreign language.

But the gentleman understood them perfectly. 'Go away girls,' he said cheerfully and in plain English. 'Another time I'd be pleased to accommodate one or two of you, but tonight I've other fish to fry and a train to catch into the bargain.' And he hurried into the station which Lucy had just vacated, almost pushing her aside as he did so.

'Well I never did, those ladies aren't . . . aren't ladies,' Lucy said under her breath. 'I think I'd better find me hotel before I make any more mistakes.' And, bag in hand, she made her way quickly along the pavement to the grand foyer of the nearest hotel.

There was a smart young man on the desk. He looked

her over very carefully, but seemed to approve of what he saw for he gave her a smile and said, 'Was you wantin' a room, miss?' in a slow but pleasant voice.

'Yes, please. Just for the one night,' Lucy said and for the first time became conscious of her own brogue, because the young man said 'Pardon?' and she had to repeat the words, speaking this time as slowly and carefully as the reception clerk.

'Ah, I understand. Sorry, miss, a room for one night. If I might make so bold I suggest that you pay now, then if you have to leave early in the morning there will be no need to waste time settling your account.'

Wearily, Lucy found money, paid him, picked up her case. But the young man whistled and a boy appeared in a smart maroon uniform and enough gold braid to make him captain of a passenger liner at least. The boy took her case and her bag from her grasp and jerked his head at her.

'Folly me, queen,' he said briefly. 'Room 101.'

Dazed with tiredness and wide-eyed at the strangeness of the very first hotel she had ever visited, let alone stayed in, to say nothing of the sheer size of it, Lucy only realised he was expecting a tip when he opened the door of Room 101 and ushered her in. She turned to thank him and found an outstretched hand practically under her nose.

'Oh, sorry,' she said. She took out her purse again, selected a coin and put it on his palm. 'Thanks very much . . . aha! Give me me bag, you young rascal.'

The boy handed over her bag, which he had slung across his shoulder to free his hands for tackling the door-key and her case. 'You're norras green as you're painted,' he said pleasantly. 'Sweet dreams, queen!'

Lucy tumbled into bed without so much as washing, though she did take a drink from the toothglass. But although she slept very deeply at first she was awoken in the early hours by strange noises from the room next door. Bed springs twanged, voices cooed and called and cursed, someone gave a couple of very loud shrieks, and then, abruptly, silence fell once more. Lucy, who had sat tremblingly upright in bed at the first sound, lay slowly down on her pillows once again. For the first time, she began to realise what life must have been like for Linnet once her mother had died. Of course it was possible that Linnet was in America, but Lucy did not think so. She knew almost nothing about her twin, had scarcely thought of her over the past twenty years, but now that she was actually in Liverpool she was getting a steadily increasing feeling that Linnet was near. That she had been in Liverpool all along – and that she, Lucy, was about to find the missing Murphy.

And alongside that feeling was this other, newer one. That far from being jealous of Linnet and envying her, she should pity her from the bottom of her heart. I had so much – Maeve, Grandad, Caitlin, Granny Mogg, she told herself. I've never in my life, until now, had to do anything by meself. Poor Linnet's been travelling alone, living alone, working alone. She's had to earn her own money, make it go round, find somewhere to live, even. And I've had my tickets paid for, my journey mapped out for me, and still I got lost, missed my train, arrived very late in the hotel, and I've absolutely hated it. Over the past day I've been frightened, sick, lost and lonely – so lonely! My sister Linnet's a brave girl to have faced a loneliness worse than any I've ever dreamed of – the loneliness of one small girl in this huge, frightening city!

Next day, Lucy left the hotel, bags in hand, and went in search of something cheaper and more suitable. Outside the hotel she hailed a taxicab and asked the driver to take her to a smaller, friendlier place than the big hotel in which she had spent the night.

'You want a boarding 'ouse, chuck,' the driver said, having given the matter some thought. 'Temp'rance, are you?'

'I'm from County Kerry,' Lucy assured him. 'A boarding house sounds nice. Will it be cheap?'

'Depends on the area. I think you'd best 'ead for a street what's quiet but central. Near the station, but not too near, 'cos o' the din. I should think Brownlow 'ill would suit, bein' as it's central but classy.' He glanced over his shoulder at her. 'An' you're young, you'll manage the climb,' he said encouragingly. 'From Ireland, are you?'

'Yes, from Kerry,' Lucy said again. She was gradually growing used to the Liverpool accent, having spent most of breakfast time simply listening to it as it surged around her, but she did realise that she would have to try to tame her own brogue a bit, if she was to be understood, that was. 'I'm searching for me sister – we're twins. I thought it would be easy to find her, but I'd not realised the city was so huge. Still, if she's in Liverpool, I'll find her – her name's Linnet Murphy.'

'Linnet. Unusual. Can't say I've 'eard of a Linnet afore,' the driver mused. 'You'll find 'er, though, if you keep askin'. Liverpool's norras big as you think, chuck.'

'It's bigger than Cahersiveen,' Lucy said and the driver chuckled, then drew in beside the kerb. 'There you are, Mrs Cordiner, The Lilacs, Brownlow 'ill. You'll be fine wi' Mrs Cordiner, she looks after 'er guests like a mother would.'

Lucy lugged her belongings out of the taxicab, paid the driver and knocked on the green front door. A large lady answered and said that she did have a room and that Miss was welcome to take a look before making up her mind.

Miss took a look and liked the place; it was clean, cheap and cheerful, what more could anyone ask? She explained her quest to Mrs Cordiner as she paid her first week's rent and Mrs Cordiner said she would put the word around for a Miss Linnet Murphy and would Miss Lucy Murphy like a cup of tea before she started out?

I'm going to be all right, Lucy told herself later, when the tea had been drunk, the house vacated, and she was on her way to the public library to see if they could help her. Mrs Cordiner's a nice woman, she'll do what she can to help and she won't cheat me. I'm going to find Linnet, I know it in me bones!

It was Linnet's day off and the day started bright and seemed likely to go on the same way. Linnet felt cheerful and happy from the moment she had jumped out of bed, not only because it was her day off but because it was sunny which must mean that summer was on its way at last.

Ever since the advent of Emma, the nurserymaid, Linnet had taken her time off without fail and since Mollie had started nursery school she did not even feel guilty at so doing. She usually went to the Sullivans' place and helped in the house, washing, ironing, cleaning, until it was time for the midday meal. Having worked hard all morning, the afternoon was usually given up to an outing of some description. Linnet treated Mrs Sullivan since she still spent very little of her salary and enjoyed giving pleasure. Besides, she was very conscious of the debt she owed the older woman. So Linnet and Mrs Sullivan took themselves off to a theatre or a cinema, or some other form of entertainment. Sometimes they took a tram ride or went on the overhead railway, at other times they treated themselves to tea and cream cakes at a posh café. In fine weather they set off as soon as Linnet arrived and went to Seaforth Sands, or New Brighton, or Woodside, anywhere within reach, in short. But today Linnet had a problem and needed Mrs Sullivan's advice, which meant, of course, that theatres and cinemas were out; she wanted quiet, a good tea, and plenty of time.

'We'll walk down the Scottie, takin' a look in the winders as we go, an' find ourselves a nice café for tea,' Mrs Sullivan said with relish. Now that her children were growing up and the older ones working, life was much easier. Roddy, Linnet knew, sent his mother home a generous allotment, as did the other boys with well-paid jobs. 'I only 'ope I can 'elp, Linnie. I don't need to tell you 'ow dear you are to me, chuck; you're the daughter I never did 'ave, that's what.'

'And you're more of a mam to me than my own ever was,' Linnet said ruefully. 'Come on then, let's window-shop!'

And for the first twenty minutes they enjoyed themselves thoroughly, just looking and dreaming. But then Linnet broached the subject which was bothering her.

'Mrs Sullivan, it's me and your Roddy. We've been going steady for ages, I'm ever so fond of him, but when he comes home however well we start off before long we're quarrelling. And I don't understand it, truly I don't, because I – well, I like him so much. He's funny and kind and very clever in his own way, and I long for his shore leave and then when it comes within two minutes we're starting to disagree, then to quarrel and then, sometimes, I give him a clack.'

'I know, queen,' Mrs Sullivan said ruefully. 'The 'ole Square knows, comes to that. But I do 'ave a thought on the marrer. When's the weddin', eh?'

Startled, Linnet gave a snort of laughter. 'We keep putting it off, because I promised Mr Cowan that I wouldn't leave him and Mollie in the lurch, and because now Roddy wants to leave the sea when we get married. I told him if he's going to come ashore then he's bound to get less money, so we'll have to save up harder and get a home of our own before we tie the knot. Well, it's all very well to say he wants to come ashore, but if he does I'm just scared we'd quarrel even worse than we do now. And I don't think I could stand it, quite honestly. I hate being cross all the time but it's beginning to be like that when Roddy's home. And I don't fancy constant bickering, because that's not good for a marriage, is it?'

'It wouldn't be, but you're wrong, chuck,' Mrs Sullivan said, stopping to peer at a display of silk blouses in a draper's window. 'I like that pink 'un, don't you? Pink used to suit me when I were young. Yes, you're wrong about quarrelling more if you were married than if you weren't. Waitin' for what they want ain't good for fellers, it's against their natural instincts to keep sayin' no to their – well, their desires, like.'

'I think I know what you mean,' Linnet agreed. Roddy's parting shot when last they quarrelled had been that if Linnet wouldn't, then he knew a girl who would. At the time she had been furious, jealous, distraught, but later, when she cooled down, she had also felt more than a twinge of guilt. She was very fond of Roddy and certainly wanted his lovemaking, could not prevent herself from responding hotly to his kisses and caresses. But then, when he tried to go further, she stopped him short. She did not want to make the mistake her mother had made, she wanted marriage and then babies, not babies first to complicate her life.

Now, she turned appealingly to her companion. 'But, Mrs Sullivan, you wouldn't want me to . . . you wouldn't expect me to let Roddy . . .'

'No, indeed,' Mrs Sullivan said hastily. 'But if you was

married, chuck, then it wouldn't arise. In a manner of speaking. I mean you wouldn't feel bound to push 'im back, would you?'

'No,' Linnet said rather doubtfully. There were definitely times when she wondered whether married life wasn't all a bit nasty, somehow, a bit crude. 'Only it – it worries me, rather. Roddy gets – gets quite rough.'

Mrs Sullivan laughed. 'Aye, men do,' she agreed. 'But it'll be all right, our Linnie, I promise you. Just marry the lad, an' let nature tek its course.'

'Right away? But we haven't got a place of our own yet and Mr Cowan needs me still, he says so every time . . .'

She broke the sentence off short. Mrs Sullivan raised quizzical brows. 'Every time you say you'd like to leave? That ain't fair, Linnet, an' well you know it. What's 'e playin' at, eh? You can't stay there for ever while poor Roddy goes wild for you, queen.'

'No, I know. But you see I'm not sure about – about Roddy and me and Mr Cowan's sensible and kind and – and what he's proposed . . .'

'Proposed? Linnet, you don't mean to tell me 'e's asked you to be 'is wife?'

'I didn't mean that, but . . . yes, he has,' Linnet said slowly. 'I like him very much but I don't love him at all, only . . . only when Roddy and I quarrel, and when Roddy says awful things and storms off, then Mr Cowan seems so quiet and sensible that I can't help thinking perhaps that's what I want and not – not all that love stuff.'

They were walking slowly along the crowded pavement, arm in arm, heads close. Mrs Sullivan gave Linnet's arm a squeeze.

'I dunno 'ow to say this, queen, but *all that love stuff*, it's what life's about, y'know. Love makes the world go round they say, and I tell you straight, wi'out love a marriage ain't worth tuppence. It wouldn't be fair to say as 'ow I think Roddy's the feller for you, bein' as 'e's me son, but I'm certain-sure that a bloke 'oo's quiet an' sensible ain't a bloke in love, whatever 'e may say. Love – love 'urts when things go wrong, it wrenches your guts, but when things go right . . . oh, then love's the crash o'drums an' trumpets, 'ot sunshine full in your face, the scent o' lilac when there's really only kippers. What are you laughin' at, young Linnet?'

'You were doing fine till you got to kippers,' Linnet wailed, mopping her streaming eyes. 'But I do understand what you mean, Mrs Sullivan. And I believe you're right. Roddy and I usually fight after we've been . . . well, you know.'

'I know,' Mrs Sullivan said. 'Here's Candwell's; time for a cuppa an' a pastry, eh?'

'Definitely,' Linnet said, following her friend into the refreshment rooms. 'I love Mrs Annie's sugar buns!'

They were shown to a window table and ordered a pot of tea for two and a selection of fancy pastries from the cheerful little waitress. Linnet began to chatter but she soon realised that Mrs Sullivan was not happy; the older woman kept starting sentences and then breaking off to stare broodingly at the pink and yellow rosebuds on the dainty china cups. Linnet leaned across the table and took Mrs Sullivan's work-worn hand in hers.

'What's the matter, Mrs S?' she said gently. 'You've gone very quiet on me!'

'I were just thinkin'. If you married that feller, that Cowan, I doubt I'd ever clap eyes on you again.'

'That's nonsense; of course you would, I'd come round just as often as I do now – more, probably,' Linnet said, but even as she spoke the words she knew she lied. Mr Cowan did not approve of what he called 'your past' and would make sure she had no time to keep popping round to Peel Square. And besides, it would be awkward, because although Mrs Sullivan was dear to Linnet she was dearer to Roddy, and Roddy and Linnet would avoid one another, it stood to reason. 'But anyway it doesn't matter, because I'm not going to marry Mr Cowan,' she added cheerfully. 'I'll promise not to, if you like. And now do choose another cake because all this talking has made me terribly hungry!'

'She's my twin,' Lucy said to everyone she came across. 'So she'll be very like me. Our mam was called little Evie and she was an actress at the theatre here.'

But although as a description it was good enough, no one seemed to know Linnet. And finally Lucy worked her way up to the theatre and asked the lady booking seats whether she knew a Miss Linnet Murphy, daughter of an actress called little Evie.

'You mean the exotic dancer,' the woman said. 'Oh aye, I remember little Evie. But she's not been here for years – went to the States wi' an American feller.'

'Yes, I know. But she left her daughter behind, didn't she?' Lucy said. 'So far as we know she's still in Liverpool somewhere – Linnet I mean – and I'm trying to find her. She's inherited some – some money from her grandfather so we have to find her.'

'Oh aye? Tell you who might know, Topsy Page. I 'member she lodged with Evie's daughter one time.'

'Oh, that's wonderful! Is she here? Can I see her?' Lucy said eagerly. It really seemed as though her quest was about to end at last.

'She's in tonight,' the woman said. 'Come round when the show's over, at about ten. Bring her a box of chocolates, she's mortal fond of sweets, and likely she'll ask you in. She's a nice enough girl.'

327

'Right,' Lucy said joyfully. 'A box of chocolates; I won't forget.'

Topsy Page remembered Linnet and was able to give Lucy the whereabouts of the rooms in Juvenal Street, but there, for the time at least, the trail ended. No one in Juvie, as it was called, could tell Lucy where the Murphy girl had gone though one young lad told her to try Peel Square.

'She were thick wi' a feller what lived there,' he said. 'I b'lieve, when 'er mam were out, she stayed wi' someone there. Or you could try the convent school. They'd know.'

Lucy tried to find Peel Square and when she did she was shocked; all those tiny, overcrowded houses built round a paved courtyard which never saw the sun, filled now with scruffy, down-at-heel kids. How could anyone live here? So she did not try very hard to run her sister to earth in this particular place.

'Lorra gairls around 'ere, chuck,' a fat woman in a droopy grey skirt and brown blouse told her at the first house she visited. 'Never know 'alf the names of 'em. Waste o' time anyroad, 'cos she ain't 'ere now. I'd know if she were.'

At the second house a man lurched out and tried to persuade her that he had Linnet tucked away in his kitchen. He caught hold of her arm and Lucy, really frightened, tore herself free and ran out of the court, telling herself that no sister of hers would have stayed in such a horrid place amongst such rough and dreadful people.

It had taken her most of the day to find Peel Square, so she went back to Brownlow Hill and ate a good dinner, determining to spend the next day at the convent school.

'The nuns'll know,' her landlady said comfortably, serving stewed apples and custard. 'They keep a track o' their pupils, the sisters do. You'll be lucky tomorrer, chuck.'

'A job in an insurance office on Exchange Flags,' Lucy murmured to herself as she left the convent the following afternoon. The sisters had been great, they remembered Linnet well enough though it had been years since they had taught her. But they couldn't tell Lucy which insurance company, so she would have to do some more foot-slogging.

It'll be tomorrow I find her, Lucy told herself, returning to her boarding house once more. 'Tomorrow will be my lucky day!'

There were a great many insurance offices on Exchange Flags and Lucy visited each one of them. And finally, at the Eagle and General, she struck gold.

'That's right, she worked here,' an elegant young lady said thoughtfully. 'She and Rose Beasley shared an office. Rose moved on six months ago – she and her feller got wed – but Miss Murphy went a while before that. Now, I wonder where she went? Not into another insurance office I don't think . . . want me to ask around?'

'Oh, please,' Lucy said gratefully. 'When shall I come back?'

The elegant one looked at her fob watch, then tapped her teeth with her pencil. 'Well, I'll put the word around – how about the day after tomorrow? Only it's a big firm, it may take me a while, and I do have a job to do as well!'

'That'll be fine,' Lucy said, though with sinking heart. She had been here nearly a week and if she didn't turn something up soon . . . and when I find her, I've got to persuade her to come back to Ireland with me, she remembered gloomily. If I were her I'd jump at the chance, but I'm not her. We've been brought up so differently that we probably don't even like the same things. She probably loves this city whereas to me its just miles of pavements and people who talk so fast I can't understand a word and live in terrible conditions. Oh, I do want Cahersiveen!

She trudged back through the streets to her boarding house but over dinner that night her thoughts took a different direction, thanks to Mr Harrigan.

Mr Harrigan was what Mrs Cordiner called 'a commercial', which was short, apparently, for commercial traveller. He proved to be a short, bald man in his fifties who travelled, he told Lucy, in patent medicines for a large pharmaceutical company. He was Irish, but no longer lived in that country since the market for his product was not so good 'over the water', but he was an enthusiast for the city of Liverpool.

'You don't like it, alanna?' he said incredulously when Lucy told him how homesick she was. 'You don't like this most beautiful of cities? Ah, but how much have ye seen of it? Have ye taken the ferry across the great River Mersey and seen it from the Woodside shore? Have you visited the art gallery, the museum, St George's Hall, the great lending library? And the theatres! Sure, the theatres of Liverpool are second only to the theatres of London – if they are second to them, which I doubt. My dear Miss Murphy, you must give the city a chance to prove itself!'

'I haven't had much time,' Lucy admitted. 'I've been trying to find my sister. But as it happens I am free tomorrow – how would you suggest I spend the day?'

'Take the ferry from the Pier Head to Woodside; once there, you'll see the most beautiful and impressive waterfront in the world, so you will. Then come back – you needn't go ashore, you can stay aboard – and get on the overhead railway and go along to Seaforth Sands. If you've missed your sea lough you ought to enjoy that. Then take a tram back to the city and get off at St George's

Hall. Take a good, long look at it – magnificent architecture! Then you can do the museum and the art gallery because they're only just across the road so they are. And if you've got any strength left, sit in St John's garden and contemplate life for half an hour, to recover yourself. Will ye do that for me, Miss Murphy? Your soul will be refreshed, I promise you.'

'Yes, I will,' Lucy said. She was sick and tired of city streets and city faces, she would enjoy a river trip. A thought struck her, however. 'The ferry – does it bounce around much? Sick as a dog I was on the ferry from Dun Laoghaire.'

Mr Harrigan laughed. 'Flat as a mill pond it will be, and us with summer truly upon us. Have a good day, Miss Murphy.'

The following day started cloudy but by the time Lucy had eaten her breakfast and set out to walk to the Pier Head the sun was peeping from behind the clouds, and as she joined the crowd shuffling along the floating road to get aboard the ferry the sky was clearing fast.

I do believe I really shall enjoy today, Lucy told herself as she stood in line to buy her ticket. I don't intend to worry, or think about Linnet, or do anything other than relax today.

Having purchased a return she went and joined the other would-be passengers who stood in little groups, waiting whilst the ferry backed into its berth. She watched idly, but presently her attention was drawn to a young woman of about her own age, standing by the railings, with her back to Lucy, looking pensively out across the water. The young woman was thin, with straight, light-brown hair. She was wearing a navy blue jacket and skirt and sensible black shoes and she was clearly waiting for the ferry, as Lucy was. I wish I knew her, Lucy thought. She looks rather nice, though since I can't see her face I don't really see why I should think that. But some people you do like instinctively, and your instincts are usually right.

She was wondering whether she could go across and strike up an acquaintance when the ferry jostled itself into position, the gang-plank came down with a crash and people began to pour ashore. Lucy moved over against the railings herself so that she wouldn't get in the way, and by the time the crowds had passed and passengers for Woodside were being allowed aboard, she had forgotten all about the girl in the navy suit.

She remembered her again aboard the ferry, though, because she decided to take a quick look at the saloons and then return to the deck; even the slight movement of the deck beneath her feet reminded her all too sharply of her recent ghastly experience on the voyage from Ireland. As she came out of the saloon and regained the deck the girl in the navy suit came towards her, clearly about to go below. Lucy moved aside and then their eyes met and they exchanged smiles. The girl in the navy suit was slim and slightly built with fawny-brown hair which swung, rain-straight, down to her shoulders and her smile was friendly, forthcoming. Lucy spoke first.

'Hello! This is me first trip on the ferry, so I've been hopin' it wouldn't make me sick. Do you come over often?'

'I wouldn't say often, but this isn't my first trip,' the girl said readily. 'I've been over before, two or three times, and I always enjoy it. What makes you think you might be sick, though? It's a short crossing, you know.'

'I was terrible sick comin' from Ireland so I was,' Lucy admitted gloomily. 'I wanted to die so I did.'

The other girl laughed.

'Well, the Mersey isn't the Irish sea exactly,' she pointed out. 'But why don't you come below with me and then we can have a cup of coffee, or a lemonade? It might settle your stomach.'

'I think it might be safer not,' Lucy said cautiously. She looked over the rail at the gently moving water, at the gulls bobbing on the surface, then glanced back at her companion. 'I'd like a coffee so I would, but I durst not go below whilst the ship's moving.'

'Well, why don't you sit down by the rail and keep your eyes fixed on Woodside – that's the further shore – and think about the land, and I'll go below and fetch a drink for both of us,' the girl said in heartening tones. 'And when I come back we'll chat and that'll keep your mind off your stomach.'

'That's awful kind,' Lucy said. 'Let me give you the money, though. How much does a coffee cost aboard this ship?'

The brown-haired one shrugged. 'I haven't the foggiest idea. Tell you what, if you're going back on the same ferry as I am you can buy the coffee in the other direction. How does that seem?'

'Grand. And I can go back on any ferry, since I'm only going for to see the Liverpool shore from the other side,' Lucy admitted. 'There's a feller in me boarding house – shocked he was that I'd not seen the waterfront properly. So I said I'd spend an idle day, just lookin' around me.'

'And I'm only going on a message – when I get to Birkenhead I'm to buy some flowers and take them to an old lady who's been ill,' the brown-haired one said comfortably. 'So if you've nothing better to do, why not come with me? It's just a walk in the sunshine, you know, and then back to Woodside and the ferry again. Now you just wait here – I shan't be two ticks.'

Lucy sat in the sunshine and fixed her eyes on the further shore as her new friend had suggested, and sure enough she did not feel at all sick, not even when a tug steamed across the ferry's bows and the ship heaved on the swell. And presently, when the girl came back with the steaming coffee she took it, sipped, and then set the cup down on the slatted wooden seat beside her.

'Well now, how can I thank you when I don't even know your name?' she said brightly. 'I'm Lucy Murphy. How do you do . . . ?'

'That's odd,' the brown-haired one said cheerfully, setting her own coffee down between them. 'I'm a Murphy, too – Linnet Murphy.'

Lucy's mouth fell open. She gaped, there was no other word for it. And when she spoke her voice was thin and high. '*Linnet*? You're Linnet Murphy? Begod, but isn't that the strangest t'ing ever?' She grabbed the other girl's hand in hers and squeezed it hard. 'There can't be two . . . but Maeve said you were the very image of me as a child, yellow hair an' all!'

'Maeve?' The brown-haired girl was laughing; she thinks I'm an Irish madwoman, Lucy thought belatedly. 'Well, now, and isn't that odd? My mammy came from Ireland, way back, and there was a Maeve in her family – her eldest sister.' She gently drew her hand out of Lucy's grasp. 'But Murphy's a common enough name, I suppose.'

'Yes, but Linnet isn't,' Lucy said triumphantly. 'My mammy was on the stage at one time. They called her little Evie.' She watched as Linnet's thin face flushed to a delicate shade of rose, as her eyes rounded. 'You're me twin sister, the person I've come to Liverpool to find,' she said triumphantly. 'And now that I come to look at you, you've a great look of Maeve about you so you have.'

'And now that I come to look at you, you're rather like my mammy,' Linnet said with a distinct wobble in her voice. 'Oh Lucy, I can't believe it – a sister of me own!'

*

Linnet couldn't believe the extent of her own good fortune. Mammy had mumbled about relatives, but she had never even hinted that Linnet had a sister let alone a twin. And it seemed impossible that this golden-haired girl with the gentle, mischievous face had come miles and miles, just to find her, and had actually done so. The two girls sat on the sunny deck and at first could only stare at each other, now and again smiling with delight. My sister, Linnet kept thinking, my very own sister – a relative of my very own!

Presently, she put it into words. 'It's like Christmas and birthdays all rolled into one,' she said. 'To have someone of my own, I mean. I've got friends, of course, and a feller – do you have a feller, Lucy? – but no relatives, not that I'd met. I didn't even know how badly I wanted a sister of my own until you turned up. But I wonder why your Maeve thought we would be alike, because we aren't at all similar, really. You're terribly pretty.'

'You're not so bad yourself! And I think other people will say we're quite alike because we've both got the same sort of eyes and the same shaped face, only our hair's a different colour and I'm a few inches taller than you,' Lucy said. 'That's odd, that is, because Maeve always told me I was the small, sickly baby and you were big and bonny.'

'People change,' Linnet said ruefully. 'My hair was fair when I was young, but it got darker as I got older. I wonder why yours didn't?'

'Lots of Irish cream and butter, and lots of Irish honey; it keeps you blonde,' Lucy said with a giggle. 'But I've not told you why I've come to find you, Linnet. Do you mind if I start at the beginning? Only it's a long story and you'll want a bit of background.'

'I don't mind at all,' Linnet said, settling herself comfortably on the wooden slatted seat. She thought she would have been quite happy to have listened to this beautiful, golden-haired girl all day – this brand-new twin sister of her very own. 'Fire ahead.'

'Well, it was like this,' Lucy said after some thought. 'My grandad – and yours, Linnet – was an old man and he'd been very sick. But the Stations were coming to our home, we live near Cahersiveen, in County Kerry, so . . .'

'What are the Stations?'

'Dear God, you're a heathen,' Lucy said, smiling. 'Forget the Stations, 'tis just a Mass said in the home and attended by everyone all about. As I was saying, the Stations were coming to Ivy Farm so of course I was very busy, and Caitlin chose the same month . . .'

'Caitlin? Is she another sister? Another relative to me?'

'Caitlin's me best friend, she's the daughter of . . . look, just let me tell it, will you? Or I'll still not be finished be nightfall. Now, as I was saying, Caitlin chose the same month to announce that she and Declan were to wed, so . . .'

It would have been idle to pretend that Lucy was not a little disappointed to find Linnet was not a double of herself; the prospect of fooling people had been in its way rather fun. But to find Linnet had straight brown hair and was smaller than she and slightly built was, by and large, probably better for their eventual friendship.

She had not, at first, thought Linnet pretty, but as they grew easier together she revised her opinion. Linnet was fascinating; she would never lack admirers even without guinea-gold curls and a bee-stung lower lip. She had that quality of unselfconscious charm which soon had Lucy in its thrall, for all she had been determined merely to feel sorry for her sister. And Linnet was also a good listener. Having been told to keep her questions for after the story she sat there, hanging on Lucy's every word, her eyes gradually widening as the story progressed.

'And he's left the farm to the pair of us?' she gasped at the end, when Lucy produced her trump card. 'A farm? But Lucy, I don't even know how to keep a garden, let alone a farm. What good would I be to you if I did come back? And I've a well-paid job here, I'm a nanny so I get to save most of my salary and – and I'm thinking about getting married before the year's end.'

'I'm not saying stay for ever, Linnet,' Lucy reminded her. 'I'm just saying come over, see how you like it, and get things settled. Couldn't your – your feller come as well? For a week or two, maybe?'

'He's a seaman, on a timber haul at the moment,' Linnet said slowly. 'We've talked about getting married but we've not set a date, only now I want to make it definite. You see, the man I work for has asked me to marry him as well and when I say no, I'm afraid things could get difficult. He's a gentleman, he won't kick me out, but – well, you know how it is.'

'I can imagine,' Lucy agreed. 'So you'd better tell him no at once and come back to Ireland with me. Explain where you're going and why, that should make things easier, if anything.'

And after a thoughtful pause, Linnet reached across and grasped Lucy's hand tightly. 'I'll come!' she declared. 'My job will go down the pan but you said our grandad had left some money, too, didn't you? That will tide me over.' She beamed at her twin, her eyes brilliant with excitement. 'And it'll mean Roddy and I can get married just as soon as we can arrange it,' she added. 'Oh Lucy, I'm so glad we found each other! Will you dance at my wedding?'

'With all my heart. And perhaps, in a year or two, you'll dance at mine,' Lucy said, and told her sister about Peder and her grandfather's hopes that she would marry

land and double the size of Ivy Farm. She tried to make
it sound just what she wanted, and thought she had
succeeded until Linnet reached out and squeezed her
hand.

'It's not Peder you want, is it?' she said shrewdly. 'But
there's someone just right for you around the corner,
Lucy. Just you wait and see.'

Chapter Twelve

As it happened, it was a lot easier for Linnet to give in her notice than she had imagined it would be.

She arrived home with a sunburnt nose after spending most of the day talking to Lucy, full of trepidation over the task to come. She intended to tell Mr Cowan, as soon as she walked through the door, that she would be returning to Ireland at the end of the week because her grandfather had died. But she could well imagine the scene which could take place when she admitted – as she must – that she would not be coming back.

And then there was his proposal of marriage. She meant to tell Mr Cowan that she had considered very carefully, as carefully as he had implored her to, and was conscious of the great honour he had done her, but did not think she would make him a suitable wife.

It sounded easy when she rehearsed the words in her head; the snag came when she began to think of Mr Cowan's lines. She could imagine all too well what his reaction would be – she feared he would be angry as well as honestly distressed. She did not intend to give way, knew, after her talk to Mrs Sullivan, that it would be very wrong to marry him, but he was a good deal older than she and a wealthy man; to turn him down was going to take courage.

So it was a surprise when she walked into the house to find Mr Cowan with Mollie and Emma, the nursery-maid, all dressed in their coats and hats, waiting in the hallway.

He knows! she thought, and opened her mouth to start explaining but was forestalled by Mr Cowan.

'Ah, Miss Murphy, at last! I was in fear and trembling that you'd not come home before we had to leave – you're very late. I've news which I scarcely know how to impart! Do you remember Mr Aloysius Paulett, Miss Murphy?'

Linnet gaped at him. 'Aloysius who?'

He clucked impatiently. 'Mr Paulett, the Chairman of the Eagle and General; you can't have forgotten him!'

'I don't think we ever met,' Linnet said slowly. 'He was in the London office, wasn't he?'

'Yes, indeed. And two days ago the poor old fellow dropped dead in the middle of a board meeting. And today I hear that they've chosen me – me, Miss Murphy – to take his place! I am to go up to London immediately, the company will put us into a company house until such time as I purchase my own property, and I will be confirmed in the position within the next couple of days. In my wildest dreams I never thought . . . but there, I've always put the company before myself, always worked hard . . . and now, it seems, this is to be my reward.'

He sounded horribly complacent, Linnet thought. She frowned across at him, trying to take it all in. 'And Mollie? What about Mollie? She's happy at school, sir, she has friends in the neighbourhood . . .'

He laughed; behind his horn-rimmed glasses his eyes glittered. 'Mollie will want for nothing! Advancement such as this will ensure her future – and, indeed, mine. I thought that you, Miss Murphy, might hold the fort for me here until such time as . . . as you decide whether you wish to come to London with – with Mollie and myself. But now I must go, the Board are sending a chauffeur driven car for us . . . I'll ring up when I have time and you can tell me what . . . what you've decided to do.'

There was anxiety in the last words and Linnet responded to it at once.

'I won't be here,' she said quickly. 'Sir, I met a close relative in the city this morning who had come to tell me my grandfather had died recently and left me money and some property. I'm returning to Ireland at the end of the week to sort things out.'

Was it relief she saw behind those glasses? He tutted in vague disapproval, but . . . yes, it was definitely relief. The girl who was good enough for a provincial insurance executive would not, Linnet thought, be the right wife for the head of the company. He could not realise it, but she was every bit as relieved as he – more, probably.

'I see; well you must go, Miss Murphy, your duty is clear, you must not consider us, we shall do very well.' He could not hide his relief, his elation, almost. 'And since you've not yet taken your annual holiday this year you must take it now – I'll pay you for the full month.' He reached into his pocket and withdrew a cheque book. He scribbled for a moment and then handed Linnet the cheque which she put into her pocket without looking at it.

'Thank you, sir. May I wish you well in your new career? Will you be returning here in a week or so? To see to the house and so on?'

'I think not. In two or three months perhaps . . . but for the next few weeks we'll be busy people won't we, Mollie, my dear?'

Mollie nodded uneasily. She was too young for such an upheaval, Linnet thought, but she could not interfere, especially since she was about to abandon both father and child.

'I see. Then I'd better say my goodbyes before you go off on your adventure.' Linnet bent and kissed Mollie, shook hands with Emma, then held out a hand to Mr Cowan.

'Goodbye, sir, and good luck.'

Almost as she spoke the front doorbell pealed and Mr Cowan all but wrenched his hand out of hers and hurried to answer it. 'Come along, Mollie. Emma, it's our car,' he said importantly. 'Oh, Miss Murphy, you'd best tell Cook not to bother with dinner if you're leaving, too.'

When the front door had closed behind them Linnet sat down on the stairs and laughed until the tears ran down her cheeks. She had said that she was leaving, but not until the end of the week. Mr Cowan, however, clearly did not intend to pay for her keep a moment longer than was necessary. Well, that was all right by her; she wanted to get away, and away she had got. There was no point in feeling sorry for Mollie, no point in missing her, since she would under no circumstances have gone with the family to London. And what was more, it was plain as plain that Mr Cowan did not intend her to do so.

So Linnet went upstairs and packed all her things into a large gladstone bag which she found in the lumber room. She left her uniforms but took her shoes since she doubted that Mr Cowan would want to hand them on to his new nanny. She went down to the kitchen and explained the situation to Cook, Mrs Eddis and the maids and then she lugged her belongings down the stairs and used the telephone in the hall to ring for a taxi.

Her twin was staying in Brownlow Hill, at a boarding house run by a Mrs Cordiner. I'll go there, Linnet decided. If they haven't got a spare room then I'll find somewhere else, but it would be nice to be under the same roof as Lucy.

The taxicab drew up on the gravel sweep outside and whilst the driver carried her bag out to the car Linnet asked him if he knew a Mrs Cordiner on Brownlow Hill.

He said he did, promised to take her there and to wait until she was sure Mrs Cordiner had a room free, and handed her carefully into the back of his vehicle.

A short while later, Linnet was standing in the hall-way of Mrs Cordiner's boarding house, paying off the cab and waiting for Mrs Cordiner to show her to her room.

'Life's full of coincidences, Miss Murphy, for I've an-other Miss Murphy stayin' wi' me this week,' Mrs Cordiner said as she ponderously ascended the stairs. 'She's in the room next door to you; and a very nice, well-brought-up young lady she is, too.'

'I'm glad to hear it, because she's my sister,' Linnet said with a twinkle. 'She came over from Ireland to find me, and find me she did.'

'Well, ain't that a thing?' Mrs Cordiner gasped. 'Said she were searchin' for a twin . . . you ain't very like each other, norrat first glance.'

'No-oo. But we've led very different lives,' Linnet said. 'Is she back yet? Only she won't be expecting me.'

As she spoke they reached the landing and a door flew open. Her twin stood there, beaming at her.

'Linnet! It *is* you! I got the oddest feeling that it was. What's happened? Was he very cross? As soon as you've seen your room come and tell me all about it!'

Naturally enough, Lucy's first thought was that now she could carry her sister back to Ireland with her without waiting until the end of the week, but Linnet speedily disabused her.

'I've got to see the Sullivans,' she said firmly. 'Mrs Sullivan is Roddy's mam and my greatest friend. They're not at all well-off, in fact I suppose at the time they took me in they were miserably poor because they had six sons and not much money coming in, but when I was in need

Mrs Sullivan rescued me and – and loved me. I couldn't go *anywhere* without letting her know, certainly not across the sea to Ireland.'

'Fair enough. Where do the Sullivans live?' Lucy enquired, and was rather shocked when Linnet said that it was indeed Peel Square.

'It is a poor neighbourhood, I know it,' Linnet admitted when her twin remarked timidly that the area seemed crowded and poverty-stricken. 'But everyone helps each other in Peel Square, not like in Sunnyside. Why, all Mr Cowan could think about this evening was his own advancement, he didn't really give a thought to Mollie being taken away from her kindergarten and her friends. And the neighbours in Sunnyside hardly know one another, though their servants are friendly enough. If I had to choose somewhere to live for ever and ever I reckon I'd take Peel Square sooner than the biggest, poshest house in Sunnyside. Now, do you want to come with me or shall I go alone?'

They had their first argument over the visit to Peel Square, but it wasn't a serious one. Over breakfast they discussed it and Lucy thought that Linnet ought to see Mrs Sullivan alone and not have someone she didn't know hovering at her shoulder all the while. Linnet agreed in one way, but she desperately wanted Mrs Sullivan to meet this brand-new sister of hers. So, in the end, they compromised. Linnet was to go in under the arch first, and Lucy would window-shop up and down Cazneau Street.

'The shops are bigger and better on the Scottie,' Linnet said, buttering toast. 'But there's a florist or two in Cazneau, ever such pretty windows they have, and there's Lewis Cann's tearooms and of course there's Laurence Meehan near the corner of St Anne's Street. You could pop in there and buy a book, then go to Cann's and have tea and buns. But if you want clothes, you'll have to go up to Great Homer, or the Scottie.'

'Cahersiveen's a grand little town so it is,' Lucy said loyally. She poured herself another cup of tea from the big metal teapot which their landlady had left on the table so that they could help themselves. 'But the shops here – Holy Mother, they're grand and big, even the small ones. Don't worry, Linnet, I'll be well-occupied for that half-hour. And I'm mortal fond of a good read – aren't we all, when we live in the country? So I'll be after taking a book or two back with me for Caitlin and me other friends. You'll be lucky if I'm not an hour behind you instead of just the half with so much to see and do.'

'Mrs Sullivan and me will settle down and gossip, or I'll give her a hand with the washing or the ironing,' Linnet said contentedly. 'Take your time, sister. We won't mind waiting on you.'

'I will. Now is breakfast over? Because if so, we really ought to get started.'

They walked to the tram stop and caught a Green Goddess which would take them to the Juvenal Street stop on Scotland Road. Linnet was happy to see her sister's eyes widen approvingly as they climbed into the tram.

'Grand, isn't it?' she said, taking her place beside Lucy on the brown leather seat. 'A few years back we only had ordinary trams with wooden slatted seats and slatted floors that the old fellers spat on, and the din they made had to be heard to be believed. But the Goddesses are wonderful, and so quiet!'

Lucy had not been on a tram before; she made enthusiastic noises but the tram's very quietness scared her and she was glad to get off when her sister jumped to her feet and made her way along the swaying aisle.

'Right you are. Now this is the Scottie – Scotland Road to you – and that there's Juvenal Street.' She pointed. 'We go through there to Cazneau and I'll show you the Peel Street entrance, then you can come back to it when you've had enough of window-shopping. Are you sure you'll be all right, chuck?'

'I'll be fine,' Lucy said at once. 'Don't worry about me. I may be a country girl but I've got a good head on me shoulders so I have. See you in an hour?'

'In an hour, then.'

And Linnet turned and dived under the arch into Peel Square, leaving Lucy in Cazneau Street.

Linnet didn't bother to knock, she simply burst into the tiny, square living room and ran through into the kitchen, where her friend was labouring over a pile of sheets with irons standing against the fire despite the heat of the day outside.

'Mrs Sullivan, you'll never guess what's happened to me!' Linnet, lit up with excitement, saw Mrs Sullivan's face grow anxious and pale. She shook her head at the older woman. 'It's all right, I've not done anything I'm going to regret for the rest of my life, I've left Sunnyside and Mr Cowan. Because my twin sister's turned up!'

'Your twin sister? Chuck, I couldn't be more pleased! Your mam were always a bit quiet, like, about your sister and there were times when I wondered . . . but you say you've met the girl, and she really is your twin? Like as two peas in a pod, are you?'

'No, not a bit,' Linnet confessed. 'She's taller than me and rounder, somehow, and she's got the most beautiful golden curls. She reminded me of my mam straight off, but she's not like her really. Too big and tall for a start, and too – well, she's not like little Evie, anyway. But she's nice, Mrs Sullivan, real nice, you'll like her, honest to God you will.'

'Any sister of yours is bound to be nice, queen,' Mrs

Sullivan said loyally, ironing away. 'So what's she doin'
in the Pool, eh? Why's she 'ere?'

'Our grandfather died recently and he left the farm to
the two of us, to be divided equally. And some money,
as well. Apparently the family thought I'd gone to New
York with Mammy, so first of all they advertised in the
local newspapers over there and Maeve – she's Mammy's
big sister – went over and looked for me. Only then Lucy
said she got this feeling that I wasn't in New York at all.
She found some old letters and read them and she said it
seemed to her that little Evie didn't talk about me much
because I wasn't with her, though folk had got the impression that Mammy had put me in lodgings in the
country because New York wasn't a good place to bring
up a child.'

'Aye, that's your mam all over,' Mrs Sullivan said
frankly, switching irons and standing the old one back
before the fire to reheat. 'She were good at givin' im-
pressions, I noticed it meself. So why didn't this sister of
yours come searchin' right away, after she'd read the
letters? Why wait till now?'

'I don't know when she read the letters,' Linnet said.
'But she came now because she had this news for me, that
I owned half of Ivy Farm. I suppose, before Grandad
died, she was pretty busy herself, what with the farm and
looking after him and everything. But she's here now,
Mrs Sullivan, and she's coming round to meet you, only
she said she'd let me get it all off my chest first – the
inheritance and everything.'

'Right, go on then, tell me,' Mrs Sullivan commanded.
'An' while you talk fold this sheet wi' me, there's a good
girl. It 'alves the work if there's two of us.'

'Course. Let me have a go with the iron whilst you sit
and listen to me telling you,' Linnet said and as soon as
the sheet was folded she seized the iron and began to pass

it briskly across a white linen sheet. 'I don't mind ironing sheets, it's the shirts and frilly petticoats I find hard. Why don't you put the kettle on?'

Mrs Sullivan chuckled but complied. 'You're just like me, chuck, you do like your cuppa,' she said approvingly. 'Go on, then . . . your twin turned up. And what about old Cowan, eh?'

'It's a long story,' Linnet warned her, shaking out the sheet and sprinkling water from the jug over it to smooth the creases. 'But I'll start right at the beginning, when I got on the ferry to go over to visit Mollie's great-aunt, in Birkenhead. Mollie didn't come with me since it was my day off, but the old girl's been kind to me and she does like a bit of company, so I set off quite early . . .'

At the end of the story Mrs Sullivan's eyes were round. 'Wharra strange thing, you two meetin' up like that,' she declared. 'The Murphy girls' first meetin' was on the Mersey! Only wi' you marryin' so soon, queen, you won't be the Murphy girls for long.' She chuckled. 'We'll call you the Mersey girls instead. And wharra strange feller that Cowan chap o' yourn must be, to go off to London at the drop of an 'at. An' 'e didn't even arst you to go along o' the rest?'

'No, he didn't mention it. I knew at once that though I might have been all right as the wife of a regional manager, there was no way he thought I'd rise to being wife of the chairman of the board. Which was so much easier, Mrs Sullivan, than having to tell him I was turning down his proposal of marriage.'

'Ye-es, I see that,' Mrs Sullivan said doubtfully. 'But 'ow 'e could jest walk out on you, queen . . .'

'He's a strange feller, I'll grant you that,' Linnet admitted. 'But it was all for the best, so let's not talk about it. Let's talk about me going to Ireland with Lucy – what do you think of *that*, eh?'

'You're actually goin'? You're leavin' us? But not for good, queen? You'll come back in a couple o' months? Roddy'll be ashore again in a fortnight, you was goin' to tell 'im mebbe you ought to get wed, wasn't you?' She sighed deeply and then snatched the kettle off the fire as it began to splutter and hop its lid. 'I dunno, I shouldn't try to influence you, but I've always loved you, queen, an' I want what's best for you, an' Roddy's 'avin' an 'ard time . . .'

'I'll be back, but I don't know exactly when. Only, Mrs Sullivan, there's money due, Lucy swears it and she's not the sort of girl to – to muddle things. So with half a farm and some money of my own, maybe things will be easier for me and Roddy. Maybe we could work on the farm, d'you think?'

'Work on a farm? Eh, queen, our Roddy's not gorra clue about farmin', we don't even 'ave a patch to grow a spud or two, norrin the square. 'Sides, farmin's gorra be in your blood, they say. Mind, we was farmers ourselves way back, 'cos my fambly come over durin' the 'forties, when the tater famine came,' Mrs Sullivan said thoughtfully. 'But that's something you'd 'ave to talk to our Roddy about. An' when'll you see 'im, at this rate?'

'Well, I thought he could take a voyage out, people do, he's mentioned it before. Then he could come over to Ireland and have a look at things,' Linnet said eagerly. 'Oh, Mrs Sullivan, we'll work something out so we will.'

'So we will? Now that's Irish if you like – you're catchin' the brogue off your sister an' she's not been wit' you a week, yet,' Mrs Sullivan said, laughing. 'Leave Roddy a letter, chuck, I'll see 'e gets it, an' if 'e can, 'e'll come to you. 'Cos 'e do love you,' she added softly. 'We all loves you, our Linnie.'

'Yes, and because of that I'd never go off and leave

you,' Linnet promised. 'Not for good, I mean. Ah, I hear a knock – that'll be my sister.'

'Good Lord, gel, you never tole me 'er name,' Mrs Sullivan shouted as Linnet headed for the front door. 'She ain't Maeve, is she?'

'No, Maeve's our eldest aunt. My sister's Lucy, Mrs Sullivan, Lucy Murphy, and I love her already. And you're going to love her, too.'

After her sister had disappeared into Peel Square, Lucy wandered up the street, going from window to window, relaxing at last after the nerve-racking search for Linnet. She had found her sister and, contrary to her expectations, they had really liked each other almost on sight. Linnet, she thought, was grand, just the sort of sister she would have chosen had she had a choice in the matter. Sharing Ivy Farm with some people would have been next to impossible, but sharing with Linnet would be fun, she was sure of it.

Not that she believed Linnet would want to share the farm, because Linnet had already said, in the sweet, shy way which Lucy so admired, that farming was something which neither she nor her feller had ever considered.

'But there must be a way to divide it so we're all doing what we want,' Lucy had said reassuringly. 'There has to be a way!'

But it was not going to be easy. Before she even left Cahersiveen, Lucy had realised that this very question was likely to arise, so she had closeted herself with her grandfather's man of business and they had discussed it at length. Mr Eamonnn was a round and cheery little man with a great deal of common sense, and he had told her at once that the farm simply could not afford to pay out half its value to her sister.

'Farming's not what it was,' he said seriously. 'As ye know, m'dear, there's a depression on, and it affects farmers worse, in many ways, than other folks. The Murphys have been all right because you feed yourselves from what you produce and sell what's left over locally, in Caher. Dear old Padraig wasn't afraid to take a chance, either. You've good acreage put down to things not every other farmer produces – your grandaddy grew what would sell – and he wasn't scared to change things around, to have a go with sheep when everyone else was still fattening cattle. But bigger spreads are havin' troubles, so they are, because of the competition from the vast farmlands in the United States and the poor wages in other parts of the world. Grain prices have plummeted, but you've been growing corn to make your own bread, not trying to export it. Why, in England they can't sell farmland at any price, but even if you sold, which you'd not find easy, then where would your living come from? For the matter of that, where would you live? I've done me best to think of a solution, alanna, but I have to tell you selling up may be the only answer.'

'If I married Peder I could mebbe take half the land . . .' Lucy had said without much hope. But Mr Eamonnn was shaking his head.

'That wouldn't do, m'dear. Your sister, who knows nothing about farming, would be left with insufficient acreage to live on. She'd still have to employ workers, you see, and the land wouldn't support 'em. And no one in their right minds would buy half a farm for the same reason. No, you can't chop Ivy Farm in half wit'out it bleeds to death.'

Lucy had shuddered involuntarily. She could not bear that the place where she had been born and bred should bleed to death.

'It's like that Egyptian feller when the two women

351

both said the baby was hers, and he said the only way to settle it was to chop the little baby in half,' she said. 'Well, Mr Eamonnn, I'll prove meself the true mother of me land – I'll not divide it, I love it too well. I'd rather me sister had it all than let it come to ruin. Have you no suggestions for what the pair of us should do?'

'You could pay your sister a small yearly income, until the value of her half of the farm was paid off,' Mr Eamonn said. He sounded doubtful. 'It wouldn't be much, at first, because it will take you a while to recover from me old friend Padraig's death, but if prices pull up, who knows? You might be rid of the debt in twenty years or so.'

'Twenty years! Well, if that's the only way . . . thanks for your help, Mr Eamonnn, I'll bear in mind what you've said.'

So now, strolling down Cazneau Street in the bright May sunshine, Lucy had to face facts. She had meant to puzzle over the dividing of the property whilst searching for her sister, but instead she had simply put it right out of her mind. And even now, when she should have been racking her brains for a solution, all she kept thinking was, 'We'll get round it somehow,' and letting her mind go back to the cheerful fact that Linnet was coming to Ireland with her, would see the farm, meet her friends and relatives and would, surely, find a solution to their problem.

Presently, in her wanderings, she found the bookshop and browsed there for a little. She bought some books, tucked them into her string shopping bag, and then continued to walk along, staring in every window as she passed, keeping to the area but not minding which streets she visited. And presently she found a little sweet shop with the legend Kettles' Confectionery over the door, and hovered in the doorway. She had meant to buy buns but wouldn't it be a much nicer gesture now, and more appreciated by the young'uns, if she bought some sweeties for the Sullivan children?

The shop was small and dim and behind the counter, squatting on a very tiny stool, was an enormous woman with a pair of spectacles perched on her button nose and a tiny, hard bun of grey hair, lanced with many hairpins, on top of her head. She was reading a newspaper but put it down when Linnet entered and surged to her feet, leaning over the counter and beaming at her customer.

'Well now, missie, what can I get you? Is it for yourself or for a pal, eh? We've gorra good range o' fancy choc'lit all done up in boxes, but o' course I allus tell folk to buy 'omemade 'ere, to get the best valuc.' She waved an expansive hand at the tall jars on the shelves behind her. 'Lickrish, annyseed, taffy . . . we makes it all in our boilin' kitchen we does, an' you'd go far before you gorranything better.'

'I'd like two pounds of taffy, please,' Lucy said recklessly. 'And could you divide it into six bags?'

'Oh, aye, course I could.' The old woman lifted a huge jar of toffee off the shelf and banged it aggressively on the counter; the pieces, which had been firmly stuck together, began to jump apart. The old woman continued to thump the jar on the counter as she spoke until the pieces within were all separated. 'Aye, this is me best taffy, this. You'll not gerrany better in the 'ole of Liverpool. Oh aye, an' you won't spend a fortune, either, 'cos it's not 'spensive. Poor but honest, us Kettles, that's what I always say. Poor but honest.'

She tipped a rattling stream of toffee chunks into her scale pan, then put two one pound weights on the scale and adjusted the flow of toffee until the two hung equal. Then she turned to the shelf behind her, replaced the toffee-jar, and began to tip the pieces, a few at a time, into six conical brown bags.

'There y'are, queen,' she said at last. 'If you gi' me one and eight we'll part friends.' She chuckled again, beaming at Lucy. 'An' you won't get better,' she added. 'Poor but honest, us Kettles.'

'There's a piece of toffee still on the scale pan,' Linnet remarked, feeling guilty because the poor old girl plainly had not realised. 'If you could put it in the last bag . . .'

'Lor, 'ow could I 'ave missed it?' the old woman marvelled. She shook her head over her own stupidity and then looked past Lucy to the doorway. 'Ah, another customer!'

Linnet glanced round but the would-be customer must have walked past and by the time she looked back Mrs Kettle – if indeed the old woman was Mrs Kettle – was carefully placing all the small brown bags in a big brown bag and handing it across the counter. Linnet counted out one and eightpence, thanked the sweetmaker, and left the little shop. She did wonder about trying the toffee, but decided, instead, to make her way to the Lewis Cann tearooms and try their cream cakes.

The cream cakes – and the coffee which accompanied them – were delicious and when she left the tearooms, with a large bag of sugar buns for the Sullivan boys as well as the taffy, she went into Turner's the Florists and selected some purple, red and white lilac for Mrs Sullivan. The girl in the shop wrapped the stems in pretty paper and charged Lucy what she thought an exorbitant sum, but the scent alone, as the sun fell on the blossom, was worth it. Ivy Farm and the old barn against which the lilac trees bloomed came into her mind so strongly that it was like a visit home and she thought again that the farm was the most important thing in her life, that she could never leave it, not even for Linnet. But if there was no other choice, if they simply had to sell up in order to get a bit of money each, then she supposed that marrying

Peder and moving five miles further inland, to Culnagap Farm, would be a good deal better than starving at her own home, or moving far away.

She didn't remember Mr Sullivan until she happened to pass a tobacconist but then she went inside and bought an ounce of pipe tobacco. Laden, she turned at last towards Peel Square. Imagine living here, she thought as she walked along the crowded pavement of Cazneau Street. Imagine what my sister has had to put up with for all these years . . . it's lucky I am that I have a choice in the matter, that I can go home to Ireland . . . that a good man wants to marry me for that matter, and has offered me the shelter of his roof.

She dived under the archway into Peel Square. Children covered the paving stones, sat on doorsteps, ran and shouted. They were dirty, badly dressed, underfed, yet Lucy found herself smiling at them. Happiness shone out of their bright, hungry eyes and was clear from every movement as they shouted, chased, shrieked. My sister was right when she said this wasn't a bad place, Lucy thought as she approached the door of No 16. There's love here, and a sort of – togetherness. These kids would stick up for each other, fight for each other, if it came to the crunch. There are worse places than Peel Square, very much worse.

Mrs Sullivan was completely won over as soon as Lucy stepped through the doorway with her arms full of lilac, the scent preceding her, warm and strong and full of sunshine.

'Flowers, for me? Oh, bless me, the scent of 'em! Oh, miss, you don't know what it means to 'ave flowers, and such lovely colours, so many . . . the smell of 'em . . .' Mrs Sullivan's eyes were brimming, she clutched the flowers to her flat bosom, then buried her nose in them. 'I've not 'ad flowers since me weddin', an' that's a few months gone I tell you.' Still clutching the lilac she hurried over to the sink. 'They've gorra go in deep, cold water, then they'll keep longer,' she said over her shoulder. 'Oh, miss, what they must 'ave cost – you shouldn't 'ave! But I'm that grateful – ain't they beautiful?'

'Don't call her miss, Mrs Sullivan, she's Lucy,' Linnet said when she could get a word in edgeways. 'She's brought sweets for the boys, too, and some baccy for Mr Sullivan – isn't she kind?'

'No I'm not,' Lucy said at once. 'It's making sure of me welcome I am ... you're me sister's favourite person, Mrs Sullivan, and that's good enough for me so it is.'

Mrs Sullivan turned from the sink. She had put one of the buckets of water on the draining board and had plunged the lilac into it. She smiled from one girl to the other, her cheeks very pink, her eyes bright now and no longer tear-filled.

'You're two of a kind, you Murphy gels,' she said. 'Or as I said to Linnet, you Mersey girls! Now, let's 'ave a cuppa whiles you tell me what you're plannin'. Because you ain't gettin' away from 'ere till I knows just when you're off to Ireland – and when you're a-comin' back!'

'You really did like Mrs Sullivan, didn't you?' Linnet said, when the two of them stood on the landing in their boarding house just before making their separate ways to bed. 'You weren't just saying it? She was so good to me when Mammy left me. If there is any money, I'm going to see she gets a share. Mr Sullivan's a nice enough feller, but he was hurt bad in an accident years ago and can't do much. She does it all, honest to God, she runs that family.'

'She's a dear, I really liked her enormously,' Lucy said reassuringly. 'I just hope you'll like our people as well when you meet them. So we'll buy you a ticket tomorrow, alanna, and we'll be back in Ireland the day after!'

'Back in Ireland . . . yes, I suppose it'll be going back for me, too,' Linnet mused. 'Though I wasn't very old when I left last time! I wish I could have met Grandad – you were very fond of him, weren't you. And Granny, of course.'

'I never knew Granny myself,' Lucy said, rather puzzled. 'She died before we were born . . . oh, you mean Granny Mogg!' she laughed. 'Aye, she was a grand old girl, you'd have liked her. But she wasn't a relative, alanna, just a tinker who was old and not strong enough to travel the roads any more. I told you about her dying, but I didn't say much about her living . . . well, she lived in an ancient, ruined castle about half, three-quarters of a mile from Ivy Farm, and Caitlin and I took care of her when – when no one else could. Tinkers don't like roofs, nor they don't like buffers – that's us, Linnet – but Granny Mogg grew fond of Cait and me. And a roof was a necessity, because she'd been terrible ill with a badness in her chest. But there, she lived to a good age and she died in her sleep.'

'Like our grandad,' Linnet said contentedly. 'I'm glad he didn't suffer, but I still wish I'd known him. Never mind, though, I know you, and I'm going to meet Caitlin, Clodagh, Kellach, Éanna . . . heaps of new people.'

'And Peder; I'm going to introduce you to Peder,' Lucy said with a touch of shyness in her voice. 'I will maybe marry him one of these days. He's a nice feller, Peder, we've known each other for always. It's may be not a bad thing to marry a feller who tipped tadpoles into your midday milk and tied a live mouse to your plait.'

'The horror! He sounds like Roddy, my feller, so I ought to be able to tell you if marrying him's the right thing for you to do. I'm going to write to Roddy when I get into bed and I'll post it in the morning. Mrs Sullivan thinks he'll take a voyage out and come over to Ireland, to Cahersiveen, and meet you. And then we'll talk over what we're going to do about the farm. But Lucy, dear Lucy, I won't have you selling up or doing anything like that because I don't think we need half the farm. Just a tiny bit of cash would be nice, especially if I don't get a job too quick when I come back here, but I don't need half the farm.'

'Who's been talking to you?' Lucy said suspiciously. 'You know nothing about it, not yet.'

Linnet laughed. 'Do I not? These walls are thin as paper, dear sister, and you talked in your sleep for hours last night! I don't want you worrying, because it isn't worth missing a night's sleep over. Half a farm sounds good, but it's much more than Roddy and I need, or expect, or deserve. You were the one who nursed Grandad, you worked on the farm, you managed it all for him. You should have the farm . . . and I mean that from the bottom of my heart.'

Lucy put her arms round her sister and gave her a hug. 'You're kind and generous, but we won't talk about it yet,' she said huskily. 'We'll go to bed and sleep well – both of us – and let decisions wait until we get home to Cahersiveen.'

When Linnet simply assumed that they would sail from Liverpool instead of catching the train to Holyhead, Lucy was dismayed.

''Tis a longer voyage,' she said apprehensively. 'I'm not sure it's a good idea at all at all.'

'Oh, you're a little longer on the sea, but it saves absolutely *hours* of messing about on trains and things,' Linnet assured her. 'I'll book us on an early morning departure though, so we won't arrive after dark.'

What could Lucy do but agree? The weather seemed set fair. So on their last morning she and her sister said their goodbyes and made their way to the docks.

'It'll be me first time on a big ship,' Linnet said excitedly as they made their way up the gang-plank. She squeezed Lucy's arm. 'Oh, isn't it thrilling? I'd be scared stiff if I was on me own, mind, but because you're with me it's just an adventure.'

'Hmm,' Lucy said doubtfully. The sea, even here in the dock, was *moving*. She did hope it did not intend to behave like that all the way from Liverpool to Ireland or Linnet might well end up wishing she was on her own!

It seemed strange to Linnet to be aboard the big Irish ferry instead of the very much smaller one which chugged several times a day across the Mersey between the Pier Head and Woodside. But that little ferry would always wear a special aura for her, because that was where she and her sister had first met. Mrs Sullivan had called them the Mersey girls – she wondered what name they would be given in Ireland.

But right now they were saying goodbye to Liverpool, watching the familiar, much loved skyline becoming smaller as they stood at the rail and waved to the tiny figure of Mrs Sullivan standing on the quayside surrounded by little Sullivans, all of them waving vigorously back.

'Look at Freddy, jumping up and down,' Lucy said in her ear. 'Or is it Toddy?'

'I don't know, they're too far away to say for sure,' Linnet said. To her horror her voice sounded shaky. 'Oh, isn't it awful, Lucy, I think I'm going to cry! And I'm only off on a lovely sort of holiday, but I never could bear saying goodbye.'

'Nor me,' Lucy said. Her voice, if anything, was shakier than her sister's. 'And I'm saying goodbye for much longer than you are, so I am. Your friend Mrs Sullivan's lovely so she is, and I don't like saying goodbye to her one little bit.'

'Let's go below and get a drink of coffee,' Linnet suggested. 'It will make us feel better. How stupid we are, standing here crying, when we're together! Come on . . . I could do with a bite, as well. They have doughnuts, I could smell 'em when we came aboard.'

'Oh, I think I'm best on deck,' Lucy said doubtfully. She remembered her last voyage on a ship and shuddered. 'We're coming out of the mouth of the Mersey now . . . here come the waves!'

'I can't see any,' Linnet said, leaning over the side and gazing down at the heaving, white flecked water below them. 'I've never been on a ship before, not at sea. Oh yes, that was a wave . . .' she turned to her sister. 'You're a bit pale, are you sure you wouldn't like to come below for a coffee and doughnut?'

'I'm going to sit down and look away from the sea,' Lucy said. She headed for a deckchair and subsided into it. 'You go if you want, I'll be all right up here.'

'I'll bring you something up,' Linnet offered. 'I shan't be long.'

Lucy closed her eyes. 'If you like,' she said wearily. 'Just a coffee, though, not a doughnut. I don't think a doughnut would be a good idea at all!'

Linnet enjoyed the voyage, though she felt terribly sorry for her sister. Lucy, pale green in the face, could neither eat her doughnut nor drink her coffee, so Linnet finished both off for her. And quite soon after Linnet had drunk the two cups of coffee and eaten the two doughnuts Lucy lost her breakfast, noisily, over the side.

'It's odd that one of us should feel splendid and the other so dreadful,' Linnet said at one point, holding her twin's head as Lucy tried in vain to turn her stomach inside out, or so at least it appeared. 'You're being iller than you need, though, queen. If you'd only eat something . . .'

A groan answered her. Lucy waved a pallid hand in the air and then subsided onto her deckchair once more, having for the moment, at least, given up the thought of being sick again.

'Yes, I know it sounds cruel, but if you'd just have a couple of plain biscuits or some seltzer . . .'

'They tried that on the way over,' Lucy quavered. 'Oh, if only the sea wasn't so rough! If only the weather would improve! Is it long before we dock?'

Linnet gazed out over a blue sea flecked with gentle white horses. Rough? This, rough? 'We dock in an hour,' she said, tactfully not mentioning the calmness of the sea or the blueness of the sky. 'Just you lie still, queen, with your eyes closed. That way you might drop asleep and sleeping helps to pass the time.'

'I'll never go aboard a ship again,' a sepulchral voice from the deckchair announced with bitterness. ''Tis clear I bring on hurricanes just by lookin' at a ship. If I'm spared I'll stay at home for the rest of me life so I will. I'm a home-girl, so I am, I don't travel well at all at all.'

Linnet made soothing noises and presently she realised that her sister had indeed fallen asleep so she sat quietly down beside her and despite her best intentions, dozed herself.

'Isn't it good to be on dry land? And isn't it strange that the moment there's firm ground beneath me feet I'm a different person?' Lucy demanded as the two of them stepped ashore at Dun Laoghaire. 'I'm starving hungry so I am – where's a café?'

'We've no time if we're to catch the train,' Linnet said doubtfully, but her sister was firm.

'I must eat or sure and I'll die,' she said simply. 'It's as empty as a drum I am and if I'm not fed I'll keel over. Come on!'

They found a down-at-heel little eating place where the food was cheap; they had floury potatoes boiled in their jackets and some sort of fish. They drank tea with it, and afterwards ate brack, which looked and tasted similar, Linnet thought, to what the Welsh call *bara brith*. Linnet, who had enjoyed the doughnuts on the ship, ate sparingly but the empty and drumlike Lucy squared her elbows and ate like – like a starving navvy, Linnet thought. She also drank huge quantities of tea . . . and then, of course, when they should have been catching the next train, having missed the one they should have caught, they needed to find a ladies' lavatory, so they missed the following train, too.

'It'll be midnight and gone before we catch a train at this rate,' Lucy moaned as they tumbled out of the lavatory and raced for the station. 'But at least no one's meeting us.'

'Then shall we get a bed for the night in Dublin and get a train in the morning?' Linnet said hopefully. She was worn out and wanted nothing more than to sleep. 'Come on, it won't cost the earth, and I've got some spare money.'

Mr Cowan's cheque, which was made out for a much larger sum of money than he had owed her, even for a month, had startled and amused Linnet. But she had cashed it quite merrily.

'He's paying me off, the old terror,' she said cheerfully, showing the cheque to Lucy. 'Just because he doesn't want to marry me any more! Well, since I was about to turn down his proposal he might just as well have saved his money, but he won't miss it and it'll come in handy for us.'

And now it really was coming in handy, for Lucy's money had run out. 'I feel awful mean, letting you pay,' she said now, following her sister across to the nearest bus stop. 'But it's worn out I am as well as penniless. We'll settle up when we're back in Caher, I promise you.'

They found a lodging house in Dominic Street and got themselves a bed for the night. It was a double bed in a tiny room, and they both fell into it in their underwear, having failed to find a lock on the rickety door.

'If anyone comes we'll crack him over the skull with our boot-heels and scream blue bloody murder,' Linnet said, shoving a chair up against the door and wedging the back of it under the handle. But Lucy was not impressed.

'This is Ireland, not Liverpool,' she mumbled, climbing into bed and heaving the covers up round her shoulders. 'Sure I am no one will come in here this night.'

'Ireland's not heaven; there are good and bad everywhere,' Linnet said rather reproachfully. 'We'd be safe enough in Liverpool from Liverpool fellers, I daresay, but there's all sorts roaming the docks.'

Both girls were proved right in a way since someone did try their door in the early hours; but what with the wedged chair and Linnet repeating some of the nastier threats she had heard Roddy using on his brothers, the door rattler decided to move on and troubled them no more that night.

The girls arrived back at Ivy Farm just as Caitlin was setting down the tea baskets on the verge of the hayfield. The men were carting hay today from the long, sloping meadows which led to the lough and Lucy stopped by the gate and set her suitcase down.

'They're our workers, and some neighbours who are

helping with the haymaking,' she told her sister. 'And that's Caitlin, the girl putting the baskets down in the shade. Haven't they a grand day for it? And we've arrived at the right moment – just in time to share their meal.'

The scene before them was enough to impress anyone, Lucy thought, with the sun beating down on the workers' heads, and everyone flushed from the heat and sweating from their toil, and the enamel buckets of tea and the loaves of buttered bread, the slices of fruit cake, the cold apple pie, spread out on the cloth in the shade of a great oak looking so appetising that she quite envied the haymakers.

The two girls leaned over the mossy five-barred gate. 'It's grand to be home so it is,' Lucy said quietly. 'It's your home too, Linnet. Do you like what you see?'

It was a fair scene indeed. The hayfield, pale gold beneath the sun, the workers sun-tanned and smiling, the trees in their summer finery casting a shade and the lough blue as the sky above and calm enough to reflect the towering hills and the little town nestling at their feet.

'I think it's beautiful,' Linnet said, her voice small and awed. 'Oh, this is a wonderful country, Lucy! I can't imagine why our mammy left, can you?'

Lucy shrugged. 'Fame and fortune, I suppose. Ah, Caitlin's turned . . . she's coming up to meet you, the word will soon go around that we're home!'

Caitlin arrived at the gate at a run. She beamed at both girls and hugged Lucy over the top of the gate. Then she stood back and held out a hand, her face wreathed in smiles. 'Welcome,' she said warmly, shaking Linnet's hand. 'You'll be Linnet – I'm glad to meet you at last. Welcome home to the both of you!' She turned to Lucy. 'Are you comin' in for a bite here, Luceen, or will you go back to the farm first? There's the kettle singin' on the hob in the kitchen and a fine cake waitin' for the first cut.'

'I think we'll go back to the farm, alanna,' Lucy said. 'Me sister's not seen it yet and we're hot and weary. But we'll come down to the meadow when we've rested up a bit.'

'Never worry,' Caitlin said. 'We'll be done here in good time, the men have worked like slaves to get the hay in before the weather breaks and we've only one more meadow to clear. Get off wit' you now then, and I'll start the tea.' She turned back to the meadow. 'Tea!' she hollered. 'Come an' dig in, fellers!'

They walked up the little, narrow lane, their feet ocuffing tiredly in the white dust. Wild roses and honeysuckle sent their perfume into the warm air and birds sang and rustled in the hedgerows.

They rounded a bend in the lane and they were on the home straight, Linnet knew it without Lucy having to say a word. Here the lane wound between tall banks, mossy and cool, the trees arching over their heads to mingle branches, plunging the walkers into a sweet, dappled shade. They walked on, Linnet staring about her with wondering eyes. This was the lane down which her mammy had carried her years ago – she was about to set eyes on Ivy Farm for the first time . . . no, not the first time, for the baby she had once been must have known it.

Suddenly, unexpectedly, Lucy turned right, between two huge, mossy stone pillars, then stopped short. She turned to her sister, her face bright with excitement. 'Well? What d'you think of it?'

The house, the farmyard, the outbuildings, lay before them. Ivy Farm was built of grey stone and ivy massed along its walls, reached out curly tendrils as far as the slates of the roof. There were two doors, one with a porch, around which the ivy had been cleared to allow another creeper to take a hold, a creeper which was covered in pale purple blooms which hung like bunches of grapes amidst the light green, ferny foliage. The second door was ajar and within, Linnet glimpsed a wide room, the floor paved, the paving gilded with great slabs of sunshine. Outbuildings surrounded the yard on two sides and they were built of stone, too, but their slate roofs were much older, dipping and rising like the waves of the sea and covered with cushions of moss, yellow flowers, a white, waxy plant.

'It's . . . it's . . .' Linnet gasped. How could she tell her sister how she felt, how beautiful was the scene before her? But Lucy seemed to understand for she smiled and moved forward, into the yard.

'It's beautiful, isn't it? The creeper round the front door is a wistaria, I've always loved it, and the plants on the roofs of the buildings are house leeks and stone crop. Follow me!'

In a dream, Linnet followed, across the yard and in through the door, to a big, untidy kitchen. Lucy dumped her bag on the floor and turned to her sister.

'Farmers never use the front door save for weddings and funerals,' she said. 'We always come straight into the kitchen. Take your coat off and sit down – you look exhausted.'

'I am,' Linnet said. She was looking round the kitchen. It was big, with windows on either side of the back door and there was an odd sort of squeaky, twittering noise . . . it seemed to be coming from a cardboard box set down close to the big black cooking range. She peered into the box and saw it was heaving with fluffy yellow chicks. She had seen day-old chicks for sale in the city so she knew what they were but had never got so close to a group of them before. She looked across at her sister, heaving the kettle off the top of the range. 'There are chicks in that box – can I touch them?'

'Course,' Lucy said, tipping the contents of the kettle into a battered old teapot. 'There's kittens, too, see the hatbox? Spit must have had them whilst I was away.'

Linnet went over to the hatbox, which was on the other side of the range. The kittens were, if it was possible, prettier than the chicks. Linnet hung over both boxes in turn, cooing incoherently. This was a farm, there would be baby cows, baby horses . . . she was so happy she almost forgot that she was on strange ground and when Lucy thrust a cup of tea into her hand she very nearly forgot to thank her.

'Lucy, do you have baby cows and baby horses as well? Oh . . . thanks for the tea, I'm dry as dust! Only I've never seen a baby cow . . .'

Lucy laughed and came and pushed her sister gently into one of the shabby, comfortable chairs, then bent over and plucked a kitten out of its nest. She plonked it on Linnet's lap and then balanced a large slice of fruit cake on the arm of the chair.

'Here, you can hold a kitten if you like – I remember when I dearly loved baby things! Then, when you've drunk your tea and eaten your cake we'll have a tour of the house. Later we'll go round outside, but I think for this afternoon the house will be quite enough for you to take in.'

'I can't believe it,' Linnet kept saying as she ate the cake and stroked the kitten and sipped at her tea. 'I just can't believe I'm here, where Mammy . . . our Mammy . . .'

Her voice broke and she ducked her head but Lucy saw the tears and knew that no matter how badly little Evie had behaved towards her, Linnet had loved her mammy. Lucy went over and sat on the arm of her sister's chair.

'It was all a long time ago, alanna,' she said gently. 'Our mammy's long gone, long gone. Now we must make our own future, but we'll never be alone again, because you've got me and I've got you. And whatever we do, wherever we roam, we'll hold each other dear in our hearts. Now, are you going to come over the house with me, or must I go by meself?'

Linnet gave a sigh, pulled a hanky from her sleeve and blew her nose, then stood up. She put the kitten back in its nest and ate the last of her cake. Then she smiled across at Lucy. 'I'm ready,' she said. 'Will I bring my bag up so you can show me where I'm to sleep tonight?'

The neighbours were delighted with Linnet.

'The image of Maeve, the little darlin',' Mrs Kelly said, sighing sentimentally. 'But Maeve was plain, useless to deny it, and she's a pretty t'ing, that sister of yours. So I don't know why they look alike, I just know they do.'

'I noticed it meself, first go off,' Lucy confessed. 'And you know what, Linnet's like Maeve in other ways, too. She catches on so quick over farming matters you'd think she'd been reared here. I show her how to do a thing once and it's there in her head for ever, I'm sure. And though she never got much chance of cooking while she was a nanny, she picks up my recipes in a moment so she does.'

'Aye. But it's because she wants to understand, to be a part of it,' Mrs Kelly said shrewdly. 'I explained about broody hens and d'you know, she's writ it down? So she won't never forget, she said.'

'I'm so glad,' Lucy said. 'I wanted her to take to it, but I never dreamed she would – not so fast, anyway. But as it is, I do think that we might make a go of it between us. You see, once Caitlin and Declan marry there will be a big gap here, and you only come in a couple of mornings a week now. So if Linnet did decide to stay there would be work for her.'

'Aye, there would. And what about her young man? She says he'll be coming on the train in a few days.'

'That's right. They're hoping to marry so Linnet wants to talk to him about it. Mrs Kelly, he's from a – a very poor area of Liverpool, he knows nothing about farming . . .'

'But he comes from farming stock, Linnet told me so.'

'Yes, but I think that was so far back – they left in the 'forties, because of the potato famine – that I doubt he's got any interest in the land at all at all.'

'Well, if he's not goin' to be a farmer, then mebbe the feller could get a job in Cahersiveen,' Mrs Kelly said with unimpaired cheerfulness. 'Or mebbe he could go to sea and come back to Ivy Farm and his wife when he was ashore. They'll be an asset to Cahersiveen, the young folk.'

'We've not met Mr Sullivan yet; he may not be nice at all,' Lucy said, but Mrs Kelly just laughed and shook her head reprovingly at the younger woman.

'Not nice, when Linnet loves him? He's a dote, I'm sure of it!'

Chapter Thirteen

Roddy got off the train at Cahersiveen station and it was raining: gentle, soft rain, the sort that gardeners love, but the sort that penetrates clothing, soaks hair, even infiltrates footwear. The sort of rain, Roddy thought ruefully as his stout seamen's boots thudded onto the platform, which meant you turned up at your destination looking like a drowned rat and squelching. Which didn't matter on some occasions and mattered very much on others. It mattered today.

A week ago he had arrived home after an exhausting voyage to find his mother in a state of high excitement.

'It's Linnet,' she had gasped almost before he was through the doorway. 'She's gone off to Ireland wit 'er sister, Lucy! The gel came for 'er, Roddy, after all these years, an' a lovely gel she is, too. Their old grandad died an' left 'em the farm between 'em so they 'ad to go back an' see to things – lawyer's things, you know. Linnet left a letter – she wants you to tek a voyage out, son, an' go over there. You'll go, won't you? Now don't gerrall obstinate an' pig-'eaded this time, just give it a bit o' thought, don't start . . .'

'I'll go.' He didn't have to think. Where Linnet was concerned there could be no thought, no reasoned judgement. He loved her, wanted her – damn it, he *needed* her, as she needed him, though whether she knew it yet was another matter. They quarrelled and fought, hurt each other, made it up, quarrelled again. But that did not mean that they weren't deeply in love, though sometimes he got so exasperated with her . . .

'You'll go, son? You'll tek a voyage out an' go over to Ireland? Well, an' I thought I'd 'ave to argufy an' explain . . . Here, read the letter, though I've telled you most, I reckon.'

She hurried across to the mantelpiece and took down a brown envelope wedged behind the clock. It had his name sprawled across it in a rather wild hand, very different from Linnet's usual neat script. He commented on it as he slung his ditty bag on the table and began to slit the envelope open.

'She were in an 'urry, judgin' by the writin'.'

'That's right, she were,' his mother agreed. She was peeling apples and the kitchen smelled sweetly of the fruit. 'It all 'appened so quick, son, you'd scarcely credit. You see, what 'appened . . . but I'd best let you read the letter.'

Roddy, reading, grunted. But the letter was a good deal clearer than his mother's garbled explanation for all that.

Dear Roddy,
My twin sister has come for me because we've inherited the farm where Mammy was born and bred. I left the Cowans because they went to London. My sister's name is Lucy and she's very, very nice. The address is Ivy Farm, Cahersiveen, County Kerry. I don't know how long I'll be here, but it would help me a lot if you would come over for a week or so. Lucy would love to meet you. Could you come? It would help me a lot. Please come.
Your Linnet.

Below was a small pencilled sketch map of the area with arrows leading from the main street, across the bridge and out to a small square labelled Ivy Farm.

Roddy read every word through twice and studied the map; then he put the letter down on his knee. He whistled thoughtfully beneath his breath, then glanced at his mother through his eyelashes. What exactly did she know? He had had his suspicions about that Cowan feller, always so quick to take Linnet out in his car, to pay her a bit extra, to dance attendance on her. But he'd not said anything to Linnet because she would have been offended and said Mr Cowan was a gentleman, as if that made any difference! Gentlemen, Roddy was sure, had exactly the same feelings, urges and the like, as fellers. Besides, Linnet wouldn't let any bloke go too far, Roddy knew that. None better. His own hopeful advances were always slapped down and briskly, too.

Mrs Sullivan looked up from her work. 'Did she tell you the Cowans 'ad moved to London? Oh, she were treated shabby there, but she just laughed – you know Linnet – and said she were glad to be out of it. So off she went to Ireland wit' a month's money in 'er pocket in lieu o' notice, 'appy as Larry.'

'Oh,' Roddy said rather feebly. 'There weren't no – no trouble, then?'

'Norra bit of it,' his mother said cheerfully. 'They parted fr . . . well, I were goin' to say they parted friends, but that ain't true. They parted as nanny an' guv'nor, I'd say.'

'Oh. Well, that's awright, I suppose,' Roddy said, having given the matter some thought. '"Cos once or twice it seemed to me . . . but there, I were wrong. There weren't nothin'. . .'

'No, nothin',' Mrs Sullivan said. 'When'll you leave, eh? End o' the week?'

'In a day or so,' Roddy said easily. 'Gorra get tickets an' that. She's give me the address so I'll tell 'er when to expect me.'

It had not taken long to arrange to miss a voyage. He said he would probably be signing on for the following one and the shipping clerk just nodded. An experienced seaman could usually get a berth, they guessed he would probably be back.

Then there was his ticket for the ferry and his train ticket, too. He packed a few things in his ditty bag, kissed his mam, bought sweets for the kids, shook hands with his dad, and left. He marched down to the dock with a silly grin on his face because not only was he going to Linnet but she had said she needed him, had almost begged him to join her in Ireland.

He had rather enjoyed being a passenger instead of a deckhand, what was more. He prowled all over the ship, talked to the seamen, got taken on the bridge. He drank a couple of pints in the bar, refused to play cards with a group of sharp-looking characters in one of the lounges, leaned over the bows and watched the mysterious land grow bigger and clearer.

The train journey across Ireland was enjoyable, too, though overlong for an impatient swain going to see his lady-love. But sailors are used to seemingly endless journeyings so Roddy took this one in his stride and passed the time by examining the scenery – lakes, bogs, rolling meadowland and wooded hillsides – as the train chugged along.

It hadn't started to rain until well past Killarney but now it seemed to have got into its stride. Because it had been so fine when he set out Roddy had not bothered to wear his seaman's cap and now it was probably right at the bottom of his ditty bag so he just shrugged his shoulders up to protect his ears and headed for the roadway which he could just see past the station's ticket office.

He did wonder about a taxi, but although he had had plenty of time on his hands both on the ferry and in the train, he found that he still needed to think. So he strode out along the street, scarcely glancing at anything or anyone, just savouring the fact that Linnet needed him, had sent for him, had signed herself 'Your Linnet' for the first time for months.

He knew that to reach the farm he must go down towards the sea lough and find Barry's Bridge. He found it easily, first passing the ruined barracks on his right just as Linnet had said, and strode across its length, once again never glancing down at the water beneath but keeping his eyes fixed on the gently rising hills ahead. She was near, now! He could feel frissons of excitement chasing up and down his spine and his face wore a broad smile despite the falling rain, the weight of his ditty bag, and a secret worry that this twin of hers, this Lucy, might resent him, be jealous of his closeness to her recently discovered sister.

The road wound on and Roddy followed it until he came to the lane leading off on his left. There was no sign to say 'Ivy Farm this way', but Roddy knew that it was because of Linnet's squiggly pencil-map, so he turned left.

He reached the mossy stone posts and turned in through them. He saw, spread out before him, the farm, the outbuildings, the yard where hens pecked and purred over their finds. He saw lilac and laburnum trees laden with blossom and a well with a slate roof and buckets standing beside it. The trees were diamonded with raindrops and the buckets, as he approached, were half full of water so that the drops rocked the surface and tinkled against the sides.

The farm was bigger, older, more impressive than he had expected. A thin, orange-striped cat came round the corner of the house at a trot, with something gripped in its mouth. It saw Roddy and in one swift, sinuous movement it turned and retreated the way it had come. I hope everyone's not goin' to be like that, Roddy thought apprehensively. I hope they won't all turn and run when they clap eyes on me! But he approached the nearest door, a plain wooden one, ignoring the more elaborate one with the porch around it. He knocked. Waited.

Linnet knew he would be arriving some time today, but not when. For once she could not bring herself to leave the house, so she told Lucy that she would do the housework and make the midday dinner and she was busy now doing just that. She scrubbed a large quantity of potatoes, threw them in a saucepan with stock made out of beef and mutton bones, added some carrots and onions, and put it to simmer on the side of the stove. Then she made an apple pie, climbing up to the apple loft and carefully picking out the best fruit because she wanted her twin to know she really could cook and – and she wanted Roddy to enjoy the pie.

And all the time she was bustling round making beds and sweeping floors and cooking, she told herself that she was not excited, that she was looking forward to seeing an old friend, showing him round, but that was all. But she knew it was not all, of course. She knew that having Roddy here would complete the scene, that once he was here she would know what she should do. It was not so much a matter of asking his opinion, it was more seeing how they got on together in this place.

If they quarrelled here, she did not know what she would do, but they would not stay. Life without Roddy wasn't bearable, but then life with him had not been any great treat, so somewhere along the line they had gone wrong. This was their chance to put things right, to make it work, and if they made a mess of it, then . . .

Then we don't deserve each other, or happiness, or any

other good thing, Linnet decided, wielding the rolling pin with a fierceness not at all in keeping with her usual cooking methods. She had some paste left over and was rolling it out, sprinkling it with sugar and currants, folding it over several times and making shortcakes. Then she brushed the cakes with the top of the milk so that they would shine and popped them in the oven. And all the time her mind was miles away, with Roddy. She wondered what train he would catch and whether he was already on his way or still wandering around Dublin. She wondered what he would think of it all when he finally arrived in Cahersiveen. She wished that it hadn't decided to rain because it would mean he would arrive soaked and cross and that would make Linnet cross and before they knew it, they would be quarrelling again.

Outside, in the quiet farmyard, a hen croodled away to herself, the rain pattered on the slates overhead, someone crossed the yard. Immediately Linnet was alert. She ran over to the window but as she was trying to press her nose to the rain-spattered pane there was a knock and she flew across to the back door and tugged it open.

He stood there, grinning at her. His hair was sleeked to his head, his face was wet . . . she flung her arms round him, hugging him breathlessly. She had not known she had felt alone here but she had, she had!

'Linnet! Oh, Linnet!'

She dragged him into the kitchen whilst his wet mouth was still searching for hers, and then they kissed, whilst the rain on his duffle coat was absorbed by her thin cotton dress and they clung closer and closer, murmuring lovewords.

'Oh, Roddy, I didn't know how badly I've missed you till this moment,' Linnet said at last, standing back from him. 'Take off your wet coat at once before you catch your death!'

'Take off your wet frock before you catch yours,' Roddy said, grinning, but he struggled out of his coat as he spoke and handed it to Linnet, who hung it on the back door. 'I'm a thoughtless feller – you'd best go upstairs, get changed.'

Linnet looked down at her pink gingham dress and laughed.

'You're right, I'm as wet as you, pretty near. Oh, Roddy, I'm that glad you've come – what d'you think?'

'Of what? The countryside's rare pretty, and the house – what I've seen of it – seems a good solid buildin'.'

Linnet shook his arm. 'You know what I mean! Bring your bag and I'll show you round and later I'll take you to the Kellys', where you'll be lodging. Then whilst you unpack I'll go and put a dry frock on. And after that we can talk.'

Downstairs again, clean and dry, Linnet bustled round making tea and talking whilst Roddy sat in one of the easy chairs and watched her with such contentment glowing from his eyes that Linnet felt tears come to her own. What had been the matter with her these past months? She had found fault with Roddy, criticised, slapped him down, when in truth all she wanted was his love. But now, with the new serenity she had found at Ivy Farm, she could see all too clearly the tensions and stresses, the uncertainties, which had made her so unfair to her love.

A part of me was proud of living in a big, posh house and having Mr Cowan wanting to marry me, she thought with deep shame. I kept seeing these little pictures of me as his wife, driving around in the car, going to all the big shops, all my old friends so envious. But I never thought about the other side of it – him as my husband. And as soon as I did, as soon as Roddy's mam made me look, then I knew I couldn't go through with it.

She poured the tea and carried the two cups over to where Roddy sat, but when she would have handed him his cup and gone over to the other chair he shook his head reprovingly at her.

'What's wrong wi' this chair?' he asked, catching hold of her and pulling her onto his lap. 'What's wrong wi' a bit o' cuddlin', eh, queen?'

'You'll spill my tea,' Linnet squeaked as the cup rocked perilously. 'This is my second clean frock today, don't go spilling my tea, Roddy!'

He took the cup from her and set it down on the floor, beside his own. 'Shan't spill a drop. Oh, Linnet, isn't this lovely? A big, clean kitchen, the stove mutterin' away, the rain patterin' on the winder pane, and – and just you an' me.'

'Yes, it is lovely,' Linnet said. She buried her face in the side of his neck. 'The whole house is lovely, isn't it?'

'Yeah. But it's only lovely because you're in it,' Roddy said frankly.

'Could you live here, with me, Roddy?' Linnet said dreamily. 'Oh, and I didn't mean to say that until you'd seen the farm and met my sister Lucy . . . oh what a fool I am!'

'I could live anywhere if you was there, queen,' Roddy said, stroking her arm. 'I could live in Africa or – or the Arctic, if you was there.'

'Silly! I'm serious, I mean could you learn to farm and live out here a long way from – well, from Liverpool and Peel Square and so on?'

'I don't know whether I'd be any use at it, but I'd 'ave a go,' Roddy said. 'I ain't afraid o' work, no seaman is. But someone 'ud 'ave to tell me what needed doin'.'

'Ye-es, but if they told you. . . ?'

'Wait an' see 'ow I shapes up,' Roddy advised her. 'Now 'ad you better introduce me to this sister o' yours?'

'They'll be coming in for tea in a few minutes, you'll meet Lucy and the others then. Tell you what, I'm learning to milk a cow, d'you want to come and watch me have a go?'

He laughed but stood up, tipping her off his lap. Then he put his arm round her waist and gave her a quick squeeze and a kiss on the soft side of her face. 'You're on! Where's this 'ere cow what's goin' to let you 'ave a go at 'er?'

'She's waiting at the gate by now, to be let through. She's a dear little thing . . . come on, then, no point in putting coats on, it's a short run to the cowshed. Follow me!'

Together they dashed out into the rainy yard, across it and into the cowshed. Linnet caught Roddy's arm.

'I'll bring her in, you wait here.'

Roddy waited and in rather less than a minute Linnet reappeared, leading a small red and white cow on a rope halter.

'She's the easiest to milk,' she said as she was tying the cow in her stall. 'She's quite happy to chew the cud whilst I try to bring the milk down. Now you watch, Roddy – it's harder than it looks.'

She fetched a milking stool and a bucket, squatted down, leaned her head against the little cow's red and white side and began to tug the long teats firmly through her fingers. The milk squirted into the bucket and Linnet turned her head and grinned lopsidedly at him.

'What d'you think of that? Good, aren't I?'

'You are,' Roddy said, very impressed. 'Can I have a go?'

'In a minute, when I've got an inch or two in the bucket,' Linnet said. 'Oh, Roddy, it's so nice to see you again – you don't know how horribly I've missed you!'

'What I don't understand, chuck, is why you should miss me worse 'ere than you did in Liverpool,' Roddy said practically. 'You never saw me for weeks at a time when I were at sea and when we did meet we quarrelled.'

'Yes, and it was mostly my fault,' Linnet said. 'And before I left I knew it was you I wanted, that if I had you . . . if we were really married, I mean . . . then we'd probably never quarrel again. So leaving the city felt like leaving you, and it was horrid, and I missed you all the time.'

Roddy crouched down beside the cow and kissed the side of Linnet's face again. The cow rolled her eyes and shifted uneasily; it was clear she did not approve of people canoodling whilst she was giving milk.

'Oh, Linnet, you don't know 'ow I've longed to 'ear you say that! And you mean it this time, d'you? Rain or shine, wet or fine, you'll marry me?'

'Course I will,' Linnet assured him. She squirted a final squirt into the bucket and turned towards him. 'If you want me to I'll come back to Liverpool with you, but if you felt you could stay here it would make me – and Lucy – ever so happy.'

'If there's work for me, and a place for us . . .' Roddy began, then pulled Linnet roughly into his arms. The stool tipped against the bucket, the bucket rolled noisily onto its side, the cow mooed and kicked out at the bucket . . . but Linnet and Roddy were oblivious. Tightly clasped in each other's arms they were kissing with total concentration. In fact they did not notice the figure in the doorway until Lucy took a step forward and cleared her throat.

'Hmm-mm! Excuse me, Linnet, but do I take it Roddy's arrived? Because if the feller who's trying to gobble you up isn't Roddy Sullivan then I've a word or two to say to the pair of ye!'

Things moved at an amazing speed once they got started. After Lucy had been introduced to Roddy the three of them had gone all round the entire farm. They had to walk a good distance since they owned the land from the lough's edge to the mountain top and Roddy wanted to see everything. And then Lucy had to explain to him how the farm had been run when her grandfather had been alive, how it had been run since, and how – she hoped – it would be run in the future, by herself, Linnet and Roddy plus the farmhands.

'And what will 'appen when you're wed?' Roddy asked at one point. 'Because you will be wed, an' sooner rather than later, I'd bet.'

Lucy smiled at Roddy. He was a nice young man, as nice as Mrs Kelly had expected him to be, but that did not give him the right to pry into her private life. Linnet, she supposed, must have told him about the ardent Peder and everyone's freely expressed expectations that the two of them would marry.

'I'm not thinking of marrying just yet,' she assured him. 'I guess you've heard I've a young man, but I'm not sure . . . But if I married and moved away then you and Linnet would have Kellach and the Kellys, though not Caitlin, of course. But as I said I'm not thinking of marrying yet.'

'Well, look, Lucy,' Roddy said, having apparently thought this over. 'We'll strike a bargain, the three of us. Linnet and I will work 'ere, doin' our very best to learn farmin' ways, for six months. We'll 'ave to marry, because . . .' Roddy blushed, to Lucy's considerable amusement. 'Well, because it's only right, see? And if we don't get wed, we'd mebbe quarrel like we did at 'ome. But we won't mess you about, we'll work as 'ard as we know, won't we, Linnie? And at the end of six months we'll see 'ow we've gorron. If we're no good to you, we'll slope off back to the Pool, but if we've managed to be useful, we'll stay wi' you and wi' Ivy Farm. Is it a bargain?'

And Lucy, agreeing, felt lighter of heart than she had done since her grandfather's death. Ivy Farm had a chance, and so did she – so did they, come to that.

'But Linnet's already very useful,' she told Roddy. 'And I've a feeling that you'll have the will to learn and the strength to stick it. So I'm thinking we'll be all right, the three of us.'

Caitlin married Declan and became Mrs Franklin the September after Roddy had taken up residence with the Kellys. She was blissfully happy in her rooms above the grocer's shop in Cahersiveen and sang the praises of married life loudly and meaningfully to the Murphy girls when she visited the farm.

Despite Roddy's words, he and Linnet had not been able to marry as quickly as they would have liked for two reasons; one was that from the moment they woke until they fell into bed each night, every day was as full as an egg. Because they were new to the work they found themselves aching in every limb as muscles they had never known they possessed came into play, and their brains ached, too, from taking in all the information which Lucy, Kellach and the Kellys bombarded them with. Another, more important reason was that Mr Sullivan had a stroke about a month after Roddy arrived at the farm and though he lingered for five or six weeks, he had then died.

Roddy and Linnet had returned to Liverpool for the funeral and had been astonished at Mrs Sullivan's well of grief and at how she seemed to have grown small and old in their absence.

'Some folk might 'ave thought 'e weren't much good,' Mrs Sullivan said sadly, as they returned home after the funeral to have a bit of a wake in the tiny house in Peel Square. 'But 'e were kind to me an' the kids, which is more'n you can say for all the old fellers. An' 'e gave me what 'e could – never spent it on 'isself whiles we went wit'out. So give 'im a chance to settle in 'is grave afore you wed, our Roddy. Let your marriage wait on 'im, until I'm over it all a bit an' can come over to Ireland an' do me part in the ceremony. Don't be rushin' into things with your mam not there to shed a tear an' wish you luck.'

And somehow, it wasn't so hard to comply with her wishes when they were so very happy, and so hearteningly busy, too.

'I never thought we could go on so well without being married,' Linnet told Roddy as the weeks slid into months. 'Besides, I wouldn't want to upset your mam, Roddy. She was more than a mother to me, she was a friend as well, and I want her at my wedding. Only – only I hope we won't have to wait too long.'

Winter came and Christmas was celebrated, the twins' first Christmas together. It was a quiet time for farming and Linnet and Roddy were by now, Lucy told them, indispensable to the welfare of Ivy Farm.

'But you've waited and worked hard and thought of others, and now you really should get married yourselves,' she said firmly one evening as the three of them sat round the fire doing the bookwork. Or rather Linnet was writing the figures down, Roddy was dictating them and Lucy was toasting bread in front of the flames. 'I don't see why you should have to wait until the spring, write to your mam, Roddy, and tell her that you're getting married in February. Send her money for her tickets and say we expect her a week before the wedding and afterwards, for another week at least. Will she bring the small children with her?'

'They ain't so small, now,' Roddy said. 'But me Auntie Bertha's moved in – didn't we tell you? – so she'll give an eye to our kids. Oh aye, February sounds grand, eh, Linnie?'

'It sounds lovely,' Linnet said wistfully. She was finding it increasingly hard to see Roddy go off to the Kelly cottage each night, though Roddy had not once hinted that she could be a little more generous if she chose. It was as though being happily together all the time had made it easier for Roddy to wait whilst it became daily more difficult for Linnet.

'Good. And Caitlin's going to have her wedding dress altered to fit you, so that's one expense you're spared, Linnet.' Lucy turned a scorched face away from the flames and handed her twin a slice of lightly burned toast. 'Here, you have this bit, and pass me another. Then Roddy had better drive into Caher tomorrow and see the priest. And you must write to Mrs Sullivan immediately, of course. And I shall start planning the wedding feast.'

Later that evening, Roddy and Linnet slipped into the moonlit yard and went for a bit of a walk, as they did every night. It stretched their legs, got them ready for bed, and allowed them some privacy for a last goodnight kiss.

'I wish your Lucy would tell Peder yes and gerron with it,' Roddy grumbled as they walked, arms round each other, down the lane towards the lough. 'He's good lookin', good company, he's gorra nice bit o' money tucked away . . . an' the honest truth is that you an' I and the fellers could make a go of this place. If your Lucy weds and moves away then there's no end to the things we could do 'ere, you an' me. Why, I've gor ideas for changin' things which would suit the land, I reckon.'

'But Lucy doesn't love Peder,' Linnet said sadly. 'It doesn't work unless you love someone, Roddy, so your plans will have to wait. She likes him all right – he's a nice person – but she doesn't love him. I mean how could you go into a bedroom and close the door and – and take your clothes off with someone you didn't love? I mean no one could, could they?'

'We-el, if she were pretty . . .' Roddy began and got thumped for his pains by a giggling Linnet.

'Roddy, how like a feller! A woman couldn't, she – she just couldn't. So don't you try and persuade her, there's a good feller. Because I'm ever so fond of Lucy and I wouldn't want her to feel we wouldn't mind if she moved on.'

'I couldn't persuade no one to do nothin',' Roddy said. 'But if she won't take the plunge with Peder, queen, there's another what will. Did you see young Bridget O'Reilly makin' eyes at Peder an' teasin' 'im to dance with 'er at the Christmas ceilidh at the O'Rorkes'? I tell you, if Lu doesn't mek 'er mind up quick she won't 'ave a choice in the matter.'

'If Lu doesn't want him then it's only fair that someone else should get him,' Linnet said at once. 'But I'll have a word with her, love.' She pulled him round the corner into the warmth of the stackyard and cuddled against him. 'Kiss me, then we'd better go in before we freeze to icicles,' she whispered. 'Oh Roddy, I can't wait until February!'

They waited, in fact, until March. And then, on a wild, sweet day, with a boisterous wind tossing Linnet's veil and sunshine gilding the churchyard one minute whilst raindrops sparkled down the next, they were married at last.

Linnet looked beautiful and no one knew – or cared – that she was wearing Caitlin Franklin's altered gown. She carried a bunch of early primroses and had a wreath of snowdrops in her shining, fawn-coloured hair and Lucy, in deep blue silk, was her bridesmaid.

Mrs Sullivan cried, everyone threw confetti, and then they went back to Ivy Farm for the wedding feast which had kept both girls cooking for days. The neighbours brought gifts, a fiddler played for the dancing and Peder O'Rorke kept trying to get the bridesmaid into a corner . . . and Bridget kept trying to do the same to him.

'We're pulling Ivy Farm back into profit and we're learning, all of us, how to live and work together,' Lucy told Mrs Sullivan, after the bridal pair had departed, in the late afternoon, for a very short honeymoon – they were staying one night – in Killarney. 'I honestly think that Roddy is a natural farmer and as for Linnet, it's in her blood from not too far back at all. They're going to make a go of it and I couldn't be happier for them.'

'You're right there,' Mrs Sullivan said. 'Well, well, we can't call you the Murphy girls any longer, Lucy. Though you'll always be the Mersey girls, to me.'

Lucy chuckled. 'I like both names,' she said. 'But I'm still the Murphy girl, and likely to be.'

'And why is that?' Mrs Sullivan asked. The guests had all departed and the two women were sitting in the kitchen with the fire banked down for the night, having a cup of cocoa before wending their way to bed. 'You could marry that feller tomorrer, if you chose. Why doncher?'

'Because I don't love him and I think it's important to love the man you marry,' Lucy said baldly. 'Respect is all very well, but I don't think it's enough, not in the long run.'

'Sometimes love comes after the weddin',' Mrs Sullivan said presently. She sipped her cocoa. 'I've known gels what goes to their weddin' bed cryin' for their mammy an' spends the next forty years wit' a smile from ear to ear.'

'But not girls who were already . . .' Lucy broke off. 'Anyway, they must have been . . .'

'Not girls who were already in love wi' someone else?' Mrs Sullivan said softly. 'Are you in love, already, queen? Well, don't the feller 'ave eyes in 'is 'ead? You're as sweet as you're pretty, so is the feller blind an' deaf not to snatch you up?'

'No. No, he isn't blind or deaf, and I think he likes me a little. But he likes his freedom more,' Lucy said rather bitterly. 'He didn't want to settle down, stay in one spot. So he left me, and he's never come back, or at least if he has he's never let me catch more than a glimpse of him. I tell meself that one day I'll get him out o' my system, out o' my mind and my heart. But that day hasn't come yet . . . sometimes I think it never will.'

The two women sat there in silence for a short while, and then Mrs Sullivan leaned over and patted Lucy's knee. 'You'll find your path,' she said. 'Dunno where it'll lead, or who'll be there to 'old your 'and, but you'll find it, one o' these days.' She stood up. 'Bless me, I'm fair wore out – it's been a long day. I'm for bed.'

'I think I'll just get a breath of air before I come up,' Lucy said. 'I shan't set my alarm tonight, I think we deserve a lie-in tomorrow. And Kellach's going to do the milking, so there's no need for us to stir ourselves.'

'Put a coat on; don't go catchin' cold,' Mrs Sullivan said. 'Eh, that pretty dress . . . it'll get mired, tharrit will.'

Lucy was still in her blue silk frock but she laughed and shook her head at the older woman. 'Oh, a bit of farmyard muck won't hurt it and it's a mild night. See you in the morning, Mrs Sullivan.'

As the moon rose in the sky Linnet and Roddy lay, for the first time in their lives together, in each other's arms. The bed was big and soft, a feather bed into which they had sunk gratefully, and now Linnet put her hot face against Roddy's cool, muscular shoulder and tried to relax and be natural with him, for they had known each other all their lives, so why should she feel so – so odd?

She hadn't understood a good deal of the rich Kerry brogue being talked around them in the hotel dining room and had gradually become convinced that every eye in the place was upon her, guessing, speculating, and that every guest in the hotel was waiting for the moment when she and Roddy disappeared into the same room and closed the door behind them.

She had blushed and mumbled and hung her head and wished herself anywhere but in the smart dining room of the best hotel in Killarney, and now, in their bed, she clung to Roddy and admitted that she was afraid, that she did not know what to do next, was not at all sure she wanted to know.

'It don't matter, queen,' Roddy said gently, when her painful whispers died away. 'A weddin's a weddin', we're man and wife. What follers is up to us, between us two, what no man may put asunder. Not now.'

'And – and must we . . . ? I'm – I'm ever so tired,' Linnet faltered. 'I love you so much, Roddy, but I'm not at all sure . . .'

'And I love you so much that if you're tired we'll go to sleep,' Roddy said comfortingly. 'We'll 'ave a bit of a cuddle an' then we'll snore so loud they'll think we've been wed for an 'undred years!'

'Oh, Roddy, I always knew you were the nicest feller

in the world,' Linnet said with an involuntary giggle. She relaxed against him, then leaned up on her elbow to kiss his cheek. 'You understand me so well and you're so kind to me!'

'I know I am,' Roddy said nobly. 'There, sweet'eart, you go to sleep if you want to, but there's no 'arm in a bit of a cuddle, first.'

Linnet agreed that there could be no harm in it at all, and so tenderly did Roddy cuddle, and so gently persuade, that long before the moon had begun to fade in the sky they were truly man and wife.

The moon was still climbing the sky when Lucy went out into the farmyard. It was very beautiful out here with a full moon shining down from the dark sky and the stars twinkling frostily. It made her think of another night ... but she ignored the twinge of sadness and walked across the yard and out between the stone pillars, turning to her left along the lane.

It was, as she had said, a mild night, with a boisterous March wind blowing. Lucy walked steadily on, her eyes fixed ahead, her thoughts far from here. She thought about Linnet and Roddy, in their hotel in Killarney, savouring their love, their nearness. She thought about Peder, in his warm farm kitchen, stockinged feet stretched out towards the fire, hair rumpled, thoughts turning to the next day's work, to his beasts, his fields. Perhaps to her in her blue dress, saying no she didn't want to walk in the woods with him, no she couldn't see him next day, and thank you but she was fond of her own company so she was and there was no point in him sitting here trying to talk to her when she had other guests ...

Cruel, cruel to treat Peder so, but sometimes she was so lonely she actually ached with loneliness. Sometimes she longed for a hand in hers, a man of her own, someone who would be, to her, what Roddy was to Linnet. Longed, in other words, for Finn Delaney with his dark eyes and his black hair, with his charm and his iron will, even for his indifference.

She had walked further than she realised because she was at Barry's Bridge. Too far; she should turn now, make her way back. Only she had such a longing to cross the bridge all of a sudden, to go at least to the middle, to look into the limpid dark waters and to see, at last, that little mermaid, combing her long, golden hair.

He came along the road in his jaunting car as he had come along half-a-dozen times a year ever since he'd left her, all those years ago. He had followed her in crowds, almost close enough to touch yet never touching. He had haunted the farm, watching from a safe distance as she went about her work. He had seen, with real dismay, the appearance of another man and had been prepared, almost, to throw off his disguise and step forward, challenge, declare himself.

But the feller wasn't interested in Lucy but in the other girl, the one they said was her twin sister. Twin sister! She was nothing like his Lucy, nothing like at all at all. No, his golden girl had no match, no equal, and she would wait for him until he was tired of wandering, until he was old and grey and wanted to settle down.

But sometimes he almost couldn't stand it, he wanted her so bad, so cruel bad! The touch, feel, sound, smell of her haunted him, her remembered face smiled at him, for him, with all its old sweetness and spirit. If only he could conquer the desire to move on, but he doubted he ever could and it wouldn't be fair to a farmer's girl to find herself with a feller who had no easement in him.

And besides, he mustn't be tied down. He was Finn Delaney, the best driver of a jaunting car ever seen in

Killarney, the only feller who could thatch a stack, plough a straight furrow, tickle a trout out of the brown pools and into his fry-pan, stand up in the jaunting car as it tore over ground so uneven and rough that others clutched at the seat in terror, or fell out onto the hard old earth below.

Oh aye, there was only one Finn Delaney. But – but he had to see her now and then, to calm his mind and ease, for a short time, the ache of longing for her.

So he came into Cahersiveen in his jaunting car and drove quietly through the moonlit streets and out to Barry's Bridge. He planned how he would tie the horse up in the long meadow which led down to the lough and prowl around the farmhouse and hide up in the big old barn where once he had slept after Granny Mogg's funeral. If he waited long enough she would come out, feed the hens, milk one or two of the cows to help out the farmhand, potter around and then go in to cook breakfast. He would see her, hear her – he would not touch her.

He turned the jaunting car onto the bridge and slowed the horse to a walk. The horse was not sorry; it was a good long run from Killarney to Cahersiveen and the horse would have much preferred its stable and a meal of hay, the harness hung up, a good stiff brush taking off the dirt of the day.

The moon was high in the sky, spreading its silver over the whole black landscape. The lough below him was as bright as a mirror, the moon swam on its surface and sent arrows and spears of white light dancing over the water.

He reined in and leaned over to look deep into the water, then looked away – and there was her face, not a foot from his, staring at him as though she could not believe her eyes. He stared back, taking in every detail of her from the dark, flowing dress to the smooth oval of her face, the lovely line of her throat.

'Finn?' It was scarcely more than a whisper but it thrilled through him like a lightning strike. 'Finn, is it really you?'

'Aye, my sweetheart, my dearest, it's really me. Is it really you, little Lucy?'

She nodded, her eyes still fixed on his face. They were dark as pits, shaded by moon-shadow, and he saw, suddenly, that her face was sad where it had once been merry, that the line of her lips drooped, that beneath the dark silk of her dress her figure was less rounded than he remembered it.

'Finn, why didn't you come back?'

'I did . . . but I kept hidden from you. I had to see you, ástor, but I dared not let you see me; it wouldn't have been right, see, when I knew we couldn't – couldn't be together.'

She lifted her chin, then put a hand on the side of the jaunting car. 'Why not? Why could we not be together?'

'Because I'm a tinker, always on the move, and you're the girl who owns all this . . .' he spread his hands, indicating the size of her acres. 'Your grandad died and you inherited; they talk, townsfolk.'

'And that is enough to stop you taking what's yours? A farm, a bit of talk?' She sounded not sad now but angry, scornful almost. He watched her small white hand on the edge of the jaunting car, saw her fingers tighten, the knuckles whiten. He looped the reins and leaned nearer her whilst the horse stood still, glad not to be galloping, to have a bit of a rest in the quiet, windy moonlight.

'Taking what's mine? Ah, Luceen . . . you don't know how I've wanted you.'

She shrugged. 'Talk, Finn, just talk. If you knew how I'd wanted you, now – that would be a very different story. Because I didn't know where you were or what you were doing, and a woman can't just go chasing after a feller, she has to wait. But you . . . you can't have wanted me at all at all.'

Her voice was light now, amused! Anger filled him, that the hugeness of his love, which had begun to take over his life, to hurt him with her absence day and night, should be reduced, by her, to mere talk. He leaned closer still, until his lips all but brushed her brow.

'Lucy Murphy, I t'ought I could live wit'out ye, I t'ought I would be better wit'out ye, but I was wrong. I need you as a bird needs the air under its wings . . . will ye come with me?'

She did not answer, but he could tell by the way she stood, by the set of her head on her slim, strong shoulders, by the look on her face, that her decision was taken, had been taken long ago.

He leaned out of the jaunting car and took her under the arms and lifted. She came easily up into the jaunting car and he stood her on the board floor and then reeled back as she threw her arms round his neck, hugging him hard, hard!

'Oh dear God, Finn, I thought I'd lost you, so I did! There's no one for me but you and I've always known it. There's no shame in me any more, I can tell you I love you, have always loved you, and if I'm makin' a fool of meself, I don't care!'

Finn gave a subdued whoop and put his hands to the back of his neck. He unhooked the bee-chain and put it, warm from his skin, round Lucy's white neck. Then he unlooped the reins and put a hard, strong arm about her waist and clicked to the horse.

'Now you're mine, alanna, for you wear Granny Mogg's gift, to be given only to my woman,' he said, and skilfully turned the jaunting car so that it faced towards the town. 'If you come wit' me now, it's an end to your

393

settled, farming life. As Finn Delaney's wife all I can offer you is the road, Lucy Murphy!'

They clattered off the bridge and Finn turned the horse's head towards Killarney, towards the grey road which wound on and on and would take them, eventually, anywhere in Ireland that they wished to go. Lucy stood beside him, slim and strong in her beautiful silk dress with her pale hair tossed by the breeze of their going and her pale face set steady as she looked at the road ahead. Finn felt a stab of guilt and slowed the horse, to give her a last chance to change her mind, get down, and she gave an impatient little yelp and snatched the reins from his hands, bringing them down sharply on the bay mare's neck.

'Giddup, horse,' Lucy Murphy said fiercely. 'Finn Delaney, are you never goin' to tell me you love me?'

Finn threw back his head and laughed and then he let her keep the reins and put both arms round her and turned her to face him and began to kiss her.

The horse, finding the reins suddenly loose on its neck, cantered on for a bit and then slowed first to a trot, then a walk, then to stillness whilst it ate the rich grass at the roadside. And in the back of the jaunting car two young people who had loved and hungered for each other for many a long year, loved, and hungered no more.